BOOKS BY JULIE GARWOOD

Gentle Warrior
Rebellious Desire
Honor's Splendour
The Lion's Lady
The Bride
Guardian Angel
The Gift
The Prize
The Secret
Castles
Saving Grace
Prince Charming
For the Roses
The Wedding
Come the Spring
Ransom
Heartbreaker
Mercy

The Clayborne Brides
One Pink Rose
One White Rose
One Red Rose

PUBLISHED BY **POCKET BOOKS**

For information regarding special discounts for bulk purchases,
please contact Simon & Schuster Special Sales at
1-800-456-6798 or business@simonandschuster.com

JULIE GARWOOD

THE GIFT

POCKET BOOKS
New York London Toronto Sydney

This book is a work of fiction. Names, characters, places and inci-
dents are products of the author's imagination or are used ficti-
tiously. Any resemblance to actual events or locales or persons living
or dead is entirely coincidental.

An *Original* Publication of POCKET BOOKS

 POCKET BOOKS, a division of Simon & Schuster, Inc.
1230 Avenue of the Americas, New York, NY 10020

ISBN: 0-671-70250-5

First Pocket Books paperback printing January 1991

32 31 30 29 28 27 26 25 24 23

POCKET and colophon are registered trademarks of
Simon & Schuster, Inc.

Printed in the U.S.A.

For Bryan Michael Garwood.
This one's all yours.

THE GIFT

Prologue

It was only a matter of time before the wedding guests killed one another.

Baron Oliver Lawrence had taken every precaution, of course, for it was his castle King George had chosen for the ceremony. He was acting as host until the king of England arrived, a duty he embraced with as much joy as he would a three-day flogging; but the order had come from the king himself, and Lawrence, ever loyal and obedient, had immediately complied. Both the Winchester family and the St. James rebels had protested his selection most vehemently. Their noise was all for naught, however, for the king was determined to have his way. Baron Lawrence understood the reason behind the decree. Unfortunately, he was the only man in England still on speaking terms with both the bride's and the groom's families.

The baron wouldn't be able to boast about that fact much longer. He believed his time on the sweet earth could well be measured in heartbeats. Because the ceremony was to take place on neutral ground, the king actually believed the gathering would behave. Lawrence knew better.

The men surrounding him were in a killing mood. One word given in the wrong tone of voice, one action perceived to be the least bit threatening could well become the spark needed to ignite the bloodbath. God only knew they were itching to get at one another. The looks on their faces said as much.

The bishop, dressed in ceremonial whites, sat in a high-backed chair between the two feuding families. He looked neither to the left, where the Winchesters were sequestered, nor to the right, where the St. James warriors were stationed, but stared straight ahead. To pass the time the clergyman drummed his fingertips on the wooden arm of his chair. He looked as though he'd just eaten a fair portion of sour fish. He let out a high-pitched sigh every now and then, a sound the baron thought was remarkably like the whinny of a cranky old horse, then let the damning silence envelop the great hall again.

Lawrence shook his head in despair. He knew he wouldn't get any help from the bishop when the real trouble broke out. Both the bride and the groom waited in separate chambers above the stairs. Only after the king had arrived would they be led, or dragged, into the hall. God help the two of them then, for all hell would surely break loose.

It was a sorry day indeed. Lawrence had actually had to post his own contingent of guards betwixt the king's knights along the perimeter of the hall just as an added deterrent. Such an action at a wedding was unheard of, yet it was just as unheard of for the guests to come to the ceremony armed for battle. The Winchesters were so loaded down with weapons they could barely move about. Their insolence was shameful, their loyalty more than suspect. Still, Lawrence was hard put to condemn the men completely. It was true that even he found it a challenge to blindly obey his leader. The king was, after all, as daft as a duck.

Everyone in England knew he had lost his mind, yet no one dared speak the fact aloud. They'd lose their tongues, or worse, for daring to tell the truth. The marriage about to take place was more than ample testimony to any doubting Thomases left in the *ton* that their leader had gone around the bend. The king had told Lawrence he was determined to have everyone in his kingdom get along. The baron didn't have an easy answer to that childlike expectation.

But for all of his madness, George was their king, and damn it all, thought Lawrence, the wedding guests should show a little respect. Their outrageous conduct shouldn't be tolerated. Why, two of the seasoned Winchester uncles were blatantly fondling the hilts of their swords in obvious anticipation of the bloodletting. The St. James warriors immediately noticed and retaliated by taking a unified step forward. They didn't touch their weapons, though, and in truth most of the St. James's men weren't even armed. They smiled instead. Lawrence thought that action was just as telling.

The Winchesters outnumbered the St. James clan six to one. That didn't give them the advantage, however. The St. James men were a much meaner lot. The stories about their escapades were legendary. They were known to tear a man's eyes out just for squinting; they liked to kick an opponent in his groin for the fun of hearing him howl; and God only knew what they did to their enemies. The possibilities were simply too appalling to think about.

A commotion coming from the courtyard turned Lawrence's attention. The king's personal assistant, a dour-faced man by the name of Sir Roland Hugo, rushed up the steps. He was dressed in festive garb, but the colorful red hose and white tunic made his imposing bulk all the more rotund-looking. Lawrence thought Hugo resembled a plump rooster. Because he was his good friend, he kept that unkind opinion to himself.

The two men quickly embraced. Then Hugo took a step back. In a hushed tone he said, "I rode ahead the last league. The king will be here in just a few more minutes."

"Thank God for that," Lawrence replied, his relief visible. He mopped at the beads of sweat on his brow with his linen handkerchief.

Hugo glanced over Lawrence's shoulder, then shook his head. "It's as quiet as a tomb in your hall," he whispered. "Have you had a time of it keeping the wedding guests amused?"

Lawrence looked incredulous. "Amused? Hugo, nothing short of a human sacrifice could keep those barbarians amused."

"I can see your sense of humor has helped you through this atrocity," his friend replied.

"I'm not jesting," the baron snapped. "You'll quit your smile, too, Hugo, when you realize how volatile the situation has become. The Winchesters didn't come bearing gifts, my friend. They're armed for battle. Yes, they are," he rushed on when his friend shook his head in apparent disbelief. "I tried to persuade them to leave their arsenal outside, but they wouldn't hear of it. They aren't in an accommodating mood."

"We'll see about that," Hugo muttered. "The soldiers riding escort with our king will disarm them in little time. I'll be damned if I allow our overlord to walk into such a threatening arena. This is a wedding, not a battlefield."

Hugo proved to be as good as his threat. The Winchesters piled their weapons in the corner of the great hall when they were confronted with the order by the infuriated king's assistant. The demand was backed up by some forty loyal soldiers who'd taken up their positions in a circle around the guests. Even the St. James rascals handed over their few weapons, but only after Hugo ordered arrows put to the soldiers' bows.

If he lived to tell the tale, no one was ever going to believe him, Lawrence decided. Thankfully, King George had no idea what extreme measures had been taken to secure his protection.

When the king of England walked into the great hall the

soldiers immediately lowered their bows, though their arrows remained securely nocked for a quick kill if the need arose.

The bishop rallied out of the chair, bowed formally to his king, and then motioned for him to take his seat.

Two of the king's barristers, their arms laden with documents, trailed in the king's wake. Lawrence waited until his leader was seated, then hurried over to kneel before him. He spoke his pledge of loyalty in a loud, booming voice, hoping his words would shame the guests into showing like consideration.

The king leaned forward, his big hands braced on his knees. "Your patriot king is pleased with you, Baron Lawrence. I am your patriot king, champion of all the people, am I not?"

Lawrence was prepared for that question. The king had taken to calling himself by that name years before, and he liked to hear affirmation whenever possible.

"Yes, my lord, you are my patriot king, champion of all the people."

"That's a good lad," the king whispered. He reached out and patted the top of Lawrence's balding head. The baron blushed in embarrassment. The king was treating him like a young squire. Worse, the baron was beginning to feel like one.

"Stand now, Baron Lawrence, and help me oversee this important occasion," the king ordered.

Lawrence immediately did as he was told. When he got a close look at his leader he had to force himself not to show any outward reaction. He was stunned by the king's deteriorating appearance. George had been a handsome figure in his younger days. Age hadn't been kind to him. His jowls were fuller, his wrinkles deeper, and there were full bags of fatigue under his eyes. He wore a pure white wig, the ends rolled up on the sides, but the color made his complexion look all the more shallow.

The king smiled up at his vassal in innocent expectation.

5

Lawrence smiled back. There was such kindness, such sincerity in his leader's expression. The baron was suddenly outraged on his behalf. For so many years, before his illness had made him confused, George had been far more than just an able king. His attitude toward his subjects was that of a benevolent father watching over his children. He deserved better than he was getting.

The baron moved to the king's side, then turned to look at the group of men he thought of as infidels. His voice shook with fury when he commanded, "Kneel!"

They knelt.

Hugo was staring at Lawrence with the most amazed expression on his face. He obviously hadn't realized his friend could be so forceful. As to that, Lawrence had to admit that until that moment he hadn't known he had it in him either.

The king was pleased with the united show of loyalty, and that was all that mattered. "Baron?" he said with a glance in Lawrence's direction. "Go and fetch the bride and groom. The hour grows late, and there is much to be done."

As Lawrence was bowing in answer to that command the king turned in his chair and looked up at Sir Hugo. "Where are all the ladies? I daresay I don't see a single lady in evidence. Why is that, Hugo?"

Hugo didn't want to tell the king the truth, that the men in attendance hadn't brought their women along because they were set on war, not merriment. Such honesty would only injure his king's tender feelings.

"Yes, my patriot king," Hugo blurted out. "I have also noticed the lack of ladies."

"But why is that?" the king persisted.

Hugo's mind emptied of all plausible explanations to give for the oddity. In desperation he called out to his friend. "Why is that, Lawrence?"

The baron had just reached the entrance. He caught the edge of panic in his friend's tone and immediately turned around. "The journey here would have been too difficult for such . . . frail ladies," he explained.

He almost choked on his words. The lie was outrageous, of course, for anyone who had ever met any of the Winchester women knew they were about as frail as jackals. King George's memory wasn't up to snuff, however, because his quick nod indicated he was appeased by the explanation.

The baron paused to glare at the Winchesters. It was their conduct, after all, that had forced the lie in the first place. He then continued on his errand.

The groom was the first to answer the summons. As soon as the tall, lanky marquess of St. James entered the hall a wide path was made for him.

The groom strolled into the hall like a mighty warrior ready to inspect his subjects. If he'd been homely, Lawrence would have thought of him as a young, arrogant Genghis Khan. The marquess was anything but homely, however. He had been gifted with dark, auburn-colored hair and clear green eyes. His face was thin, angular, his nose already broken in a fight he had, of course, won. The slight bump on the bridge made his profile look less pretty and more ruggedly handsome.

Nathan, as he was called by his immediate family, was one of the youngest noblemen in the kingdom. He was just a scant day over fourteen years. His father, the powerful earl of Wakersfield, was out of the country on an important assignment for his government and therefore couldn't stand beside his son during the ceremony. In fact, the earl had no idea the marriage was taking place. The baron knew he was going to be furious when he heard the news. The earl was a most unpleasant man under usual conditions, and when provoked he could be as vindictive and evil as Satan. He was known to be as mean as all the St. James relatives put together. Lawrence supposed that was the reason they all looked up to him for guidance on important matters.

Yet while Lawrence thoroughly disliked the earl, he

couldn't help but like Nathan. He'd been in the boy's company several times, noticed on each occasion that Nathan listened to the views the others had to give, and then did what he felt was best. He was just fourteen, yes, but he had already become his own man. Lawrence respected him. He felt a little sorry for him, too, for in all their visits together Lawrence had never once seen him smile. He thought that was a pity.

The St. James clan never called the marquess by his given name, though. They referred to him simply as "boy," for in their eyes he had still to prove his worth to them. There were tests he would have to conquer first. The relatives didn't doubt the lad's eventual success. They believed he was a natural leader, knew from his size that he would be a giant of a man, and hoped, above all other considerations, that he would develop a streak as mean as their own. He was family, after all, and there were certain responsibilities that would fall on his shoulders.

The marquess kept his gaze directed on the king of England as he made his way over to stand in front of him. The baron watched him closely. He knew Nathan had been instructed by his uncles not to kneel before his king unless commanded to do so.

Nathan ignored their instructions. He knelt on one knee, bowed his head, and stated his pledge of loyalty in a firm voice. When the king asked him if he was his patriot king, a hint of a smile softened the boy's expression.

"Aye, my lord," Nathan answered. "You are my patriot king."

The baron's admiration for the marquess increased tenfold. He could see from the king's smile that he was also pleased. Nathan's relatives weren't. Their scowls were hot enough to set fires. The Winchesters couldn't have been happier. They snickered in glee.

Nathan suddenly bounded to his feet in one fluid motion. He turned to stare at the Winchesters for a long, silent moment, and the look on his face, as cold as frost, seemed to chill the insolence right out of the men. The marquess didn't turn back to the king until most of the Winchesters were intently staring at the floor. The St. James men couldn't help but grunt their approval.

The lad wasn't paying any attention to his relatives. He stood with his legs braced apart, his hands clasped behind his back, and stared straight ahead. His expression showed only boredom.

Lawrence walked directly in front of Nathan so that he could nod to him. He wanted Nathan to know how much his conduct had pleased him.

Nathan responded by giving the baron a quick nod of his own. Lawrence hid his smile. The boy's arrogance warmed his heart. He had stood up to his relatives, ignoring the dire consequences that were sure to come, and had done the right thing. Lawrence felt very like a proud father—an odd reaction to be sure, for the baron had never married and had no children to call his own.

He wondered if Nathan's mask of boredom would hold up throughout the long ceremony. With that question lurking in the back of his mind he went to fetch the bride.

He could hear her wailing when he reached the second story. The sound was interrupted by a man's angry shout. The baron knocked on the door twice before the earl of Winchester, the bride's father, pulled it open. The earl's face was as red as a sunburn.

"It's about time," the earl bellowed.

"The king was delayed," the baron answered.

The earl abruptly nodded. "Come inside, Lawrence. Help me get her down the stairs, man. She's being a mite stubborn."

There was such surprise in the earl's voice, Lawrence almost smiled. "I've heard that stubbornness can be expected of such tender-aged daughters."

"I never heard such," the earl muttered. "'Tis the truth

this is the first time I've ever been alone with Sara. I'm not certain she knows exactly who I am," he added. "I did tell her, of course, but you will see she isn't in the mood to listen to anything. I had no idea she could be so difficult."

Lawrence couldn't hide his astonishment over the earl's outrageous remarks. "Harold," he answered, using the earl's given name, "you have two other daughters, as I recall, and both of them older than Sara. I don't understand how you can be so—"

The earl didn't let him finish. "I haven't ever had to be with any of them before," he muttered.

Lawrence thought that confession was appalling. He shook his head and followed the earl into the chamber. He spotted the bride right away. She was sitting on the edge of the window seat, staring out the window.

She quit crying as soon as she saw him. Lawrence thought she was the most enchanting bride he'd ever seen. A mop of golden curls framed an angelic face. There was a crown of spring flowers on her head, a cluster of freckles on the bridge of her nose. Tears streamed down her cheeks, and her brown eyes were cloudy with more.

She wore a long white dress with lace borders around the hem and wrists. When she stood up the embroidered sash around her waist fell to the floor.

Her father let out a loud blasphemy.

She repeated it.

"It's time for us to go downstairs, Sara," her father ordered, his voice as sour as the taste of soap.

"No."

The earl's outraged gasp filled the room. "When I get you home I'm going to make you very sorry you've put me through this ordeal, young lady. By God, I'm going to land on you, I am. Just you wait and see."

Since the baron didn't have the faintest idea what the earl meant by that absurd threat, he doubted Sara understood any better.

She was staring up at her father with a mutinous expression on her face. Then she let out a loud yawn and sat down again.

"Harold, shouting at your daughter isn't going to accomplish anything," the baron stated.

"Then I'll give her a good smack," the earl muttered. He took a threatening step toward his daughter, his hand raised to inflict the blow.

Lawrence stopped in front of the earl. "You aren't going to strike her," he said, his voice filled with anger.

"She's my daughter," the earl shouted. "I'll damn well do whatever it takes to gain her cooperation."

"You're a guest in my home now, Harold," the baron replied. He realized he was also shouting then and immediately lowered his voice. "Let me have a try."

Lawrence turned to the bride. Sara, he noticed, didn't seem to be at all worried by her father's anger. She let out another loud yawn.

"Sara, it will all be over and done with in just a little while," the baron said. He knelt down in front of her, gave her a quick smile, and then gently forced her to stand up. While he whispered words of praise to her he retied the sash around her waist. She yawned again.

The bride was in dire need of a nap. She let the baron tug her along to the door, then suddenly pulled out of his grasp, ran back to the window seat, and gathered up an old blanket that appeared to be three times her size.

She made a wide path around her father as she hurried back to the baron and took hold of his hand again. The blanket was draped over her shoulder and fell in a heap on the ground behind her. The edge was securely clasped under her nose.

Her father tried to take the blanket away.

Sara started screaming, her father started cursing, and the baron developed a pounding headache.

"For God's sake, Harold, let her have the thing."

"I'll not," the earl shouted. "It's an eyesore. I won't allow it."

"Let her keep it until we reach the hall," the baron commanded.

The earl finally conceded defeat. He gave his daughter a good glare, then took up his position in front of the pair and led the way down the stairs.

Lawrence found himself wishing Sara was his daughter. When she looked up at him and smiled so trustingly he wanted to take her into his arms and hug her. Her disposition underwent a radical change, however, when they reached the entrance to the hall and her father once again tried to take her blanket away.

Nathan turned when he heard the noise coming from the entrance. His eyes widened in astonishment. In truth, he was having difficulty believing what he was seeing. He hadn't been interested enough to ask any pertinent questions about his bride, for he was certain his father would have the documents overturned as soon as he returned to England, and for that reason he was all the more surprised by the sight of her.

His bride was a hellion. Nathan had trouble maintaining his bored expression. The earl of Winchester was doing more shouting than his daughter was. She, however, was far more determined. She had her arms wrapped around her father's leg and was diligently trying to take a fair chunk out of his knee.

Nathan smiled. His relatives weren't as reserved. Their laughter filled the hall. The Winchesters, on the other hand, were clearly appalled. The earl, their unspoken leader, had pulled his daughter away from his leg and was now involved in a tug of war over what resembled an old horse blanket. He wasn't winning the battle, either.

Baron Lawrence lost the last shreds of his composure. He grabbed hold of the bride, lifted her into his arms, snatched the blanket away from her father, and then marched over to

Nathan. With little ceremony he shoved the bride and the blanket into the groom's arms.

It was either accept her or drop her. Nathan was in the process of making up his mind on the matter when Sara spotted her father limping toward her. She quickly threw her arms around Nathan's neck, wrapping both herself and her blanket around him.

Sara kept glancing over his shoulder to make certain her father wasn't going to grab her. When she was certain she was safe she turned her full attention to the stranger holding her. She stared at him for the longest while.

The groom stood as straight as a lance. A fine sweat broke out on his brow. He could feel her gaze on his face yet didn't dare turn to look at her. She just might decide to bite him, and he didn't know what he would do then. He made up his mind that he would just have to suffer through any embarrassment she forced on him. He was, after all, almost a man, and she was, after all, only a child.

Nathan kept his gaze directed on the king until Sara reached out to touch his cheek. He finally turned to look at her.

She had the brownest eyes he'd ever seen. "Papa's going to smack me," she announced with a grimace.

He didn't show any reaction to that statement. Sara soon tired of watching him. Her eyelids fell to half mast. He stiffened even more when she slumped against his shoulder. Her face was pressed up against the side of his neck.

"Don't let Papa smack me," she whispered.

"I won't," he answered.

He had suddenly become her protector. Nathan couldn't hold onto his bored expression any longer. He cradled his bride in his arms and relaxed his stance.

Sara, exhausted from the long ride and her strenuous tantrum, rubbed the edge of her blanket back and forth under her nose. Within bare minutes she was fast asleep.

She drooled on his neck.

The groom didn't find out her true age until the barrister began the reading of the conditions for the union.

His bride was four years old.

Chapter One

London, England, 1816

It was going to be a clean, uncomplicated kidnapping.

Ironically, the abduction would probably hold up in the courts as a completely legal undertaking, save for the niggling breaking and entering charges, of course, but that possibility wasn't the least significant. Nathanial Clayton Hawthorn Baker, the third marquess of St. James, was fully prepared to use whatever methods he deemed necessary to gain success. If luck was on his side, his victim would be sound asleep. If not, a simple gag would eliminate any sounds of protest.

One way or another, legal or nay, he would collect his bride. Nathan, as he was called by those few friends close to him, wasn't going to have to act like a gentleman—a blessing, that, considering the fact that such tender qualities were completely foreign to his nature anyway. Besides, time was running out. There were only six weeks left before he would be in true violation of the marriage contract.

Nathan hadn't seen his bride since the day the contracts were read fourteen years earlier, but the picture he'd painted in his mind wasn't fanciful. He didn't have any illusions about the chit, for he'd seen enough Winchester women to know there wasn't any such thing as a pick of the litter. They were all a sorry lot in both appearance and disposition. Most were pear-shaped, with big bones, bigger derrières, and, if the stories weren't exaggerated, gigantic appetites.

Although having a wife by his side was about as appealing to him as a midnight swim with the sharks would be, Nathan was fully prepared to suffer through the ordeal. Perhaps, if he really put his mind to the problem, he could find a way to meet the conditions of the contract without having to stay with the woman day and night.

For most of his life Nathan had been on his own, refusing to receive counsel from any man. Only his trusted friend Colin was privy to his thoughts. Still, the stakes were too high for Nathan to ignore. The booty the contract afforded after one year's cohabitation with Lady Sara more than made up for any repulsion he might feel or any inconvenience he might have to endure. The coins he would collect by the crown's decree would strengthen the fledgling partnership he and Colin had formed the summer before. The Emerald Shipping Company was the first legitimate business either man had ever attempted, and they were determined to make it work. The reason was simple to understand. Both men were tired of living on the edge. They'd fallen into the business of pirating quite by accident —had done fairly well for themselves, too—yet they felt that the risks involved were no longer worth the aggravation. Nathan, operating as the infamous pirate Pagan, had made quite a legend for himself. His list of enemies could carpet a good-sized ballroom. The bounty on his head had increased to such an outlandish amount that even a saint would be tempted to turn traitor for the reward. Keeping Nathan's other identity a secret was becoming more and more difficult. It was only a matter of time before he was caught, if they continued with their pirating escapades, or so Colin relentlessly nagged, until Nathan finally agreed.

Exactly one week after that momentous decision had been

made the Emerald Shipping Company was founded. The offices were located in the heart of the waterfront, the furnishings sparse. There were two desks, four chairs, and one filing cabinet, all blistered from a previous fire. The former tenant hadn't bothered to cart them away. Since coins were at a premium, new furniture was at the bottom of their list of purchases. Additional ships for their fleet came first.

Both men understood the ins and outs of the business community. They were both graduates of Oxford University, although as students neither had anything to do with the other. Colin never went anywhere without a pack of friends in attendance. Nathan was always alone. It was only when the two men were partnered as operatives in a deadly game of secret government activities that a bond formed between them. It took a long while, a year or so, before Nathan began to trust Colin. They had risked their lives for each other and for their beloved country, only to be betrayed by their own superiors. Colin had been stunned and outraged when the truth became known. Nathan hadn't been surprised at all. He always expected the worst in people and was rarely disappointed. Nathan was a cynical man by nature and a fighter by habit. He was a man who thoroughly enjoyed a good brawl, leaving Colin to clean up the mess.

Colin's older brother, Caine, was the earl of Cainewood. He'd married Nathan's younger sister, Jade, just the year before, and in so doing unknowingly strengthened the bond between the two friends. Colin and Nathan had become brothers by marriage.

Because Nathan was a marquess and Colin was the brother of a powerful earl, both men were invited to all the affairs of the *ton*. Colin mingled quite easily with the staunch upper crust and used each occasion to mix pleasure with the business of building their clientele. Nathan never attended any of the parties, which was, as Colin suggested, probably the reason he was invited. It was a fact that society didn't consider Nathan a very likable man. He certainly wasn't bothered by the *ton*'s opinion of him, though, for he much preferred the comfort of a seedy tavern on the wharf to the stiffness of a formal salon.

In appearance the two men were just as different. Colin was, as Nathan liked to remark whenever he wanted to prick his temper, the pretty one in the partnership. Colin was an attractive man with hazel eyes and a strong patrician profile. He'd taken to the unsavory habit of wearing his dark brown hair as long as his friend's, a lingering leftover from his pirating days, but that minor fashion sin didn't detract from the perfection of his unscarred face. Colin was almost as tall as Nathan was, but much leaner in build, and as arrogant as Brummell when the occasion called for it. The ladies of the *ton* thought Colin incredibly handsome. Colin had a noticeable limp due to an accident, but that even seemed to add to his appeal.

When it came to appearance, Nathan hadn't been as blessed. He looked more like a warlord from the ancient days than a modern Adonis. He never bothered to bind his auburn-colored hair in a leather thong behind his neck the way Colin usually did but left it to fall past his shoulders as was its natural inclination. Nathan was a giant of a man, muscular in both shoulders and thighs, with nary a pinch of fat on his frame. His eyes were a vivid green—an attention-getter, to be sure, if the ladies weren't in such a hurry to get away from his dark scowl.

To outsiders the two friends were complete opposites. Colin was considered the saint, Nathan the sinner. In reality, their dispositions were very much alike. Both kept their emotions locked inside. Nathan used isolation and a surly temper as his weapons against involvement. Colin used superficiality for the same reason.

In truth, Colin's grin was as much a mask as Nathan's scowl. Past betrayals had trained the two men well. Neither man believed in the fairy tale of love or the nonsense of living happily ever after. Only fops and fools believed in such fantasies.

Nathan's scowl was in full evidence when he walked into the office. He found Colin lounging in a wingback chair with his feet propped up on the window seat.

"Jimbo has two mounts ready, Colin," Nathan said, referring to their shipmate. "You two have an errand to do?"

"You know what the mounts are for, Nathan. You and I are going to ride over to the gardens and have a look at Lady Sara. There's going to be quite a crush of people in attendance this afternoon. No one will see us if we keep to the trees."

Nathan turned to look out the window before answering. "No."

"Jimbo will watch the office while we're away."

"Colin, I don't need to see her before tonight."

"Damn it all, you need to get a good look at her first."

"Why?" Nathan asked. He sounded genuinely perplexed.

Colin shook his head. "To prepare yourself."

Nathan turned around. "I don't need to prepare myself," he said. "Everything's ready. I already know which window belongs to her bedchamber. The tree outside will hold my weight; I tested it to be sure. There isn't a lock on her window to worry about, and the ship is ready to sail."

"So you've thought of everything, have you?"

Nathan nodded. "Of course."

"Oh?" Colin paused to smile. "And what if she won't fit through the window? Have you considered that possibility?"

That question got just the reaction Colin wanted. Nathan looked startled, then shook his head. "It's a large window, Colin."

"She might be larger."

If Nathan was chilled by that possibility, he didn't let it show. "Then I'll roll her down the stairs," he drawled.

Colin laughed over that picture. "Aren't you at all curious to see how she turned out?"

"No."

"Well, I am," Colin finally admitted. "Since I won't be

going along with you two on your honeymoon, it's only decent to satisfy my curiosity before you leave."

"It's a journey, not a honeymoon," Nathan countered. "Quit trying to bait me, Colin. She's a Winchester, for God's sake, and the only reason we're sailing is to get her away from her relatives."

"I don't know how you're going to stomach it," Colin said. His grin was gone, his concern obvious in his expression. "God, Nathan, you're going to have to bed her in order to produce an heir if you want the land, too."

Before Nathan could comment on that reminder Colin continued. "You don't have to go through with this. The company will make it with or without the funds from the contract. Besides, now that King George has officially stepped down the prince regent will surely rule to overturn the contract. The Winchesters have been waging an intense campaign to sway his mind. You could turn your back on this."

"No." His tone was emphatic. "My signature's on that contract. A St. James doesn't break his word."

Colin snorted. "You can't be serious," he replied. "The St. James men are known to break just about anything when the mood strikes them."

Nathan had to agree with that observation. "Yes," he said. "Regardless, Colin, I won't turn my back on this matter any more than you would take the money your brother offered. It's a point of honor. Hell, we've been over this before. My mind's made up."

He leaned against the window frame and let out a long, weary sigh. "You aren't going to let up unless I agree to go, are you?"

"No," Colin answered. "Besides, you'll want to count the number of Winchester uncles there so you'll know how many you have to contend with this evening."

It was a paltry argument, and they both knew it. "No one's going to get in my way, Colin."

That statement was made in a soft, chilling tone of voice.

Colin grinned in reaction. "I'm well aware of your special talents, friend. I just hope to God there isn't a bloodbath tonight."

"Why?"

"I'd hate to miss all the fun."

"Then come along."

"I can't," Colin answered. "One favor deserves another, remember? I had to promise the duchess I'd attend her daughter's recital, heaven save me, if she could find a way to get Lady Sara to attend her party this afternoon."

"She won't be there," Nathan predicted. "Her bastard father doesn't let her attend any functions."

"Sara will be there," Colin predicted. "The earl of Winchester wouldn't dare offend the duchess. She specifically requested that Lady Sara be allowed to join in the festivities."

"What reason did she give?"

"I haven't the faintest idea," Colin answered. "Time's wasting, Nathan."

"Damn." After muttering that expletive Nathan pulled away from the frame. "Let's get it done, then."

Colin was quick to take advantage of his victory. He strode out the door before his friend could change his mind.

On their way across the congested city he turned to ask Nathan, "Aren't you wondering how we'll know which one is Sara?"

"I'm sure you have it all figured out," he remarked dryly.

"That I do," Colin returned in a gratingly cheerful voice. "My sister Rebecca has promised she'll stay close to Lady Sara all afternoon. I've hedged my bets, too."

He waited a long minute for Nathan to inquire as to how he'd done that, then continued. "If Rebecca is waylaid from her duty, I've lined up my other three sisters to take turns stepping in. You know, old boy, you really could show a little more enthusiasm."

"This outing is a complete waste of my time."

Colin didn't agree, but he kept that opinion to himself.

Neither man spoke again until they'd reached the rise above the gardens and reined in their mounts. The cover of the trees shielded them well, yet they had a clear view of the guests strolling about the gardens of the duchess's estate below.

"Hell, Colin, I feel like a schoolboy."

His friend laughed. "Leave it to the duchess to go overboard," he remarked when he noticed the crowd of musicians filing toward the lower terrace. "She hired an entire orchestra."

"Ten minutes, Colin, and then I'm leaving."

"Agreed," Colin placated. He turned to look at his friend. Nathan was scowling. "You know, she might have been willing to leave with you, Nathan, if you'd—"

"Are you suggesting I send another letter?" Nathan asked. He raised an eyebrow over the absurdity of that possibility. "You do recall what happened the last time I followed your advice, don't you?"

"Of course I remember," Colin answered. "But things might have changed. There could have been a misunderstanding. Her father could have—"

"A misunderstanding?" Nathan sounded incredulous. "I sent the note on a Thursday, and I was damn specific, Colin."

"I know," Colin said. "You told them you were going to collect your bride the following Monday."

"You thought I should have given her more time to pack her belongings."

Colin grinned. "I did, didn't I? In defense of my gentlemanly behavior, I must say I never imagined she'd run away. She was quick, too, wasn't she?"

"Yes, she was," Nathan replied, a hint of a smile in his voice.

"You could have gone after her."

"Why? My men followed her. I knew where she was. I just decided to leave her alone a little longer."

"A stay of execution, perchance?"

Nathan did laugh then. "She's only a woman, Colin, but yes, I do suppose it was a reprieve of sorts."

"There was more to it than that, though, wasn't there? You knew she would be in danger as soon as you claimed her. You won't admit it, Nathan, but in your own way you've been protecting Sara by leaving her alone. I'm right, aren't I?"

"You just said I wouldn't admit it," he countered. "Why bother to ask?"

"God help the two of you. The next year is going to be hell. You'll both have the world trying to do you in."

Nathan shrugged. "I'll protect her."

"I don't doubt that."

Nathan shook his head. "The daft woman actually booked passage on one of our own ships to run away from me. That still chafes. A bit of an irony, wouldn't you say?"

"Not really," Colin answered. "She couldn't have known you owned the ship. You did insist upon remaining a silent partner in the company, remember?"

"We wouldn't have any clients otherwise. You know damn well the St. James men aren't liked by the members of the *ton*. They're still a little rough around the cuffs." His grin told his friend he found that trait appealing.

"It's still odd to me," Colin announced, switching the topic. "You had your men follow Lady Sara—watch out for her, too—yet you never bothered to ask any of them to tell you what she looked like."

"You didn't ask any of them either," Nathan countered.

Colin shrugged. He returned his attention to the crowd below. "I suppose I thought you'd decide the contract wasn't worth the sacrifice. After all, she . . ." He completely lost his train of thought when he spotted his sister strolling toward them. Another woman walked by her side. "There's Becca," he said. "If the silly chit would just move a little to the left . . ." That remark went unfinished. Colin's indrawn breath filled the air. "Sweet Jesus . . . could that be Lady Sara?"

Nathan didn't answer him. In truth, he doubted he was capable of speech right then. His mind was fully consumed taking in the vision before him.

She was enchanting. Nathan had to shake his head. No, he told himself, she couldn't possibly be his bride. The gentle lady smiling so shyly at Rebecca was simply too beautiful, too feminine, and too damn thin to belong to the Winchester clan.

And yet there was a hint of a resemblance, a nagging reminder of the impossible four-year-old he'd held in his arms, something indefinable that told him she really was his Lady Sara.

Gone was the wild mop of honey-colored curls. Her hair was shoulder-length, still given to curl, but as dark as chestnuts. Her complexion looked pure to him from the distance separating them, and he wondered if she still had the sprinkle of freckles across the bridge of her nose.

She'd grown to only average height, judging by the fact that she was eye level with Colin's younger sister. There certainly wasn't anything average about her figure, however. She was rounded in all the right places.

"Look at all the young bucks moving in," Colin announced. "They're like sharks circling their prey. Your wife seems to be their target, Nathan," he added. "Hell, you'd think they would have the decency to leave a married woman alone. Still, I suppose I can't really fault them. My God, Nathan, she's magnificent."

Nathan was fully occupied watching the eager men chase after his bride. He had an almost overwhelming urge to beat the foppish grins off their faces. How dare they try to touch what belonged to him?

He shook his head over his illogical reaction to his bride.

"Here comes your charming father-in-law," Colin said. "God, I didn't realize how bowlegged he is. Look how he shadows her," he continued. "He isn't about to let his prize out of his sight."

Nathan took a deep breath. "Let's ride, Colin. I've seen enough."

Not a hint of emotion was in his voice. Colin turned to look at him. "Well?"

"Well, what?"

"Damn it, Nathan, tell me what you think."

"About what?"

"Lady Sara," Colin persisted. "What do you think of her?"

"The truth, Colin?"

His friend gave a quick nod.

Nathan's smile was slow, easy. "She'll fit through the window."

Chapter Two

⁓

Time was running out.

Sara was going to have to leave England. Everyone would probably think she'd run away again. They'd begin to call her coward, she supposed, and although that slander would sting, she was still determined to go through with her plans. Sara simply didn't have any other choice. She'd already sent two letters to the marquess of St. James requesting his assistance, but the man to whom she was legally wed hadn't bothered to respond. She didn't dare try to contact him again. There simply wasn't enough time left. Aunt Nora's future was at stake, and Sara was the only one who could—or, more specifically, who would—save her.

If the members of the *ton* believed she was running away from the marriage contract, so be it.

Nothing ever turned out the way Sara imagined it would. When her mother had asked her to go to Nora's island the previous spring to make certain she was all right Sara had immediately agreed. Her mother hadn't received a letter from her sister in over four months, and fear about her health was beginning to make Sara's mother ill. In truth,

Sara was just as concerned about her mother's health as she was about her aunt's. Something had to be amiss. It simply wasn't like her aunt to forget to write. No, the monthly packet of letters had always been as dependable as the inevitable rain on the annual Winchester picnics.

Sara and her mother agreed that neither one of them would confide the real reason behind her sudden departure. They settled on the lie that Sara was simply going to visit her older sister Lillian, who lived in the colonies of America with her husband and infant son.

Sara had considered telling her father the truth, then discarded the notion. Even though he was certainly the most reasonable of the brothers, he was still a Winchester through and through. He didn't like Nora any better than his brothers did, though for his wife's sake he wasn't as vocal in his opinions.

The Winchester men had turned their backs on Nora when she disgraced them by marrying beneath her station. The marriage to her groom had taken place fourteen years earlier, but the Winchesters weren't a forgiving lot. They put great store in the expression "an eye for an eye." Revenge was as sacred to them as the commandments were to most of the bishops, even when the infraction was as slight as a brief month of public embarrassment. Not only would they never forget their humiliation, they would also never, ever forgive.

Sara should have realized that fact sooner. She never would have allowed Nora to come home for a visit otherwise. Heaven help her, she'd actually believed that time had softened her uncles' attitude. The sad truth was quite the opposite. There wasn't a happy reunion allowed between the sisters. Sara's mother didn't even get to speak to Nora. As to that, no one did, for Nora had simply vanished a scant hour after she and Sara had left the ship.

Sara was nearly out of her mind with worry. The time had finally come to put her plan into action, and her nerves were at the screaming point. Her fear had become an almost tangible thing, tearing at her determination. She was accustomed to letting other people take care of her, but the shoe was on the other foot, as Nora liked to say, and Sara needed to be the one in charge. She prayed to God she was up to the challenge. Nora's life depended upon her success.

The horrendous pretense Sara had had to endure the past two weeks had become a nightmare. Each time she heard the door chime sound she was certain the authorities had come to tell her Nora's body had been found. Finally, when she thought she couldn't stand the worry another minute, her faithful servant Nicholas had found out where her uncles had hidden Aunt Nora. The gentle woman had been closeted away in the attic of her Uncle Henry's townhouse until all the arrangements could be made with the court for guardianship. Then she was going to be spirited away to the nearest asylum, with her fat inheritance divided between the other men in the family.

"The bloody leeches," Sara muttered to herself. Her hand shook when she clipped the latch shut on her satchel. She told herself it was anger and certainly not fear that made her tremble so. Every time she thought about the terror her aunt must be going through she became infuriated all over again.

She took a deep, calming breath as she carried her satchel over to the open window. She tossed the garment bag down to the ground. "That's the last of it, Nicholas. Hurry now before the family returns. Godspeed, friend."

The servant collected the last bag and rushed toward the waiting hack. Sara closed the window, doused the candle, and climbed into bed.

It was almost the midnight hour when her parents and her sister Belinda returned from their outing. When Sara heard the footsteps in the hallway she rolled onto her stomach, closed her eyes, and feigned sleep. A moment later she heard the squeak of the door as it was opened and knew her father was looking in to see that his daughter was where she was supposed to be. It seemed to Sara an eternity passed before the door was pulled shut again.

Sara waited another twenty minutes or so to let the household settle down for the night. Then she slipped out from under the covers and collected her belongings from where she'd hidden them under the bed. She needed to be inconspicuous on her journey. Since she didn't own anything black, she wore her old dark blue walking dress. The neckline was a little too revealing, but she didn't have time to worry about that problem. Besides, her cloak would conceal that flaw. She was too nervous to braid her hair and had to settle on tying it behind her neck with a ribbon so it would stay out of her way.

After she'd placed the letter she'd written to her mother on the dressing table she wrapped her parasol, white gloves, and reticule in her cloak. She tossed those possessions out the window, then climbed out on the ledge.

The branch she wanted to grasp was just two feet away but a good three to four feet below her. Sara said a quick prayer she'd make it as she wiggled closer to the edge. She sat there a long while until she could summon up enough courage to jump. Then, with a whimper of fear she couldn't contain, she pushed herself off the ledge.

Nathan couldn't believe what he was seeing. He was just about to climb up the giant tree when the window opened and various articles belonging to a woman came flying down. The parasol hit him on his shoulder. He dodged the other items and moved deeper into the shadows. The moon gave him sufficient light to see Sara when she climbed out on the ledge. He was about to shout a warning, certain she was going to break her neck, when she suddenly jumped. He raced forward to catch her.

Sara caught hold of a fat branch and held on for dear life. She said another prayer to keep herself from crying out. Then she waited until she quit swinging back and forth so violently and slowly wiggled her way toward the trunk.

"Oh, God, oh, God, oh, God." She whispered that litany all the way down the tree. Her dress got tangled up in another branch, and by the time her feet finally touched the ground the hem of her gown had worked its way up and over her head.

Sara righted her dress and let out a long, ragged sigh. "There now," she whispered. "That wasn't so horrible after all."

Lord, she thought, she was starting to lie to herself. She knelt down on the ground, gathered up her possessions, mumbling all the while, and wasted precious minutes putting on her white gloves. Dusting her cloak off took a bit longer. After she'd adjusted the garment around her shoulders she untwisted the strings of her reticule, slipped the satin cords around her wrist, tucked the parasol under her arm, and finally walked toward the front of the house.

She stopped quite suddenly, certain she heard a sound behind her. Yet when she whirled around she didn't see anything but trees and shadows. Her imagination was getting the better of her, she decided. It was probably just her own heartbeat making all the ruckus in her ears.

"Where is Nicholas?" she muttered to herself a short time later. The servant was supposed to be waiting for her in the shadows next to the front stoop. Nicholas had promised to escort her to her Uncle Henry Winchester's townhouse. Something must have happened to waylay him, she decided.

Another ten minutes passed before Sara accepted the fact that Nicholas wasn't going to return to fetch her. She didn't dare wait any longer. There was too much risk of being found out. Since her return to London two weeks before her father had taken to the habit of looking in on her during the night. There would be hell to pay when he realized she'd run away again. Sara shivered just thinking about the consequences.

She was completely on her own. That admission made her heartbeat go wild again. She straightened her shoulders and then started walking toward her destination.

Uncle Henry's townhouse was just three short blocks

away. It shouldn't take her any time at all to walk over there. Besides, it was the middle of the night, and surely the streets would be deserted. Villains needed their rest, too, didn't they? Lord, she certainly hoped so. She would fare all right, she told herself as she hurried down the street. If anyone tried to waylay her, she'd use her parasol as a weapon to defend herself. She was determined to go to any length to save her Aunt Nora from having to spend one more night under her uncle's sadistic supervision.

Sara ran like lightning the first full block. A stitch in her side forced her to slow down to a more sedate pace. She relaxed a little when she realized she was actually quite safe. There didn't seem to be anyone else on the streets that night. Sara smiled over that blessing.

Nathan followed behind. He wanted to appease his curiosity before he grabbed his bride, tossed her over his shoulder, and headed for the wharf. In the back of his mind was the irritating thought that she might be trying to run away from him again. He discarded that notion as foolish, for she couldn't possibly know about his plans to kidnap her.

Where was she going? He mulled that question over in his mind while he continued to trail her.

She did have gumption, though. He found that revelation astonishing, since she was a Winchester. Yet she'd already shown him a glimpse of real courage. He'd heard her cry out in obvious fear when she'd thrown herself off that ledge. The woman had gotten herself caught up in the branches, too, then prayed her way down to the ground in a low, fervent voice that had made him smile. He'd gotten a healthy view of her long, shapely legs while she was in such an unseemly position and had to restrain himself from laughing out loud.

It soon became evident to him that she was still blissfully oblivious to his presence. Nathan couldn't believe her naïveté. If she'd only bothered to look behind her, she certainly would have seen him.

She never bothered to look back. His bride rounded the first corner, passed a dark alley at a brisker pace, then slowed down again.

She hadn't gone unnoticed. Two burly men, their weapons at the ready, slithered out of their makeshift home like snakes. Nathan was right behind them. He made certain they heard his approach, then waited until they were turning around to confront him before he slammed their heads together.

Nathan tossed the garbage back into the alley, his gaze directed on Sara all the while. The way his bride strolled down the street should be outlawed, he thought to himself. The sway of her hips was too damn enticing. Just then he saw another movement in the shadows ahead. He rushed forward to save Sara once again. She'd just turned the second corner when his fist slammed into her would-be attacker's jaw.

He had to intervene on her behalf yet again before she finally reached her destination. He assumed she was going to call on her Uncle Henry Winchester when she paused on the bottom step of his residence and stared up at the dark windows a long while.

Of all her relatives, Nathan thought Henry was the most disreputable, and he couldn't come up with a single logical reason why Sara would want to call on the spineless bastard in the middle of the night.

She wasn't there for a visit. Nathan came to that conclusion when she crept around to the side of the townhouse. He followed her, then lounged against the side gate to keep other intruders out. He folded his arms across his chest and relaxed his stance while he watched her fight her way through the shrubs and breach the house through the window.

It was the most inept burglary he'd ever witnessed.

She spent at least ten minutes working the window all the way up. That simple accomplishment was a short victory, though. She was just about to hoist herself up onto the ledge when she tore the hem of her gown. Nathan heard her cry of distress, then watched her turn and give full attention to her gown. The window slid back down while Sara lamented over the damage.

If she had a needle and thread handy, he thought she might very well sit down next to the shrubs and repair the dress.

She finally turned back to her purpose, though. She thought she was being quite clever when she used her parasol to prop the window open. She adjusted the strings of her reticule around her wrist before she jumped up to grab hold of the ledge. It took her three tries before she made it. Getting in through a window proved to be far more difficult than getting out through one. She fairly knocked the wind out of herself before she finally made it. She wasn't at all graceful, either. When Nathan heard the loud thud he decided his bride had landed on either her head or her backside. He waited only a minute or two before he silently climbed in after her.

He adjusted to the darkness quickly. Sara didn't make the adjustment quite as swiftly, however. Nathan heard a loud crash that sounded like glass hitting stone, followed by an unladylike expletive.

Lord, she was loud. Nathan strolled into the foyer just in time to see Sara rush up the steps to the second story. The crazed woman was actually muttering to herself.

A tall, willow-thin man Nathan assumed was one of the servants drew his attention then. The man looked ridiculous. He was dressed in a white knee-length nightshirt. He carried an ornately carved candlestick in one hand and a large crust of bread in the other. The servant lifted the candlestick above his head and started up the steps after Sara. Nathan clipped him on the back of his neck, reached over his head to take the candlestick out of his hand so it wouldn't make a clatter when it hit the floor, then dragged the servant into a dark alcove adjacent to the stairs. He stood next to the crumpled form a long minute while he listened to all the racket coming from above the stairs.

Sara would never make a proper thief. He could hear the doors being slammed shut and knew it was his bride making all the noise. She was going to wake the dead if she didn't quiet down. And what in God's name was she looking for?

A shrill scream rent the air. Nathan let out a weary sigh. He started toward the stairs to save the daft woman once again, then suddenly stopped when she appeared at the landing. She wasn't alone. Nathan moved back into the alcove and waited. He understood the reason for her errand. Sara had her arm around another woman's stooped shoulders and was assisting her down the stairs. He couldn't see the other woman's face, but he could tell from her slow, hesitant walk that she was either very feeble or in terrible pain.

"Please don't cry, Nora," Sara whispered. "Everything's going to be fine now. I'm going to take good care of you."

When the pair reached the foyer Sara took off her cloak, adjusted it around the other woman's shoulders, and then leaned forward to kiss her on her forehead.

"I knew you would come for me, Sara. I never doubted. I knew in my heart that you would find a way to help me."

Nora's voice cracked with emotion. She mopped at the corners of her eyes with the backs of her hands. Nathan noticed the dark bruises on her wrists. He recognized the marks. The old woman had obviously been tied up.

Sara reached up to adjust the pins in her aunt's hair. "Of course you knew I would come for you," she whispered. "I love you, Aunt Nora. I would never let anything happen to you. There," she added in as cheerful a tone of voice as she could manage, "your hair looks lovely again."

Nora grasped Sara's hand. "Whatever would I do without you, child?"

"That's a foolish worry," Sara answered. She kept her

voice soothing, for she knew her aunt was in jeopardy of losing her control. Sara was actually in much the same condition. When she'd seen the bruises on her aunt's face and arms she'd wanted to weep.

"You came back to England because I asked you to," Sara reminded her. "I thought you would have a happy reunion with your sister, but I was wrong. This atrocity is all my fault, Nora. Besides, you must know you're never going to have to do without me."

"You're such a dear child," Nora answered.

Sara's hand shook when she reached for the door lock. "How did you find me?" Nora asked from behind.

"It doesn't matter now," Sara said. She worked the lock free and opened the door. "We're going to have all the time in the world to visit after we've boarded the ship. I'm taking you back home, Nora."

"Oh, I can't leave London just yet."

Sara turned around to look at her aunt. "What do you mean, you can't leave just yet? Everything's been arranged, Nora. I've booked passage with the last of my funds. Please don't shake your head at me. Now isn't the time to turn difficult. We have to leave tonight. It's too dangerous for you to stay here."

"Henry took my wedding band," Nora explained. She shook her head again. The silvery cluster of hair at the top of her head immediately sagged to one side. "I won't leave England without it. My Johnny, God rest his soul, gave me orders never to take it off the day we were wed fourteen years ago. I can't go home without my wedding band, Sara. It's too precious to me."

"Yes, we must find it," Sara agreed when her aunt started to weep again. She was alarmed by the wheeze in her aunt's voice, too. The dear woman was obviously having difficulty catching her breath. "Do you have any idea where Uncle Henry might have hidden it?"

"That's the true blasphemy," Nora answered. She leaned

35

against the banister in an effort to ease the ache in her chest, then said, "Henry didn't bother to hide it. He's wearing it on his little finger. Sporting it like a trophy, he is. Now, if we could determine where your uncle is drinking tonight, we could fetch the band back."

Sara nodded. Her stomach started aching at the thought of what she was going to have to do. "I know where he is," she said. "Nicholas has been following him. Now, are you up to a short walk to the corner of the block? I didn't dare order the hack to wait out front for fear Uncle Henry would come home early."

"Of course I'm up to a walk," Nora answered. She moved away from the banister. Her gait was stiff as she slowly made her way to the door. "Heavens," she whispered. "If your mother could see me now, she'd die of shame. I'm about to take a walk in the dead of night dressed in my nightgown and a borrowed cloak."

Sara smiled. "We aren't going to tell my mother, though, are we?" She let out a gasp when she saw her aunt grimace. "You're in terrible pain, aren't you?"

"Nonsense," Nora scoffed. "I'm already feeling much better. Come along now," she ordered in a brisker tone. "We mustn't linger here, child." She clutched the rail and started down the steps. "It will take more than a Winchester to do me in."

Sara started to pull the door shut behind her, then changed her mind. "I believe I shall leave this door wide open in the hope that someone will come along and help himself to Uncle Henry's possessions. I dare not get my hopes up, though," she added. "There don't seem to be any villains on the streets tonight. On my walk over here I saw nary a one."

"Good Lord, Sara, you actually walked over here?" Aunt Nora asked, clearly appalled.

"I did," Sara answered. There was a hint of a boast in her voice. "I kept my guard up, of course, so you can quit your frown. I didn't have to use my parasol once to fend off anyone with ill intentions, either. Oh, heavens, I've left my lovely parasol in the window."

"Leave it be," her aunt ordered when Sara started back up the steps. "We're pressing our luck against the devil if we stay here much longer. Now give me your arm, dear. I'll hold onto you while we make this short walk. You really walked over here, Sara?"

Sara laughed. "To tell you the full truth, I do believe I ran most of the way. I was very frightened, Nora, but I made the journey without mishap. Do you know, I believe all this talk about our streets being so unsafe is just exaggeration."

The two ladies strolled arm in arm down the dark, narrow street, Sara's laughter trailing behind them. The hack was waiting for them at the corner. Sara was assisting her aunt inside the black vehicle when a hopeful assailant came rushing toward them. Nathan intervened by simply moving forward into the moonlight. The man took one look at him, did a hasty turnaround, and blended back into the shadows again.

Nathan thought the old woman might have gotten a look at him. She had glanced back over her shoulder just when he'd moved forward, but he decided her eyesight must have dimmed with age when she turned around again without shouting a warning to her niece.

Sara certainly hadn't noticed his presence. She had a heated discussion over the fare with the driver, finally agreed to his exorbitant fee, and then joined her aunt inside the vehicle. The hack was in motion when Nathan grabbed hold of the back rail and swung himself up on the ledge. The vehicle rocked from the added weight before picking up speed again.

Sara was certainly making her own kidnapping easy work. Nathan had heard her tell her aunt that they would be leaving London by ship. He therefore assumed their destination was the wharf. Then the hack veered off onto one of the side streets near the waterfront and came to an abrupt stop in front of one of the most notorious taverns in the city.

She was going after the damn wedding band, he supposed with a growl of irritation. Nathan jumped down from the ledge and moved into the light further behind the hack. He wanted the men loitering in front of the tavern to get a good look at him. He braced his legs apart for a fight, moved his right hand to the hilt of the coiled whip hooked to his belt, and scowled at the sizable group.

They noticed him. Three of the smaller ones edged their way back inside. The other four leaned back against the stone wall. Their gazes were directed on the ground.

The driver climbed down from his perch, received fresh instructions, and hurried inside. He came back outside a scant minute later, muttered that he'd best be getting a giant bonus for all the trouble he'd had to endure, and then climbed back up to his seat.

Another few minutes elapsed before the door of the tavern opened again. A sour-faced man with a grossly distended belly came outside. He was dressed in rumpled, soiled clothing that was ripe from wear. The stranger slicked his greasy hair back from his brow in a pitiful attempt at grooming as he swaggered over to the carriage.

"My employer, Henry Winchester, is too sotted to come outside," he announced. "We come to this part of town when we don't want to be noticed," he added. "I'm here in his stead, m'lady. Your driver said there be a woman in need of something, and I'm thinking I'm just the man you're needing."

The disgusting man scratched his groin while he eagerly waited for a reply to his offer.

The stench radiating from the foul-smelling man came in through the window. Sara almost gagged in reaction. She placed her perfumed hankerchief over her nose, turned to her aunt, and whispered, "Do you know this man?"

"I most certainly do," her aunt answered. "His name's

Clifford Duggan, Sara, and he's the one who helped your uncle waylay me."

"Did he strike you?"

"Yes, dear, he did," Nora answered. "Several times, as a matter of fact."

The servant under discussion couldn't see inside the dark carriage. He leaned forward to get a better look at his prize.

Nathan walked over to the side of the carriage. His intent was to tear the man from aft to stern for daring to leer at his bride. He stopped when he saw the white-gloved fist fly through the open window and connect quite soundly with the side of the man's bulbous nose.

Clifford hadn't been prepared for the attack. He let out a howl of pain, staggered backwards, and tripped over his own feet. He landed with a thud on his knees. While he spewed one crude blasphemy after another he diligently tried to regain his feet.

Sara pressed her advantage. She threw the carriage door open, catching the villain in his midsection. The servant did a near somersault before landing in the gutter on his backside.

The men lounging against the wall hooted in appreciation of the spectacle they'd just witnessed. Sara ignored her audience as she climbed out of the carriage. She turned to hand her reticule to her aunt, took another minute to remove her gloves and pass those through the window to her aunt, too, and then finally gave her full attention to the man sprawled on the ground.

She was simply too infuriated to be afraid. She stood over her victim looking very like an avenging angel. Her voice shook with fury when she said, "If you ever mistreat a lady again, Clifford Duggan, I swear to God you'll die a slow, agonizing death."

"I ain't never mistreated a lady," Clifford whined. He was trying to catch his breath so he could pounce on her. "How would you be knowing my name?"

Nora leaned out the window. "You're a shameful liar, Clifford," she called out. "You're going to burn in hell for all your sins."

Clifford's eyes widened in astonishment. "How did you get out—"

Sara interrupted his question by giving him a sound kick. He turned his gaze back to her. His expression was insolent. "You think you got the meat to hurt me?" he sneered. He glanced back at the men leaning against the wall. In truth, the servant was more humiliated than injured by her paltry attack. The snickers echoing behind him stung far more than her little slap. "The only reason I ain't retaliating is because my employer will want to beat you good and sound afore he lets me have you."

"Do you have any idea how much trouble you're in, Clifford?" Sara asked. "My husband is going to hear about this atrocity, and he will certainly retaliate. The marquess of St. James is feared by everyone, even ignorant pigs like you, Clifford. When I tell him what you've been up to he'll give you equal measure. The marquess does whatever I tell him to do just like that." She paused to snap her fingers for effect. "Oh, I can see I've gotten your full attention with that promise," she added with a nod when Clifford's expression changed. The man looked downright terrified. He had quit trying to regain his feet and was actually scooting backward on his backside.

Sara was inordinately pleased with herself. Her bluff had worked quite well. She didn't realize that Clifford had just gotten a good look at the giant standing a scant ten feet behind her. She thought she'd just put the fear of a St. James into the servant. "A man who strikes a lady is a true coward," she announced. "My husband kills cowards as easily as he would a bothersome gnat, and if you doubt me, just remember he is a St. James through and through."

"Sara, dear," Nora called out. "Would you like me to accompany you inside?"

Sara didn't take her gaze off Clifford when she gave her aunt answer. "No, Nora. You aren't dressed for the occasion. I won't be long."

"Hurry, then," Nora called out. "You'll catch a chill, dear."

Nora continued to lean out the window, but her gaze was directed at Nathan. He returned her wide-eyed stare with a brisk nod before turning his attention back to his bride.

Nora was quick to notice how the big man was keeping the hounds at bay. His mere size was intimidating. It didn't take her any time at all to realize he was actually providing safety for Sara. Nora thought about calling a warning to her niece, then discounted the notion. Sara had enough to worry about. Nora would wait to mention the savior when she was finished with her important errand.

Nathan kept his attention on Sara. His bride was certainly full of surprises. He was having difficulty coming to terms with that fact. He'd seen what cowards the Winchesters were. The men in the family always did their dirty work under cover of darkness, or when a man's back was turned. Sara, however, wasn't acting at all like a Winchester. She was courageous in her defense of the old woman. And Lord, was she in a fury. He didn't think he would have been surprised if she'd pulled out a pistol and shot her victim between his eyes. She was definitely angry enough.

Sara skirted the servant, paused to give him a good glare, and then hurried on inside the tavern.

Nathan immediately walked over to Clifford. He grabbed him by his neck, lifted him high into the air, and then flung him against the stone wall.

His audience scattered like mice to avoid being hit. Clifford struck the wall with a loud splat, then crumpled to the ground in a dead faint.

"My good man?" Nora called out. "I do believe you'd better go inside now. My Sara's bound to need your assistance yet again."

Nathan turned to scowl at the woman who dared to issue him an order. Just then the whistles and hoots of laughter coming from inside the tavern gained his full attention. With a growl of frustration over what he considered a damned inconvenience he slowly uncoiled his whip and walked toward the door.

Sara located her uncle who was hunched over his ale at a round table in the center of the establishment. She made her way through the throng of customers to get to him. She thought she would use shame and reason to get Aunt Nora's ring back. Yet when she actually saw the silver band on his finger her mind emptied of all reasonable ploys. There was a full pitcher of dark ale on the table. Before Sara could contain herself she lifted the pitcher and emptied the contents over her uncle's balding head.

He was too far gone from drink to react swiftly. He let out a loud bellow, interrupted himself with a rank belch, and then staggered to his feet. Sara had worked the wedding band off his finger before his mind had cleared sufficiently to ward her off.

It took him a long while to focus on her properly. Sara slipped the ring on her own finger while she waited.

"My God . . . Sara? What are you doing here? Is something amiss?" Uncle Henry stammered out his questions in a bluster. The effort cost him what little strength he had left. He slumped back down in his chair and squinted up at her with bloodshot eyes. Henry noticed the empty pitcher. "Where's my ale?" he shouted to the barkeep.

Sara was thoroughly disgusted with her uncle. Even though she doubted he'd remember a single word of her lecture, she was determined to let him know what she thought about his sinful conduct.

"Is something amiss?" She repeated his question in a derisive tone. "You are despicable, Uncle Henry. If my father knew what you and his other brothers were doing to Nora, I'm certain he'd call the authorities and have you all carted off to the gallows."

"What say you?" Henry asked. He rubbed his forehead while he tried to concentrate on the conversation. "Nora? You're ranting at me because of that worthless woman?"

Before Sara could chastise him for making that shameful remark he blurted out, "Your father was in on the plan from the very beginning. Nora's too old to take care of herself. We know what's best for her. Don't try throwing a tantrum with me, girl, for I'm not going to tell you where she is."

"You do not know what's best for her," Sara shouted. "You wanted her inheritance, and that's the real reason. Everyone in London knows about your gaming debts, Uncle. You found an easy way to pay them off, didn't you? You were set to lock Nora away in an asylum, weren't you?"

Henry's gaze darted back and forth between the empty pitcher and his niece's outraged expression. It finally dawned on him that she had poured his ale over his head. He touched his collar just to be sure, and when he felt the sticky wetness there he became livid. His own anger made his head start pounding. He was in desperate need of another drink. "We are going to put the bitch away, and you can't do anything about it. Now get on home before I put my hand to your backside."

A snicker sounded behind her. Sara turned around to glare at the customer. "Drink your refreshment, sir, and stay out of this." She whirled back to her uncle only after the stranger turned his gaze to his goblet. "You're lying about my father," she stated. "He would never be a party to such cruelty. As for striking me, do so and suffer my husband's wrath. I'll tell him," she threatened with a nod.

Sara had hoped that since her empty threat about her husband's retaliatory methods had been so successful with the hired servant Clifford, the same bluff might work on her sotted relative.

It was a vain hope. Henry didn't look at all intimidated. He let out a loud snort. "You're as crazed as Nora if you believe a St. James would ever come to your defense. Why, I could beat you good, Sara, and no one would give a notice, least of all your husband."

Sara stood her ground. She was determined to gain her uncle's promise to leave Nora alone before she left the foul-smelling tavern. Her fear was that he or one of his brothers would send someone after her aunt and drag her back to England. Nora's inheritance from her father's estate was sizable enough to make the journey worth the nuisance.

She was so incensed with her uncle, she didn't notice that some of the customers were slowly edging their way toward her. Nathan noticed. One man he judged to be the leader of the pack actually licked his lips in apparent anticipation of the morsel he thought he would soon get to devour.

Sara suddenly realized the futility of her plan. "Do you know, Uncle Henry, I've been trying to find a way to get you to promise to leave Nora alone, but I now realize my own foolishness. Only a man of honor would keep his promise. You're too much of a swine to keep your word. I'm wasting my time here."

Her uncle reached up to slap her. Sara easily dodged him. She stopped backing away when she bumped into something quite solid, turned around, and found herself surrounded by several disreputable-looking men. All of them, she immediately noticed, were in desperate need of a bath.

Everyone was so mesmerized by the beautiful lady they never noticed Nathan. He thought they might be too consumed with lust to think about caution. In time they would realize that error, of course. Nathan leaned back against the closed door in the corner and waited for the first provocation.

It came with lightning speed. When the first infidel grabbed hold of Sara's arm Nathan let out a roar of outrage. The sound was deep, guttural, deafening. Effective, too. Everyone in the tavern froze—everyone but Sara. She jumped a good foot, then whirled around toward the sound.

She would have screamed if her throat hadn't closed up

on her. In truth, she was having difficulty catching her breath. Her knees buckled when she spotted the big man standing in front of the door. Sara grabbed hold of the table to keep herself from falling down. Her heart was slamming inside her chest, and she was certain she was about to die of sheer fright.

What in God's name was he? No, not what, she corrected herself, but who. She was nearly frantic. He was a man—yes, a man—but the biggest, the most dangerous-looking, the most . . . oh, God, he was staring at her.

He motioned to her with the crook of his finger.

She shook her head.

He nodded.

The room began to spin. She simply had to get hold of her wits again. She desperately tried to find something about the giant that wasn't so horribly terrifying. She realized then that someone was clutching her arm. Without taking her gaze away from the big man trying to stare her into a faint she slapped the hand away.

The giant looked as if he bathed. There was that much. His hair appeared to be clean, too. It was a dark bronze in color, as bronzed as his face and arms. Dear Lord, she thought, his upper arms and shoulders were so . . . muscular. So were his thighs. She could see the sleek bulge of steel indecently outlined by his snug britches. But they were clean britches, she told herself. Villains usually wore only crumpled, smelly garments, didn't they? Therefore, she reasoned illogically, *he* couldn't be a villain. That conclusion made her feel better. She was actually able to take a breath. All right, she thought to herself, he isn't a villain; he's just a warlord, she decided when she'd finished her thorough inspection, perhaps even a Viking warrior from the length of his hair. Yes, he was simply a barbarian who had somehow transported himself across time.

Her mind had snapped, she concluded then. The green-eyed warlord motioned to her to come to him again. She looked behind her to make certain he wasn't motioning to someone else. There wasn't anyone there.

He meant her, all right. Her stomach lurched. She blinked. He didn't disappear. She shook her head in a bid to clear her mind of the vision from hell.

He crooked his finger at her again. "Come to me."

His voice was deep, commanding, arrogant. God help her, she started walking toward him.

And then all hell broke loose. The sound of the whip cracking in the air, the scream of pain from the fool who tried to touch her as she moved past him echoed in Sara's ears. She never looked toward the commotion. Her gaze was locked on the man who was methodically destroying the tavern.

He made it look so easy. A simple flip of his wrist that didn't seem to cost him the least amount of effort made such a lasting impression on his audience.

She also noticed that the closer she got to him, the deeper his scowl became.

The warlord obviously wasn't in a good mood. She decided to humor him until she could regain her composure. Then she was going to run outside, jump into the hack with Nora, and race to the waterfront.

It was a fine plan, she told herself. The problem, of course, was getting the Viking away from the door first.

She realized she'd stopped to stare at him again when he motioned for her to move. She felt a restraining hand on her shoulder, glanced down at it, then heard the crack of the whip.

Sara was suddenly in full flight. She ran to him, determined to get there before her heart completely failed her.

She came to a swaying stop directly in front of him, tilted her head back, and stared up at those piercing green eyes until he finally looked down at her. On impulse she reached out and pinched his arm just to make certain he really wasn't a figment of her imagination.

He was real, all right. His skin felt like steel, but warm

steel. The look in those beautiful eyes saved her from insanity, though. The color was hypnotizing, intense.

Odd, but the longer she stared at him, the safer she felt. She smiled with acute relief. He raised an eyebrow in reaction. "I knew you weren't a villain, Viking."

Sara was suddenly weightless. She felt as though she were floating through a dark tunnel and on her way toward the bronzed Viking standing in the sun.

Nathan caught her before she hit the floor. His bride was in a full faint when he tossed her over his shoulder. He scanned the tavern for any leftovers he might have missed. There were bodies all over the wooden floor. That wasn't good enough, he thought. He had an almost overwhelming urge to mark the bastard uncle who was cowering under the table. He could hear the choked sobs coming from the man.

Nathan kicked the table across the room in order to see his prey. "Do you know who I am, Winchester?"

Henry was locked in fetal position. When he shook his head his jowls rubbed back and forth against the floor-boards.

"Look at me, bastard."

His voice sounded like thunder. Henry looked up. "I'm the marquess of St. James. If you ever come near my wife or that old woman, I'll kill you. Do we understand each other?"

"You're . . . him?"

The bile had risen in Henry's throat, making speech nearly impossible. He started gagging. Nathan gave him a sound shove with the tip of his boot, then turned and walked out of the tavern.

The barkeep peeked out from his hiding place behind the grill and looked at the devastation around him. There wouldn't be any more ale purchased that dark night, for nary a one of his customers was in any condition to drink. They covered his floor like discarded peanut shells. It was a sight he wouldn't soon forget. He wanted to remember every single detail so he could relate the happening to his friends.

He already knew how he was going to tell the ending, too. The Winchester dandy crying like an infant would provide a good, hearty laugh for his future customers. The sound of gagging pulled the barkeep from his musings. The high and mighty Winchester was puking all over his floor.

The tavern owner's shout of anger mingled with Aunt Nora's gasp of fear. When she saw her niece draped over the stranger's shoulder her hand flew to her bosom.

"Is Sara hurt?" she cried out. Her mind was already picturing the worst.

Nathan shook his head. He opened the door of the carriage, then paused to grin at the old woman. "She fainted."

Nora was too relieved at that news to take exception to the fact that the man was amused over her niece's condition. She moved over to make room for Sara. Nathan placed his bride on the opposite seat, however. Nora gave her niece a quick once-over to make certain she was still breathing, then turned to look at their savior again. She watched him recoil the whip and hook it to his belt.

Nora hadn't expected him to join them inside the vehicle. When he did so she squeezed herself into the far corner. "Sara can sit next to me," she offered.

He didn't bother to answer her. He did, however, take up all the space across from her. Then he lifted Sara onto his lap. Nora noticed how very gentle he was when he touched her niece. His hand lingered on the side of Sara's cheek when he pressed her face into the crook of his neck. Sara let out a little sigh.

Nora didn't know what to make of the man. The carriage was in full motion before she tried to engage him in conversation.

"Young man, my name's Nora Bettleman. The dear lady you just saved is my niece. Her name is Sara Winchester."

"No," he said in a hard voice. "Her name is Lady St. James."

After making that emphatic statement he turned his gaze to the window. Nora continued to stare at him. The man had a nice, strong profile. "Why are you helping us?" she asked. "You won't convince me you're in the employ of the Winchester family," she added with a firm nod. "Could one of the St. James men have hired you?"

He didn't answer her. Nora let out a sigh before turning her attention to her niece. She wished Sara would hurry up and finish with her swoon so she could sort out the confusion.

"I've come to depend upon the child you're cradling in your arms, sir. I cannot abide the thought of anything ill happening to her."

"She isn't a child," he contradicted.

Nora smiled. "No, but I still consider her such," she admitted. "Sara's such an innocent, trusting soul. She takes after her mother's side of the family."

"You aren't a Winchester, are you?"

Nora was so pleased that he was finally conversing with her, she smiled again. "No," she answered. "I'm Sara's aunt on her mother's side. I was a Turner before I married my Johnny and took his name."

She glanced over to look at Sara again. "I don't believe she's ever fainted before. Of course, the last two weeks must have been a terrible strain on her. There are shadows under her eyes. She obviously hasn't been sleeping well. The worry about me, you see," she added with a little wheeze. "Still, she must have seen something quite frightening to make her swoon. What do you suppose . . ."

She quit her speculation when she caught his grin. The man was certainly on the peculiar side, for he smiled over the oddest remarks.

And then he explained himself. "She saw me."

Sara started to stir. She felt dizzy still, disoriented, yet wonderfully warm. She rubbed her nose against the heat, inhaled the clean, masculine scent, and let out a sigh of contentment.

"I do believe she's coming around," Nora whispered. "Thank the Lord."

Sara slowly turned her gaze to her aunt. "Coming around?" she asked with an unladylike yawn.

"You swooned, dear."

"I didn't," Sara whispered, clearly appalled. "I never faint. I . . ." She stopped her explanation when she realized she was sitting on someone's lap. Not someone, she realized. His lap. The color drained from her face. Memory was fully restored.

Nora reached over to pat her hand. "It's all right, Sara. This kind gentleman saved you."

"The one with the whip?" Sara whispered, praying she was wrong.

Nora nodded. "Yes, dear, the one with the whip. You must give him your appreciation, and for heaven's sake, Sara, don't faint again. I don't have my smelling salts with me."

Sara nodded. "I won't faint again," she said. To insure that promise she decided she'd better not look at him again. She tried to move off his lap without his noticing, but as soon as she started to scoot away he increased his grip around her waist.

She leaned forward just a little. "Who is he?" she whispered to Nora.

Her aunt lifted her shoulders in a shrug. "He hasn't told me yet," she explained. "Perhaps, dear—if you tell him how thankful you are—well, then he just might give us his name."

Sara knew it was rude to talk about the man as though he weren't even there. She braced herself before she slowly turned to look at his face. She deliberately stared at his chin when she said, "Thank you, sir, for coming to my defense inside the tavern. I shall be in your debt forever."

He nudged her chin up with his thumb. His gaze was inscrutable. "You owe me more than gratitude, Sara."

Her eyes widened in alarm. "You know who I am?"

"I told him, dear," Nora interjected.

"I don't have any coins left," Sara said then. "I used all I had to book passage for our journey. Are you taking us to the harbor?"

He nodded.

"I do have a gold chain, sir. Will that be payment enough?"

"No."

The abruptness in his answer irritated her. She gave him a disgruntled look for being so ungallant. "But I don't have anything more to offer you," she announced.

The hack came to a stop. Nathan opened the door. He moved with incredible speed for such a big man. He was outside the carriage and assisting Nora to the ground before Sara had straightened her gown. The man had all but tossed her into the corner of the hack.

His arms were suddenly around her waist again. Sara had only enough time to grab her reticule and her gloves before she was hauled out of the carriage like a sack of feed. He dared to put his arm around her shoulders and pull her up against his side. Sara immediately protested that liberty. "Sir, I happen to be a married woman. Do remove your arm. It isn't decent."

He obviously suffered from a hearing impairment, for he didn't even glance at her when she'd given that order. She was about to try again when he let out a piercing whistle. The moonlit area had been completely deserted until that moment. Within a blink of an eye she found herself completely surrounded by men.

Nathan's loyal crew stared at Sara. They acted as though they'd never seen a pretty woman before. He looked down at his bride to see how she was reacting to their stares of obvious adoration. Sara wasn't paying any attention to the men, though. She was occupied glaring up at him. Nathan almost smiled in reaction.

He gave her a quick squeeze to get her to quit her show of insolence, then turned his attention to the old woman. "Do you have any baggage?"

"Do we, Sara?" Nora asked.

Sara tried to shove herself away from her anchor before answering. "I told you I was a married woman," she muttered. "Now unhand me."

He didn't budge. She gave up. "Yes, Nora, we do have baggage. I borrowed some of my mother's things for you to wear. I'm certain she won't mind. Nicholas stored the bags at the Marshall storefront. Shall we go and claim them?"

She tried to take a step forward and found herself hauled up against the giant again.

Nathan found his man Jimbo in the back of the crowd and motioned to him. A tall, dark-skinned man walked over to stand in front of Sara. Her eyes widened at the sight of the near-giant. She stared at him a long minute, then came to the conclusion that he might have been attractive if it weren't for the odd-looking gold earring looped through his ear.

He must have felt her stare on him, for he suddenly turned his full attention on her. He folded his massive arms across his chest and gave her a good scowl.

She scowled back.

A sudden sparkle appeared in his midnight-dark eyes, and he gifted her with a full smile. She didn't know what to make of that strange behavior.

"Have two men see to the baggage, Jimbo," Nathan ordered. "We'll board the *Seahawk* at first light."

Sara couldn't help but notice that the Viking had included himself in her plans.

"My aunt and I will be perfectly safe now," she said. "These men seem to be . . . pleasant enough, sir. We've wasted enough of your valuable time."

Nathan continued to ignore her. He motioned to another man. When a thick-muscled though squat-framed older man came forward, Nathan nodded toward Nora. "Take care of the old woman, Matthew."

Nora let out a gasp. Sara thought it was because they were about to be separated from each other. Yet before she could argue with their unwanted protector Nora straightened her shoulders and slowly walked over to the enormous man.

"I'm not an old woman, sir, and I take grave exception to such an insult. I'm only one year past fifty, young man, and feeling as spry as can be."

Nathan's eyebrow rose a fraction, but he kept his smile contained. A strong gust of wind would topple the old woman, so frail did she appear to him to be, yet she had the tone of voice of a commander.

"You should apologize to my aunt," Sara said.

She turned back to her aunt before he had time to react to that statement. "I'm certain he didn't mean to hurt your feelings, Nora. He's just rude."

Nathan shook his head. The conversation was ridiculous to him. "Matthew, move," he ordered in a clipped voice.

Nora turned to the man hovering by her side. "And just where do you think you're taking me?"

In answer, Matthew lifted Nora into his arms.

"Put me down, you rascal."

"It's all right, lovey," Matthew replied. "You look a might peaked to me. You don't weigh more than a feather."

Nora was about to protest again. His next question changed her mind. "Where did you get those bruises? Give me the name of the bloody infidel, and I'll be happy to cut his throat for you."

Nora smiled at the man holding her. She judged his age to be near her own and had also noticed what a fit man he appeared to be. She hadn't blushed in years, yet she knew from the sudden heat in her cheeks that she was certainly blushing at that moment. "Thank you, sir," she stammered out as she patted the bun back into place on top of her head. "That is certainly a kind offer."

Sara was astonished by her aunt's behavior. Why, she was fluttering her eyelashes and acting very like a flirt at her first ball! She watched the pair until they were out of sight, then noticed that the crowd of men had also vanished. She was suddenly all alone with her contrary savior.

"Is my Aunt Nora going to be safe with that man?" she demanded to know.

His answer was a low growl of obvious irritation. "Does one grunt mean yes or no?" she asked.

"Yes," he answered with a sigh when she poked him in his ribs.

"Please let me go."

He actually did as she asked. Sara was so surprised she nearly lost her balance. Perhaps, she decided, if she could maintain her pleasant tone of voice, she could get him to obey other commands. It was certainly worth a try.

"Am I going to be safe with you?"

He took his sweet time answering her. Sara turned until she was standing face-to-shoulders in front of him. The tips of her shoes touched the tips of his boots. "Please answer me," she whispered in a sweet, coaxing tone of voice.

He didn't seem to be impressed with her attempt to have a pleasant conversation. His exasperation, on the other hand, was evident. "Yes, Sara. You'll always be safe with me."

"But I don't want to be safe with you," she cried out. She realized how foolish that statement sounded as soon as the words were out of her mouth, and she hastily tried to correct herself. "What I mean to say is that I do always want to be safe. Everyone wants to be safe. Even villains . . ."

She stopped rambling when he grinned at her. "I want to be safe without you. You aren't planning to sail with Nora and me, are you? Why are you staring at me like that?"

He answered her first question and ignored her second one. "Yes, I'm sailing with you."

"Why?"

"I want to," he drawled. He decided to wait a little longer before giving her the particulars. Her cheeks were flushed again. Nathan couldn't decide if the cause was fear or temper.

His bride still had freckles on the bridge of her nose. He was pleased by that fact. It made him remember the little hellion he'd held in his arms. She wasn't a little girl any longer, though. She'd grown up quite nicely, too. She was, however, obviously still a bit of a hellion.

She actually nudged him in his chest to gain his attention again. "I'm sorry, sir, but you simply cannot travel with Nora and me," she announced. "You're going to have to find another boat. It wouldn't be safe for you to be on the same vessel with me."

That strange statement gained his full attention. "Oh? And why is that?"

"Because my husband won't like it," she announced. She nodded when he looked incredulous, then continued. "Have you heard of the marquess of St. James? Oh, of course you have. Everyone knows about the Marquess. He's my husband, Viking, and he's going to pitch a fit when he finds out I'm traveling with a . . . protector. No, I'm afraid it won't do. Why are you smiling?"

"Why did you call me Viking?" he asked.

She shrugged her shoulders. "Because you look like one."

"Should I call you shrew?"

"Why?"

"You're acting like one."

She felt like screaming in frustration. "Who are you? What do you want with me?"

"You still owe me, Sara."

"Oh, Lord, are you going to harp on that issue again?"

His slow nod infuriated her. He was thoroughly enjoying himself. When Sara realized that fact her bluster of indignation evaporated. She knew then that she was never going to get him to make sense. The man was daft. The sooner she got away from this barbarian, she thought, the better. First, however, she would have to find a way to placate him.

"All right," she agreed. "I owe you. There, we are in

complete agreement. Now then, please tell me exactly what it is you think I owe you, and I shall endeavor to make payment."

He moved forward so that he could catch her in the event she fainted on him again before he gave her an answer. "My name's Nathan, Sara."

"And?" she asked, wondering why he'd suddenly decided to tell her his name.

She was slow to catch on. His sigh was long, weary. "And you, Lady St. James, owe me a wedding night."

Chapter Three

〜

She didn't faint; she screamed. Nathan didn't try to quiet her down. When he couldn't stand the grating noise another second he simply dragged her over to the Emerald Shipping Company offices. He left the hysterical woman in her aunt's capable hands. Because he believed he was capable of gentlemanly behavior upon rare occasion, he didn't start laughing until he was once again outside.

Nathan had thoroughly enjoyed her reaction to his announcement. Lady Sara wasn't at all subtle. He doubted he would ever have to worry about knowing what was on her mind. Nathan, conditioned to sneakiness all his life, found his straightforward bride refreshing. Loud, he added as an afterthought, but refreshing all the same.

After he took care of a few remaining details Nathan joined the last of the crew aboard the ship. Jimbo and Matthew were waiting on deck for him. They were both scowling, but Nathan decided to let them get away with their show of insolence. He had saddled the loyal men with the chore of getting Sara and Nora settled in their cabins.

"Did she finally quit screaming?" Nathan asked.

"When I threatened to put a gag in her mouth," Jimbo answered. The big man increased his frown and added, "She hit me then."

Nathan let his exasperation show. "I assume she isn't too frightened any longer," he replied dryly.

"I'm not so certain she ever was frightened," Matthew interjected. The older man grinned. "Didn't you notice the fire in her eyes when you dragged her into the offices? She looked bloody furious to me."

Jimbo reluctantly nodded. "After you left she kept shouting that it was all just a cruel jest. Not even her sweet-tempered aunt could calm her down. Your lady actually demanded that someone pinch her so she'd wake up and find it was all just a black nightmare."

"Aye, she did," Matthew agreed with a chuckle. "Felix took her to heart, too. For all his bulk, the boy isn't very cunning."

"Felix touched her?" Nathan was more incredulous than angry.

"No, he didn't touch her," Jimbo rushed out. "He tried to give her a little pinch, that's all. He thought he was being accommodating. You know how the boy likes to please. Your little bride turned into a wildcat as soon as he went for her. I wager Felix won't be so eager to obey next time she gives an order."

Nathan shook his head in vexation. He started to turn away. Matthew stopped him with his next remark. "Perhaps Lady Sara will do better if we put her in with her aunt."

"No."

Nathan realized how abrupt he'd sounded when both men smiled at him. "She stays in my cabin," he added in a much softer tone of voice.

Matthew paused to rub his chin. "Well now, boy, that could be a problem," he drawled. "She doesn't know it's your cabin."

Nathan wasn't at all concerned about that announcement. He frowned at Matthew, but only because the seaman had used the ridiculous nickname "boy" when he'd addressed him. Nathan knew his unspoken censure wouldn't do him any good, though. Both Matthew and Jimbo called him that insulting nickname whenever they were alone with him. They didn't think he was seasoned enough to merit the name "captain" in private. Nathan had inherited the pair when he'd taken over the vessel. The two men had quickly proven to be invaluable. They knew all the ins and outs of pirating and had shown him the way. He knew they thought of themselves as his guardians. God only knew they'd told him so often enough. Still, they'd put their lives on the line countless times in the past to save his backside. Their loyalty far outweighed their irritating habits.

Since the two men were staring at him with such expectant looks on their faces, Nathan said, "She'll find out soon enough whose cabin she's in."

"The aunt is in a poor way," Matthew said then. "I'd wager a couple of her ribs are cracked. As soon as she falls asleep I'm going to strip her raw and bind her tight around the middle."

"The Winchesters did the damage, didn't they?" Jimbo asked.

Nathan nodded. "Which bastard brother was it?" Matthew asked that question.

"It appears that Henry was behind the scheme," Nathan explained. "But I would imagine the other brothers were aware of what was going on."

"Are we going to take Nora home?" Matthew asked.

"We're charted in that direction," Nathan answered. "I don't know what the hell else to do with the woman. Is she strong enough to make the journey?" he asked Matthew. "Or are we going to have to bury her at sea?"

"She'll do all right," Matthew predicted. "There's a tough hide underneath all those bruises. Yes, if I coddle her real nice, she'll make it." He nudged Jimbo in his side, then added, "Now I'm having to nursemaid two weaklings."

Nathan knew he was being baited. He turned and walked

away. From behind Jimbo called out, "He's referring to you, boy."

Nathan raised his hand high into the air to make an obscene gesture before disappearing down the stairs. The men's hearty laughter followed him.

The next several hours were spent on chores for every hand aboard the *Seahawk*. The cargo was secured, the jib raised, the anchor weighed, and the eight cannons given a last spit and oiling before the command was given to sail.

Nathan did his part until his stomach became so queasy he was forced to stop. Jimbo took over command of the forty-two seamen when Nathan went below again.

It was a ritual getting seasick the first couple of days out. Nathan had learned to put up with the inconvenience. He was certain no one besides Matthew and Jimbo were aware of his problem, but that fact didn't ease his embarrassment at all.

From past experience he knew he had another hour or two before he was completely out of commission. Nathan decided to look in on his bride to make certain she was all right. If luck was on his side, she would be sound asleep, and the inevitable confrontation could be put off until later. God knew she should be exhausted. His bride had been awake for over twenty-four hours, and the tantrum she'd thrown when she found out that he was indeed her husband surely had worn her out. Still, if she wasn't sleeping, Nathan determined to have it out with her and get it over and done with. The sooner the rules were set down for her, the sooner she could come to terms with his expectations for their future together.

She would probably get hysterical on him again, Nathan guessed. He braced himself against the inevitable pleading and weeping and opened the door.

Sara wasn't asleep. As soon as Nathan walked into the cabin she bounded off the bed and stood there with her hands clenched at her sides, facing him.

It was apparent she wasn't quite over her fear or her anger

yet. It was damp and stuffy inside the cabin. He shut the door behind him, then walked over to the center of the large square room. He could feel her staring at him when he reached up and lifted the square trap built into the ceiling. He propped the makeshift window open with a stick wedged into the third groove.

Fresh sea air and sunlight flooded the cabin. Nathan's stomach lurched in reaction. He took a deep breath, then walked back over to the door and leaned against it. In the back of his mind lurked the possibility that his bride might just decide to take flight. He wasn't in any condition to go chasing after her, and therefore he blocked the only exit.

Sara stared at Nathan a good long while. She could feel herself shaking and knew it was only a matter of time before her fury got the upper hand. She was determined to hide her anger from him, though, no matter what the cost. Showing any emotion in front of the barbarian would certainly be a poor beginning.

The expression on Nathan's face was one of resignation. His arms were folded in front of his chest, his stance relaxed.

She thought he looked bored enough to fall asleep. That didn't sit well. His intense stare was making her toes curl, too. Sara forced herself to stare back. She wasn't about to cower in front of him, and if anyone was going to win the rude staring contest, it was going to be she.

Nathan thought his bride seemed quite desperate to hide her fear from him. She wasn't doing a very good job of it, for her eyes were already getting misty, and she was trembling.

Lord, he hoped he was up to another round of hysterics. His stomach was railing against the pitch of the ship. Nathan tried to block the feeling and concentrate on the matter at hand.

Sara was a beautiful woman. The streamers of sunlight made her hair look more golden than brown. There was a pick of the litter in the Winchester family after all, he thought to himself.

She was still dressed in the unappealing dark blue gown.

The neckline was too damned low, in his opinion. He thought about mentioning that fact to her later, after she'd gotten rid of some of her fear, but her sudden frown changed his inclination. It was imperative that she understood who was in charge.

He stood in the shadows of the door, but she could still see the long, wicked scar running the length of the side of his right arm. The white mark against such bronzed skin was noticeable. Sara stared at it a long minute while she wondered how he'd come by such a horrible injury, then she let out a soft little sigh.

He was still dressed in a pair of indecently snug fawn-colored britches. It was a miracle to her that he could even breathe. His white shirt was unbuttoned to the waist, the cuffs rolled up to his elbows, and the casualness of his attire irritated her almost as much as his sudden frown. She thought about waiting until later to tell him that one simply didn't wear such unseemly attire when one was traveling aboard such a fine vessel, but his intense frown changed her inclination. It was imperative that he understand what was expected of him now that he was married.

"You dress like a tavern wench."

It took a full minute for the insult to penetrate. At first Sara was too astonished to react. Then she let out a loud gasp.

Nathan hid his smile. Sara didn't look as if she was going to weep. In truth, she looked like she wanted to kill him. It was a nice beginning. "You're falling out of your neckline, bride."

Her hands immediately covered the top of her gown. Her face was flaming red in the space of a heartbeat. "It was the only dress that was dark enough to conceal me when I walked along . . ." She stopped her explanation as soon as she realized she was actually defending herself.

"Conceal?" Nathan drawled. "Sara, it doesn't conceal anything. In future you will not wear such revealing gowns.

The only one who sees your body will be me. Do you understand me?"

Oh, she understood all right. The man was a cad, she concluded. How easily he'd turned the tables on her, too. Sara shook her head. She wasn't about to let him put her in such a vulnerable position when he had so much accounting to do.

"You look like a barbarian," she blurted out. "Your hair's much longer than is fashionable, and you dress like a . . . villain. Guests traveling aboard such a fine boat should keep their appearances impeccable. You look like you've just carried in the crops," she added with a nod. "And your scowl is downright ugly."

Nathan decided he was finished with foolish banter and homed in on the true matter at hand.

"All right, Sara," he began. "Get it over and done with."

"Get what over and done with?"

His sigh was long, weary, absolutely infuriating to her. She desperately tried to hold onto her temper, but the urge to shout at him was making her head pound and her throat ache. Her eyes stung with tears. He had so much explaining to do before she would ever consider forgiving him, she thought, and he had damn well better get on with it before she decided his sins were too mortal ever to be forgiven at all.

"The fit of weeping and begging," Nathan explained with a shrug. "It's obvious to me that you're afraid," he continued. "You're about to start crying, aren't you? I know you must want me to take you back home, Sara. I've decided to save you the humiliation of pleading by simply explaining that no matter what you say or do, you're staying with me. I'm your husband, Sara. Get used to it."

"Will it bother you if I weep?" she asked in a voice that sounded like someone was choking her.

"Not in the least," he said. It was a lie, of course, for it would bother him to see her upset, yet he wasn't about to admit to that fact. Women generally used that kind of information against a man and burst into tears every time they wanted something.

Sara took a deep breath. She didn't dare speak another word until she'd gained control of herself. Did he actually think she would beg? By God, he was a horrid man. Intimidating, too. He didn't seem to possess an ounce of compassion.

She continued to stare at him while she gathered her courage to ask him all the painful questions she'd stored up inside her for such a long time. She doubted that he would tell her the truth, but she still wanted to hear what he had to say for himself.

He thought she looked ready to cry. Sara was apparently back to being terrified of him, he decided. Hell, he hoped she wouldn't faint again. He had little patience with the weaker sex, yet found he didn't want Sara to be too frightened of him.

In truth, he felt a little sorry for her. She couldn't possibly want to be married to him. He was a St. James, after all, and she had been raised a Winchester. She had certainly been trained to hate him. Poor Sara was just a victim in the scheme, a pawn the daft king had used to try to right the differences between the two feuding families.

Still, he couldn't undo the past for her. His signature was on that contract, and he was bound and determined to honor it.

"You might as well understand that I'm not going to walk away from this marriage," he stated in a hard voice. "Not now, not ever."

After making that statement he patiently waited for the fit of hysterics sure to come.

"What took you so long?"

She'd spoken in such a soft whisper, he wasn't certain he heard her correctly. "What did you say?"

"Why did you wait so long?" she asked him in a much stronger voice.

"Wait so long to do what?"

He looked completely bewildered to her. She took another deep breath. "To come for me," she explained. Her voice shook. She gripped her hands together in a bid to hang onto her temper, then said, "Why did you wait so long to come and get me?"

He was so surprised by her question, he didn't immediately respond. That Nathan didn't even think she merited a response was the last blow to her pride that Sara was going to take. In a near shout Sara demanded, "Do you have any idea how long I've waited for you?"

His eyes widened in surprise. His bride had just shouted at him. He stared at her in a way that made her think he thought she'd lost her mind.

And then he slowly shook his head at her. Her composure shattered. "No?" she shouted. "Was I so insignificant to you that you couldn't even be bothered getting around to the chore of coming for me?"

Nathan was stunned by her questions. He knew he shouldn't let her raise her voice to him, but her comments so astonished him, he wasn't certain what to say.

"You actually want me to believe you're angry because I didn't come for you sooner?" he asked.

Sara picked up the nearest object she could get her hands on and threw it at him. Fortunately, the chamberpot was empty. "Angry?" she asked in a roar worthy of a commander. "What makes you think I'm angry, Nathan?"

He dodged the chamberpot and the two candles that followed, then leaned back against the door. "Oh, I don't know," he drawled. "You seem troubled."

"I seem . . ." She was too incensed to stammer out another word.

Nathan's grin was in full evidence when he nodded. "Troubled," he finished for her.

"Do you own a pistol?"

"Yes."

"May I borrow it?"

He forced himself not to laugh. "Now why would you want to borrow my pistol, Sara?"

"I want to shoot you, Nathan."

He did laugh then. Sara decided she hated him. The bluster went out of her. She wanted to weep with frustration. Perhaps her relatives had been right after all. Perhaps he did despise her, maybe even as much as her parents told her he would.

She gave up the battle and sat down on the bed again. She folded her hands in her lap and kept her gaze downcast. "Please leave my cabin. If you wish to explain your sorry conduct to me, you may do so tomorrow. I'm too weary to listen to your excuses now."

He couldn't believe what he was hearing. She dared to give him orders. "That isn't how our marriage works, Sara. I give the orders, and you obey them."

His voice had been hard, angry. It was deliberate, of course, for he wanted her to understand he meant what he said. He thought he was probably frightening her again. She started wringing her hands in obvious agitation, and though he felt a bit guilty because he had to resort to such intimidating tactics, the issue was far too important to soften his approach. Nathan promised himself that no matter how pitiful she looked or sounded when she started crying, he would not back down.

Sara continued to wring her hands for a long minute, pretending that it was her husband's stubborn neck she had between her fingers. The fantasy helped to lighten her mood.

Nathan nagged her back to reality when he growled, "Did you hear me, bride?"

God, she hated the name "bride!" "Yes, I heard you," she answered. "But I don't really understand. Why is that how this marriage works?"

The tears were back in her eyes again. Nathan suddenly felt like an ogre. "Are you trying to bait me?" he asked.

She shook her head. "No," she answered. "I just supposed our marriage was going to go along in the opposite direction.

Yes, I always did," she added in a rush when he frowned intently at her.

"Oh? And just how did you think this marriage was going to go along?"

He actually seemed to be interested in her opinion. Sara immediately took heart. She lifted her shoulders in a dainty shrug. "Well, I supposed that it would always be my duty to tell you what I wanted."

"And?" he prodded when she quit her explanation.

"And it would always be your duty to get it for me."

She could tell from his dark expression he didn't like hearing that opinion. She could feel herself getting riled up again. "You're supposed to cherish me, Nathan. You did promise."

"I did not promise to cherish you," he countered in a shout. "For God's sake, woman, I didn't promise you anything."

She wasn't about to let him get away with that lie. She jumped to her feet to confront him again. "Oh, yes, you did promise," she shouted back. "I read the contract, Nathan, from start to finish. In return for the land and the treasury you're supposed to keep me safe. You're also supposed to be a good husband, a kind father, and most of all, Viking, you're supposed to love and cherish me."

He was at a loss for words. He suddenly felt like laughing again. The twisted turn in the topic was exasperating. Exhilarating, too.

"You really want me to love and cherish you?"

"I most certainly do," she replied. She folded her arms across her chest. "You promised to love and cherish me, Nathan, and by God, you're going to."

She sat down on the bed again and took her time straightening the folds in her gown. The blush that covered her cheeks told of her embarrassment.

"And what are you supposed to be doing while I'm loving and cherishing you?" he asked. "What are your promises, bride?"

"I didn't promise anything," she answered. "I was only four years old, Nathan. I didn't sign the contract. You did."

He closed his eyes and counted to ten. "Then you don't believe you have to honor your father's signature? The promises he made on your behalf aren't binding?"

"I didn't say that," she whispered. She let out a loud sigh, then added, "Of course I will honor them. They were given in my name."

"And what are they?" he demanded.

She took a long time answering him. She looked thoroughly disgruntled, too. "I have to love and cherish you, too," she muttered.

He wasn't satisfied. "And?"

"And what?" she asked, pretending ignorance.

He decided then and there that his bride was trying to make him crazed. "I also read the contract through from start to finish," he snapped. "Don't try my patience."

"Oh, all right," she countered. "I have to obey you, too. There, are you happy now?"

"Yes," he returned. "We're now back where we started," he said then. "As I instructed you before, I will be the one to give the orders, and you will be the one to obey them. And don't you dare ask me why again."

"I will try to obey your orders, Nathan, when I think they're reasonable."

His tolerance was at an end. "I don't give a damn if you think they're reasonable or not," he roared. "You will do as I say."

She didn't seem at all upset that he'd raised his voice to her. Her voice was quite mild when she said, "You really shouldn't use blasphemies in a lady's presence, Nathan. It's common, and you happen to be a marquess."

The look on his face was chilling. Sara felt completely defeated. "You hate me, don't you?"

"No."

She didn't believe him. Lord, the mere sight of her was making him ill. His complexion had a gray cast to it. "Oh, yes, you do hate me," she argued. "You can't fool me. I'm a Winchester, and you hate all the Winchesters."

"I do not hate you."

"You don't have to shout at me. I'm only trying to have a decent conversation, after all, and the least you could do is control your temper." She didn't give him time to shout at her again. "I'm very weary, Nathan. I would like to rest now."

He decided to let her have her way. He opened the door to leave, then turned around again.

"Sara?"

"Yes?"

"You aren't at all afraid of me, are you?"

He looked quite astonished. It was as though the truth had just dawned on him. She shook her head. "No."

He turned around again so she wouldn't see his smile.

"Nathan?"

"What?"

"I was a little afraid of you when I first saw you," she admitted. "Does that make you feel better?"

His answer was to shut the door.

The minute she was alone again she burst into tears. Oh, what a naïve fool she'd been. All those wasted years of dreaming about her wonderful knight in golden armor coming to claim her for his bride. She'd imagined him to be a gentle, understanding, sensitive man who was thoroughly in love with her.

Her dreams mocked her. Her knight was more tarnished than golden. He had just proven to be as understanding, as compassionate, as loving as a goat.

Sara continued to feel sorry for herself until exhaustion overcame her.

Nathan looked in on her again an hour later. Sara was sound asleep. She hadn't bothered to remove her clothes but slept on top of the multicolored quilt. She rested on her stomach, her arms thrown wide.

A feeling of contentment settled inside him. It was a

strange, altogether foreign feeling, but he found he actually liked seeing her in his bed. He noticed Nora's wedding band was still on her finger. Odd, but he didn't like seeing that at all. He pulled the ring off her finger just to rid himself of his own irrational irritation and put the band in his pocket.

He turned his attention to taking Sara's clothes off. After he'd unbuttoned the long row of tiny clasps down her back he eased the gown off. Her shoes and stockings came next. He was awkward with the task, and the petticoats almost defeated him. The knot in the string was impossible to untie. Nathan used the tip of his knife to cut the string away. He kept at the chore until he'd stripped his bride of all but her silk chemise. The white garment was extremely feminine, with lace edging the scooped neckline.

He gave in to his urge and brushed the back of his hand down her back.

Sara didn't wake up. She let out a little sigh in her sleep and rolled over onto her back just as Nathan was tossing the rest of her garments on the nearby chair.

Nathan didn't have any idea how long he stood there staring at her. She looked so innocent, so trusting, so damned vulnerable when she slept. Her eyelashes were black, thick, startling against the creaminess of her skin. Her body was magnificent to him. The fullness of her breasts, only partially concealed by the flimsy chemise, aroused him. When he realized he was physically reacting to her he turned to leave the cabin.

What in God's name was he going to do with her? How could he ever maintain his distance from someone as enticing as his bride?

Nathan put those questions aside when a wave of seasickness hit him. He waited until his stomach quit lurching so violently, then lifted the blanket from the hook and covered Sara. His hand touched the side of her face, and he couldn't help but smile when she instinctively rubbed her cheek against his knuckles. She reminded him of an affectionate little kitten.

She turned, and her mouth touched his skin. Nathan abruptly pulled his hand away. He left the room and went to look in on Sara's aunt. Nora appeared to be sleeping peacefully. She looked pale, and her breathing was labored, but she didn't seem to be in much pain. Her expression was serene. Nathan remembered the ring in his pocket. He walked over to the side of the bed, lifted her hand, and slipped the band back on.

Nora opened her eyes and smiled at him. "Thank you, dear boy. I'll rest much easier now that I have my Johnny's ring back."

Nathan acknowledged her gratitude with a curt nod, then turned and walked back to the door. "You think I'm a sentimental fool, don't you?" she called out.

His smile was quick. "Aye," he answered. "I do."

His blunt honesty made her chuckle. "Have you spoken to Sara yet?" she asked.

"I have."

"Is she all right?" Nora asked. She wished he'd turn around so she could see his expression.

"She's sleeping," Nathan announced. He opened the door and started out.

"Wait," Nora called out. "Please don't leave yet."

He reacted to the tremor he heard in her voice and immediately turned around again.

"I'm very frightened," Nora whispered.

Nathan shut the door and walked back over to the old woman's side. His arms were folded across his chest. He looked relaxed, save for the frown on his face. "You needn't be afraid," he told her. His voice was soft, soothing. "You're safe now, Nora."

She shook her head. "No, you misunderstand," she explained. "I'm not afraid for myself, dear boy. My worry is for you and Sara. Do you have any idea what you're letting yourself in for? You can't possibly know what those men are capable of. Not even I understood the depths to which they would sink for greed. They'll come after you."

Nathan shrugged. "I'll be ready," he answered. "The Winchesters aren't a challenge to me."

"But dear boy, they—"

"Nora, you don't know what I'm capable of," he countered. "When I tell you I'll be able to handle any challenge, you'll just have to believe me."

"They'll use Sara to get to you," Nora whispered. "They'll hurt her if they have to," she added with a nod.

"I protect what's mine." His voice was hard, emphatic.

His arrogance actually calmed her, too. She slowly nodded. "I believe you will," she said. "But what about the Winchester women?"

"Do you mean all of them, or one specifically?"

"Sara."

"She'll do all right," he said. "She isn't a Winchester any longer. She's a St. James. You insult my capabilities when you worry about her safety. I take care of my possessions."

"Possessions?" she repeated. "I've never heard a wife referred to in quite that fashion."

"You've been away from England long years, Nora. Nothing's changed in all that while, though. A wife is still a husband's possession."

"My Sara's very tenderhearted," Nora said, turning the topic a bit. "These past years haven't been easy for her. She's been considered an outsider because of the marriage contract. Some would say she was a leper in her own family. Sara was never allowed to attend any of the functions young ladies so look forward to. The fuss was always made over her sister Belinda."

Nora paused to take a breath, then continued. "Sara's fiercely loyal to her parents and her sister, of course, though for the life of me I can't understand why she would give any of them the time of day. You'd best beware of Sara's sister, for she's as cunning as her Uncle Henry. They're cut from the same evil bolt."

"You worry too much, Nora."

"I just want you to understand . . . Sara," she whispered.

The wheeze was back in her voice, and it was obvious that she was becoming weary. "My Sara's a dreamer," she continued. "Look at her drawings, and you'll understand what I'm saying. Her head's in the clouds most of the time. She sees only the goodness in people. She doesn't want to believe her father is like his brothers. I place the blame on Sara's mother, of course. She's lied to her daughter all these years, made up excuses for each and every sin the others committed."

Nathan didn't comment.

"Dear boy," she began again.

His sudden frown stopped her. "Madam, I'll make a pact with you," Nathan said. "I'll refrain from calling you old woman if you'll quit calling me your dear boy. Are we in agreement?"

Nora smiled. She was squinting up at the giant of a man. His very presence seemed to swallow up the room. "Yes, calling you dear boy was rather foolish," she agreed with a chuckle. "Do I have your permission to call you Nathan?"

"You do," he answered. "As for your concerns about Sara, they're all ill-founded. I will not allow anyone to hurt her. She's my wife, and I will always treat her kindly. In time she'll realize her good fortune."

His hands were clasped behind his back like a general's, and he was pacing the small room.

"There is also the telling fact that you protected her from those thugs the other evening," Nora said. "I know you'll take good care of her. I only hope you'll consider her tender feelings, too, Nathan. You see, Sara's actually very shy. She keeps her thoughts bottled up inside her. It's very difficult to know what she's feeling."

Nathan raised an eyebrow over that announcement. "Are we talking about the same woman, madam?"

Nora's grin was telling. She paused to pat a stray hair back into her bun. "I happened to overhear a little of your conversation with my niece," she confessed. "I'm not in the habit of eavesdropping," she added, "but it was a rather

73

loud discussion the two of you were having, and actually they were mostly Sara's comments I overheard. Just a snatch here and there," she added. "Tell me this, Nathan. Will you?"

"Will I what?"

"Love and cherish her?"

"You heard that particular snatch, did you?" He couldn't contain his grin when he remembered the militant way his bride had dared to challenge him.

"I do believe your entire crew overheard Sara's remarks. I must have a little chat with her about her unladylike bellowing. I've never heard her raise her voice before, yet I cannot truly fault her. You did take your time coming to claim her. She's been stewing over your . . . forgetfulness. You must believe me when I tell you it isn't at all in her nature to raise her voice to anyone."

Nathan shook his head. He turned and walked out of the cabin. He was pulling the door shut behind him when Nora called out, "You've still to answer me. Will you love and cherish her?"

"Do I have a choice, madam?"

He shut the door before she could answer him.

Sara awakened a short time later to the horrid noise of someone retching. The tortured sound made her own stomach queasy. She sat up with a start. Her first thought was for Nora. The rolling motion of the ship must have made her aunt sick.

Sara immediately tossed the cover aside and rushed to the door. She was still so sleepy, she felt completely disoriented. She didn't even realize she was only partially dressed until she tripped over one of her petticoats.

One of Nathan's maids had obviously been at work. Sara saw that her trunk had been placed next to the far wall and realized she must have slept through its delivery. She blushed over the realization that a man had come into her cabin while she'd been asleep. She hoped the maid had covered her with the blanket before the visitation had taken place.

She heard a sound in the hallway and opened the door. Nathan was just walking past when she peeked outside. He never bothered to glance her way, just reached out and pulled the door closed again when he strode by.

Sara wasn't offended by his rudeness, and she wasn't worried about her aunt any longer. When she had seen the color of Nathan's complexion she'd known immediately, of course. Her fierce Viking husband looked as green as the sea.

Could it be possible? she asked herself. Was the invincible, ill-mannered marquess of St. James afflicted with seasickness?

Sara would have laughed out loud if she hadn't been so exhausted. She went back to bed and took a long nap, getting up only briefly to eat dinner with Nora before returning yet again to her bed for more badly needed sleep.

The air inside the chamber cooled considerably during the night, and Sara woke up shivering. She tried to pull the quilt up around her shoulders, but the blanket was caught on something quite solid. When Sara finally opened her eyes she found the cause. The blanket was tangled up in Nathan's long, naked legs.

He was sleeping next to her.

She almost had heart failure. She opened her mouth to scream. He clamped his big hand over half her face.

"Don't you dare make a sound," he ordered.

She pushed his hand away. "Get out of my bed." The command came out in a furious whisper.

He let out a weary sigh before responding to that command. "Sara, you happen to be sleeping in my bed. If anyone's going to leave, it's going to be you."

He sounded sleepy to her, and mean. Sara was actually comforted by his callous attitude. She guessed he was so exhausted he only wanted to sleep, and her virtue was therefore still safe.

"Very well," she announced. "I'll go and sleep with Nora."

"No, you won't," he answered. "You aren't going to leave this cabin. If you wish to, bride, you may sleep on the floor."

"Why do you persist in calling me bride?" she demanded. "If you have to call me something other than my name, then call me wife, not bride."

"But you aren't my wife yet," he responded.

She didn't understand. "I most certainly am your wife . . . aren't I?"

"Not until I've bedded you."

A long silent minute passed before she responded to that statement.

"You may call me bride."

"I don't need your permission," he growled. He reached out to take her into his arms when she started shivering again, but she pushed his hands away.

"My God, I can't believe this is happening to me," she cried out. "You're supposed to be kind, gentle, understanding."

"What makes you think I'm not?" he couldn't resist asking.

"You're naked," she blurted out.

"And that means I'm not—"

She wanted to hit him. Her face was turned away from him, but she could hear the laughter in his voice. "You're embarrassing me," she announced. "On purpose."

His patience was at an end. "I am not deliberately trying to embarrass you," he snapped. "This is just how I sleep, bride. You'll like it, too, once—"

"Oh, God," she said on a groan.

She decided she was through with the shameful conversation. She scooted down to the bottom of the bed so that she could get out, as one side was blocked by the wall, and the other side was blocked by Nathan. It was too dark inside the cabin to find her wrapper. Nathan had kicked one of the covers off the bed, though. Sara grabbed it and wrapped it around herself.

She didn't know how long she stood there glaring at his back. His deep, even breathing indicated he was sound asleep.

She was freezing in no time. Her thin nightgown offered little protection against the chill in the room.

She was miserable. She sat down on the floor, tucked her bare feet under the blanket, and then stretched out on her side.

The floor felt as though it were covered with a layer of ice. "All married couples have separate chambers," she muttered. "I have never, ever been treated so poorly in all my days. If this is your idea of how you plan to cherish me, you're already failing, Nathan."

He heard every word of her whispered tirade. He held his smile when he said "You're a quick learner, bride."

She didn't know what he was talking about. "And what is it you think I've learned so quickly?" she asked.

"Where your place is," he drawled. "It took my dog much longer."

Her scream of outrage filled the cabin. "Your dog?" She came to her feet in one swift action, then poked him in his shoulder. "Move over, husband."

"Climb over, Sara," he ordered. "I always sleep on the outside."

"Why?" she asked before she could stop herself.

"For protection," he answered. "If the cabin is breached, the enemy will have to get through me in order to get to you. Now will you go to sleep, woman?"

"Is this an old rule or a new one?"

He didn't answer her. She poked his shoulder again. "Have there been other women in this bed, Nathan?"

"No."

She didn't know why, but she was immensely pleased with that surly denial. Her anger dissipated when she realized her husband really meant to try to protect her. He was still an ogre, but he would do his best to keep her safe. She got into bed and squeezed herself up against the wall.

The bed soon began to shake from her shivers. Nathan's tolerance was gone. He reached out and roughly pulled her into his arms. Sara was literally covered by his warmth. And his nakedness. He draped one of his heavy legs over both of hers, immediately warming the lower half of her body. His chest and arms took care of the rest of her.

She didn't protest. She couldn't. His hand was clamped over her mouth. She snuggled closer to him, tucked the top of her head under his chin, and closed her eyes.

The instant Nathan removed his hand from her mouth, she whispered, "If anyone is going to sleep on the floor, it's going to be you."

His low grunt of irritation was his only response. Sara smiled to herself. She was feeling much better. She let out a yawn, moved even closer to her husband, and let him take her shivers completely away.

She fell asleep feeling warm and safe . . . and just a little bit cherished.

It was a nice beginning.

Chapter Four

Sara felt much better when she awakened the following morning. She'd finally caught up on her rest, and she felt ready to take on the world. More directly, she felt strong enough to talk to her Viking husband again.

She had come up with a wonderful plan during the night, and she was certain that once she'd explained exactly what she wanted from her husband, he would agree. Oh, he'd probably grumble and growl, but in the end he'd see how much it meant to her, and he would give in.

There were several issues that needed to be discussed, but she decided she would get the most worrisome one over and done with first.

She wanted a courtship and a proper marriage. No matter how rude and arrogant he became when she explained her request to him, she was determined to hold onto her temper. She would simply use a sweet tone of voice and be as logical as possible.

Lord, she did dread the task ahead of her. Nathan wasn't a very easy man to talk to. Why, he acted as though it was a chore to be in the same room with her.

That realization led to a dark thought. What if he really didn't want to be married to her?

"Nonsense," she muttered to herself. "Of course he wants to be married to me."

That attempt to bolster her confidence didn't last long. She was so accustomed to thinking of Nathan as her husband that she had never once considered being married to anyone else. She'd grown up with the idea, and because she had such an easygoing, accepting nature, she never questioned her fate.

But what about Nathan? He didn't seem to be the type of man who accepted much of anything without putting up a fight.

She guessed that she would continue to fret about the situation until she'd talked to him.

She dressed with care, determined to look her best when she confronted Nathan. It took her almost an hour to unpack her possessions. The dark green walking dress was her first choice, but she couldn't shake all the wrinkles out of the skirt, so she settled on wearing her light pink gown. The neckline wasn't nearly as revealing as the one Nathan had rudely remarked upon, and she thought that fact might put him in a good mood.

Their cabin was actually quite nice. It was much larger than the one she'd visited Nora in. Why, her chamber was actually three times the size. The ceiling was much higher, too, adding to the feeling of spaciousness.

It was sparsely furnished, though. There was a twisted metal grate in the corner of the cabin. Sara assumed that was the hearth, though she admitted she didn't care for the modern design overly much. In the opposite corner of the room was a tall white screen. There were hooks on the wall behind it to hold clothing, and a washstand with a porcelain pitcher and bowl set on top. In the corner opposite the bed was her trunk. A table and two chairs took up the center of the room, and a large mahogany desk was set against the wall.

Yes, the room was sparsely furnished, she mused, but it would certainly do for the next month or two, depending upon the weather. If the sea remained calm, the journey to her aunt's island shouldn't take them too long.

Sara removed Nathan's clothes from the hooks, folded them, and put them on her trunk. She then hung up her gowns. She also removed the papers and charts from the top of his desk and put her sketch pads and charcoals there instead.

After donning the pink gown and matching shoes she brushed her hair and tied it behind her neck with a pink ribbon. She grabbed her matching pink parasol from her trunk and then went to look in on Nora. She hoped her aunt would be feeling rested enough to stroll along the upper decks. Sara wanted to go over her prepared speech with her aunt before confronting Nathan.

Nora was sound asleep, however, and Sara didn't have the heart to wake her.

When she left her aunt's cabin she noticed that the dark, narrow hallway actually widened into a large rectangular room. Sunlight filtered down the steps and made the wooden floors sparkle. The pristine area was devoid of furniture, but there were a multitude of black iron hooks protruding from the ceiling. She wondered what in heaven's name the area was used for, or if it was just wasted space. Her attention was turned when one of the crew came lumbering down the steps.

The man tucked his head under the low overhand, then came to an abrupt stop when he spotted her. Sara recognized the man from the wharf but decided to pretend that she didn't. After all, she had acted most unladylike, and that incident was best forgotten.

"Good day, sir," she announced with a curtsy. "My name is Lady Sara Winchester."

He shook his head at her. She didn't know what to make of that.

"You're Lady St. James."

She was too surprised by his boldness to correct him for contradicting her. "Yes," she agreed. "I am Lady St. James now, and I thank you for reminding me."

The big man shrugged. The gold earring in his earlobe fascinated her. So did the fact that he seemed to be a little wary of her. Perhaps the seaman just wasn't used to visiting with gentle ladies of breeding. "I'm very happy to make your acquaintance, sir," she said.

She waited for him to tell her his name. He stood staring down at her for a long minute before he finally responded. "We met last night, Lady St. James," he said. "You hit me, remember?"

She remembered. She gave him a disgruntled look for bringing up her bad behavior, then slowly nodded. "Yes, I do remember, sir, now that you mention it, and for that shame I must apologize to you. My only excuse is that I was in a bit of a startle at the time. What is your name?"

"Jimbo."

If she thought that name odd, she didn't remark upon it. She reached out and clasped his right hand in both of hers. The feel of her soft skin against his calluses startled him. Her parasol fell to the floor, but Jimbo was still too surprised by her touch to fetch it, and she was too intent on gaining his friendship to fetch it herself. "Do you forgive me, sir, for hitting you?"

Jimbo was rendered speechless. The woman he'd met two nights before was a far cry from the soft-spoken lady standing so humbly before him. Lord, she was a fair sight, too. She had the prettiest brown eyes he'd ever seen.

He got hold of his thoughts when she gave him a puzzled look. "Does it matter to you if I forgive you or not?" he muttered.

Sara gave his hand an affectionate squeeze before she let go. "Oh, my, yes, Mister Jimbo. Of course it matters. I was very rude."

He rolled his eyes heavenward. "All right, I forgive you.

You didn't do any real damage," he added in a grumble. He was feeling as awkward as a schoolboy.

Sara's smile melted his frown away. "I do thank you, sir. You have a kind heart."

Jimbo threw back his head and shouted with laughter. When he was able to regain his composure he said, "Be sure to mention my . . . kind heart to the captain. He'll appreciate hearing such high praise."

She thought that was a fine idea. "Yes, I will mention it," she promised.

Since the seaman seemed to be in such a pleasant mood, she decided to ask him a few questions. "Sir? Have you seen the maids about this morning? My bed has still to be made up, and I have several gowns that need attention."

"We don't have any maids aboard this vessel," Jimbo returned. "Fact is, you and your aunt are the only women traveling with us."

"Then who . . ." She stopped that question in midsentence. If there weren't any maids, who had taken her clothes off her? The answer came to her in a flash. Nathan.

Jimbo watched as a fine blush covered her cheeks and wondered what she was thinking about.

"I have one other question to ask you, sir, if you're patient enough to listen."

"What?" he countered abruptly.

"What is this room called? Or does it have a specific name?" She made a sweep with her hand to indicate the area around her. "I thought it was just a hallway, yet now, with the light streaming down the steps, I can see it's much larger. It would make a wonderful salon," she added. "I hadn't noticed that folding screen when I first boarded, and I . . ."

She quit her speech when Jimbo moved the screen off to the side and secured it in the buckles and straps against the wall next to the stairs. "This is the wardroom," Jimbo told her. "Or so it's called on all true frigates."

The hallway was completely gone, and once the screen

had been moved Sara could see the steps leading down to another level. "Where do those steps lead?"

"The wine and water are stored on the level below us," Jimbo answered. "Lower still is the second hold, where we keep the ammunition."

"Ammunition?" she asked. "Why would we need ammunition?"

Jimbo smiled. "You didn't chance to notice the cannons, m'lady, when you boarded?"

She shook her head. "I was a little upset at the time, sir, and I didn't pay much attention to details."

A little upset was certainly the understatement of the year, Jimbo thought. The woman had been in a rage.

"We have eight cannons in all," Jimbo announced. "That's way below the usual number for most ships, but our aim is always on target, and we don't need more. This ship is a scaled-down version of a frigate the captain took a liking to," he added. "The ammunition stores are kept below the water level in the event of an attack. They're safer from explosion that way."

"But Mister Jimbo, we aren't at war now. Why would the captain have such weapons on board? What is the need?"

Jimbo shrugged. Sara's eyes suddenly widened. "Pagan." She blurted out the name of the infamous pirate and then nodded. "Yes, of course. How cunning of our captain to be prepared for the villains who roam the seas. He thinks to defend us against all the pirates, doesn't he?"

It was a mighty effort, but Jimbo was able to hide his smile. "You've heard of Pagan, have you?"

She let him see her exasperation. "Everyone has heard of that villain."

"Villain? Then you don't like Pagan?"

She thought that had to be the oddest question ever put to her. The sparkle in his eyes puzzled her, too. He seemed to be vastly amused, and that didn't make any sense at all. They were talking about the horrid pirate, not sharing the latest jest making the rounds in London.

"I most certainly don't like the man. He's a criminal, sir. Why, there's a bounty the size of England on his head. You're obviously given to a romantic nature if you believe all those silly stories about Pagan's goodness."

The piercing sound of a whistle interrupted her lecture. "What is that noise?" she asked. "I heard it earlier when I was dressing."

"That's the boatswain piping the change," he explained. "You'll be hearing the sound every four hours, night and day. It's the notice of the change of duty."

"Mister Jimbo?" she asked when he started to turn away from her.

"Lady Sara, you don't have to call me mister," he grumbled. "Jimbo will do fine."

"Then you must quit calling me Lady Sara," she countered. "We are friends now, and you may simply call me Sara." She grabbed his arm. "May I ask you just one last question?"

He glanced over his shoulder. "Yes?"

"Last evening . . . or was it the night before? Well, I noticed that you seemed to be in my husband's employ. Is that correct?"

"Yes."

"Do you happen to know where Nathan is? I would like to have a word with him."

"He's aft."

She looked startled but was quick to recover. Then she shook her head at him. The censure in her expression gained his full attention. He turned completely around. "He's aft, I'm telling you."

"Yes, he might very well be daft, Jimbo," she began. She paused to pick up her parasol and then walked around the big man. "But you're most disloyal when you voice that thought aloud. I'm Nathan's wife now, and I won't listen to such talk. Please don't show such disrespect again."

Matthew came down the stairs just in time to hear his

friend mutter something about respect. Lady Sara smiled as she made her way past him.

"What was that all about?" Matthew asked his friend. "I thought I heard you—"

Jimbo cut him off with a glare. "You aren't going to believe this, but I just promised not ever to tell anyone Nathan was aft."

Matthew shook his head. "She's a strange one, isn't she, Jimbo? I'm wondering how such an innocent could have come from such a mean-hearted family."

"Sara isn't anything like our Jade," Jimbo announced. He was referring to Nathan's younger sister. "In all our travels together I never once saw Jade cry."

"No, she never cried." There was pride in Matthew's voice. "But this one . . . I didn't know a woman could carry on the way she did that first night."

"Screaming like a hellion, too," Jimbo interjected. "Now, Jade," he continued, "she never screamed."

"Never," Matthew agreed. His voice was emphatic.

Jimbo suddenly grinned. "The two are as different as fire and snow," he said. "Still, they do have one thing in common."

"What's that?"

"They're both damn fair in looks."

Matthew nodded.

The comparison between the two ladies was cut short when a shrill scream reached them. They both knew it was Sara making all the racket. "She's a piece of work, isn't she?" Matthew drawled out.

"A damned loud piece of work," Jimbo muttered. "Wonder what's got her all riled up this time."

Odd, but both men were eager to get back up on deck to see what was happening. They were both smiling, too.

Sara had just located Nathan. He was standing behind a spoked wheel. She was about to call out to him when he turned his back on her and pulled off his shirt.

She saw the scars on his back. Her reaction was instinctive. She let out a shout of outrage.

"Who did that to you?"

Nathan immediately reacted. He grabbed hold of his whip and turned to confront the threat. It didn't take him any time at all to realize there wasn't any enemy trying to harm his bride. Sara stood all alone.

"What is it?" he roared at her while he tried to calm his heartbeat. "I thought someone was . . ."

He stopped himself in mid-bellow, took a deep breath, and then said, "Are you in pain, madam?"

She shook her head.

"Don't you ever scream like that again," he ordered in a much softer tone of voice. "If you wish my attention, simply ask for it."

Sara's parasol fell to the deck when she walked over to her husband. She was still so stunned by what she'd seen, she wasn't even aware she'd dropped it. She stopped when she was just a scant foot away from Nathan. He saw the tears in her eyes. "Now what is it?" he demanded. "Did someone frighten you?" Damn, he didn't have the patience for this, he told himself.

"It's your back, Nathan," she whispered. "It's covered with scars."

He shook his head. No one had ever dared mention his disfigurement to him. Those who'd seen his back pretended not to notice.

"Thank you for telling me," he snapped. "I never would have known . . ."

Hell, she started to cry. His sarcasm was obviously too much for her, he decided. "Look, Sara," he muttered in true exasperation. "If the sight of my back offends you, go below."

"It doesn't offend me," she answered. "Why would you say such a mean thing?"

Nathan motioned to Jimbo to take over the wheel, then

clasped his hands behind his back so he wouldn't grab her. The urge to shake some sense into the woman fairly overwhelmed him. "All right, then, why did you scream?"

His voice was as brisk as the wind. Sara guessed he was a little sensitive about his marks. "I was very angry when I saw the scars, Nathan. Did you have an accident?"

"No."

"Then someone deliberately did this thing to you?" She didn't give him time to answer. "What monster inflicted such pain? My God, how you must have suffered."

"For God's sake, it happened a long time ago."

"Was it Pagan?" she asked.

"What?" he asked.

He looked startled. Sara thought her guess had been right after all. "It was Pagan who did that to you, wasn't it?"

Jimbo started coughing. Nathan turned to glare him into silence. "Why in God's name would you think it was Pagan?" he asked Sara.

"Because he's mean enough," she answered.

"Oh?" he asked. "And how would you know that?"

She shrugged. "I heard that he was."

"It wasn't Pagan."

"Are you absolutely certain, Nathan? No one knows what the villain looks like. Perhaps it was Pagan, and you just didn't realize it because he didn't give you his true name."

He let her see his exasperation. "I know who did it."

"Will you tell me who it was, then?"

"Why?"

"So I can hate him."

His anger vanished. Such loyalty stunned him. "No, I won't tell you who it was."

"But it wasn't Pagan."

She could drive a man to drink, Nathan thought to himself. "No," he answered once again.

"Nathan, you don't have to shout at me."

He turned his back on her in dismissal. Jimbo moved

away from the wheel. Sara waited until she and her husband were all alone and then moved closer.

He felt the touch of her fingertips on the top of his right shoulder. He didn't move. The feathery light caress down his back was incredibly gentle, and provocative, too. He couldn't ignore it, or the strange feelings her touch evoked.

"I wouldn't have poked you in your back last night if I'd known about your injury," she whispered. "But I couldn't see in the dark, and I didn't . . . know."

"For God's sake, woman, it doesn't hurt now. It happened years ago."

His abrupt tone startled her. Her hand dropped back to her side. She moved over to stand beside him. Her arm touched his. She looked up at his face and simply waited for him to look at her again. His expression could have been chiseled in stone, she thought to herself. He looked just the way she pictured a Viking. The ripple of muscles cording his shoulders and his upper arms were those of a fit warrior. His chest was covered with dark curly hair that tapered to a V at the waistband of his breeches. She didn't dare look any lower, for to do so would be brazen, and when she returned her attention to his face again she found him watching her.

She blushed. "Nathan?"

"What?"

Did he always have to sound so resigned when he talked to her? Sara forced herself to sound pleasant when she apologized. "I'm sorry if I hurt your feelings."

He didn't think that comment was worthy of a response.

"Will the captain mind?" she asked then.

"Mind what?"

"Mind that you're directing his boat for him."

His smile was heartwarming to her. "It isn't a boat, Sara. You may call the *Seahawk* a ship or a vessel, but you must never call her a boat. It's an insult, bride, and we captains take grave exception to hearing such blasphemy."

"We captains?"

He nodded.

"Oh, Nathan, I didn't realize," she blurted. "Then we're rich?"

"No."

"Well, why not?"

Hell, he thought, she looked disgruntled. Nathan quickly told her how he and his friend Colin had started the shipping company together, why they'd decided that he should remain a silent partner, and he ended his brief summary with the fact that in approximately ten months time, give or take a month or two, their company would take a turn into sure profits.

"How can you be so certain that in just a year we'll be rich?"

"The contract I signed."

"Do you mean a contract for shipping services?"

"No."

Her sigh was dramatic. "Please explain, Nathan."

He ignored her request. She nudged him. Lord, getting anything out of him was such a strain. "If you're so certain about this, I'll be happy to help you."

He actually laughed. Sara took heart. Her offer to lend a hand had obviously pleased him. Her voice was filled with enthusiasm when she said, "I could help you with the books. I'm really quite good with figures. No?" she added when he shook his head. "But I want to help."

He let go of the wheel and turned to face her. Lord, she was a fair sight today, he thought to himself as he watched her try to manage her wild curls. The wind was high, making the task impossible. She was dressed in pink. Her cheeks were flushed, adding to the lovely picture. His gaze settled on her mouth. Her lips were just as rosy as the rest of her.

He gave in to his sudden urge. Before she could back away from him he grabbed hold of her shoulders. He pulled her up against his chest, then threaded one hand through the curls behind her neck. Her hair felt like silk to him. He made a fist of the curls, then jerked her head back so her face was tilted up toward him. He told himself that it was only for his own peace of mind that he was going to kiss her, knowing full well that once he explained the special task she was going to have to undertake she'd start screaming again.

"We'll each have a special duty to perform," he told her. His mouth was getting closer to hers. "It's my duty to get you pregnant, Sara, and it will be your duty to give me a son."

His mouth settled on top of hers just in time to capture her outraged gasp.

Sara was simply too stunned to react at first. His mouth was hard, hot, incredibly demanding. He was drowning her with his warmth, his taste, his wonderful masculine scent.

Nathan wanted her response. She didn't disappoint him. When his tongue moved inside her mouth to mate with hers, her knees went weak. She put her arms around his neck and clung to him even as she tried to wiggle out of his embrace.

She didn't realize she was kissing him back, didn't know the sounds she heard belonged to her.

Only when Nathan had her full cooperation did he gentle the kiss. God, she was soft. He could feel the heat inside her, wanted to get closer, closer. His hands moved to cup her derrière, and he slowly lifted her off the ground until her pelvis was touching his own, then pulled her tight against his arousal.

His mouth slanted over hers again and again. He wanted to be inside her. Nathan knew he was close to losing all sense of discipline. His hunger was demanding to be appeased.

The whistles and hoots of laughter penetrated his mind then. His crew was obviously enjoying the spectacle he was giving them. Nathan tried to pull away from Sara.

She wouldn't let go of him. She pulled on his hair to get him to deepen the kiss again. He gave into her silent plea with a low growl. The kiss they shared was openly carnal, but when her sweet tongue rubbed against his he forced himself to stop.

They were both out of breath when they drew apart. Sara

couldn't seem to keep her balance. She fell back against the wooden ledge adjacent to the wheel. One hand rested on the swell of her bosom, and she let out a ragged little whisper. "Oh, my."

As soon as their captain had quit touching his bride the men returned to their duties. Nathan glared at several backs before he looked at Sara again. He couldn't help but feel extremely satisfied when he saw the bemused look on her face. It made him want to kiss her again.

He had to shake his head over his own lack of discipline. He decided he'd wasted enough time on his bride and turned his attention back to the wheel. He scowled when he noticed his hands were shaking. The kiss had obviously affected him a little more than he'd thought.

It took Sara much longer to recover. She was trembling from head to foot. She had no idea a kiss could be so . . . thorough.

He certainly hadn't been affected, she thought when she saw the horridly bored look on his face again.

She suddenly felt like crying and didn't understand why. Then she remembered the obscene remarks he'd made about her special duty. "I'm not a brood mare," she whispered. "And I'm not at all certain I like you touching me."

Nathan glanced back over his shoulder. "You could have fooled me," he drawled. "The way you kissed me—"

"I believe I hated it."

"Liar."

It was an insult, yes, but the way he'd said the word actually warmed her heart. He made it sound very like an endearment.

That didn't make any sense. Was she so desperate for a word of kindness from the Viking that she now responded to insults? Sara could feel herself blushing. She stared at her shoes and folded her hands demurely in front of her. "You can't kiss me again," she announced, wishing her voice had sounded a little more forceful and less breathless.

"I can't?"

His amusement was apparent. "No, you can't," she told him. "I've decided that you're going to have to court me first, Nathan, and then we must have a proper ceremony performed by a true minister before you may kiss me again."

She hadn't looked at him when she made that emphatic speech, but when she was finished she glanced up to gauge his reaction. His expression, unfortunately, didn't tell her anything. She frowned at him. "I believe our marriage could be challenged in the courts unless we say our vows to each other in front of a man of God."

He finally let her see his reaction. She wished she'd been left guessing. Lord, his scowl was as hot as the noon sun beating down on them.

But his eyes . . . the color was so vivid, so true, so mesmerizing. When he was looking directly into her eyes he made her forget to breathe. A sudden thought settled in her mind. Her Viking was actually very handsome.

Why hadn't she noticed that before? she asked herself. Good God, was she beginning to find him appealing?

Nathan pulled her from her thoughts when he said, "Are you thinking you've found a way to breach this contract?"

"No."

"Good," he countered. Almost as an afterthought he added, "As I instructed you before, I'm not about to dissolve this contract, Sara."

She disliked his arrogant tone. "I already knew that before I was so instructed."

"You did?"

"Yes, I did."

"How?"

She started to shake her head at him again, but Nathan stopped that action when he hauled her back into his arms. He firmly grabbed hold of her hair.

"Unhand me, Nathan. You make my head ache when you tug on my hair like that."

He didn't let go, but he did begin to rub the back of her neck. His touch was very soothing. Sara had to catch herself from letting out a telling little sigh.

"You realize how much I want the money and the land, don't you, Sara?" he asked. "That's why you know I won't walk away from the contract."

"No."

Nathan didn't know why he pressed her for an explanation. His curiosity was caught, however, because she was acting so damn shy. The woman didn't make any sense to him, and he was determined to understand how her mind worked.

"Then why did you know I would want to be married to you?"

"Well, why wouldn't you?" she whispered.

"Why wouldn't I?"

"Nathan, I'm everything a husband could want in a wife," she blurted out. She tried to sound as arrogant, as self-assured as he did whenever he talked to her. "Truly," she added with a vehement nod.

"Is that so?"

She could see the laughter in his eyes. Her bluster of pride immediately began to evaporate. "Yes, I am," she said.

A fine blush covered her cheeks. How could anyone sound so arrogant and look so shy at the same time? he wondered. She was such a contradiction to him. "Would you care to tell me why you think you're everything I could want?"

"Certainly," she replied. "For one, I'm pretty enough. I'm not plain," she added in a rush. "I'll admit I'm not a raving beauty, Nathan, but that shouldn't signify."

"You don't believe you're a . . . raving beauty?" he asked, amazed.

She gave him a good frown, for she was certain he was deliberately baiting her. "Of course not," she said. "You must have a cruel streak inside you to taunt me over my appearance. I'm not overly ugly, Nathan. Just because I have

brown hair and brown eyes doesn't necessarily mean I'm
. . . homely."

His smile was tender. "Sara, haven't you ever noticed how
men stop and stare when you pass by?"

She wished she could strike him. "If you mean to imply
that I'm that unappealing, well, sir," she muttered.

"Well, what?" he asked when she seemed to be at a loss for
words.

"You're no prize either, husband."

He shook his head. He wasn't married to a vain woman.
That fact pleased him considerably. "You're right," he
announced. "I have seen prettier women, but as you just
said, that shouldn't signify."

"Lest you think you make me feel completely inferior
with that rude remark, you're mistaken," she returned. The
blush had moved to her voice. "I'm really all a man could
want. Dare you smile at me? I mean what I say. I've been
trained to be a good wife, just as you've been trained to be a
good provider. It's the way of things," she ended with a
deliberate shrug.

The vulnerability in her expression was apparent. She had
pricked his curiosity, too. The woman said the damnedest
things. "Sara, exactly what is it that you've been trained to
do?"

"I can run a household with ease, no matter the number
of servants you employ," she began. "I can sew a straight
stitch without pricking my finger, plan a formal dinner party
for as many as two hundred," she exaggerated, "and accomplish any other duty associated with the running of a large
estate."

She was certain she'd impressed him with her list. She'd
even impressed herself. Most of what she'd just boasted of
was pure fabrication, of course, as she didn't really have the
faintest idea if she could run a large estate or not, but
Nathan couldn't possibly know about her inadequacies,
could he? Besides, just because she'd never entertained

anyone before didn't necessarily mean she couldn't organize a party for two hundred guests. She believed she could accomplish any goal if she really put her mind to the challenge. "Well?" she asked when he didn't make any comment. "What think you of my accomplishments?"

"I could hire someone to run my household," he countered. "I don't have to be married to have a comfortable home."

He almost laughed out loud, for the look of disappointment on her face was comical.

She tried not to feel defeated by his remark. "Yes, but I can also engage in intelligent conversation with your guests on any current topic. I happen to be very well-read."

His grin stopped her. His conduct, she decided, was proving just what one would expect from a man bearing his name. Nathan was turning out to be as despicable as the rest of the St. James men. He was certainly as muleheaded.

"You could not hire anyone with such a fine education," she muttered.

"And that's it?" he asked. "There isn't anything else you've been trained to do?"

Her pride was like a shredded gown pooled around her ankles. Wasn't there anything she could say that would impress the man?

"Such as?"

"Such as pleasing me in bed."

Her blush intensified. "Of course not," she stammered out. "You're supposed to teach me how . . ." She paused to step on his foot. Hard. "How dare you think I would be trained in that . . . that . . ."

She couldn't go on. The look in her eyes confused him. He couldn't decide if she was about to burst into tears or try to kill him. "A mistress could see to those duties, I suppose," he said just to goad her.

Lord, he thought, she really was a joy to tease. Her reactions were so uninhibited, so . . . raw. He knew he should quit his game. She was getting all worked up, but he was enjoying himself too much to stop just yet.

"You will not have a mistress."

She'd shouted that statement. He deliberately shrugged. She stepped on his foot again. "No matter how pretty she is, no matter how . . . talented she may be, no matter what," she said. "I won't have it."

She didn't give him time to respond to that statement but continued. "As for sleeping next to me, Nathan, well, you can just forget such notions in future. I'm going to be properly courted by you and wed before a minister first."

She waited a long minute for his agreement. "Well?" she demanded.

He shrugged again.

How could she have thought he was the least bit appealing? Lord, she wished she had enough strength to give him a sound kick in his backside. "This is a very serious matter we're discussing," she insisted. "And if you shrug at me once more, I swear I'll scream again."

He didn't think it was the time to mention the fact that she was already screaming. "Not we," he said in soft, soothing voice. "You're the one who thinks this is a serious matter," he explained. "I don't."

She took a deep breath and tried one last time. "Nathan, please try to understand my feelings," she whispered. "I've decided that it isn't decent for you to sleep with me." She was too embarrassed to continue with that particular bend in the topic. "Are you going to marry me or not?"

"I already did."

Lord, she was furious with him. Her face was as red as sunburn, and she couldn't meet his gaze. She was staring intently at his chest. The subject was obviously extremely distressing to him.

And yet she persisted. "Look," she muttered. "It's really very simple to understand, even for a St. James. I want to be properly courted, Nathan, and you aren't going to touch me until we've said our vows in front of a man of God. Do you hear me?"

"I'm certain he heard you clear, miss," came a shout from behind her. Sara shoved herself away from Nathan and turned around to find an audience of some ten men smiling at her. All had paused in their duties, she noticed, and all were nodding at her. Most were actually a fair distance away.

"Aye, I'd wager he caught every word," called another. "You ain't going to let the captain touch you until you're wed proper. Ain't that right, Haedley?"

A baldheaded, bent-shouldered man nodded. "That's what I heard," he shouted back.

Sara was mortified. Lord, she must have been screaming like a shrew.

She decided to blame Nathan. She turned around to glare at him. "Must you embarrass me?"

"You're doing a fair job on your own, bride. Go back to the cabin," he ordered. "Take that gown off."

She was immediately waylaid by that command. "Why? Don't you like it?" she asked.

"Take everything off, Sara. I'll be down in a few minutes."

Her heart almost failed her when the fullness of what he'd just said settled in her mind. She was simply too furious to try to reason with him any longer. Without a word of farewell she turned around and slowly walked away from him.

She passed Jimbo on her way toward the steps. "You were correct, Mister Jimbo," she said in a hoarse whisper. "Nathan is daft."

The seaman wasn't given time to reply, for Lady Sara was already gone.

She didn't start in running until she reached the wardroom area. Sara picked up her skirts and ran like lightning then. She didn't pause at her cabin door but continued on to the far corner, where Aunt Nora's quarters were located.

For all his bulk and age, Matthew could still be quick when the occasion called for such action, and he reached the door at the same time Sara did.

"Lady Sara, I'm hoping you won't disturb sweet Nora with a visit now," he said from behind.

She hadn't heard his approach. She let out a loud gasp and turned around. "You gave me a startle," she began. "You shouldn't sneak up on someone, sir. What is your name?"

"Matthew."

"I'm pleased to meet you," she returned. "As for my aunt, well, I just wanted to look in on her."

"I'm taking care of your aunt," Matthew interjected. "She isn't up to visitors today. She's tuckered out."

Sara immediately felt guilty. She had fully intended on pouring her heart out to her aunt so that she could gain her assistance in dealing with Nathan. Her own problems seemed paltry, however. "Nora isn't truly ill, is she?" she asked, fear obvious in her voice. "I saw the bruises, but I thought—"

"She's going to heal just fine," Matthew announced. He was pleased by her caring attitude. "Nora's needing plenty of rest, though. She shouldn't move about neither. Her ribs were cracked—"

"Oh God, I didn't know."

"Now, now, don't start in weeping," Matthew pleaded. Lady Sara's eyes were already looking misty to him. He didn't know what he'd do if she went full-blown on him. The thought of having to comfort the captain's wife made his stomach tighten up. "It ain't as bad as all that," he announced with a nod for emphasis. "I've wrapped her tight around the middle. She just needs rest is all. I don't want her fretting about anything, either," he added. He gave her a knowing look when he made that last remark.

Sara immediately concluded he'd guessed what her mission was. She bowed her head in contrition and said, "I was going to burden her with a special problem that has developed. I won't bother her, of course. I don't want to worry her. When she awakens will you please tell her that I'll come to visit her as soon as she asks for me?"

Matthew nodded. Sara took hold of his hand. The show of affection rattled him. "Thank you for helping Nora. She's such a good-hearted woman. She has suffered so, Mister Matthew, and all because of me."

Lordy, she looked like she was about to burst into tears again. "Now, now, you didn't do the damage to your aunt," Matthew said. "You aren't the one who kicked her in the ribs. I was told it was your father and his brothers behind the foul deed."

"My Uncle Henry was behind this treachery," she returned. "Still, I'm just as responsible. If I hadn't insisted that Nora come back to England with me . . ."

She didn't go on with her explanation. She gave Matthew's hand another quick squeeze, then surprised a smile out of him when she made a formal curtsy and told him how pleased she was to have him on her staff.

Matthew mopped his brow as he watched her walk back to her cabin. He grunted over the foolishness of it all, for the fact that he was actually nervous because she had almost cried was simply ludicrous. Still, he was smiling when he strolled away.

Sara continued to think about Nora until she opened the door to her cabin. As soon as she spotted the big bed the problem of Nathan became uppermost in her thoughts.

She didn't dare waste another minute. She shut the door, bolted it, and then dragged her heavy trunk over to the entrance, straining her back with the effort.

She hurried over to the table, thinking she'd put that piece of furniture up against the trunk to add to her fortress.

No matter how much grit she put to the chore, she couldn't get the table to budge. She finally located the cause. The legs had been nailed to the floor. "Now why would anyone want to do such a thing?" she muttered to herself.

She tried to move the desk and found that it had also been

nailed to the floor. The chairs, thankfully, weren't stationary. They were heavy, though. Sara dragged one over to the trunk and spent precious minutes struggling with the weight until she'd lifted the awkward piece of furniture and had it propped up on top.

She stood back to observe her work. She rubbed her lower back, trying to take the sting away. She knew that blocking the door was only a temporary measure, but she still felt she'd been very clever. It didn't take her long to discard that bit of praise, however, when she realized how childishly she was behaving. Yes, she thought to herself, her conduct was infantile, but then so was Nathan's. If he wasn't going to be reasonable, why should she? Perhaps by nightfall her Viking would come to his senses and realize her request had validity. And if the muleheaded man didn't agree, well, she was determined to stay inside the cabin until he gave in. If she starved to death, so be it.

"I like it better the other way."

Sara jumped a foot, then whirled around. She found Nathan lounging against the edge of the desk, smiling at her.

He didn't wait for her question but simply pointed up to the trapdoor. "I usually come in through the top," he explained in a soft whisper. "It's quicker."

She might have nodded, but she couldn't be sure. She leaned back against the trunk and stared at him. Oh, God, now what was she going to do?

His bride couldn't seem to find her voice. Nathan decided to give her a little more time to calm down before he pressed her. The color was completely gone from her face, and there was the real possibility that she might swoon on him again.

"I assume you were trying to change the room around?"

His voice had been pleasant, soothing. She wanted to scream. "Yes," she blurted out instead. "I like it better this way."

He shook his head. "It won't do."

"It won't?"

"You might not have noticed, but the trunk and the chair

are actually blocking the door. Besides, I don't think either one of us will want to sit . . . up there."

His remarks were ridiculous, of course. They both knew why the door was blocked. Sara pretended to give the matter her full attention, however, in an attempt to save her pride. "Yes, I do believe you're right," she announced. "The furniture is blocking the door. I only just noticed. Thank you so much for pointing out that fact to me." She didn't pause for breath when she added, "Why is the table nailed to the floor?"

"You tried to move that, too?"

She ignored the laughter in his voice. "I thought it would look much nicer in front of the trunk. The desk, too," she added. "But I couldn't move either one."

He stood up and took a step toward her. She immediately backed away. "When the pitch of the sea gets rough, the furniture moves," he explained. He took another step toward her. "That's the reason."

She felt as though she was being stalked. Nathan's long hair swayed about his shoulders when he moved. The muscles in his shoulders seemed to roll with his pantherlike swagger. She wanted to run away from him, and yet in the back of her mind was the honest admission that she wanted him to catch her. She thoroughly liked the way he kissed her . . . but that was all she was going to like.

From the look on Nathan's face she knew he would like a lot more from her. His intimidating tactics were making her daft. She frowned at him for confusing her.

He smiled back.

She'd made a half circle of the cabin but trapped herself at the head of his bed. Nathan stopped when he saw the fear in her eyes. He let out a long sigh.

She thought he might be having second thoughts, yet before she could grasp the joy in that possibility his big hands were on her shoulders, and he was pulling her toward him.

He tilted her chin up, forcing her to look into his eyes. His

102

voice was actually very gentle when he said, "Sara, I know this is difficult for you. If there was more time, perhaps we could wait until you knew me a little better. I won't lie to you and tell you I could or would court you, though, for in truth I don't have the patience or the experience for such a chore. Still, I don't want you to be afraid of me." He paused to shrug, then smiled at her. "It shouldn't matter to me if you're afraid or not, but it does."

"Then . . ."

"There isn't time," he interrupted. "If you hadn't run away from me eight months ago, you'd be carrying my son now."

Her eyes widened over that announcement. Nathan thought she was reacting to his mention of a babe. She was such an innocent, and he knew she didn't have any experience in sexual matters. And Lord, that did please him.

"I didn't run away from you," she blurted out. "Whatever are you talking about?"

That denial surprised a frown out of him. "Don't you dare lie to me." He gave her shoulders a little squeeze to emphasize his words. "I will not abide it, Sara. You must always be completely honest with me."

She looked as furious as he'd sounded. "I'm not lying," she returned. "I never ran away from you, Viking. Never."

He believed her. She looked too sincere, and thoroughly outraged.

"Sara, I sent a letter to your parents informing them of my intent to come for you. I sent the messenger on a Friday. You were supposed to be ready the following Monday. I even gave the hour. You left for your aunt's island on Sunday morning, the day before. I simply put two and two together."

"I didn't know," she returned. "Nathan, my parents must not have received your letter. Neither one said a word to me. It was such a chaotic time. My mother was worried sick about my Aunt Nora, her sister. Nora always wrote at least one letter a month, but Mother hadn't received a missive in

such a long time. She was making herself ill worrying about
Nora. When she suggested I go to her sister and find out
what was wrong, well, I immediately agreed, of course."

"Just when did your mother confide this worry in you?"
he asked.

His cynicism irritated her. She knew what he was thinking and frowned in reaction. "A few days before I left," she
admitted. "But she wouldn't have confided her concerns to
me if I hadn't caught her crying. And she was most reluctant
to burden me. Very reluctant," she added. "Do you know,
now that I reflect upon it, I'm certain I was the one who
suggested I go to Nora's island."

A sudden thought turned her attention. "How did you
know my true destination? My family told everyone I had
gone to the colonies to visit my older sister."

He didn't bother to explain that his men had been
following her, and he didn't mention that she'd booked
passage on one of his ships. He simply shrugged. "Why
couldn't they have told the truth about the matter?"

"Because Nora was in disgrace," Sara said. "She married
her groom and fled from England over fourteen years ago. I
was certain everyone would have forgotten the scandal, but
as it happens, no one did."

Nathan turned the topic back to the letters. "So you
didn't know that Nora hadn't written to your mother until
two days before you left?"

"Mother didn't want me to worry," Sara said. "I won't
allow you to think that my mother had anything to do with
trickery. My father or my sister might have tried to intercept
your missive, Nathan, just to make you wait a little longer,
but my mother would never have gone along with such
deceit."

Nathan found her defense of her mother honorable.
Illogical, but honorable all the same. For that reason he
didn't force her to accept the truth. Her belief that her father
was innocent, however, irritated the hell out of him.

And then it dawned on him that she hadn't tried to run away from him. He was so pleased over that revelation, he quit frowning.

Sara stared up at her husband while she tried to think of another way to convince him that her mother was completely innocent of any treachery. And then the truth of what he had just told her settled in her mind.

He hadn't forgotten her.

Her smile was captivating. He didn't know what to make of the sudden change in her. She threw herself against his chest, wrapped her arms around his waist, and hugged him. He grunted in reaction. He was more confused than ever by her bizarre behavior. Yet he found he liked the sudden show of affection she was showing him, liked it very much.

Sara let out a little sigh, then moved back from her husband.

"What was that all about?" he asked, grimacing inside over the hard edge in his voice.

She didn't seem to notice. She patted her hair back into place as she whispered, "You didn't forget me." She tossed a strand of curls back over her shoulder in a motion he found thoroughly feminine, then added, "Of course, I knew you hadn't. I was certain there was just a little misunderstanding of sorts, because I . . ."

When she didn't continue, he said, "Because you knew I wanted to be married to you?"

She nodded.

He laughed.

She gave him a disgruntled look, then said, "Nathan, when I couldn't find Nora I sent several notes to your residence asking for your assistance, and you never responded. I did wonder then . . ."

"Sara, I don't have a residence," Nathan announced.

"Of course you do," she argued. "You have the townhouse. I saw it once when I was out for a ride in . . . why are you shaking your head at me?"

"My townhouse was burned to the ground last year."

"No one told me!"

He shrugged.

"I should have sent the message to your country home, then," she said. "All right," she added in a mutter. "Now why are you shaking your head?"

"The country home was also destroyed by fire," he explained.

"When?"

"Last year," he answered. "About a month before my townhouse was gutted."

She looked appalled. "You have had your share of mishaps, haven't you, Nathan?"

They weren't mishaps, but he didn't tell her that. The fires had been deliberately set by his enemies. They'd been looking for incriminating letters. Nathan had been working for his government, and at the end of the investigation the bastards had been dealt with, but he hadn't had time to right the damage to his estate just yet.

"You actually wrote to me asking my assistance in locating Nora?" he asked.

She nodded. "I didn't know who else to turn to," she admitted. "I think it was your Uncle Dunnford St. James who was behind this trickery," she added.

"Which trickery?" he asked.

"He probably intercepted the missive you sent to my parents."

He let her see his exasperation. "I think it was your father who was behind that scheme."

"And just why would you think that?"

"Because Attila the Hun's been dead for years," he said. "And your father is the only other man mean enough to come up with such a vile plan."

"I won't listen to such slander against my father. Besides, I'm just as certain it was Dunnford."

"Oh? And is he the one who beat your aunt?"

Her eyes immediately filled with tears. He regretted his question at once. She turned to stare at his chest before answering. "No," she whispered. "That was the work of my Uncle Henry. He's the one you saw inside the tavern the other night. And now you know the truth about me," she ended with a pitiful wail.

Nathan lifted her chin up with the crook of his finger. His thumb rubbed her smooth skin. "What truth?"

She stared into his eyes a long minute before answering. "I come from bad stock."

She'd hoped to gain a quick denial, even a bit of praise. "Aye, you do."

The man didn't have a sympathetic bone in his body, she thought. "Well, so do you," she muttered. She pushed his hand away from her chin. "We really shouldn't have children."

"Why not?"

"Because they could end up turning out like my Uncle Henry. Worse, they could behave like your side of the family. Even you have to admit that the St. James men are all mean-looking and just as mean-hearted. They're villains," she added with a nod. "Every last one of them."

He wouldn't admit to any such thing, of course, and he made his position known at once. "For all their rough behavior, they're damned honest. You know when you've got them riled. They're very straightforward."

"Oh, they're straightforward, all right," she countered.

"What's that supposed to mean?"

She knew she was getting him riled up again, but she didn't care. "Your Uncle Dunnford was straightforward when he shot his own brother, wasn't he?"

"So you heard about that, did you?" He tried hard not to smile. Sara looked so disapproving.

"Everyone heard about it. The incident took place on the steps of his townhouse in the middle of the morning, with witnesses strolling by."

Nathan shrugged. "Dunnford had good reason," he drawled.

"To shoot his brother?" She sounded incredulous.

He nodded.

"And what was his reason?" she asked.

"His brother woke him up."

She was waylaid by his sudden grin. He was back to looking handsome to her. She found herself smiling.

"Dunnford didn't kill his brother," Nathan explained. "He just made it a little inconvenient for him to sit for a couple of weeks. When you meet him, you'll—"

"I did meet him once," Sara interrupted. She was suddenly out of breath. The way he was staring at her made her feel so strange inside. "I met his wife, too."

She was still smiling at him. There was a mischievous glint in her eyes. He took heart. She wasn't acting at all afraid of him. He tried to think of a way to bring the topic around to the most important matter in his mind: bedding her.

He was gently rubbing her shoulders in an absentminded fashion. Sara didn't think he was even aware of what he was doing, for he had a faraway look in his eyes. She thought he might be thinking about his relatives.

She wanted him to rub away the sting at the base of her back, and since he was looking so preoccupied she decided to take advantage of his inattention. She moved his right hand to her spine. "Rub there, Nathan. My back aches from moving the furniture."

He didn't argue over her request. He simply did as she asked. He wasn't very gentle until she told him to ease his touch a little. Then she moved both his hands to the base of her spine. When he began to rub there she leaned against him and closed her eyes. It felt like heaven.

"Better?" he asked after a few minutes of listening to her sighs.

"Yes, better," she agreed.

He didn't stop rubbing her back, and she didn't want him to. "When did you meet Dunnford?" he asked. His chin dropped to rest on the top of her head. He inhaled her sweet, feminine scent.

"I met him at the gardens," she answered. "Both your uncle and your aunt were there. It was a frightening experience I shall never forget."

He chuckled. "Dunnford does look like a barbarian," he said. He slowly pulled her closer to him by pressing against her spine. She didn't resist. "My uncle's a big man, muscular. He's given to bulk in his shoulders. Yes, I suppose he could be a little frightening."

"So is his wife," Sara interjected with a smile. "I couldn't tell them apart."

He pinched her backside for being so insolent. "Dunnford has a mustache."

"So does she."

He pinched her again. "The St. James women aren't as fat as the Winchester women," he countered.

"The Winchester ladies are not fat," she argued. "They're just . . . fit."

It was high time they confronted the true issue here, she decided. She took a deep breath, then said, "Nathan?"

"Yes?"

"I'm not going to take my clothes off."

That announcement got his full attention. "You're not?"

She moved back a fraction of an inch so she could see his expression. His smile was slow, easy. It gave her courage to set down the rest of her rules. "No, I'm not," she said. "If we must do this thing, I'm keeping my clothes on. Take it or leave it, Nathan."

She worried her lower lip while she waited for his reaction. Nathan thought she might be frightened again. That chafed him. "For God's sake, Sara, I'm not going to hurt you."

"Yes, you will," she whispered.

"And just how would you know?"

"Mother said it always hurts." Sara's cheeks turned scarlet.

"It doesn't always hurt," he snapped. "The first time might be a little . . . uncomfortable."

"You just contradicted yourself," she cried out.

"You don't have to act as though—"

"I'm not going to like it much either," she interrupted. "You might as well understand that right this minute. How long does it take? Minutes or hours?" she asked. "I would like to try to prepare myself."

He wasn't rubbing her backside now. He was gripping her. Hard. He looked a little startled by her question. Sara pushed her advantage. "I have only one little favor to ask of you. Couldn't you please wait until tonight to do this thing? Since you're so determined, couldn't you at least give me a few more hours to come to terms with my fate?"

Come to terms with her fate? Nathan felt like throttling her. She acted as though she was going to an execution. Hers. He frowned even as he gave in. "All right," he said. "We'll wait until tonight, but that is the only favor I'm willing to give you, Sara."

She leaned up on tiptoes and kissed him. Her lips rubbed against him for just a fleeting instant, and when she moved back she was looking damned pleased with herself.

"What the hell was that supposed to be?"

"A kiss."

"No, Sara," he growled. "This is a kiss."

He hauled her up against his chest, tilted her face up, and slammed his mouth down on hers. He wasn't at all gentle, but in truth she didn't mind at all. She melted against him and let him have his way. After all, she thought to herself, she'd just gotten her victory, and she guessed he was entitled to one, too.

Odd, but it was the last thought she could hold. The kiss became one of blatant ownership. The intensity, the raw intimacy made her weak in the knees. She clung to her husband and let out a little whimper of sheer bliss when his tongue moved inside her mouth.

He squeezed her backside and lifted her up against his pelvis. Her hips instinctively cuddled his hardness. He pulled. She pushed.

The feeling was erotic, arousing. Nathan quit trying to subdue her when he realized he had her full cooperation. Lord, she was responsive. She was tugging on his hair even as she tried to get closer to him.

He pulled back quite suddenly, then had to hold her up until she recovered from the kiss. He was arrogantly happy over that telling fact.

And damn, he wanted her. He pushed Sara down the bed and turned to leave. He had to move the chest and chair before he could get to the door.

Sara had gathered her wits by the time he'd gotten the door open. "In future, Nathan," she began, grimacing over the shiver in her voice, "I would really appreciate it if you wouldn't come into our chamber by way of the chimney. I promise I won't bolt the door again," she added when he turned around and gave her an incredulous look.

"Come in through what?" he asked, thinking he surely hadn't heard her correctly.

"The chimney," she explained. "And you still didn't answer my question. Is this thing you're so determined to do going to take minutes or hours?"

Her question turned his attention, and he was no longer interested in explaining that the trapdoor wasn't a chimney. He'd explain that fact to the ignorant woman later. "How the hell would I know how long it's going to take?" he muttered.

"Do you mean you've never done it before?"

Nathan closed his eyes. The conversation had gotten out of hand.

"Well, have you?"

"Yes." He sounded disgusted. "I've just never timed it before," he snapped.

He was pulling the door shut behind him when he suddenly turned back and smiled at her.

She was amazed by the quick change in him. "Sara?" he asked.

"Yes?"

"You aren't going to hate it."

The door closed on that promise.

Chapter Five

&

Sara didn't see Nathan for the remainder of the day. She kept busy by righting the cabin and sorting through the rest of her possessions. Since she didn't have a lady's maid, she made the bed herself, dusted the furniture, and even borrowed a broom to sweep the dust from the floor. She remembered the parasol she'd left up on the deck, but when she went to fetch it she couldn't find it anywhere.

By sundown her nerves were at the breaking point. She hadn't been able to come up with any suitable plan to gain another reprieve. Sara was a little ashamed of her own cowardice. She knew that the bedding would have to happen sometime, knew that she would continue to dread it until it was over and done with, but those realizations didn't ease her fear.

When the knock sounded at her door she almost screamed. She quickly regained her composure when she realized that Nathan certainly wouldn't knock. No, he'd barge right in. The cabin belonged to him, after all, and she supposed he had the right to come in unannounced.

Matthew was waiting outside her door. She curtsied to the

seaman and invited him inside. He declined her offer with a shake of his head. "Your Aunt Nora's waiting to have a visit with you now," he announced. "While you're in her cabin I'll have Frost bring in the tub. The captain thought you might be wanting a bath, so he ordered us to bring fresh water. It's a treat you won't be getting too often," he added. "You'd best enjoy it."

"That was very thoughtful of Nathan," Sara returned.

"I'll be sure to tell him you thought so," Matthew replied for lack of anything better to say. He walked by Sara's side, feeling both awkward and ridiculously shy. He blamed his condition on the fact that he wasn't used to being treated like an equal except by Nathan. He'd never had a lady curtsy to him either. There was also her enchanting smile, he admitted. His shoulders slumped forward a little. Lord, he was falling under the pretty's spell just like that ox Jimbo had.

When they reached Nora's door Matthew forced himself out of his stupor and muttered, "Don't you tire her out, all right?"

Sara nodded, then waited for Matthew to open the door for her. He was a bit slow to catch on until she motioned to show what she wanted. She thanked him after he'd thrown the door wide, then walked inside. Matthew pulled the door closed behind her.

"Matthew had the most bewildered look on his face," Nora called out.

"I didn't notice," Sara admitted. She smiled at her aunt as she hurried over to the side of the bed to kiss her. Nora was propped up by a mound of fat pillows.

"I did notice what a worrier he is, though, and all on your behalf, Aunt," Sara announced. She pulled up a chair, sat down, and brushed the crinkles out of her gown. "I believe he's become your champion."

"He's a handsome man, isn't he, Sara? He has a kind heart, too. His nature is very like my late husband's, though the two men are nothing alike in appearance."

Sara held her smile. "You're a little smitten with Matthew, aren't you, Nora?"

"Nonsense, child. I'm too old to be smitten."

Sara let the subject go. "Are you feeling better today?"

"Yes, dear," Nora answered. "And how are you feeling?"

"Fine, thank you."

Nora shook her head. "You don't look fine to me," she announced. "Sara, you're sitting on the edge of that chair, looking like you'll bolt at the first provocation. Is it Nathan worrying you?"

Sara slowly nodded. "I was also worried about you, of course," she confessed. "But now that I see you, I realize you're going to be fine."

"Don't change the topic," Nora ordered. "I want to talk about Nathan."

"I don't."

"We're going to all the same," Nora countered. The cheer in her tone took the sting out of her remark. "How are you and your husband getting along?"

Sara lifted her shoulders in a dainty shrug. "As well as can be expected, given his disposition."

Nora smiled. "Has he kissed you yet?"

"Nora, you shouldn't be asking me that question."

"Answer me. Has he?"

Sara looked at her lap when she answered. "Yes, he did kiss me."

"Good."

"If you say so."

"Now, Sara, I know Nathan isn't exactly what you imagined he would be, but if you'll only look below the gruff exterior, I believe you'll find yourself a good man."

Sara was determined to keep the conversation light. "Oh?" she teased. "And how would you know what I imagined him to be?"

"In your wildest dreams you couldn't possibly have imagined yourself married to Nathan. He's a bit overwhelming at first sight, isn't he?"

"Oh, I don't know," Sara whispered.

"Of course you do," Nora returned. "You fainted when you saw him that first time, didn't you?"

"I was exhausted," Sara argued. "Nora, he wants to . . sleep with me," she suddenly blurted out.

Nora didn't seem to be at all surprised by that announcement. Sara was acutely relieved that her aunt wasn't embarrassed. She desperately needed her advice.

"That would be his natural inclination," Nora announced. "Are you afraid, Sara?"

"A little," Sara answered. "I know what my duty is, but I don't know him very well, and I did want a courtship."

"What is it you're worried about?"

Sara shrugged.

"Do you think he's going to hurt you?"

Sara shook her head. "It's the most peculiar thing, Aunt. Nathan's such a ferocious-looking man when he's frowning at me, which is most of the time, but in my heart I know he won't hurt me. He even told me he didn't want me to be afraid of him."

"Good."

"But he won't wait until I get used to the idea," Sara explained.

Nora smiled. "I would expect that he wouldn't want to wait, Sara. You are his wife, and I could see the way he watched you that first night. He wants you."

Sara could feel herself blushing. "What if I disappoint him?"

"I don't believe you will," Nora soothed. "He'll see to it that you don't."

"We have to have a child if Nathan is going to get the second half of the treasury set aside by the king, and since he was forced to wait to come for me . . . did you know he thought I had run away from him?" Sara explained what she'd learned, and when she'd finished Nora was frowning.

"Aren't you pleased Nathan tried to come for me?"

"Of course. I'm frowning because I believe your parents have deceived you yet again."

"Nora, you can't believe—"

"As I told you before," Nora interrupted, "I never quit writing to your mother. I will even allow for the possibility that one or two of my letters got lost, but certainly not all six of them. No, it was all a lie, Sara, to get you out of England."

"Mother wouldn't agree to such a lie."

"Of course she would," Nora muttered. "My poor sister is afraid of her husband. She always was, and she always will be. We both know it, Sara, and it's pointless to pretend to each other. Get your head out of the clouds, child. If Winston told her to lie to you, she would. Now enough about your sorry parents," she rushed on when Sara looked as if she was about to interrupt. "I want to ask you a question."

"What is it?"

"Do you want to be married to Nathan?"

"It doesn't matter what I want."

"Do you or not?"

"I've never thought about being with anyone else," Sara answered hesitantly. "I don't really know how I feel, Nora. I dislike the notion of any other woman having him, though. Do you know I didn't realize that until he mentioned the word 'mistress' to me? I reacted most vehemently to that proposal. It's all very confusing."

"Yes, love is always confusing."

"I'm not talking about love," Sara countered. "It's just that I've been trained to think of Nathan as my husband all these years."

Nora let out an inelegant snort. "You were trained to hate the man. They thought they'd raised another one just like your sister Belinda, but they couldn't do it, could they? You don't hate Nathan at all."

"No, I don't hate anyone."

"All these years you've protected him in your heart, Sara,

just as you've protected your mother whenever you had a chance. You listened to their lies about Nathan, and then you discarded them."

"They think I hate him," Sara confessed. "I pretended to agree with everything my relatives told me about him so they would leave me alone. Uncle Henry was the worse. Now he knows the truth. When I confronted him in the tavern, when I saw your band on his fat little finger, well, I lost my temper. I boasted that Nathan would retaliate and added to that lie by telling him that Nathan and I had been on the best of terms for a long while."

"Perhaps it wasn't all a lie," Nora said. "I do believe Nathan would retaliate on my behalf in future, Sara. And do you know why?"

"Because he realizes what a dear, sweet lady you are," Sara answered.

Nora rolled her eyes heavenward. "No, dear, I don't believe he realizes that just yet. He'll watch out for me because he knows how much you love me. Nathan is the kind of man who takes care of the people close to him."

"But Nora—"

"I'm telling you he's already beginning to care for you. Sara."

"You're being fanciful."

The conversation came to an abrupt end when Matthew came into the room. He gave Nora a wide smile and a slow wink. "It's time for you to have a rest," he told her.

Sara kissed her aunt goodnight and went back to her cabin. The bath was ready for her. She took her time soaking until the water turned cold, then dressed in her white nightgown and matching wrapper. She was sitting on the side of the bed, brushing the tangles out of her hair, when Nathan came into the room.

Two younger men followed him inside. The seamen nodded at her, then lifted the tub between them and carried it out. Sara clutched the top of her robe against her neck in an attempt at modesty until the men left, then resumed brushing her hair.

Nathan shut the door and bolted it.

He didn't say a word to her. He didn't have to. The look on his face told her all she needed to know. The man was determined, all right. There wouldn't be any more favors doled out, no more hasty reprieves. She started trembling.

Nathan had had a bath, too, she realized. His hair was still wet. It was slicked back behind his neck. His unforgiving profile wasn't softened at all. He wasn't wearing a shirt either. Sara stared at him while she continued to brush her hair, wondering what in God's name she could talk about to ease the tension inside her.

Nathan stared back at her while he pulled the chair out from the table, sat down, and slowly removed his boots. The socks came off next. Then he stood up, facing her still, and began to unbutton his pants.

She closed her eyes.

He smiled over her shyness. It didn't deter him, though. He took off the rest of his clothes and tossed them on the chair.

"Sara?"

She didn't open her eyes when she answered. "Yes, Nathan?"

"Take your clothes off."

His voice was soft, tender, he thought. He was trying to ease a little of her fear away. There wasn't any doubt in his mind that she was afraid, for she was ripping that brush through her hair with such vigor that she had to be giving herself one hell of a headache. She'd knock herself senseless if she didn't calm down.

She wasn't soothed by his voice, however. "We've already had this discussion, Nathan," she announced as she slammed the brush against her temple again. "I told you I was keeping my clothes on."

She'd tried to make her voice firm, determined. The effort

didn't work. Even she could hear the tremor in her hoarse whisper. "All right?" she asked.

"All right," he agreed with a sigh.

His easy agreement calmed her. She quit brushing her hair. She still wouldn't look at him when she stood up and slowly crossed the room. She made a wide path around him, her gaze directed on the floor.

After she put her brush away she took a deep breath and turned around. She was determined to pretend his nakedness didn't bother her. She was his wife, she reminded herself, and she shouldn't be carrying on like a silly, innocent chit.

The problem, of course, was that she *was* an innocent. She'd never seen a naked man before. Lord, she was nervous. I'm a woman now, not a child, she told herself There's absolutely no reason to be embarrassed.

Then she got a rather thorough look at her husband, and all thoughts about being worldly flew out the chimney. Nathan was in the process of closing the trap in the ceiling. He was half turned away from her, but she still saw quite enough of his physique to make her forget how to breathe.

The man was all muscle and steel. Bronzed, too. It suddenly dawned on her that his backside was almost as dark as the rest of his body. How did he get that private area bronzed?

She wasn't about to ask him that question, though. Perhaps after they'd been married some twenty or thirty years she'd feel comfortable enough to broach that topic.

Perhaps, too, one day in the future she might be able to look back on the night of agony and have herself a good laugh.

She certainly wasn't laughing at the moment. She watched Nathan light the candle. The soft glow made his skin glisten. She was grateful that he had his back turned to her when he saw to that task. Was he deliberately giving her time to get accustomed to his size?

If that was his aim, it wasn't working, she thought to

herself. The man could masquerade as a tree. He was certainly big enough.

Sara let out a little sigh when she realized how childishly she was behaving. Her only saving grace was the fact that he wasn't going to know how terrified she was. She averted her face so he couldn't see her blush, then said, "Are we going to bed now?"

She was pleased with herself. She'd sounded very nonchalant when she'd asked that question.

He thought she sounded like she'd just swallowed a spike. He knew he was going to have to find a way to deal with her fear before he bedded her.

The question, of course, was how. He let out a sigh and turned to take her into his arms. She ran to the bed. He grabbed hold of her shoulders and slowly forced her around to face him.

His bride certainly wasn't having any difficulty meeting his gaze, he thought. No, he didn't have to nudge her chin up to get her full attention. Nathan held his smile. He doubted Sara would have lowered her gaze even if he told her there was a snake slithering across her feet.

"Does my nakedness upset you?" He asked the obvious, thinking to attack the problem head on.

"Why would you think that?"

His hands moved to the sides of her neck. He could feel her pulse pounding under his thumb. He kept his touch gentle. "You like it when I kiss you, don't you, Sara?"

She seemed surprised by that question. "Do you?" he asked again when she continued to stare at him.

"Yes," she admitted. "I do like you to kiss me."

He looked arrogantly pleased.

"But I don't believe I'm going to like the other thing at all," she said, thinking to give him fair warning once again.

He didn't look offended by her honesty. He leaned down and kissed her on her forehead, then kissed the bridge of her nose. His mouth brushed against hers for a fleeting second. "I'm going to like it," he told her in a low growl.

She didn't have a ready comeback for that comment, so she was silent. She kept her mouth closed, too, when his mouth settled on hers again.

He felt as if he were kissing a statue. He wasn't deterred, though. He sighed against her mouth and slowly tightened his hold around her neck. When her skin began to sting she opened her mouth to order him to let go of her. That demand got all tangled up in her confused mind, however, when his tongue moved inside to touch hers.

Her response was nice. The ice inside her began to melt. Nathan softened his hold as soon as she opened her mouth for him. His thumbs made lazy circles along the sides of her neck. He was deliberate in his bid to overwhelm her and thought he was succeeding when she moved closer to him and put her arms around his neck.

Her sigh of pleasure mingled with his growl of need. He didn't let up on his gentle attack. The kiss was long, hard, damned thorough. His mouth slanted hungrily over hers again and again while his tongue stoked the fire inside her.

The kiss seemed endless. Because she was innocent of such new feelings it didn't take him long at all to rid her of her shyness, her resistance. He tried to contain his own hunger, but when her fingers threaded through his damp hair and he felt the sensual, feathery-light caress the flame inside him began to burn.

He wasn't very deliberate. He'd tamed her and was suddenly impatient. Sara let out a ragged moan when he pulled her arms away from his neck. His mouth continued to plunder hers, but it wasn't enough. She wanted to get close to his heat again, to wrap herself around his warmth. He wasn't cooperating. He kept blocking her arms and tugging on her at the same time. She didn't understand what he wanted from her, couldn't seem to sort it all out in her mind, for she was too occupied kissing him, and simply too overwhelmed by the strange, wonderful feelings rioting inside her.

"Now you can put your arms around me again," he

whispered when he ended the kiss. His smile was filled with tenderness. Lord, she was transparent. Her bemused expression hid nothing from him. Passion and confusion were there for him to see. Nathan had never known a woman who could respond with such openness, such abandon.

It shook him a little when he realized how very much he wanted to please her. The innocent trust she willingly gave to him made him feel as though he could conquer the world.

He was going to have to conquer her first. "Don't be afraid," he whispered in a deep, husky voice. He stroked the side of her face with the backs of his fingers, smiling anew over the way she instinctively tilted her face to the side to gain more of his caress.

"I'm trying not to be afraid," she whispered back. "It does ease my worry because I know you care about my feelings."

"And when did you come to that conclusion?"

He wondered over the sudden sparkle that came into her eyes. She seemed to be amused about something.

"When you agreed that I could keep my clothes on."

Nathan's sigh was long. He decided it wasn't the time to mention the fact that he'd just removed her robe and nightgown. He guessed she'd find out soon enough.

"I'm not a very patient man, Sara, when I want something as badly as I want you."

He put his arms around her waist and pulled her up against him. Skin touched skin. Her eyes widened in reaction, but before she could get her wits about her to decide if she liked the feeling or not, his mouth settled on top of hers again.

The man certainly knew how to kiss. She didn't make him force her mouth open—instead she quickly became the aggressor. Her tongue rubbed against his first. He grunted in reaction. She thought that sound might mean he liked her show of boldness, and she became all the more wanton.

The kiss was wild. He wanted to rekindle the passion between them. When she began to make those erotic little whimpers in the back of her throat he knew he'd accomplished his goal. She was already hot for him again. And Lord, the sound made him ache to be inside her.

Her hands gripped his shoulders. Her soft breasts rubbed against his chest. He lifted her up and pulled her tight against his arousal, then drowned out the gasp that intimacy caused with another long, hot kiss.

Sara couldn't seem to catch hold of a thought. The sensations his kiss caused were so strange, so wonderful, so consuming. She couldn't even hold onto her shyness. She knew he'd taken her clothes off, had deliberately baited him when she'd reminded him that he'd promised she could leave them on. It was trickery on her part, but her reason had made perfectly good sense to her at the time. She wanted him to slow down, to give her time to get used to his body, his heat, his touch.

She didn't have any idea how they'd gotten over to the bed, but Nathan was suddenly pulling the covers back. His mouth left hers when he lifted her up and gently placed her on her back in the center of the sheets. He didn't give her time to try to shield her nudity from him but followed her down on the bed, covering her from head to foot with his warm body.

It was too much, too soon. Sara began to feel trapped and totally at his mercy. She didn't want to be afraid, and she didn't want to disappoint him.

The haze of passion cleared in an instant. She didn't want to do this anymore.

But she didn't want him to quit kissing her either. And God, she was frightened.

He'd probably take exception if she started screaming. For that reason she kept her mouth closed in an effort to contain the shout locked in her throat.

His knee tried to nudge her legs apart. She wouldn't allow that intimacy and began to struggle against him. She slapped his shoulders, too. He immediately stopped trying. He propped himself up on his elbows to ease his weight away from her, then began to nibble on the side of her neck. She liked that. His breath was warm, sweet, teasing against her ear. She shivered in reaction. In a dark whisper he told her how much she pleased him, how much she made him want her, and even told her how beautiful he thought she was. When he was finished with his words of praise he was certain he'd coaxed her into accepting him completely.

He was mistaken. As soon as he tried to nudge her thighs apart again she went completely rigid on him. He gritted his teeth in frustration.

The feel of her soft skin made him wild with his own need to be inside her. But she wasn't ready for his invasion yet. His forehead was beaded with perspiration from the effort of holding back. Each time his hands moved to touch her breasts she tensed up on him. His frustration soon made his hunger acutely painful.

It would only be a matter of minutes before he completely lost his control. God, he didn't want to hurt her. He was feeling desperate to thrust inside her heat, but she was going to be hot for him, wet, ready, when he finally made her his.

She sure as hell wasn't ready now. She was pinching his shoulder and trying to get him to move away from her.

He decided to let her have her way for just a minute or two. Nathan rolled to his side, thinking to put a little distance between them before he completely lost his sanity, forced her thighs apart, and drove into her.

He thought he only needed a couple of minutes to regain his discipline. When his heart quit slamming inside his chest, when it didn't hurt so much to breathe, when the god-awful ache in his loins abated a little, he would try again.

Wooing a virgin was damned hard work, he thought, and since he had absolutely no expertise with either wooing or with bedding virgins, he felt completely inadequate.

Perhaps one day in the future, when he was an old, old man, he might be able to look back on this night of sweet torture and have himself a good laugh. At the moment he wasn't in the mood to laugh, though. He wanted to grab hold of his bride and shake some sense into her while he demanded at the same time that she not be afraid of him.

The contradiction in those conflicting thoughts made him shake his head.

Sara was trembling from head to foot. As soon as he moved away from her the helpless feeling of being trapped vanished. She wanted him to kiss her again.

The look on Nathan's face worried her, though. He looked like he wanted to shout at her. She took a deep breath, then rolled to her side to face him. "Nathan?"

He didn't answer her. His eyes were closed, his jaw clenched tight.

"You told me you were a patient man."

"Sometimes."

"You're upset with me, aren't you?"

"No."

She didn't believe him. "Don't frown," she whispered. She reached out to touch his chest.

He reacted as though she'd just burned him. He visibly flinched. "Don't you want to do this any longer?" she asked. "Have you quit wanting me?"

Not want her? He wanted to grab hold of her hand and force her to feel how very much he wanted her. He didn't, of course, for he was certain she'd become terrified again.

"Sara, just give me a minute," he said in a clipped voice. "I'm afraid . . ." He didn't finish that explanation, didn't tell her he was afraid he would hurt her if he touched her. That admission would only increase her fear, so he kept silent.

"You don't have to be afraid," she whispered.

He couldn't believe what he was hearing. He opened his eyes to look at her. She couldn't really think . . . and yet the tenderness in her eyes indicated she did believe he was afraid.

"For God's sake, Sara, I'm not afraid."

Her fingers slowly trailed down his chest. He caught hold

of her hand when she reached the flat of his stomach. "Stop that," he ordered.

"You've only taken experienced women to your bed, haven't you, Nathan?"

His answer was a low grunt.

She smiled. "Nathan, you like kissing me, don't you?"

He'd asked her that very question not fifteen minutes earlier, when he'd been trying to rid her of her fear. God's truth, he would have laughed if he hadn't been in so much pain. The woman was treating him as though he were the virgin.

He was about to straighten out her thinking when she edged closer to him. He suddenly realized that his bride was no longer afraid of him. "Do you?" she persisted.

"Yes, Sara, I like kissing you."

"Then kiss me again, please."

"Sara, kissing isn't the only thing I had in mind. I want to touch you. Everywhere."

He waited for her to go rigid on him again. God, he wished he had the patience for this. His nerves felt as though they were about to snap, and all he could think about was spilling his seed inside her.

He closed his eyes and growled.

And then he felt her take hold of his hand. He opened his eyes just as she placed his hand on the side of her full breast.

He didn't move for a long minute. She didn't either. They stared into each other's eyes. He waited to see what she would do next. She waited for him to get on with his duty.

Sara soon became impatient with him. He was gently stroking her breasts. The feeling made her tingle inside. It made her reckless, too. She rubbed her toes against his legs and slowly leaned up to kiss him.

"I hate the feeling of being trapped," she whispered between feathery-light kisses. "But I don't feel trapped now, Nathan. Don't give up on me yet, husband. This is a new experience for me. Truly."

JULIE GARWOOD

He gently caressed the side of her face. "I'm not going to give up," he whispered. There was a bit of laughter in his voice when he added, "Truly."

She sighed against his mouth and kissed him just the way she wanted to. When her tongue moved inside to mate with his, Nathan's control snapped. He became the aggressor again, deepening the kiss even more with wild abandon.

He kept up the gentle assault until she rolled onto her back and tried to bring him with her. Nathan didn't give in to her demand but leaned down to kiss the fragrant valley between her breasts. His mouth teased first one and then the other nipple until they were both hard nubs. His tongue drove her wild. When she couldn't stand the sweet torment any longer she grabbed hold of his hair and began to tug on him.

She felt as if she'd been hit with hot lightning when he finally took her nipple into his mouth. She arched up, demanding more. He began to suckle.

A warm knot formed in the pit of her stomach. "Nathan, please," she moaned. She didn't have any idea what she was begging him for, only knew the incredible heat was driving her beyond reason.

He turned to her other breast even as his hand slid down between her thighs. She didn't clench against him but let out another ragged groan.

He leaned up on one elbow so he could watch her expression. She tried to hide her face in the crook of his shoulder. He reached out and caught hold of her hair.

"I like the way you respond to me," he whispered. "Do you like the way I'm touching you?"

He already knew the answer. He could feel how ready she was for him. How hot. His fingers rubbed against the nub hidden between her folds until she was slick with moisture. His finger slowly eased up inside her.

Her hands had been fisted at her sides until that minute. She came apart then. She stroked his shoulders, his back.

128

Her nails scraped his backside. "Nathan," she whispered. "Don't do that. It hurts. Oh, God, don't stop."

She continued to contradict herself by arching up against his hand. Nathan could barely understand what she was saying to him. He shook with raw desire to have her.

He silenced her weak protest with a kiss and moved to cover her. She didn't try to lock her legs together but moved to cuddle his hardness between her thighs.

He twisted her hair in his hand to hold her steady for his kiss. The way she rubbed her pelvis against him drove him crazy. He wasn't being gentle. She wouldn't let him. Her nails stung. He liked that. She was moaning, too. He liked that even more.

He slowly eased into her but stopped when he felt the thin shield of her resistance. He lifted his head up enough so that he could look into her eyes.

"Put your legs around me," he ordered, his voice harsh with determination.

When she did as he commanded he let out a low growl. And still he hesitated.

"Look at me, Sara."

She opened her eyes and stared into his.

"You're going to belong to me. Now and forever."

Her eyes were misty with passion. She reached up to clasp the sides of his face. "I have always belonged to you, Nathan. Always."

His mouth covered hers again. He thrust deep inside her in one swift motion, thinking to get the pain he knew she'd feel over and done with as quickly as possible.

"Hush, baby," he whispered when she cried out. He was fully embedded in her. Her tight heat surrounded him, squeezed him. "God, that feels good," he said with a groan.

"No, it doesn't feel good," she cried out. She tried to shift positions to ease the throbbing pain, but he held her hips and wouldn't let her move.

"It will feel better in a minute," he told her. His breathing was labored. He sounded out of breath to her. His face rested in the hollow of her shoulder. He nipped at her skin with his teeth, tickled her at the same time with his tongue. The sweet torture made her forget some of the pain.

"Don't push against me like that, Sara," he ordered. His voice was harsh, strained. "I'm not stopping now. I can't."

His tongue rubbed her earlobe. She quit struggling and let out a sigh of pleasure.

"The pain won't last long," he whispered then. "I promise."

She reacted more to the tenderness, the caring in his voice than to the promise he'd just given her. She hoped he was right, though. She still hurt. The throbbing was insistent, but after a minute it did begin to lessen. Yet when he started to move again the pain immediately returned.

"If you don't move, it isn't so terrible," she whispered.

His groan was harsh.

"All right, Nathan?" she pleaded.

"All right," he answered, responding to the worry in her voice. It was a lie, of course, but she was too innocent to understand how much he needed to move. "I won't move."

Her hands began to stroke his hair, the back of his neck. His fever was burning out of control, and the pain of having to hold back was demanding to be appeased.

She couldn't seem to quit touching him. "Nathan, kiss me."

"The pain's gone now?"

"Almost."

He deliberately withdrew just a little when he moved to kiss her again, then just as slowly eased back inside her.

"You moved," she cried out.

Instead of agreeing with her he kissed her. When he tried to withdraw again her nails dug into his hard thighs. She was trying to keep him still against her. He ignored her protests and sought to make her burn the way he was burning. His hand slipped down between their joined bodies, and his thumb slowly stoked the fire inside her.

Her head fell back on the pillows, and her grip on his thighs relaxed.

And then she began to move. Her hips pushed up against his. Her actions were instinctive, primal, uncontrollable.

She soon became demanding, too. He responded to her by slowly pulling back and thrusting more powerfully inside.

She squeezed him tight and arched up against him just as forcefully. The mating ritual took over. The bed creaked from the rocking motion. Their bodies glistened with perspiration in the candlelight. Her sweet moans blended with his raw growls.

They were both wild to find fulfillment. He couldn't stop his own climax, nor the near shout he gave when he spilled his hot seed inside her.

His head dropped against her shoulder in complete surrender to the blazing orgasm that overtook him.

He knew she was close to finding her own release. His thrusts continued to be just as forceful, and when he felt her tense against him, he forced her orgasm by driving hard into her again.

She screamed. His name.

His ears rang from the noise. He collapsed on top of her, giving her his full weight in an attempt to stop her trembling.

Neither one of them moved for a long, long while. Nathan was too content. She was too exhausted.

She felt a trickle of moisture near her ear, reached up to touch it, and only then realized she'd been crying. Lord, she'd really lost her composure, hadn't she? She was too pleased to worry about that, though. And too satisfied. Why hadn't anyone ever told her how wonderful making love would be?

Her husband's heartbeat pounded in unison with her own. She let out a happy sigh. She was his wife now.

"You can't call me bride anymore," she whispered against his neck. On impulse she tickled his skin with the tip of her tongue. The taste of him was salty, male, wonderful.

"Am I too heavy for you?"

He sounded weary to her. She answered him, yes, he was getting heavy, and he immediately rolled onto his back.

She didn't want him to leave her just yet. She wanted him to hold her, to tell her what a fine woman she was, to give her the words of praise and love all new wives longed to hear. She wanted him to kiss her again, too.

She didn't get anything. Nathan's eyes were closed. He looked peaceful and sleepy.

She didn't have any idea of the war Nathan was waging with himself. He was desperately trying to understand what had just happened to him. He'd never lost control so completely. She'd bewitched him. Confused him, too. He was feeling vulnerable, and damn, that feeling scared the hell out of him.

Sara rolled onto her side. "Nathan?"

"What?"

"Kiss me again."

"Go to sleep."

"Kiss me goodnight."

"No."

"Why not?"

"I'll want you again if I kiss you," he finally explained. He didn't bother to look at her but stared at the ceiling. "You're too tender."

She sat up in bed, flinching over the discomfort she felt between her thighs. He was right. She was tender. It didn't seem to matter, though. She still wanted him to kiss her.

"You're the one who made me tender," she muttered. She poked him in his shoulder. "I specifically remember telling you not to move."

"You moved first, Sara. Remember that?" he drawled.

She blushed. She took heart. He wasn't sounding too

surly. She cuddled up against him, wishing he'd put his arms around her. "Nathan, isn't the after as important as the during?"

He didn't know what she was talking about. "Go to sleep," he ordered for the second time. He jerked the covers up over the two of them, then closed his eyes again.

She threw her arm over him. She was exhausted. Frustrated, too. She told him so.

He laughed. "Sara, I know you found fulfillment."

"That isn't what I'm talking about," she whispered.

She waited for him to ask her to explain what she'd meant, then gave up when he kept silent. "Nathan?"

"Hell, what now?"

"Please don't take that mean tone with me."

"Sara . . ." he began in a warning tone of voice.

"After you took those other women to your bed, well, after . . . what did you do?"

What in God's name was she getting at? "I left," he snapped.

"Are you going to leave me?"

"Sara, this is my bed. I'm going to sleep."

Her patience was at an end. "Not before I explain proper etiquette to you," she announced. "After a man finishes . . . that, he should tell his wife what a fine woman she is. Then he should kiss her and hold her close. They fall asleep in each other's arms."

He couldn't stop himself from smiling. She said the damnedest things. Sounded like a general, too. "It's called lovemaking, Sara, and how would you know what's proper and what isn't? You were a virgin, remember?"

"I just know what's proper," she countered.

"Sara?"

"Yes?"

"Don't shout at me."

He turned to look at her. Hell, she looked as if she was going to cry. He didn't have the patience to deal with her tears. God, she was vulnerable . . . and beautiful. Her mouth was all rosy and swollen from his kisses.

He reached over and hauled her into his arms. After giving her a quick kiss on the top of her head he pushed her face down into the crook of his shoulder and muttered, "You're a fine woman. Now go to sleep."

He didn't sound like he meant what he said, but she didn't care. He was holding her close. He was stroking her back. She thought that was a little telling. She snuggled up against him and closed her eyes.

His chin rested on the top of her head. Each time the memory of their lovemaking came into his thoughts he blocked it. He wasn't ready to let his emotions get the upper hand. He was simply too disciplined to let a woman get that close.

He was just drifting off to sleep when she whispered his name again. He squeezed her to let her know he wanted her to keep quiet. She whispered his name again.

"Yes?" he answered with a deliberate yawn.

"Do you know what this holding and hugging each other is called?"

She wasn't going to let up on him until she told him what was on her mind. Nathan squeezed her again, then gave in. "No, Sara, what's it called?"

"Cherishing."

He groaned. She smiled. "It's a good start, isn't it?"

His snore was her only answer. Sara wasn't bothered that he had rudely fallen asleep in the middle of her fervent speech. She'd simply explain it all to him again the next day.

She couldn't wait for morning light. She was going to find a hundred ways to make Nathan realize his good fortune. She already knew she was the perfect mate for him. He didn't know it yet, but eventually, with patience and understanding, he'd realize how much he loved her. She was certain.

She was his wife, his love. Their marriage was true in

every sense. There was a bond between them. Marriage was a sacred institution, and Sara was determined to protect and cherish her vows.

She fell asleep holding him tight. The next day was going to be the official start of her new life as Nathan's wife. It was going to be a day in heaven.

Chapter Six

It was a day in hell.

Nathan had already left the cabin by the time she awakened. He'd opened the chimney lid for her, and the room was flooded with fresh air and sunshine. It was much warmer than the day before. After she bathed, she dressed in a lightweight royal-blue gown with white linen borders and then went to find her husband. She wanted to ask him where the fresh sheets were kept so that she could change the bedding. She also wanted him to kiss her again.

Sara had just reached the top step on the way to the main deck when she heard a man's shout. She hurried forward to see what all the commotion was about and almost tripped over the fallen man sprawled on the deck. The older seaman had obviously taken quite a fall, for he was sleeping soundly.

The parasol she hadn't been able to find the day before was twisted between his feet. Jimbo was bent on one knee over the prostrate man. He slapped the side of the man's face twice in an attempt to waken him.

In a matter of seconds a crowd gathered around their

friend. Each immediately offered a suggestion or two as to how Jimbo could bring the man around.

"What the hell happened?"

Nathan's booming voice sounded directly behind Sara. She didn't turn around when she answered his question. "I believe he tripped on something."

"It weren't something, m'lady," one of the crew announced. He pointed to the deck. "It were your parasol that caught up in his legs."

Sara was forced to accept full responsibility. "Yes, it was my parasol," she said. "His injury is my fault. Will he be all right, Jimbo? I really didn't mean to cause this mishap. I—"

Jimbo took pity on her. "No need to carry on so, Lady Sara. The men know it was just an accident."

Sara glanced up to look at the crowd. Most were nodding and smiling at her. "No need to get yourself in a dither, m'lady. Ivan will get his wits back in a minute or so."

A man with a full orange beard nodded. "Don't be fretting," he interjected. "It weren't that bad. The back of his head broke his fall."

"Murray?" Jimbo called out. "Bring me a bucket of water. That ought to bring him around."

"Will Ivan be able to cook up our meal tonight?" The man Sara remembered was named Chester asked that question. He was frowning at Sara.

She frowned back. It was apparent he blamed her for the unfortunate circumstance. "Is your stomach more important to you than your friend's health?" she asked. She didn't give him time to answer her but knelt down beside the sleeping man and gently patted his shoulder. The elderly man didn't respond. His mouth was gaping.

"My God, Jimbo, have I killed him?" she whispered.

"No, you didn't kill him," Jimbo returned. "You can see he's breathing still, Sara. He'll just have a fair head split when he wakes up, that's all."

Nathan lifted Sara to her feet and pulled her back away

from the crowd. She didn't want to leave. "I'm responsible for this accident," she said. Her gaze was fully directed upon Ivan, but she could still see the nods from the men surrounding her. She felt herself blush in reaction to their easy agreement. "It was an accident," she cried out.

No one contradicted her. That made her feel a little better. "I should take care of Ivan," she announced then. "When he opens his eyes I must tell him how sorry I am for forgetting my parasol."

"He won't be in the mood to listen," Nathan predicted.

"Aye," Lester agreed. "Ivan the Terrible isn't one to forgive a slight for a good long while. He loves a good grudge, doesn't he, Walt?"

A slightly built man with dark brown eyes nodded agreement. "This is more than a slight, Lester," he muttered. "Ivan's going to be in a rage."

"Is Ivan the only cook?" Sara asked.

"He is," Nathan told her.

She finally turned around to look at her husband. Her blush was high, and she really didn't know if the heat in her cheeks was due to the fact that this was their first encounter since their night of intimacy or because she'd caused such commotion.

"Why do they call him Ivan the Terrible?" she asked. "Is it because he has a mean temper?"

He barely spared her a glance when he answered. "They don't like his cooking," he said. He motioned for one of the men to toss the contents of the bucket in Ivan's face. The cook immediately started sputtering and groaning.

Nathan nodded, then turned and walked away from the group.

Sara couldn't believe he'd leave without a word to her first. She felt humiliated. She turned back to Ivan and stood wringing her hands while she waited for her chance to apologize. She silently vowed she would find Nathan and give him another lesson in proper etiquette.

As soon as Ivan sat up Sara knelt down beside him. "Pray

forgive me, sir, for causing you this injury. It was my parasol that caused you to trip, though if you'd only been looking where you were going, I'm certain you would have noticed it. Still, I beg your forgiveness."

Ivan was rubbing the back of his head while he glared at the pretty woman trying to give him a bit of the blame for his near brush with death. The worry in her expression kept his surly retort inside. That, and the fact that she was the captain's woman.

"It wasn't much of a hit I took," he muttered instead. "You didn't do it on purpose, now did you?"

There was a faint Scottish brogue in his voice. Sara thought he sounded quite musical. "No, of course I didn't do it on purpose, sir. Are you strong enough to stand? I'll help you to your feet."

She could tell from his wary expression that he didn't want her assistance. Jimbo pulled the cook up, but as soon as he let go Ivan began to sway. Sara was still kneeling at his side. She reached out to grab her parasol from between his feet just as another crewman reached out to steady his friend. Poor Ivan was suddenly caught in a tug-of-war of sorts, for the captain's wife was pushing against his legs. He ended up sprawled on his backside.

"Get away from me, all of you," he roared. His voice didn't sound at all musical. "You won't be getting my soup tonight, men. My head's aching, and now my arse is stinging, too. Damned if I'm not taking to my bed."

"Watch your tongue, Ivan," Jimbo ordered.

"Yes," another man called out. "We got us a lady present."

Jimbo lifted Sara's parasol and handed it to her. He turned to leave, but her next words so startled him that he turned around again.

"I'm going to prepare the soup for the men."

"No, you aren't," Jimbo told her. His hard tone of voice didn't leave room for argument. "You're the captain's woman, and you won't be doing such common work."

Because she didn't want to get into a disagreement with Jimbo in front of the rest of the men she waited until he'd left. Then she smiled at the men watching her. "I'm going to make a lovely soup for everyone. Ivan? Will it make you feel better to have the rest of the day off and rest? It's the very least I can do to repay you for this accident."

Ivan cheered up considerably. "You ever make soup before?" he asked her with a half grin, half scowl.

Since everyone was staring at her, she decided to lie. How difficult could it be to make soup? "Oh, my, yes, many times," she boasted. "I helped our cook make many wonderful dinners."

"Why would a fine lady like yourself be doing such common work?" Chester asked.

"It was very . . . boring in the country," she countered. "It gave me something to do."

They looked as if they believed that lie. "If you're strong enough to direct me to your kitchen, Ivan, I'll get started right away. A good soup needs to simmer long hours," she added, hoping she was right.

Ivan allowed her to take hold of his arm. He continued to rub the back of his head with his other hand as he directed her toward the work area. "It's called a galley, m'lady, not the kitchen," he explained. "Slow down, lass," he added in a grumble when she rushed ahead of him. "I'm still seeing two of everything."

They walked down one dark corridor after another until she was completely disoriented. Ivan knew his way, of course, and led her right to his sanctuary.

He struck two candles, secured them in glass globes, and then sat down on a stool against the wall.

There was a giant oven in the center of the room. It was surely the largest she'd ever seen. When she made that comment to Ivan he shook his head. "It isn't an oven, it's the galley stove. There's an open pit on the other side. You've got to walk around the corner to get a look at it.

That's where I cook my meat on a sturdy spit. On this side you can see the giant coppers sunk down low in the top. There are four in all, and every one of them needed to make my beef soup. There's the meat—some went bad. I've already separated the tainted half from the good beef. Most is simmering in the water I added before I went up on deck to have a word with Chester. It gets a might stifling down here, and I needed a breath of fresh sea air."

Ivan waved a hand toward the pile of bad meat he'd left on the sidebar, thinking to tell her that as soon as he was feeling a little better he'd toss the garbage overboard, but he forgot all about explaining when his head started in pounding again.

"There isn't much else to do," he muttered as he regained his feet. "Just chop up those vegetables and add the spices. Of course, you know all that. Do you want me to stay until you learn your way around my galley?"

"No," Sara answered. "I'll do just fine, Ivan. You go and have Matthew take a look at that bump. Perhaps he has some special medicine he can give you to ease your ache."

"That he does, lass," Ivan replied. "He'll be giving me a pint full of grog to ease my aches and pains, or I'll be knowing the reason why."

As soon as the cook took his leave Sara went to work. She was going to make the finest soup the men had ever eaten. She added the rest of the meat she found on the sidebar, a little of each to each copper. She then sprinkled a fair amount of the spices she found in the cubbyhole below the coppers into each vat. One bottle was filled with crushed brown leaves. The aroma was quite pungent, so she only added a little dash of that.

Sara spent the rest of the morning and part of the afternoon in the galley. She thought it a little odd that no one had come looking for her. That thought led to Nathan, of course.

"The man didn't even give me a proper greeting," she

muttered to herself. She mopped at her brow with the towel she'd tied around her waist and pushed the damp strands of hair back over her shoulders.

"Who didn't give you a proper greeting?"

The deep voice came from the doorway. Sara recognized Nathan's low growl.

She turned around and frowned at him. "You didn't give me a proper greeting," she announced.

"What are you doing here?"

"Making soup. What are you doing here?"

"Looking for you."

It was warm in the galley, and she was sure that was the reason she was suddenly feeling so lightheaded. It couldn't be a reaction to the way he was looking at her.

"Have you ever made soup before?"

She walked over to stand in front of him before giving her answer. Nathan leaned against the doorway, looking as relaxed as a panther about to spring.

"No," she said. "I didn't know how to make soup. I do now. It wasn't difficult."

"Sara . . ."

"The men were all blaming me for Ivan's mishap. I had to do something to win their loyalty. Besides, I want my staff to like me."

"Your staff?"

She nodded. "Since you don't have a house and you don't have servants, well, you *do* own this ship, and so your crew must also be my staff. When they taste my soup they'll like me again."

"Why do you care if they like you or not?" he asked.

He straightened away from the wall and moved closer to her. Hell, he thought, he was drawn to her like a drunk drawn to drink. It was all her fault for looking so damned sweet and pretty.

Her face was flushed from the heat in the galley. Strands of her curly hair were wet. He reached out and gently

142

brushed a curl away from the side of her face. He seemed to be more surprised by the spontaneous touch than she was.

"Nathan, everyone wants to be liked."

"I don't."

She gave him a disgruntled look for disagreeing with her. He took another step toward her. His thighs touched hers. "Sara?"

"Yes?"

"Do you still hurt because of last night?"

Her blush was instantaneous. She couldn't look him in the eye when she answered him but stared intently at his collarbone. "It did hurt last night," she whispered.

He tilted her face up with his thumb. "That isn't what I asked you," he said in a soft whisper.

"It isn't?"

"No," he replied.

"Then what is it you wanted to know?"

She sounded out of breath to him. She needed some fresh air, he decided. Hell, he didn't want her fainting on him again. "I want to know if you hurt now, Sara," he said.

"No," she answered. "I don't hurt now."

They stared at each other a long, silent minute. Sara thought he might want to kiss her, but she couldn't be sure. "Nathan? You still haven't given me a proper greeting."

She put her hands on the front of his shirt, closed her eyes, and waited.

"What the hell is a proper greeting?" he asked. He knew exactly what she wanted from him, but he wanted to see what she would do next.

She opened her eyes and frowned at him. "You're supposed to kiss me."

"Why?" he asked, baiting her again.

Her exasperation was obvious. "Just do it," she commanded.

Before he could ask another aggravating question she clasped the sides of his face with her hands and pulled his head down toward her. "Oh, never mind," she whispered. "I'll do it myself."

He didn't offer any resistance. But he didn't take over the duty either. Sara placed a chaste kiss on his mouth, then leaned back. "This would feel much better if you cooperated, Nathan. You're supposed to kiss me back."

Her voice was low, sensual, as soft as her warm body pressed against his. A man could only take so much teasing. Nathan lowered his head and slowly rubbed his mouth over hers. He caught her sigh when he opened her mouth and deepened the kiss.

She was already melting in his arms. He was once again nearly undone by her easy response to his touch. His tongue dueled with hers, and he couldn't contain his low growl of pleasure.

When he finally pulled back from her she slumped against him. He couldn't stop himself from putting his arms around her and holding her tight. She smelled like roses and cinnamon.

"Who taught you how to kiss?" he demanded in a rough whisper. It was an illogical question, he supposed, given the fact that she'd been a virgin when he'd taken her to his bed, but he was compelled to ask anyway.

"You taught me how to kiss," she answered.

"You never kissed anyone before me?"

She shook her head. His anger dissipated in a flash. "If you don't like the way I kiss . . ." she began.

"I like it."

She quit protesting.

He suddenly pulled completely away from her, grabbed hold of her hand, and dragged her over to the candles. He blew both flames out and then headed for the corridor.

"Nathan, I can't leave the galley," she announced.

"You need a nap."

"I what? I never take naps."

"You do now."

"But what about my lovely soup?"

"Damn it, Sara, I don't want you cooking again."

She frowned at his broad back. Lord, he was bossy. "I already explained why I took on this duty," she muttered.

"Do you think you can win the men's loyalty with a bowl of slop?"

If he slowed down just a little, she thought, she would be able to kick him in the back of his legs. "It isn't slop," she shouted instead.

He didn't argue with her. He continued to drag her along all the way back to their cabin. She was a bit surprised when he followed her inside.

He shut the door behind him and bolted it.

"Turn around, Sara."

She gave him a good frown for being so dictatorial, then did as he commanded. He was much quicker unbuttoning the gown than he had been the last time.

"I really don't want to have a nap," she told him again.

He didn't quit prodding her until her gown fell to the floor. It still hadn't dawned on her that he really wasn't interested in forcing her to sleep. He stripped her down to her chemise, but when he tried to remove that garment she pushed his hands away.

Nathan stared at her a long minute. Her body was simply perfection to him. Her breasts were full, her waist narrow, and her legs long, shapely, exquisite.

His hot stare soon made her uncomfortable. Sara tugged on the straps of her chemise, trying without much success to conceal a little more of her breasts.

She quit feeling embarrassed when he unbuttoned his shirt. That action gained her full attention. "Are you taking a nap, too?"

"I never take naps."

He tossed his shirt aside, leaned back against the door, and began to pull his boots off. Sara backed up a space.

"You aren't just changing your clothes, are you?"

His grin was lopsided, endearing. "No."

"You don't want to . . ."

145

He didn't look at her when he answered. "Oh, yes, I want to," he drawled.

"No."

His reaction was immediate. He stood to his full height and walked toward her. His hands were on his hips. "No?"

She shook her head.

"Why the hell not?"

"It's daylight," she blurted out.

"Damn it, Sara, you aren't afraid again, are you? Honest to God, I don't think I can go through that ordeal again."

She was outraged. "Ordeal? You call making love to me an ordeal?"

He wasn't going to let her stray from answering his question. "Are you afraid?" he demanded.

He looked as though he dreaded her answer. Sara suddenly realized she had a way out if she wanted it, but she immediately discarded that idea. She wasn't going to lie to him.

"I wasn't afraid last night," she announced. She folded her arms across her chest and then added, "You were."

That remark wasn't worthy of a retort. "You said you didn't hurt anymore," he reminded her as he moved forward another step.

"I'm not tender now," she whispered. "But we both know I will be if you persist in getting your way, Nathan."

His smile indicated his amusement. "Will that be so unbearable?"

A warm knot was already forming in the pit of her stomach. All the man had to do was look at her in that special way of his and she came apart.

"Are you going to want to . . . move again?"

He didn't laugh. She looked so worried, and he didn't want her to think he was mocking her feelings. He wasn't going to lie, either. "Yeah," he drawled as he reached for her. "I'm going to want to move again."

"Then we aren't going to do anything but nap."

The little woman really needed to understand who was husband and who was wife, Nathan thought to himself. He decided he'd explain all about her duty to obey him later. All he wanted to do was kiss her. He threw his arm around her shoulders, dragged her over to the trap, and didn't let go of her when he reached up and pulled the wooden door shut.

The cabin was pitched into darkness. Nathan paused to kiss Sara. It was a hot, wet, lingering kiss that let her know with certainty that he was going to get his way.

Then he turned to light the candles. Her hand stayed his action. "Don't," she whispered.

"I want to see you when you . . ."

He stopped his explanation when he felt her hands on his waistband. Sara's hands were shaking, but she got the buttons to his breeches undone in little time. Her fingers brushed against his hard stomach. His indrawn breath told her he liked that. It made her bolder. She rested the side of her face against his chest, then slowly edged the waistband down. "You wanted to see me when I what, Nathan?" she whispered.

It took all he had to concentrate on what she was saying. Her fingers were slowly easing their way down toward his groin. He closed his eyes in sweet agony.

"When you find fulfillment," he said on a low groan. "God, Sara, touch me."

His body was rigid now. Sara smiled to herself. She had no idea her touch could so arouse him. She pushed his clothing down a little further. "I am touching you, Nathan."

He couldn't take the torment any longer. He took hold of her hand and placed it where he needed her touch most.

She wanted to stroke him. He wouldn't let her. His growl was deep, guttural. "Don't," he ordered. "Just hold me, squeeze me, but don't . . . oh, God, Sara, stop now."

He sounded as if he was in pain. She pulled her hand away. "Am I hurting you?" she whispered.

He kissed her again. She put her arms around his neck

and held him close. When he moved to the side of her neck and began to place wet kisses below her earlobe she tried to touch his hard arousal again.

He took hold of her hand and put it on his waist. "It's too soon for me to lose my control," he whispered. "You make it unbearable."

She kissed the base of his neck. "Then I won't touch you there, Nathan, if you promise not to move around so much when you make love to me."

He laughed. "You'll want me to move," he told her.

He pulled her back up against his chest. "You know what, Sara?" he said between fervent kisses.

"What?"

"I've decided I'm going to make you beg."

He was as good as his word. By the time the two of them were in bed and he was settled between her thighs she was begging him to end the sweet torment.

The fire of passion inside her was completely out of control. Nathan did hurt her when he finally moved inside her. She was so tight, so hot, it was blissful agony for him to slow down. He tried to be a gentle lover, knowing how tender she was, and he didn't move at all until she began to writhe underneath him.

She found her release before he did, and her tremors gave him his own orgasm. He hadn't spoken a word during the mating. She never quit talking. She rambled on and on, tender words of love. Some made sense. Others didn't.

When he finally collapsed on top of her, when he finally regained his ability to think at all, he realized she was crying.

"God, Sara, did I hurt you again?"

"Only a little," she whispered shyly.

He leaned up to look into her eyes. "Then why are you crying?"

"I don't know why," she answered. "It was so . . . amazing, and I was so . . . ."

He stopped her rambling by kissing her. When he next

looked into her eyes he smiled. She looked thoroughly bemused again.

This one could get to his heart, he suddenly realized. The sound of the boatswain's whistle announcing the change of the watch was like a warning bell going off inside Nathan's mind. It was dangerous to be so attracted to his wife, foolish . . . irresponsible. To care for the woman would make him vulnerable, he knew. If he'd learned anything of consequence in his escapades, it was to protect himself at all costs.

Loving her could destroy him.

"Nathan, why are you frowning?"

He didn't answer her. He got out of bed, dressed with his back to her, and then walked out of the cabin. The door closed softly behind him.

Sara was too stunned by his behavior to react for a long minute. Her husband had literally fled the cabin. It was as though he had a demon chasing him.

Had their lovemaking meant so little to him that he couldn't wait to leave her? Sara burst into tears. She wanted, needed his words of love. God, he treated her as though she was nothing but a receptacle for his passion. Fast spent, fast forgotten. A whore was treated better than he'd just treated her, she thought to herself. Women of the night at least earned a shilling or two.

She hadn't even merited a growl of farewell.

When her tears were spent she took her frustration out on the bed. She made a fist and slammed it into the center of Nathan's pillow, taking great satisfaction in pretending it was her husband's head. Then she pulled his pillow against her bosom and held it tight. Nathan's scent clung to the pillowcase. So did hers.

It didn't take her long to realize how pitiful she was being. She tossed the pillow aside and turned her attention to righting the cabin.

She stayed in the room the remainder of the afternoon. She dressed in the same blue dress, and when the cabin was cleaned she sat down in one of the chairs and began to make a sketch of the ship using her pad and charcoals.

Sketching took her mind off Nathan. Matthew interrupted her when he knocked on the door to ask if she wanted to eat her dinner with the first or second change in the watch. She told him she would wait and share her meal with her aunt.

Sara was eager to find out what the men thought about her soup. The aroma had been quite nice when she'd finished stirring in all the spices. It should have a hearty flavor, she thought, for it had simmered long hours.

It was only a matter of time before the men came to thank her. She brushed her hair and changed her gown in preparation for their visitations.

Her staff would soon be completely loyal to her. Making the soup was a giant step in that direction, anyway. Why, by nightfall they would all think she was very, very worthy.

Chapter Seven

B y nightfall they thought she was trying to kill them.

The watch turned at six that evening. The first group filed into the galley to collect their dinner just a few minutes later. The men had put in a hard day's work. The decks had been scoured, the hammocks scrubbed, netting mended, and half the cannons had been given another thorough cleaning. The seamen were weary, and their hunger was fierce. Most ate two full bowls of the heavily flavored soup before they were appeased.

They didn't start getting sick until the second watch had just eaten their share.

Sara had no idea the men were ill. She was getting impatient, though, for no one had come along to tell her what a fine job she'd done.

When a hard knock sounded at her door she rushed to answer it. Jimbo stood at the entrance, frowning at her. Her smile faltered.

"Good evening, Jimbo," she began. "Is something wrong? You look very unhappy."

"You haven't had any soup yet, have you, Lady Sara?" he asked.

His obvious concern didn't make any sense to her. She shook her head. "I was waiting to share my dinner with Nora," she explained. "Jimbo, what is that horrid sound I'm hearing?"

She looked out the door to see if she could locate the sound.

"The men."

"The men?"

Nathan suddenly appeared at Jimbo's side. The look on her husband's face made her breath catch in the back of her throat. He looked bloody furious. Sara instinctively backed up. "What's the matter, Nathan?" she asked, her alarm obvious. "Is something wrong? Is it Nora? Is she all right?"

"Nora's fine," Jimbo interjected.

Nathan motioned Jimbo out of the way, then stalked into the cabin. Sara continued to back away from him. She noticed his jaw was clenched tight. That was a bad sign.

"Are you upset about something?" she asked Nathan in a faint whisper.

He nodded.

She decided to be more specific. "Are you upset with me?"

He nodded again. Then he kicked the door shut.

"Why?" she asked, trying desperately not to let him see her fear.

"The soup." Nathan's voice was low, controlled, furious.

She was more confused by his answer than frightened. "The men didn't care for my soup?"

"It wasn't deliberate?"

Since she didn't have any idea what he meant by that question, she didn't answer. He could see the confusion in her eyes. He closed his own and counted to ten. "Then you didn't deliberately try to kill them?"

She let out a loud gasp. "Of course I didn't try to kill them. How could you think such a vile thing? The men are all part of my staff now, and I certainly wouldn't try to harm them. If they didn't like my soup, I'm sorry. I had no idea they were such persnickety eaters."

"Persnickety eaters?" He repeated those words in a roar. "Twenty of my men are now hanging over the sides of my ship. They're retching up the soup you prepared for them. Another ten are writhing in agony in their hammocks. They're not dead yet, but they sure as hell are wishing they were."

She was appalled by what he was telling her. "I don't understand," she cried out. "Do you mean to suggest that my soup wasn't any good? The men are ill because of me? Oh, God, I must go and comfort them."

He grabbed hold of her shoulders when she tried to rush past him. "Comfort them? Sara, one or two of them just might comfort you right off the ship."

"They wouldn't throw me overboard. I'm their mistress."

He felt like shouting. Then he realized he already was. He took a quick breath. "The hell they wouldn't toss you overboard," he muttered.

Nathan dragged her over to the bed and pushed her down on the quilt. "Now, wife, you're going to tell me just how you made that damned soup."

She burst into tears. It took Nathan almost twenty minutes to find the cause, and it wasn't Sara who finally gave him sufficient information. He couldn't make head or tail out of her incoherent explanation. Ivan remembered the tainted meat he'd left on the sidebar. He remembered, too, that he hadn't told Sara it was bad.

Nathan locked Sara inside the cabin so she couldn't cause any more mischief. She was furious with him because he wouldn't let her go and apologize to the men.

He didn't come to bed that night, as he and the other healthy men had to take over the next watch. Sara didn't understand that duty called and believed he was still too angry with her to want to sleep next to her.

She didn't know how she was ever going to find the

courage to face her staff again. How could she convince them that she hadn't deliberately tried to do them in? That worry turned to anger in short time. How could the men believe such a sinful thing about their mistress anyway? Why, they besmirched her character by believing she would hurt them. Sara determined that once she won their trust again she would sit them all down and have a firm talk with them about their tendency to jump to conclusions.

Nathan was slow to forgive her error, too. He came down to the cabin the following morning. He glared at her but didn't speak a word. He fell asleep on top of the covers and slept the morning away.

She couldn't stand the confinement long. She couldn't stand his snoring either. It was half past the noon hour when she slipped out of the room. She went up on deck, opened her blue parasol, and set out for a brisk walk.

It turned out to be a humiliating experience. Each man she approached turned his back on her. Most still had a gray cast to their complexions. All of them had scowls. She was in tears by the time she reached the narrow steps to the highest deck. She was scarcely aware of where she was going and only wanted to get as far away from the dark frowns as possible, if only for just a few minutes.

The highest level was filled with ropes and masts. There was barely room to walk. Sara found a corner near the tallest sail, sat down, and put her opened parasol between two fat ropes.

She didn't know how long she sat there trying to think of a plan to persuade the men to like her again. Her face and arms soon turned pink from the sun. It wasn't at all fashionable for a lady to walk around with a bronzed complexion. Sara decided she'd better go back down and look in on her Aunt Nora.

It would be nice to visit with someone who cared about her. Nora wouldn't blame her. Yes, a pleasant visit was just the thing she needed.

She stood up and tugged on her parasol only to find that

the delicate spokes had become caught up in ropes. It took her a good five minutes to loosen the knots in the ropes enough to work the parasol partially free. The wind was high again, making the task more difficult. The sound of the sails slapping against the posts was loud enough to drown out her frustrated mutters. She gave up on the task when the material of her parasol tore. She decided then to ask Matthew or Jimbo for assistance.

Sara left the parasol dangling in the ropes and made her way back down the steps.

The crash, when it came, nearly toppled her over the side of the ship. Chester caught her in the nick of time. Both of them turned to the noise on the upper deck just in time to see one of the masts slam into a larger one.

Chester took off running, shouting for assistance as he raced up the steps. Sara decided she'd better get out of the way of the sudden chaos around her. She waited until several more men had rushed past her, then made her way down to Nora's cabin. Matthew was just coming out of the room when Sara strode past him.

"Good day, Matthew," she said in greeting. She paused to curtsy, then added, "I'll only stay a few minutes. I just wanted to see how my aunt is doing today. I promise I won't wear her out."

Matthew grinned. "I believe you," he replied. "But I'm still coming back in a half hour's time to check on Nora."

The booming crash shook the vessel then. Sara grabbed hold of the door to keep herself from pitching forward to her knees. "Heavens, the wind is fierce today, isn't it, Matthew?"

The seaman was already running toward the steps. "That wasn't the wind," he shouted over his shoulder.

Sara shut the door to Nora's cabin just as Nathan came charging out of his quarters.

Her aunt was once again propped up with pillows behind her back. Sara thought she looked a little more rested and said so. "The color's back in your cheeks, Nora, and your bruises are beginning to fade to yellow now. You'll be strolling around the decks with me in no time at all."

"Yes, I do feel better," Nora announced. "How are you faring, Sara?"

"Oh, I'm just fine," she answered. She sat down on the side of the bed and took hold of her aunt's hand.

Nora frowned at her. "I heard about the soup, child. I know you aren't doing fine."

"I didn't eat any of the soup," Sara blurted out. "But I do feel terrible about the men. I didn't mean to make them ill."

"I know you didn't mean to," Nora soothed. "I told Matthew so. I took up your defense, Sara, and told him you didn't have a malicious thought in your head. Why, you'd never do such a terrible thing on purpose."

Sara's frown matched her aunt's. "I think it's horribly rude of my staff to think such evil thoughts about their mistress. Yes, I do. Why, they're as contrary as their captain, Nora."

"What about Nathan?" Nora asked. "Is he blaming you, too?"

Sara shrugged. "He was a little upset about the soup, of course, but I don't believe he thinks I poisoned the men on purpose. He's probably being a little more understanding because he didn't eat any of it. Anyway, I've decided I don't care what the man thinks of me. I'm more upset with him than he is with me. Yes, I am," she added when Nora began to smile. "He isn't treating me at all well."

She didn't give her aunt time to respond to that dramatic statement. "Oh, I never should have said that. Nathan's my husband, and I must always be loyal to him. I'm ashamed of myself for—"

"Has he harmed you?" Nora interrupted.

"No, of course not. It's just that . . ."

A long minute passed while Nora tried to guess what was the matter and Sara tried to think of a way to explain.

When Sara started blushing Nora surmised that the

problem had something to do with the intimate side of their marriage. "He wasn't gentle with you when he bedded you?"

Sara looked down at her lap before answering. "He was very gentle."

"Then?"

"But afterwards he didn't . . . that is, the second time— well, after—he just left. He didn't say a single tender word to me, Nora. In fact, he didn't say anything at all. A whore is treated with more consideration."

Nora was too relieved that Nathan had been gentle with Sara to take issue over his lack of thoughtfulness. "Did you say any tender words to him?" she asked.

"No."

"It would seem to me that Nathan might not know how to give you what you want. He might not know you need his praise."

"I don't need his praise," Sara countered in a disgruntled voice. "I would just like a little consideration. Oh, heaven help me, that's not the truth. I do need his words of praise. I don't know why I seem to need them, but I do. Nora? Do you notice how the boat is tilted to one side now? I wonder why Nathan doesn't straighten it out."

It took her aunt a minute to make the switch in topics. "Yes, it is at an angle, isn't it?" she responded. "But you did say the wind was brisk today."

"We don't seem to be clipping along either," Sara interjected. "I hope we don't topple over," she added with a sigh. "I never did learn how to swim. That shouldn't signify, though. Nathan can't let me drown."

Nora smiled. "Why can't he?"

Sara seemed surprised by that question. "Because I'm his wife," she blurted out. "He promised to protect me, Nora."

"And you have ultimate faith that he will?"

"Of course."

The vessel suddenly shifted again, pitching them even

further toward the water line. Sara saw how startled Nora was; her aunt was gripping her hand. She patted Nora and said, "Nathan is the captain of this vessel, Nora, and he wouldn't let us fall over into the ocean. He knows what he's doing. Don't worry."

A sudden roar filled the cabin. It was her name being bellowed. Sara grimaced in reaction, then turned to give Nora a thoroughly disgruntled look. "Do you see what I mean, Nora? The only time Nathan says my name, he screams it. I wonder what has him in a snit now. The man has such a sour disposition. It's a wonder I can put up with him."

"Go and see what he wants," Nora suggested. "Don't let him frighten you with his shouts. Just remember to look below the bluster."

"I know," Sara said with a sigh. She stood up and brushed the wrinkles out of her gown. "Look below the surface, and I'll find myself a good man," she added, repeating her aunt's suggestion of the day before. "I will try."

She kissed Nora and hurried out into the corridor. She almost bumped into Jimbo. The big man grabbed hold of her to steady her. "Come with me," he ordered.

He started to lead her toward the steps that led down to the lower level. She pulled back. "Nathan is calling for me, Jimbo. I must go to him. He's up on deck, isn't he?"

"I know where he is," Jimbo muttered. "But he needs a few more minutes to calm himself down, Sara. You can hide down here until he—"

"I'm not hiding from my husband," Sara interrupted.

"Damned right you're not."

Sara jumped a foot when Nathan's booming voice sounded behind her. She turned around and valiantly tried to manage a smile. After all, there was a member of her staff standing right beside her, and for that reason personal irritations should be placed aside. The scowl on her husband's face changed her inclination, though. She no longer cared that Jimbo was watching. She scowled back. "For heaven's sake, Nathan, must you sneak up on me like that? You gave me a good scare."

"Sara," Jimbo began in a whisper, "I wouldn't be . . ."

She ignored the seaman's mutterings. "And while I'm on the topic of your bad habits, I might as well point out that I'm getting mighty sick of your shouting at me all the time. If you have something you wish to say to me, kindly speak in a civil tone of voice, sir."

Jimbo moved to stand by her side. Matthew suddenly appeared out of the shadows and took up his position on her other side. In the back of Sara's mind was the astonishing fact that both men were actually trying to protect her.

"Nathan wouldn't ever hurt me," she announced. "He may want to, but he would never touch me, no matter how angry he is."

"He looks like he wants to kill you," Jimbo countered in a low drawl. He actually grinned, for he found Sara's gumption worthy. Wrongheaded, he added to himself, but worthy still.

Nathan was trying to calm down before he spoke again. He stared at Sara and took several deep breaths. He counted.

"He always looks like he wants to kill someone," Sara whispered back. She folded her arms in front of her, trying her damnedest to look irritated and not worried.

Nathan still hadn't said a word. The look in his eyes made her skin burn. In truth, he did look like he wanted to throttle her.

Look below the surface, her aunt had suggested. Sara couldn't manage that feat. She couldn't even hold Nathan's gaze for more than a heartbeat or two. "All right," she muttered when she couldn't stand his hot glare any longer. "Did someone else have some of my soup? Is that the reason you're in such a state, husband?"

The muscle flexed in the side of his jaw. She decided she

shouldn't have asked him that question after all. It only reminded him of the confusion she'd caused the day before. Then she noticed he was holding her parasol.

Nathan's right eyelid twitched. Twice. God, he was developing an affliction, he noted, thanks to his innocent wife's mischief. He still couldn't trust himself to speak to her. He took hold of her hand and pulled her into their cabin. He slammed the door, then leaned on it.

Sara walked over to the desk, turned, and leaned against it. She was trying to look nonchalant. "Nathan, I cannot help but notice that you're once again upset about something," she began. "Are you going to tell me what's bothering you, or are you going to continue to stand there and glare at me? Lord, you do strain my patience."

"I strain *your* patience?"

She didn't dare nod in answer. He'd roared that question at her, and she guessed he didn't want an answer.

"Does this look familiar?" he demanded in a rough voice. He lifted her parasol but kept his gaze fully directed on her.

She stared at the parasol and noticed right away that it had been broken in half.

"Did you break my lovely parasol?" she demanded. She looked incensed.

His eyelid twitched again. "No, I didn't break it. When the first mast let loose it broke your damned parasol. Did you untie the latchings?"

"Please quit your shouting," she protested. "I cannot think when you're yelling at me."

"Answer me."

"I might have untied a few of the fatter ropes, Nathan, but I had good reason. That's a very expensive parasol," she added with a wave of her hand toward him. "It got caught up, and I was trying to . . . Nathan, exactly what happens when the ropes become untied?"

"We lost two sails."

She didn't comprehend what he was telling her. "We what?"

"Two sails were destroyed."

"And that is why you're so upset? Husband, you have at least six others on this boat. Surely—"

"*Ship,*" he roared. "It's a ship, not a boat."

She decided to try to placate him. "I meant to say ship."

"Do you have any more of these things?"

"They're called parasols," she replied. "And yes, I do have three more."

"Give them to me. Now."

"What are you going to do with them?"

She rushed over to her trunk when he took a threatening step toward her. "I can't imagine why you would need my parasols," she whispered.

"I'm throwing them in the ocean. With any luck they'll cripple a couple of sharks."

"You cannot throw my parasols in the ocean. They match my gowns, Nathan. They were made just for . . . it would be a sin to waste . . . you can't." She ended her tirade in a near wail.

"The hell I can't."

He wasn't shouting at her any longer. She should have been happy over that minor blessing, but she wasn't. He was still being too mean-hearted to suit her. "Explain why you want to destroy my parasols," she demanded. "Then I might give them to you."

She located the third parasol in the bottom of the trunk, but when she straightened and turned to confront him again she clutched all three against her bosom.

"The parasols are a menace, that's why."

She looked incredulous. "How could they be a menace?"

She was looking at him as though she thought he'd lost his mind. He shook his head. "The first parasol crippled my men, Sara," he began.

"It only crippled Ivan," she corrected.

"Which is why you made the damn soup that crippled the rest of my crew," he countered.

He had a valid point there, she had to admit, but she

thought it was terribly unkind of him to bring up the topic of her soup again.

"The second parasol crippled my ship," he continued. "Haven't you noticed we aren't gliding across the waters now? We had to drop anchor in order to see to the repairs. We're easy prey for anyone sailing past. That's why your other damned parasols are all going into the ocean."

"Nathan, I didn't mean to cause these mishaps. You're acting as though I did everything on purpose."

"Did you?"

She reacted as though he'd just slapped her backside. "No," she cried out. "God, you're insulting."

He wanted to shake some sense into her. She started crying.

"Quit that weeping," he demanded.

Not only did she continue to cry, but she threw herself into his arms. Hell, he'd been the one to make her weep in the first place, he thought, and she certainly should have been upset with him just a little, shouldn't she?

Nathan didn't know what to make of her. Her parasols littered the floor around his feet, and she was clinging to him as she sobbed wet tears all over his shirt. He put his arms around her and held her close even as he tried to understand why in God's name he wanted to comfort her.

The woman had damn near destroyed his ship.

He kissed her.

She tucked her face in the side of his neck and quit crying. "Do the men know I broke the ship?"

"You didn't break it," he muttered. God, she sounded pitiful.

"But do the men think I—"

"Sara, we can fix the damage in a couple of days," he said. It was a lie, for it would take them close to a week to see to the repairs, but he'd softened the truth just a little to ease her worry.

He decided then that he had lost his mind. His wife had caused nothing but chaos since the moment she'd boarded his ship. He kissed the top of her head and began to rub her backside.

She leaned against him. "Nathan?"

"Yes?"

"Does my staff know I caused this mishap?"

He rolled his eyes heavenward. Her staff, indeed. "Yes, they know."

"Did you tell them?"

He closed his eyes. There had been such censure in her voice. She thought he was being disloyal to her, he surmised. "No, I didn't tell them. They saw the parasol, Sara."

"I wanted them to respect me."

"Oh, they respect you all right," he announced. His voice had lost its angry bite.

She heard the smile in his voice and felt a quick rush of hope until he added, "They're waiting for you to bring on the plague next."

She thought he was teasing her. "They don't believe that nonsense," she replied.

"Oh, yes, they do," he told her. "They're making wagers, Sara. Some think it will be boils first, then the plague. Others believe—"

She pushed away from him. "You're serious, aren't you?"

He nodded. "They think you're cursed, wife."

"How can you smile at me when you say such sinful things?"

He shrugged. "The men are superstitious, Sara."

"Is it because I'm a woman?" she asked. "I've heard that seamen think it's bad luck to have a woman on board, but I didn't credit such foolishness."

"No, it isn't because you're a woman," he answered. "They're used to having a woman on board. My sister Jade used to be mistress of this ship."

"Then why—"

"You aren't like Jade," he told her. "They were quick to notice."

She couldn't get him to elaborate. A sudden thought

changed her direction. "Nathan, I'll help with the repairs," she said. "Yes, that's it. The men will realize I didn't deliberately—"

"God save us all," he interrupted.

"Then how am I going to win their confidence again?"

"I don't understand this obsession with winning the men over," he returned. "It makes absolutely no sense."

"I'm their mistress. I must have their respect if I'm going to direct them."

He let out a loud sigh, then shook his head. "Direct yourself to bed, wife, and stay there until I come back."

"Why?"

"Don't question me. Just stay inside this cabin."

She nodded agreement. "I won't leave this cabin save for going to visit with Nora, all right?"

"I didn't say—"

"Please? It's going to be a long afternoon, Nathan. You might be too busy to come home for hours yet. You didn't come to bed at all last night. I tried to wait up for you, but I was very weary."

He smiled because she'd called their cabin home. Then he nodded. "You'll wait up for me tonight," he ordered. "No matter what the time."

"Are you going to want to shout at me again?"

"No."

"All right, then," she promised. "I'll wait up for you."

"Damn it, Sara," he countered. "I wasn't asking. I was telling."

He grabbed her and squeezed her shoulders. It was actually more of a caress. She pushed his hands away and wrapped her arms around his waist again.

"Nathan?" she whispered.

Her voice sounded shaky to him. His hands dropped to his sides. He thought she might be afraid he'd hurt her. He was about to explain that no matter how much she provoked him he would never, ever raise a hand against her. But Sara suddenly leaned up on tiptoes and kissed him. He was so surprised by the show of affection he didn't know how to respond.

"I was very upset with you when you left the cabin so quickly after we had . . . been so intimate."

"Do you mean after we made love?" he asked, smiling over the shyness in her voice.

"Yes," she replied. "I was very upset."

"Why?"

"Because a wife likes to hear that she . . ."

"Satisfied her husband?"

"No," she returned. "Don't mock me, Nathan. Don't make what happened between us so cold and calculated either. It was too beautiful."

He was shaken by her fervent speech, knew she believed what she'd said with all her heart. He found himself inordinately pleased with her. "Yes, it was beautiful," he said. "I wasn't mocking you," he added in a rougher tone. "I was just trying to understand what it is you want from me."

"I want to hear that you . . ."

She couldn't go on.

"That you're a fine woman?"

She nodded. "I'm at fault, too," she admitted. "I should have given you a few words of praise, too."

"Why?"

He really looked bewildered to her. That did irritate her. "Because a husband needs to hear such words, too."

"I don't."

"Yes, you do."

He decided he'd wasted enough conversation on his confusing wife and bent on one knee to collect the parasols.

"May I please have those back?" she asked. "I'll destroy them myself right away. I don't want my staff to see you throw them overboard. It would be most humiliating."

He reluctantly agreed, though only because he was certain she couldn't do any real damage with the useless things as long as they stayed inside the cabin. Still, just to be on the safe side, he made her give him her promise.

"The parasols won't leave this chamber?"

"They won't."

"You will destroy them?"

"I will."

He was finally satisfied. He actually began to feel a little more peaceful. By the time he left the cabin he was convinced his wife couldn't possibly wreck anything else.

Besides, he reasoned, what more could she do?

Chapter Eight

She set his ship on fire.

She'd lulled them into a state of feeling safe again. A full eight days and nights passed without a single mishap taking place. The men were still wary of Sara, but they weren't scowling nearly as often. Some were even whistling every now and again as they saw to their daily tasks. Chester, the doubting Thomas of the crew, was the only one who continued to make the sign of the cross whenever Sara strolled past.

Lady Sara pretended she didn't notice.

Once the sails had been repaired they made good catch-up time. They were just a week or so away from Nora's island home. The weather had been accommodating, though the heat was nearly unbearable in the early afternoons. The nights continued to be just as chilly, however, and thick quilts were still needed to take the shivers away.

All and all, things were looking calm.

Nathan should have realized it wouldn't last. It was late Friday night when he finished giving directions for the watch. He interrupted Jimbo's conversation with Matthew

167

to give them fresh orders for the drill and the firing of the cannons they would practice tomorrow.

The three of them were standing directly in front of the trapdoor that led down to Nathan's cabin. For that reason Jimbo kept his voice low when he said, "The men are beginning to forget this talk about your wife being cursed, boy." He paused to glance behind him, as if that action would assure him that Sara couldn't overhear, then added, "Chester is still telling everyone mischief trails in three. We'd best continue to keep a close watch on Sara until—"

"Jimbo, no one would dare touch the captain's wife," Matthew muttered.

"I wasn't suggesting anyone would," Jimbo countered. "I'm just saying that they could still hurt her feelings. She's a bit tenderhearted."

"Did you know she considers us all part of her staff?" Matthew remarked. He grinned, then stopped himself. "Lady Sara obviously has you in the palm of her hand, if you're so concerned about her feelings." He started to continue on that same topic when the scent of smoke caught his attention. "Am I smelling smoke?" he asked.

Nathan saw the stream of gray smoke seeping up around the edges of the trapdoor before the other two men did. He should have shouted fire to alert the others of the danger. He didn't. He bellowed Sara's name instead. The anguish in his voice was gut-wrenching.

He threw open the hatch. A thick black sheet of smoke billowed up through the opening, blinding the three men. Nathan shouted Sara's name again.

Matthew shouted, "Fire!"

Jimbo went running for the buckets, yelling his own order for seawater on the double, while Matthew tried to keep Nathan from going below by way of the trap.

"You don't know how bad it is," he shouted. "Use the steps, boy, use the—"

Matthew quit his demand when Nathan slipped down through the opening, then turned to run down the steps.

Nathan could barely see inside the cabin, for the smoke was so thick it blackened his vision. He groped his way over to the bed to find Sara.

She wasn't there. By the time he'd searched the cabin his lungs were burning. He staggered back to the trap again and used the buckets of seawater Jimbo handed down to him to flood the flames out.

The threat was over. The near miss they'd all had made the men shake. Nathan couldn't seem to control his heartbeat. His fear for his wife's safety had all but overwhelmed him. Yet she wasn't even inside the cabin. She hadn't been overcome by smoke. She wasn't dead.

Yet.

Matthew and Jimbo flanked Nathan. All three men stared at the corner of the room to gauge the damage done.

Several of the planks under the potbellied stove had fallen through the floor to the next level. There was now a gaping, glowing hole in the floorboards. Two of the four walls had been licked black all the way to the ceiling by the scorch of the fire.

The damage to the cabin wasn't what held Nathan mesmerized, though. No, his full attention was riveted on the remains of Sara's parasols. The spokes still glowed inside the two remaining metal fittings of the stove.

"Did she think this was a hearth?" Matthew whispered to Jimbo. He rubbed his jaw while he considered that possibility.

"I'm thinking she did," Jimbo answered.

"If she'd been asleep, the smoke would have killed her," Nathan said, his voice raw.

"Now, boy," Jimbo began, certain that the boy was getting himself all worked up, "Sara's all right, and that's what counts. You're sounding as black as the soot on these walls. You've only yourself to blame," he added with a crisp nod.

Nathan gave him a murderous stare. Jimbo wasn't the least intimidated. "I heard Sara call the trap a chimney. Had myself a good laugh over that comment, too. I thought you set her straight."

"I don't suppose he did," Matthew interjected.

Nathan wasn't at all calmed by Jimbo's argument. He sounded as if he was close to weeping when he bellowed, "She set my ship on fire."

"She didn't do it on purpose," Matthew defended.

Nathan wasn't listening. "She set my ship on fire," he repeated in a roar.

"We heard you plain the first time, boy," Jimbo interjected. "Now calm yourself and try to reason this little accident through."

"I'm thinking it's going to take him a few more minutes before he can think at all," Matthew said. "The boy always was a hothead, Jimbo. And Sara did set the fire. That's a fact, all right."

The two men turned to leave the cabin. They both thought Nathan needed to be alone for a spell. Nathan's shout stopped them in their tracks. "Bring her to me. Now."

Jimbo motioned for Matthew to stay where he was and then rushed out the doorway. He didn't give Sara any warning of the problem at hand when he found her in Nora's cabin but simply informed her that her husband would like to have a word with her.

Sara hurried back to her cabin. Her eyes widened when she saw all the water on the floor. A loud gasp followed after she noticed the gaping hole in the corner.

"My God, what has happened here?"

Nathan turned to look at her before answering. "Fire."

Understanding came in a flash. "Fire?" she repeated in a hoarse whisper. "Do you mean the fire in the hearth, Nathan?"

He didn't answer her for a long, long minute. Then he slowly walked over to stand directly in front of her. His hands were close enough to grab her by the neck.

He resisted that shameful temptation by clasping his hands behind his back.

She wasn't looking at him. That helped. Her gaze was still fully directed on the damage to the cabin. She worried her lower lip with her teeth, and when she began to tremble Nathan guessed she'd realized exactly what she'd done.

He was wrong. "I never should have left the hearth unattended," she whispered. "Did a spark . . ."

He shook his head.

She looked into his eyes then. Her fear was obvious.

He immediately lost some of his rage. Damn if he'd have her afraid of him. It was an illogical thought, given the circumstances, yet there it was, nagging him to ease his scowl.

"Sara?" His voice sounded quite mild.

He sounded furious to her. She forced herself to stay where she was, though the urge to back away from him was nearly overpowering. "Yes, Nathan?" she replied, her gaze directed on the floor.

"Look at me."

She looked. He saw the tears in her eyes. The sight tore the rest of his fury right out of him.

His sigh was long, ragged.

"Was there something you wanted to say to me?" she asked when he continued to stare intently at her.

"It isn't a hearth."

Nathan walked out of the cabin. Sara stared after him a long minute before turning around to look at Matthew and Jimbo.

"Did he just say that the hearth isn't a hearth?"

The two men nodded in unison.

Her shoulders slumped. "It looks like a hearth."

"Well, it isn't," Matthew announced. He nudged Jimbo in his side. "You explain it."

Jimbo nodded, then told Sara that the metal parts stacked in the corner of the cabin had been carted back from Nathan's last trip. They were to be used to repair the old stove in the Emerald Shipping Company offices. Nathan had just forgotten to take the parts off the ship when they'd docked, Jimbo continued, though he was certain the captain wouldn't be forgetting next time.

Matthew finished up the explanation by telling Sara that the trap was simply an air duct and nothing more. It wasn't a chimney.

Lady Sara's face looked as red as fire by the time the two men had given her their explanations. She then thanked them for their patience. She felt like an ignorant fool. "I could have killed everyone," she whispered.

"Aye, you could have," Matthew agreed.

She burst into tears. The two men were nearly undone by the emotional show. Jimbo glared at Matthew.

Matthew suddenly felt like a father trying to comfort his daughter. He took Sara into his arms and awkwardly patted her on her back.

"There now, Sara, it's not so bad," Jimbo said, trying to soothe her. "You couldn't have known it wasn't a hearth."

"An idiot would have known," she cried out.

The two men nodded to each other over the top of Sara's head. Then Matthew said, "I *might* have thought it was a hearth if I . . ." He couldn't go on because he couldn't think of a plausible lie.

Jimbo came to his aid. "Anyone would have thought it was a hearth if he wasn't used to sailing much."

Nathan stood in the doorway. He couldn't believe what he was seeing. Jimbo and Matthew, two of the most bloodless pirates he'd ever had the honor to work with, were now acting like nursemaids. He would have laughed if his attention hadn't wandered over to the fire damage just then. He frowned instead.

"When you're through beating bruises in my wife's back, Matthew, you might want to have some of the men clean up this mess."

Nathan turned to Jimbo next. "The planks went through the lower level, too. See to righting the damage, Jimbo. Matthew, if you don't get your hands off my wife, I'll . . ."

He didn't have to finish that threat. Matthew was halfway

out the door by the time Nathan reached Sara. "If anyone is to comfort my wife, it's going to be me."

He jerked Sara into his arms and shoved her face against his chest. Jimbo didn't dare break into a smile until he'd exited the room. He did let out a rich chuckle after he'd closed the door behind him, however.

Nathan continued to hold Sara for a few more minutes. His irritation got the better of him then. "God, wife, aren't you through crying yet?"

She mopped her face on the front of his shirt, then eased away from him. "I do try not to cry, but sometimes I can't seem to help it."

"I've noticed," he remarked.

He dragged her over to the bed, shoved her down, and then felt sufficiently calm to give her a firm lecture on the one overriding fear each and every seaman harbored. Fire. He paced the room, his big hands clasped behind his back, while he gave his speech. He was calm, logical, thorough.

He was shouting at her by the time he'd finished. She didn't dare mention that fact to him, though. The vein in the side of his temple throbbed noticeably, and she concluded her husband wasn't quite over his anger.

She watched him pace and shout and grumble, and in those minutes when he was being his surly self she realized how very much she really loved him. He was trying to be so kind to her. He didn't know he was, of course, but there he stood, blaming himself, Jimbo and Matthew, and even God for bringing on the fire because no one had bothered to explain ship life to her.

She wanted to throw herself into his arms and tell him that even though she had always loved him, the feeling had become much more . . . vivid, much more real. She felt such peace, such contentment. It was as though she'd been on a journey all those years while she waited for him and was home at last.

Nathan drew her attention by demanding she answer him. He had to repeat his question, of course, for she'd been daydreaming and had no idea what he'd asked. He only looked a little irritated by her lack of attention, and Sara guessed he was finally getting used to her. God only knew she was getting used to his flaws. The man was all bluster. Oh, his scowl, when set upon her fully, could still give her the hives, but Nora had been right after all. There really was a good, kind man behind the mask.

Nathan finally finished his lecture. When he asked her she immediately gave him her promise that she wouldn't touch anything else on his ship until they were in port.

Nathan was content. After he left the cabin Sara spent long hours scrubbing the mess. She was exhausted by the time she'd changed the bedding and had her own bath, but she was determined to wait up for her husband. She wanted to fall asleep in his arms.

Sara pulled her sketch pad from the trunk, sat down at the table, and drew a picture of her husband. The paper didn't seem big enough to accommodate his size. She smiled over that fanciful notion. He was just a man. Her man. The likeness was remarkably well done, she thought, though she refused to put a frown on his face. She'd captured his Viking stance, too, with his muscular legs braced apart and his hands settled on his hips. His hair flowed down behind his neck, and she wished she had her colors so she could show the magnificence of his auburn hair and his beautiful green eyes. Perhaps when they reached Nora's home she could buy new supplies so that she could do a proper sketch of her husband.

It was well after midnight when Nathan came back down to the cabin. Sara was sound asleep. She was curled up like a kitten in the chair. Her long curly hair hid most of her face, and she looked utterly feminine to him.

He didn't know how long he stood there staring at her. God, it felt right to have her close to him. He couldn't understand why he felt such contentment, even admitting that it was a dangerous reaction, for there wasn't any way in hell he would allow a woman to mean more to him than baggage would.

She was simply a means to an end, he told himself. And that was all.

Nathan stripped, washed, then went over to the table. He saw the sketch pad and gently pried it out of her grasp. Curiosity caught him, and he slowly thumbed through the work she'd done. There were a good ten or twelve drawings completed. They were all sketches of him.

He didn't know how to react. The drawings were amazingly well done. She'd certainly captured his size, his strength. But then her mind had taken a fanciful turn, he decided, for damn if he wasn't smiling in every last one of them.

Sara really was a hopeless romantic. The old woman had told him that Sara's head was in the clouds most of the time. He knew that comment wasn't exaggeration.

Yes, his wife was a foolish dreamer. And yet he stood there, lingering over one particular drawing for a long, long while. It was all wrong, of course, but it still held him mesmerized.

The picture showed him from the back, standing on the deck, next to the wheel, looking off into the fading sunset. It was as though she'd sneaked up behind him to catch him unawares. His hands were clasped on the wheel. He was barefoot and shirtless. Only a hint of his profile was visible, just enough to tell that he was supposed to be smiling.

There weren't any scars on his back.

Had she forgotten about them, or had she decided she didn't want to include his scars in her work? Nathan decided the issue wasn't important enough to think about any longer. He had scars, and she'd damn well better accept them. He shook his head over that ridiculous reaction, then lifted Sara into his arms and put her to bed.

Nathan left the trap open so that the cabin would be rid of the lingering smoke, and he stretched out next to her.

She immediately rolled over and cuddled up against his side. "Nathan?"

"What?"

He made his voice as harsh as possible so she'd realize that he didn't want to talk to her.

His message was lost on her. She scooted closer to him and put her hand on his chest. Her fingers toyed with the thick hair until he flattened his own hand on top of hers. "Stop that," he ordered.

She put her head down on his shoulder. "Why do you think I'm having such a difficult time adjusting to ship life?" she asked in a whisper.

He answered her with a shrug that would have sent her flying into the wall if he hadn't been holding her.

"Do you think it might be because I'm not used to running a vessel?"

He rolled his eyes heavenward. "You aren't supposed to run my ship," he answered. "I am."

"But as your wife I should—"

"Go to sleep."

"Help," she said at the very same time.

She kissed the side of his neck. "I'll do much better when we're on land, Nathan. I can run a large household, and—"

"For God's sake, Sara, you don't have to run through your list of accomplishments again."

She stiffened against him, then relaxed. She must have finally decided to obey him, he thought to himself. The woman was going to go to sleep.

"Nathan?"

He should have known better, he told himself. She wasn't going to sleep until she was good and ready.

"What is it?"

"You forgot to kiss me goodnight."

God, she was aggravating. Nathan let out a weary sigh. He knew he wouldn't get any sleep until he gave in to her. His wife could be quite singleminded. She was more nuisance than not, he told himself. At the moment he was hard pressed to think of any redeeming qualities she might possess. Why, she was as stubborn as a mule, as bossy as a mother-in-law, and those were just two of the numerous flaws he'd already noticed.

He did kiss her, though, fast and hard, just to get her to quit nagging him. Damn but she tasted good, he thought. He had to kiss her again. He used his tongue. So did she. The kiss was far more thorough, more arousing.

She squeezed herself up against him. The provocation was too much to resist. She was all soft and feminine. He had to make love to her then. He didn't even make her nag him into doing that duty. She was still a little resistant, though. When he ordered her to take her nightgown off and turned to light the candle she asked him to leave them in darkness. He told her no, that he wanted to watch her, and she turned crimson before trying to hide her body from him by pulling the covers up to her chin.

He tossed the blankets aside and set about the task of wooing the shyness out of her. In no time at all she became quite brazen. She wanted to touch him everywhere with her hands and her mouth. He let her have her way, of course, until he was so hot for her he was shaking with his desire.

Lord, she was the most incredibly giving woman he'd ever touched. There was always such honesty in her reactions, such trust. That worried him. She didn't hold anything back, that sweet temptress of his, and when he finally settled himself between her silky thighs she was wet and hot and begging him to come to her.

He wanted to take it slow and easy, to make each thrust last forever, but she made him forget his good intentions by squeezing him tightly inside her. The sting of her nails drove him wild, and the erotic little whimpers she made soon forced him to let go of his own control.

He spilled his seed into her at the moment she found her own release. He held her close, absorbing her shudders with his own.

The scent of their lovemaking clung to the air between them. The feeling of peace was there, too.

He tried to roll away from her. She wouldn't let him. Her arms were tightly wrapped around his waist. The restraint was puny, but he decided to stay for a few more minutes, until she'd calmed down just a little. Her heartbeat still sounded like a drumbeat, as did his own.

He could feel the wetness on his shoulder, knew she'd cried again. That amused him. Sara always ended up crying when she found her own release. She always screamed, too. His name. She'd excused her behavior by telling him they were tears of joy she wept because she'd never experienced such bliss.

Neither had he, he thought to himself. For the second time that night the realization worried him.

"I love you, Nathan."

That scared the hell out of him. He reacted to her whispered pledge as though he'd just been slashed with a whip. His accommodating body went from warm flesh to cold steel in the space of a heartbeat. She let go of him. He rolled over onto his side away from her. She suddenly found herself staring at his back.

She waited for him to acknowledge her words of love. Long minutes passed before she accepted the fact that he wasn't going to say anything. His snoring helped her come to that conclusion.

She felt like crying. She didn't, though, and found a small victory in that new strength. Then she concentrated on finding something else to be pleased about.

At least he hadn't left the cabin after they'd made love, she thought to herself. She supposed she should be thankful for that. But in truth, she wasn't overly thankful.

She was shivering. Sara rolled away from Nathan's heat and reached for the quilts. When she was finally settled under the blankets she and Nathan were back to back.

She felt lonely, vulnerable. And it was all his fault, she thought to herself. He was the one who was making her feel so miserable. She decided then and there that if it wasn't her sole duty to love him with all her heart, she just might hate him. Lord, he was coldhearted. Stubborn, too. He had to know how much she needed to hear his words of love and yet he refused to give them to her.

He did love her, didn't he? Sara thought about that worry a long while. Then Nathan rolled over and took her into his arms again. He grumbled in his sleep as he roughly pulled her up against his chest. Her hair was caught under his shoulder. His chin rubbed the top of her head in what she thought was an affectionate gesture, and she suddenly didn't mind that he'd forgotten to tell her he loved her.

She closed her eyes and tried to go to sleep. Nathan did love her, she told herself. His mind was just having a little difficulty accepting what his heart already knew . . . had always known, she corrected herself, from the moment they were wed to each other.

In time her husband would realize. Why, it was only because he had such a cranky disposition that it was taking him longer to accept than it would most ordinary husbands.

"I do love you, Nathan," she whispered against his neck.

His voice was gruff from sleep yet tender when he said, "I know, baby. I know."

He was snoring again before she could gather enough nerve to ask him if he'd been pleased by her fervent declaration.

She still couldn't go to sleep. She spent another hour trying to think of a way to make Nathan realize his good fortune in having her for his wife.

The way to Nathan's heart certainly wasn't through his stomach, she decided. He wasn't about to eat anything she prepared for him. The man was distrustful by nature, and her soup had soured him on her cooking skills.

She finally settled on a sound plan. She'd sneak up on her husband by way of his staff. If she could prove her value to the crew, wouldn't Nathan begin to see how wonderful she really was? It shouldn't be difficult to convince the men how goodhearted and sincere their mistress was. Yes, they were a superstitious lot to be sure, but men were only men, after all, and gentle words and kind actions would surely woo their loyalty.

Why, if she really put her mind to the problem she could certainly find a true method to win the men's loyalty in less than a week.

Chapter Nine

They were all wearing cloves of garlic around their necks by the end of the week in an attempt to ward off Lady Sara's mischief.

She'd spent the entire seven days trying to gain their confidence. When she found out why they were wearing the smelly necklaces she was so disgusted with her staff that she quit trying to win them over.

She also quit running back to her cabin whenever they glared at her. She just pretended she hadn't noticed. She wasn't about to let any of them know how upsetting their conduct was to her. She kept her composure and her tears firmly in check.

Only Nathan and Nora knew how she really felt. Sara kept both of them informed about her injured feelings. Nathan did his best to ignore the situation. Nora did her best to soothe her niece.

The problem, of course, was that each minor accident, no matter what the cause, was blamed solely on Sara's very presence. They thought the woman was cursed, and that was

181

that. The minute Chester noticed a fresh wart on his hand he blamed Sara. His hand had brushed against hers, he remembered, when they passed on deck.

How could she reason against such idiocy? Sara put that question to Nathan at least twice a day. His answers never made a lick of sense, though. He either grunted with what she interpreted as true irritation or shrugged with what she knew was total indifference to her plight. He was as sympathetic as a goat, and each time he finished giving her his oblique opinion she kissed him just to be contrary.

By the following Monday Sara didn't think her life could get any bleaker. But then, she hadn't counted on the pirates. They attacked the ship on Tuesday morning.

It started out to be a nice, sunny, peaceful day. Matthew was taking Nora for a stroll along the decks. Nora's arm was linked through Matthew's, and the two of them took turns whispering to each other and laughing like children. The elderly couple had become extremely close over the past weeks. Sara thought Matthew was just as smitten as Nora appeared to be. He had taken to smiling quite a lot, and Nora seemed to be blushing just as often.

When Sara set out on her stroll Jimbo walked beside her. She was never allowed to be alone. She believed it was because her staff had turned so belligerent on her. When she made that comment to Jimbo, though, he shook his head.

"That might be a little part of it," he said, "but the full truth is that the captain doesn't want anything else broken, Sara. That's why you've got yourself a guard trailing you day and night."

"Oh, the shame of it all," Sara cried out.

Jimbo had difficulty holding back his grin. Sara was certainly given to drama. He didn't want her to think he was laughing at her, though. "Now, now, it isn't that terrible," he remarked. "You needn't sound so forlorn."

Sara was quick to rally. Her face heated up, and she let him see her irritation. "So that's how it's to be, is it?" she asked. "A few little mishaps and I'm now condemned by my staff as a witch and condemned by my own husband as a defiler of property? Jimbo, must I remind you that nothing out of the ordinary has happened since the fire, and that was over seven days ago. Surely the men will come to their senses in time."

"Nothing out of the ordinary?" Jimbo repeated. "You cannot be serious, Sara. Have you forgotten Dutton's little mishap, then?"

He would have to bring up that unfortunate incident. Sara gave him a disgruntled look. "He didn't drown, Jimbo."

Jimbo rolled his eyes heavenward. "No, he didn't drown," he agreed. "But it was mighty close."

"And I did apologize to the man."

"Aye, you did," Jimbo said. "But what about Kently and Taylor?"

"Which ones are they?" Sara asked, deliberately feigning ignorance.

"The ones you knocked stupid two days ago when they slipped on the cannon grease you spilled," he reminded her.

"You cannot place the blame for that solely on my shoulders."

"I can't?" he asked. He was eager to hear the excuse she would give to explain away those injuries. "You did spill the grease, didn't you?"

"Yes," she admitted. "But I was on my way to fetch a rag to mop up the mess when those men rushed past me. If they hadn't been in such a hurry to get away from me, they would have stopped, of course, and I could have warned them about the slippery deck. So you see, Jimbo, the blame really belongs on their superstitious shoulders."

The shouted warning of a ship in the distance stopped their conversation. Within a blink of the eye the deck was filled with men running to their posts.

Sara didn't understand what all the commotion was about. Nathan bellowed her name before Jimbo could give her a proper explanation.

"Nathan, I didn't do it," she cried out when she saw him

striding toward her. "Whatever has happened, I swear to you that I had nothing to do with it."

That vehement speech gave Nathan pause. He actually smiled at her before grabbing hold of her hand and dragging her toward their cabin.

"I know you're not responsible," he told her, "though the men will probably blame you all the same."

"What is it they're going to blame me for this time?" she asked.

"We're about to have some unwanted guests, Sara."

"Unwanted?" she whispered.

They reached their cabin. Nathan pulled her inside but left the door open. It was obvious he wasn't planning on staying long. "Pirates," he explained.

The color immediately left her face.

"Don't you dare faint on me," he ordered, though he was already reaching out to catch her in the event she decided not to obey him.

She pushed his hands away. "I'm not going to swoon," she announced. "I'm furious, Nathan, not frightened. Damn if I'll let my staff think I've brought on pirates, too. Make them go away, Nathan. I'm not up to another upset."

They were in for quite a battle, Nathan knew, but he wasn't going to share that information with his wife. In truth, he was worried, for he knew he should have used the faster clipper for their journey. They would never be able to outrun the bastards closing in on them. The *Seahawk* was too bulky and too weighted down to accomplish that feat.

"Give me your promise that you'll be careful," Sara demanded.

He ignored that command. "Matthew took Nora below," he said. "Stay here until he comes for you."

After giving her that order he turned and strode out the doorway. Sara ran after him. He was forced to stop when she threw her arms around his waist. It was either that or drag her up the steps with him. Nathan turned around then, peeling her hands away as he moved. "For God's sake, woman, now isn't the time to demand a good-bye kiss," he roared.

She was about to tell him, no, that certainly wasn't the reason she'd stopped him, but he waylaid her intent by giving her a quick kiss.

When he pulled away she smiled at him. "Nathan, now isn't the time to be . . . romantic," she said. "You have a fight on your hands. Do see to it."

"Then why did you stop me?" he demanded to know.

"I wanted you to promise me you'd be careful."

"You're deliberately trying to make me crazy, aren't you, Sara? It's all a plot to make me lose my mind, isn't it?"

She didn't answer that ridiculous question. "Promise me, Nathan. I won't let go of your shirt until you do. I love you, and I'll worry unless you give me your word."

"Fine," he countered. "I'll be careful. Happy now?"

"Yes, thank you."

She turned and hurried back into her cabin to prepare herself for the coming battle. She rushed over to the desk drawers, intending to find as many weapons as possible. If the pirates were actually successful in breaching the ship, Sara was determined to help her husband any way that she could.

She found two loaded pistols in the bottom drawer and one wickedly sharp dagger in the center slot. Sara tucked the knife into the sleeve of her gown and put the pistols in a blue reticule. She wrapped the strings of the purse around her wrist just as Matthew came charging into the cabin. A loud booming sound echoed in the distance. "Was that one of our cannons or one of theirs?" Sara asked, her voice shivering with her worry.

Matthew shook his head. "It was one of theirs," he answered. "They missed their mark. They aren't close enough to do any damage yet. That's the reason we aren't firing our own cannons, Sara. Come with me now. I've got Nora safely tucked away below the water level. You can wait it out there with her."

Sara didn't argue, knowing full well that Nathan was behind the order, but she felt very cowardly. It didn't seem honorable to her to hide.

It was pitch black in the hull. Matthew went down the rickety steps first. He lifted her over the first rung, explaining that the wood was filled with rot and would be replaced just as soon as he had time for the chore.

When they reached the bottom and turned a sharp corner the soft glow of a single candle led the way to where Nora patiently waited.

Sara's aunt was settled on top of a wooden box. Her bright red shawl was draped around her shoulders. The older woman didn't look at all afraid. "We're about to have an adventure," she called out to her niece. "Matthew, dear, do be careful."

Matthew nodded. "It would be an adventure all right, if we didn't have such precious cargo on board," he announced.

"What precious cargo?" Sara asked.

"I believe he's referring to you and me, dear," Nora explained.

"Aye," Matthew agreed. He started back up the squeaky steps. "Now we've got to defend instead of offend," he added. "It's going to be a first for the crew."

Sara didn't know what he was talking about. It was apparent that Nora did understand, though. Her smile said as much. "What do you suppose Matthew meant by that remark, Aunt?" she asked.

Nora briefly considered telling Sara, then just as quickly discarded the notion. She decided that her niece was too innocent to understand. Sara still saw everything as good or evil. In her idealistic mind there weren't any shades of gray. In time she would come to understand that life wasn't that simple. Then she would be able to accept the fact that Nathan had led a rather colorful life. Nora hoped she would be there when Sara was told she was married to Pagan. She smiled just thinking about her niece's reaction to that news.

"I believe the crew would fight more vigorously if they didn't have to keep us safe," Nora said.

"That doesn't make any sense," Sara argued.

Nora agreed but changed the topic instead of saying so. "Is this where the munitions are kept?"

"I believe it is," Sara answered. "Do you suppose those kegs are filled with powder?"

"They must be," Nora said. "We must watch the candle flame. If a fire started down here—well, I needn't tell you what could happen. Don't let me forget to blow out the flame when Matthew comes to fetch us."

The ship suddenly felt as though it had just let out a giant belch. It shook from aft to stern. "Do you think they hit us with that shot?" Sara asked.

"It certainly felt as though they did," Nora answered.

"Nathan had better finish this quickly. My nerves cannot take such an upset. Nora, you and Matthew have become very close, haven't you?"

"What a time you've chosen to ask me that," Nora said with a little chuckle.

"I just wanted to take our minds off the worry at hand," Sara replied.

"Yes, that might be a good idea. And you're right, Matthew and I have become quite close. He's such a gentle, understanding man. I'd quite forgotten how comforting it is to be able to confide my thoughts and worries in someone who cares about me."

"I care about you, Aunt."

"Yes, dear, I know you do, but it isn't at all the same. You'll understand what I'm saying when you and Nathan become a little closer."

"I fear that day will never come," Sara returned. "Does Matthew confide in you as well?" she asked.

"Oh, yes, often."

"Has he talked about Nathan much?"

"Several times," Nora admitted. "Some things were given in confidence, of course, and so I cannot speak about—"

"Of course you can," Sara interrupted. "I'm your niece, after all, and anything you would tell me wouldn't go any further. You do trust me, don't you, Nora?"

Sara kept up her prodding for another ten minutes or so before Nora finally relented. "Matthew told me all about Nathan's father. Did you ever meet the Earl of Wakersfield?"

Sara shook her head. "It's said that he died when Nathan was just a boy, Nora. I couldn't have been more than a babe. I did hear that he was knighted, though."

"Yes, he was knighted. It was all a sham, though. Matthew told me that the earl actually betrayed his country while he was in service. Yes, that's true, Sara," she added when her niece let out a gasp. "It's a horrifying story, child. Nathan's father was in cahoots with two other infidels, and the three thought they could overturn the government. They called themselves the Tribunal, and as Matthew related the sequence of events to me, they almost pulled off their treacherous scheme. Nathan's father had second thoughts, though. His conscience got him killed before the truth was let out."

Sara was horrified by what she'd just learned. "Poor Nathan," she whispered. "The shame must have been unbearable."

"No, not at all," Nora returned. "You see, no one knows the full truth. It's still believed that the earl was killed in a carriage accident. There hasn't been any scandal. I warn you that if your family got wind of this, they'd use the information to get the prince to overturn your marriage contract."

"Oh, it's too late for that," Sara returned.

"You're being naïve if you believe that it's too late, Sara. The circumstances were so unusual, what with the king not feeling at all well."

"He was daft," Sara whispered.

"And you were only four years old," her aunt whispered back.

"Still, we are living as man and wife now. I don't believe the prince regent would dare overturn—"

"He can dare whatever he wants to dare," Nora argued.

"Your worry doesn't signify," Sara interjected. "I'm not going to tell anyone about Nathan's father, so my parents aren't ever going to find out. I won't even let Nathan know that I know, all right? He'll have to confide in me first."

Nora was appeased. "Do you know I also found out how Nathan's back was injured?"

"I believe someone took a whip to him," Sara returned.

"No, it wasn't a whip," Nora countered. "His back was scarred by fire, not a whip. You only have to look to realize that, child."

Sara felt sick to her stomach. "Oh, God, was it deliberate? Did someone burn him on purpose?"

"I believe so, but I can't be certain. I do know a woman was involved. Her name was Ariah. Nathan met her when he was visiting a foreign port in the east."

"How did Nathan meet this woman?"

"I wasn't given the details," Nora admitted. "I do know that this Ariah has rather loose morals. She dallied with Nathan."

Sara let out a little gasp. "Do you mean to say that Nathan was intimate with this harlot?"

Nora reached out and patted Sara's hand. "Nathan was just sowing his oats, dear, before he settled down. There's no need to get yourself all worked up."

"Do you think he loved her?"

"No, of course he didn't love her. He was already pledged to you, Sara. Nathan strikes me as being terribly sensible. He wouldn't have allowed himself to fall in love with the woman. And I'll wager you my inheritance that when Ariah was finished with him he most likely hated her. Matthew told me that the woman used Nathan to manipulate her other lover. Yes, it's true," she added in a rush when Sara looked disbelieving. "According to Matthew, Ariah was a master at her game. For that reason I do believe Nathan was tortured by her command. Thank the Lord, he was able to escape. It was during a small revolution, you see, and those sympathetic to the anarchists aided him when they released the other prisoners. Then Jimbo and Matthew took over Nathan's care."

"Nathan has certainly had a time of it, hasn't he?" Sara whispered. Her voice shook with emotion. "He must have been very young when that horrid woman betrayed him. I believe he loved her, too, Nora."

"I believe he didn't," Nora countered.

Sara let out a weary sigh. "It would be nice if it was just a dalliance," she said. "And if they did share the same bed, well, he wasn't really being unfaithful to me, because we hadn't started our married life together. You know, it's all beginning to make sense to me now."

"What is beginning to make sense?"

"I hadn't confided this to you before, but I have noticed that Nathan seems to be very concerned with protecting his feelings. Now I think I understand why. He doesn't trust women. I cannot fault him. If your fingers are burned once, you won't put your hand near the fire again, will you?"

"It was a long time ago," Nora replied. "Nathan is a grown man now, Sara, and surely he has sorted all this out in his mind."

Sara shook her head. "How else can you explain his attitude? Nathan doesn't like it at all when I tell him I love him. He stiffens up on me and goes all cold. And he's never once told me he cares for me. He just might still hate all women—except me, of course."

Nora smiled. "Except you?"

"I believe he does love me, Nora. He's just having difficulty knowing that he does."

"Give him time, dear. Men take so much longer to figure things out. It's because they're such stubborn beasts, you see."

Sara was in wholehearted agreement with that remark. "If I ever chance to meet this Ariah woman, I'll—"

"You've a good chance of meeting up with her," Nora

interjected. "She has been living in London for the past year or so. Matthew says she's looking for yet another sponsor."

"Does Nathan know she's in England?"

"I would imagine so," Nora countered.

The noise became too loud for the two of them to continue the discussion. While Nora fretted about the battle Sara worried over the information her aunt had just shared with her.

Another twenty or thirty minutes passed. Then a chilling silence filled the ship. "If I could just see what's happening, I wouldn't be so worried," Nora whispered.

Sara thought that was a fine idea. "I'll just sneak up to the cabin level and see if everything is all right."

Nora was vehemently against that suggestion. The hatch opened in the middle of their argument and the two women fell silent. They both began to pray that it was Matthew coming down to collect them. Yet when no one called down to them they drew the terrifying conclusion that the enemy had indeed taken over the ship. Sara motioned to Nora to squeeze herself into the corner behind a large crate, then turned and blew out the candle. She worked her way over to the side of the steps to wait for her chance to fell the villains.

God, she was scared. That didn't stop her, though. Her first consideration was Nathan. If the enemy really was on board, was her husband dead or alive? She pictured him lying in a pool of blood, then forced herself to block the horrid thought. She wouldn't be any help to her husband if she let her imagination get the better of her.

A bit of light shone down when the hatch was fully opened. It was no thicker than a straight pin, but still enough for Sara to see two men wearing brightly colored scarves on their heads coming down the stairs.

The first pirate missed the weak rung in the steps. The second one didn't. He let out a low blasphemy when he fell through the narrow opening. The man ended up wedged between the slats. His feet dangled below him, and his arms were pinned to his sides.

"What the hell?" the first man muttered when he turned around. "You got yourself trapped, don't you?" he added with a snicker. He was reaching out to pull the board free but came to a sudden stop when he felt a quick breeze brush his face.

The enemy was in the process of turning around again when Sara slammed the butt of her pistol into the back of his skull. She was apologizing when he crumpled to the ground.

He didn't cry out. She did. Then she noticed that he was still breathing, and she immediately calmed down, relieved to see that he wasn't dead.

Sara lifted the hem of her dress and daintily jumped over the fallen man. She hurried up the steps to confront her second victim. The ugly man was squinting up at her with the most astonished look on his face. If he hadn't been staring directly at her, she might have been able to hit him, too. She didn't have the heart for such treachery, though, for the villain was already pinned down and at her mercy, so she ended up tearing a piece of fabric from her petticoat and stuffing the thing into his mouth to keep him from crying out for help. Nora came to her assistance then and helped her tie up the man from arms to feet.

Her aunt seemed to be taking the situation quite well. Sara thought Nora just didn't understand the severity of their circumstance. If men had breached the munitions hold, then others had to be on board, too.

"Look, dear, I've found some rope. Shall I tie up the other gentleman for you?"

Sara nodded. "Yes, that would be a splendid idea. He might wake up at any moment. Do put a rag in his mouth, too. Here, use some of my petticoat. The thing's quite ruined now."

She paused to tear another long strip, then handed it to her aunt. "We wouldn't want him shouting for help, now would we, Nora?"

"We most certainly wouldn't," her aunt agreed.

Sara tried to press one of the pistols into her hands, but her aunt declined the weapon. "You might need both when you save Matthew and Nathan, dear."

"You've certainly placed a burden upon my shoulders," Sara whispered. "I'm not so certain I can save anyone."

"Go along now," Nora ordered. "You have the element of surprise on your side, Sara. I'll wait here until you've finished your task."

Sara would have hugged her aunt farewell, but she was afraid one of the pistols might discharge.

She prayed all the way up to the cabin level. The wardroom area was deserted. Sara was about to look inside her cabin when she heard the sounds of men starting down the steps. She squeezed herself into the triangular corner behind the folded screen and waited.

Jimbo came stumbling down the stairs first. Sara got a good look at her friend by peeking through the seam in the screen. Jimbo had a fair-sized cut in his forehead. Blood trickled down the side of his face. He couldn't wipe the blood away, for his hands were tied behind his back, and he was surrounded by three pirates.

The sight of the injury made Sara forget to be afraid. She was furious.

Sara saw that Jimbo was looking toward the steps. She heard additional footsteps, and then Nathan came into view. Like the shipmate, Nathan had his hands tied behind his back. Sara was so thankful he was still alive, she started shaking. The look on her husband's face made her smile a little, too. He looked downright bored.

She watched him give Jimbo a nod. It was so quick, so fleeting, she knew she would have missed it if she hadn't been watching him so closely. Then Jimbo turned his head just a little toward the screen.

She guessed then that Nathan knew she was hiding there. Sara looked down, saw that the bottom of her dress was half-protruding, and quickly pulled her skirt back.

"Take them inside the cabin," a mean voice ordered.

Nathan was being shoved forward again. He stumbled, turned in what looked like an attempt to keep himself from falling to his knees, and ended up pushing against the corner of the screen. His hands were just a foot or so away.

"Here comes Banger with the grog," another man called out. "We can have us a toast while we see to the killing. Perry, you going to let their captain die first or last?"

While that question was being asked Sara put one of the pistols into Nathan's hands. When he didn't immediately take advantage of the edge she'd given him she gave him a little nudge.

He didn't show any reaction to her prodding. She waited another minute, and when he still didn't fire she remembered his hands were tied.

She recalled the dagger in the sleeve of her gown, too, and immediately went to work cutting through the thick ropes. She accidentally pricked his skin twice. Then Nathan grabbed hold of the blade with his fingers and took over the task.

It seemed that an eternity had passed, yet she knew not even a full minute had actually gone by.

"Where the hell is the captain?" another voice shouted. "I'm wanting my grog."

So they were waiting for their leader before they began their murderous festivities, Sara concluded.

Why was Nathan waiting? His hands were free, but he was acting as though they weren't. He held the knife by the blade, probably so that he would be ready to hurl the thing when the time came. The pistol was in his other hand, pointed to the floor.

He looked ready to do battle, all right, but still he waited. He was squeezing her against the wall. Sara was surprised the hinges to the screen he pressed against hadn't already snapped from his weight.

Nathan was obviously giving her his silent message to stay put.

As if she was in the mood to go anywhere, she thought to herself. Lord, she was getting worried again. Why didn't her husband take over the advantage now? Was he waiting for the number of pirates to double from five to ten before he acted? Sara decided then to give him a little message of her own. She reached around the side of the screen and pinched him in his backside.

He didn't react. She pinched him again. She pulled her hand back when she heard the sound of another man coming down the stairs. It was obviously the leader of the pirates, for one of his men called out to him that it was high time they all had a taste of grog before getting on with their work.

One of the other villains rushed across the wardroom and opened the door to her cabin. He went inside, then came rushing back a scant second or two later. The infidel was holding one of her gowns in his hands. It was her light blue dress, her very favorite, and the filthy man had his hands all over it.

She vowed she'd never wear that gown again.

"We got us a woman on board, Captain," the foul man called out.

Their leader stood with his back to Sara so she couldn't get a proper look at his face. She was a little thankful for that reprieve. His size alone was terrifying enough. The man stood shoulder to shoulder with Nathan.

The captain let out a low, disgusting snicker that made Sara feel as though there were bugs crawling all over her skin. "Find the bitch," he ordered. "When I'm finished with her you men can each take a turn."

Sara put her hand over her mouth to keep herself from gagging.

"Ah, Captain," another man called out, "she'll be dead afore we get our chance."

A round of snickers followed that remark. Sara wanted to weep. She'd heard all she wanted to hear about their foul plans. She pinched Nathan again. Harder. She nudged him, too.

He finally gave in to her request. He moved like lightning. He turned into a blur when he rushed toward the two men standing in front of their cabin door. Yet even as he was moving he threw his knife. The blade found its mark between the eyes of a villain lounging by the steps. The shot from his pistol brought down another infidel.

Nathan slammed his shoulders into the two men blocking the door. The force of the blow sent both infidels inside. Nathan followed them. He made short work of the battle by knocking their heads together.

Jimbo used his head to fell the pirates' leader. His hands were still tied behind his back, and the hit only knocked the captain off balance. He was quick to recover. He clipped Jimbo on the side of his neck and shoved him to the floor. The captain kicked him aside. It wasn't a terribly accurate kick, though, for the leader wasn't really watching what he was doing. His full attention was centered on digging the pistol out of his pocket.

Nathan had just started out the doorway when the leader raised his pistol. There was venom in his voice when he hissed, "You're going to die slow and painfully."

Sara was too outraged to be afraid. She skirted her way around the screen and silently moved to stand directly behind the villain's back. Then she pressed the tip of her pistol against the base of his skull. "You're going to die quick and easy," she whispered.

When the leader felt the touch of cold steel he went as rigid as a day-old corpse. Sara was pleased by that reaction. So was Nathan, she noticed. He actually smiled.

She smiled back. Things weren't looking so very bleak, she thought. Still, she didn't know if she'd be able to kill the man. It was a test she didn't want to fail. Her husband's life was dependent upon her courage, after all.

"Nathan?" she called out. "Would you like me to shoot between the ears or in the neck this time?"

That bluff worked nicely. "This time?" her victim strangled out.

It wasn't good enough, though. He was still pointing his pistol at Nathan.

"Yes, this time, you stupid man," she said. She tried to make her voice sound as mean as possible, and thought she'd succeeded rather well, too.

"What's your preference?" Nathan called out. He deliberately leaned against the side of the doorway, giving the appearance of being very relaxed.

"The neck," Sara answered. "Don't you remember the mess it was cleaning up after the last one? The stains didn't come out for a week. Still, this infidel seems to have a smaller brain. Oh, you decide. I'm ever obedient."

The leader's hand fell to his side, and his pistol dropped to the floor. Sara thought victory was secure, yet before Nathan could get to the man he suddenly whirled around. The back of his fist slammed into her left cheek in an awkward move to knock the pistol out of her hand.

Sara heard Nathan's roar. She staggered backwards, tripped over Jimbo's big feet, and promptly discharged the pistol. A howl of pain followed that sound, and her enemy grabbed at his face.

It seemed to take her a long, long time to fall to the floor. Everything was in slow motion, and her last thought before she let her faint overtake her was a horrifying one. Good God, she'd shot the villain in his face.

Sara awakened a few minutes later. She found herself in bed with Matthew and Jimbo both leaning over her. Matthew held a cold cloth to the side of her face. Jimbo fanned her with one of the charts from Nathan's desk.

Her husband wasn't there. As soon as Sara realized that fact she tossed the coverlet aside and tried to stand up. Jimbo pressed her back down. "Stay put, Sara. You took quite a hit. The side of your face is already swelling up."

She ignored his instructions. "Where's Nathan?" she asked. "I want him here with me."

Before Jimbo could answer her he found himself sitting on the bed. Sara snatched the cold cloth away from Matthew and began to clean the cut in Jimbo's forehead.

"The woman's little, but she's mighty when she's riled, isn't she, Matthew?" Jimbo muttered, trying to sound surly. "Quit your fussing over me," he grumbled.

She didn't pay any attention to that dictate. "Matthew, do you think he's going to be all right? The cut doesn't look overly deep to me, but perhaps . . ."

"He'll be fine," Matthew answered.

Sara nodded. Then she turned the topic back to her other worry. "A husband should comfort his wife when she's been felled," she announced. "Anyone with an ounce of sense would know that. Matthew, go and fetch Nathan. By God, he's going to comfort me, or I'll know the reason why."

"Now, Sara," Matthew interjected, using his soothing tone of voice, "your husband happens to be the captain of this ship, and he's having to see to a few important . . . details right now. Besides, you wouldn't want his company just yet. The boy's in a killing rage."

"Because the pirates boarded his fine ship?"

"Because the bastard struck you, Sara," Jimbo muttered. "You were sleeping, Sara, after that hit, so you didn't get to see your husband's face. It was a sight I won't soon forget. I've never seen him so furious."

"That's nice to know," Sara whispered.

The two shipmates shared a look of true exasperation. Sara ignored the men, for she'd just remembered the mortal sin she'd committed. "Oh, God, I shot their leader in his face," she cried out. "I'm damned to hell now, aren't I?"

"You were saving your husband at the time," Jimbo interjected. "You won't be going to hell, Sara."

"He'll be . . . ugly for the rest of his days," she whispered.

"Nay, Sara, he already was ugly," Matthew told her.

"I wished you'd killed the bastard," Jimbo said. "As it is, you just shot his nose—"

"My God, I shot his—"

"You're getting her all worked up, Jimbo," Matthew muttered.

"Did I shoot that poor man's nose completely off his face?"

"Poor man?" Jimbo scoffed. "He's the devil's own, that one. Do you know what would have happened to you if—"

"The bastard's still got a nose," Matthew interjected. He gave his friend a dark scowl. "Quit worrying her, Jimbo," he ordered before turning back to Sara. "You just put a little hole in his nose, that's all."

"You saved the day, Sara," Jimbo told her then.

That remark did cheer her up considerably. "I did save the day, didn't I?"

Both men nodded.

"Does my staff know I . . ." She quit her question when they nodded again. "Well, then, they can't think me cursed any longer, can they?"

Before either man could answer that question she asked another. "What details did Nathan have to see about?"

"Retaliation," Jimbo announced. "It will be an eye for an eye, Sara. They were going to kill us—"

He never finished his explanation. Lady Sara let out an outraged gasp and ran out of the cabin. Both Jimbo and Matthew chased after her.

Nathan was standing by the wheel. The pirates who'd tried to take over their ship were lined up across the deck. Nathan's men surrounded them.

Sara hurried over to her husband's side. She touched his arm to gain his attention. He didn't look at her but kept his gaze directed on the leader of the pirates standing a few feet away from him.

When Sara looked at the man she instinctively took a step forward. The villain had a rag in his hands and was holding it against his nose. She wanted to tell him she was sorry she'd injured him. She also wanted to remind him that it was all his fault, for if he hadn't struck her, the pistol wouldn't have gone off.

Nathan must have guessed her intention. He grabbed her arm in a hold that stung and literally jerked her up against his side.

"Go back below," he ordered in a soft don't-you-dare-argue-with-me tone of voice.

"Not until you tell me what you're going to do to them," she announced.

Nathan might have been able to soften the truth for his gentle wife's benefit if he hadn't glanced down at her first. As soon as he saw the swelling on the side of her face his rage returned full force. "We're going to kill them."

He turned back to his crew before giving her his order again. "Go back to our cabin, Sara. It will be over in a few minutes."

She wasn't going anywhere. She folded her arms in front of her and stiffened her posture. "You will not kill them."

She'd shouted that command. She'd gained her husband's full attention, too. And his wrath. He looked like he wanted to kill her.

"The hell I won't," he countered in a low growl.

Sara heard several grunts of approval from Nathan's men. She was about to repeat her disapproval, but Nathan took the bluster right out of her when he suddenly reached out and gently touched the side of her face. He leaned down just a little and then whispered, "He hurt you, Sara. I have to kill him."

It all made perfectly good sense to him, and he thought he'd been very reasonable by taking the time to explain his determination to her. She didn't understand, though. The incredulous look on her face indicated as much.

"Do you mean to tell me that you would kill everyone who has ever struck me?" she asked.

He didn't care for the censure in her voice. "Damn right," he muttered.

"Then you're going to have to kill half my family," she blurted out.

Lord, she really shouldn't have said that, she realized. He looked bloody furious again. Yet his voice was surprisingly mild when he gave her his answer. "You give me the names, Sara, and I'll retaliate. I promise you. No one touches what belongs to me."

"Aye, m'lady," Chester bellowed. "We mean to kill every last one of these bastards. It's our right," he added.

"Chester, if you use another blasphemy in my presence, I'll wash your mouth out with vinegar."

She gave the seaman a hard glarc until he nodded, then turned back in time to catch Nathan's grin. "Nathan, you're the captain," she said. "Only you can make this important decision. Since I'm your wife, I should be able to sway you, shouldn't I?"

"No."

Oh, he was a stubborn one, she thought. "I won't have it," she shouted. The urge to stomp his foot was fairly over-whelming. "If you kill them, you're no better than they are. You'll all be villains then, Nathan, and since I'm your wife, I would also be a villain."

"But m'lady, we *are* villains." Ivan the Terrible made that statement.

"We are not villains," Sara announced. "We are all law-abiding, loyal citizens of the crown."

Sara's distress finally penetrated Nathan's fury. He put his arm around her shoulders. "Now, Sara—"

"Don't you dare now-Sara me," she interrupted. "Don't use that condescending tone of voice, either. You aren't going to be able to soothe me into allowing murder."

He wasn't in the mood to soothe or discuss, but he knew he was going to have to get her to go below before he unleashed his anger full force. He thought about ordering Jimbo to drag her down the stairs, then changed his mind and settled on an alternative plan of action. "Democracy will rule in this instance," he announced. "I'll put it to the vote of my men, Sara. Will that appease you?"

He was fully prepared for an argument before she gave in and was quite surprised when she immediately nodded. "Yes, that will certainly appease me."

"Fine," he replied. He turned back to the crew. "All those in favor—"

The hands were already going up into the air when Sara interrupted. "Just one minute, if you please."

"Now what?" Nathan growled.

"I have something to say to my staff before this vote is taken."

"Hell."

"Nathan, did I or did I not save the day?"

That question caught him off guard. Sara pressed her advantage. "Jimbo said I saved the day. Now I would like to hear you admit it, too."

"I had a plan," Nathan began. "But . . . hell, Sara, yes," he added with a sigh. "You saved the day. Happy now?"

She nodded.

"Then go below," he ordered again.

"Not just yet," she replied. She turned and smiled at her staff. She couldn't help but notice how impatient the men looked. That didn't deter her, however. "You all know that I was the one who untied Nathan," she called out. She realized that statement not only sounded like a boast but also made her husband sound a bit incapable. "Though, of course, he would have . . . untied himself if I hadn't beat him to the task, you see, and he did have a plan—"

"Sara," Nathan began in a warning tone of voice.

She quit rambling, straightened her shoulders, and then said, "And I shot the leader, though I'll admit to you that I didn't mean to hurt the man. Now he'll carry a scar for the rest of his days, and that should be enough punishment for anyone."

"It was a paltry hit at best," one of the men called out. "The shot went clean through his nostrils."

"She should have blown his head off," another shouted.

"Aye, she should have blinded him at the very least," yet another called out.

My God, they were a bloodthirsty lot, she thought. Sara took a deep breath and tried again. She waved her hand toward the pirate's leader and said, "That man has suffered enough."

"Yes, Sara," Matthew interjected with a grin. "He'll be thinking of you every time he's wanting to blow his nose."

A hearty round of laughter followed that remark. Then Chester took a threatening step forward. His hands were on his hips when he bellowed, "He won't be thinking about anything much longer. None of them will. They'll all be fish bait if the vote goes the way I'm thinking it will."

The vehemence in his tone unnerved Sara. She instinctively backed away from him until she was literally leaning against her husband's chest.

Nathan couldn't see her face, but he knew she was afraid. Without a thought as to why he was doing so he put his arm across her shoulders. She rested her chin on his wrist.

His touch had taken her fear away. She glared at Chester and said, "Were you born with a sour disposition, sir?"

The seaman didn't have a ready answer for that question and shrugged in reaction.

"All right, then," Sara shouted. "Have your vote." She pushed Nathan's arm away and took a step forward. "Just remember this," she hastily added when the hands shot back up in the air. "I'm going to be very disappointed if any of you vote in favor of death. Very disappointed," she added in a dramatic tone of voice. "If, on the other hand, you vote to toss the villains overboard and let them swim back to their ship, I would be very pleased. Does everyone understand my position?"

She scanned her audience until each man had given her a nod.

"That's it?" Nathan asked. He sounded incredulous. "That's all you have to say to sway the men?"

He actually smiled at her. She smiled back. "Yes, Nathan. You may vote now. I don't think you should be allowed to vote, though."

"Why not?" he asked before he could stop himself.

"Because you aren't thinking straight now."

The look on his face told her he didn't understand. "You see, Nathan, you're still very angry because . . . your dear wife was injured."

"My dear wife?"

She gave him a disgruntled look. "Me."

God, she was exasperating. "I know who the hell my wife is," he grumbled.

"Just leave it to your crew to decide," she prodded.

He agreed just to get her to leave. Sara forced a smile when she picked up her skirt and strolled toward the steps.

"Stay inside your cabin, Sara, until this is finished," Matthew ordered.

She could feel every man's gaze on her. She knew they were all waiting until she was out of sight before going forward with their shameful intentions. Jimbo had even closed the trapdoor to her cabin, she noticed, probably so that the horrid noise wouldn't reach her.

She didn't feel at all guilty for what she was about to do. Her motives were as white as fresh snow. She couldn't let her staff murder the pirates, no matter how dastardly their behavior had been; and once her men rid themselves of their anger they'd be thankful she'd intervened.

Sara stopped when she reached the top step. She didn't turn around. Her voice was very pleasant when she called out to her husband. "Nathan? I won't be waiting in the cabin, but do send someone to tell me how the voting went. I want to know if I should be disappointed or not."

Nathan frowned over that odd request. He knew she was up to something, but he couldn't imagine what she could possibly do to sway the men's minds.

"Where will you be waiting, m'lady?" Jimbo called out.

Sara turned around so that she could see their expressions when she gave her answer. "I'll be waiting in the galley."

It didn't take most of the men any time at all to catch her meaning. They looked horrified. Nathan, she noticed, was grinning at her. She glared back. Then she addressed her staff. "I didn't want to have to resort to such tactics, men, but you've left me with no alternative. The vote had better not disappoint me."

A few of the less astute seamen still didn't understand the hidden threat. Chester fell into that group. "What would you be doing in the galley, m'lady?"

Her answer was immediate. "Making soup."

Chapter Ten

❧

The vote was unanimous. No one wanted Sara to be disappointed. The pirates were tossed overboard and allowed to swim back to their ship.

Nathan did have the last word, however, or rather the last action. He ordered two cannons made ready and took great satisfaction in putting a large hole in the pirates' vessel. When Sara asked what the noise was he told her they were simply emptying the cannons.

The *Seahawk* had suffered damage as well. Most of the repairs that needed to be seen to at once were above the water line. The very same sails Sara had nearly destroyed with her parasol had been sliced in half by one of the enemy's cannon shots.

The crew set about righting as much of the damage as possible. They smiled as they worked—a rarity—and every one of them had tossed his necklace of garlic cloves away. They were feeling safe again, for they believed the curse had been removed.

Their mistress had saved their hides. Why, even sour-tempered Chester was singing her praises.

Sara went with Matthew to fetch Nora from the hold, and it wasn't until the hatch was opened that she remembered the captives trapped below. Nathan waited until Sara had turned to leave the deck, then slammed his fist into the midsection of each man. The loud groans caught Sara's attention, yet when she turned around and asked her husband what the awful noise was he simply shrugged at her and then graciously helped the doubled-over captives to take flight over the rail.

Sara took great delight in retelling the sequence of events to Nora. Her aunt was an appreciative audience of one. She praised her niece for her courage and her cunning.

"I cannot let you believe I was completely courageous," Sara confessed. She stood with her aunt in the middle of the wardroom area. She'd already shown Nora where she'd hidden behind the screen. "I was terrified all the while," she added with a nod.

"That doesn't signify," Nora countered. "You helped your husband. It means all the more because you were afraid and yet you didn't fail him."

"Do you know Nathan hasn't said a word of praise to me?" Sara said. "I hadn't realized that until this very minute. You would think—"

"I would think he hasn't had time to say thank you, Sara, and I doubt he will when he does have the time. He's a bit . . ."

"Stubborn?"

Nora smiled. "No, dear, not stubborn, just proud."

Sara decided he was a little of both. The rush of excitement was over, but Sara's hands started shaking. She felt sick to her stomach, too, and the side of her face was throbbing quite painfully.

She wasn't going to worry Nora, though, and so she kept her aches and pains to herself.

"I know you've heard the whispers comparing you to Nathan's sister," Nora said.

She hadn't heard any such whispers, but she pretended

she had just so that her aunt would continue. Sara nodded and said, "Jade was mistress of this vessel for a long while, and the men were very loyal to her."

"I know their comments must have hurt your feelings, child," Nora said.

"Which comments are you referring to?" Sara asked. "I've heard so many."

"Oh, that you cry all the time," Nora answered. "Jade never cried. She kept her emotions under lock and key, or so Matthew likes to boast. She was extremely courageous, too. I've heard such wonderful stories about the feats she and her men accomplished. But you've heard all that," Nora continued with a wave of her hand. "I'm not bringing up this topic to make you think the men still believe you inferior, Sara. No, quite the opposite is the case now. Why, you've won their hearts and their loyalty today. They won't be making comparisons in future, I'll wager. They've seen you're every bit as courageous as their Jade."

Sara turned to go into her cabin. "I believe I'll have a little rest, Aunt," she whispered. "The excitement has worn me out."

"You do look pale, Sara. It was quite a morning, wasn't it? I believe I'll go find Matthew and, if he isn't too busy, spend a few minutes with him. Then I'm going to have a rest, too."

Sara's light blue walking dress was on the floor of the cabin. As soon as she shut the door behind her and spotted the gown she remembered how the infidel had clutched it in his arms. She remembered all the foul words they'd said, too.

It was finally settling in. The realization of what could have happened made her stomach lurch. "I mustn't think about all the possibilities," she whispered to herself.

Nathan could have been killed.

Sara unbuttoned her gown and took the garment off. Her petticoats, shoes, and stockings came next. She was excruciatingly exact with her task. Her gaze kept returning to the gown on the floor, though, and she couldn't block the memories.

They'd really meant to kill her husband.

Sara decided she needed something to do to take her mind off her fear. She cleaned the cabin. Then she took a sponge bath. By the time she was finished with that task the trembling had eased up just a little.

Then she noticed the dark bruise on the side of her face.

The terror returned full force. How could she ever live without Nathan? What if she hadn't thought to take the pistols with her to the hold? What if she'd stayed below with Nora and hadn't . . .

"Oh, God," she whispered. "It's all a mockery. I'm such a coward."

She leaned over the washstand and stared into the mirror. "An ugly coward."

"What did you say?"

Nathan asked that question. He'd entered the room without making any noise. Sara jumped a foot, then turned to look at him. She tried to hide the right side of her face by pulling her hair forward.

She realized she was crying. She didn't want Nathan to notice, though. She bowed her head and walked toward the bed. "I believe I'll have a nap," she whispered. "I'm very weary."

Nathan blocked her path. "Let me see your face," he ordered.

His hands rested on her hips. Sara's head was still bowed, and all he could see was the top of her head. He could feel her trembling. "Does it hurt, Sara?" he asked, his voice gruff with concern.

Sara shook her head. She still wouldn't look up at him. Nathan tried to nudge her chin up. She pushed his hand away. "It doesn't hurt at all," she lied.

"Then why are you crying?"

The tenderness in his voice made her trembling increase. "I'm not crying," she whispered.

Nathan was getting worried. He wrapped his arms around her waist and pulled her close. What the hell was going on inside her mind now? he wondered. Sara had always been so transparent to him. He never had to worry about what she was thinking. She always told him. Whenever she had a problem or a worry he knew about it immediately. And as soon as she'd blurted out whatever was on her mind she demanded that he fix it.

Nathan smiled to himself. And damn if he didn't always fix it, too, he thought.

"I would like to rest now, Nathan," she whispered, turning his thoughts back to her.

"You will tell me what's bothering you first," he ordered.

She burst into loud tears.

"Are you still not crying?" he asked in exasperation.

She nodded against his chest. "Jade never cries."

"What did you say?"

She wouldn't repeat herself. She tried to move away from him then, but Nathan wouldn't let her. He was more forceful, more determined. He held her secure with one arm and pushed her chin up. His touch was gentle when he brushed the hair away from her face.

When he saw the dark swelling on her cheek his expression turned murderous. "I should have killed the bastard," he whispered.

"I'm a coward."

She blurted out that confession, then nodded vehemently when he looked incredulous. "It's true, Nathan. I didn't realize it until today, but now I know the truth about myself. I'm not at all like Jade. The men are right. I don't measure up."

He was so surprised by her fervent speech that he didn't realize he'd let go of her until she'd turned and hurried over to the bed. She sat down on the side and stared at her lap.

"I'm going to have my nap now," she whispered again.

He was never going to understand her. Nathan shook his

head and tried not to smile. It would injure his wife's feelings if she thought he was mocking her. Sara was pulling her hair over the right side of her face. It was obvious she was embarrassed about the bruise. "I'm not just a coward, Nathan. I'm an ugly one. Jade has green eyes, doesn't she? The men say her hair is as red as fire. Jimbo said she's beautiful."

"Why the hell are we talking about my sister?" Nathan asked. He regretted his gruff tone of voice immediately. He wanted to ease Sara's distress, not increase it. In a much softer voice he said, "You aren't a coward."

She looked up at him so that he could see her frown. "Then why are my hands shaking, and why do I feel like I'm going to be sick? I'm so afraid right now, and all I can think about is what could have happened to you."

"What could have happened to me?" He was stunned by her admission, humbled. "Sara, you were also at risk."

She acted as though she hadn't heard him. "They could have killed you."

"They didn't."

She started crying again. He let out a sigh. This was going to take time, he decided. Sara needed more than just a quick denial. She needed him to touch her.

And he needed to touch her as well. Nathan stripped out of all his clothes but his pants. He'd unbuttoned them and was about to pull them off, but then he decided he didn't want Sara to know what his intent was just yet. It would only turn her attention, and he wanted to address the problem first.

Sara stood up when Nathan sat down. She watched him get comfortable. He leaned against the wood behind the pillows. One leg was stretched out, the other bent at the knee. He pulled her in front of him, then settled her between his legs. Her back rested against his chest, and with prodding her head fell back against his shoulder. Nathan's arm was around her waist. She wiggled her backside against him until she was comfortable. The movement made him grit his teeth. His wife still didn't have any idea how provocative she could be. She didn't realize how quickly she could make him want her.

"Now you don't have to hide your face from me," he whispered. He gently brushed her hair away from the side of her face, leaned down, and kissed the side of her neck. Sara closed her eyes and tilted her head just a little to give him better access.

"Nathan? Did you see how quickly that man turned on me? If the pistol hadn't discharged, I couldn't have defended myself. I don't have the strength. I'm puny."

"You don't have to have strength to defend yourself," he replied.

That remark made absolutely no sense to her. "I hit Duggan, but afterwards my hand stung for the longest time. It was a paltry hit, too. Yes, one must have strength if one is going to—"

"Who's Duggan?"

"The man with Uncle Henry at the tavern the first night we met," Sara explained.

Nathan remembered. He smiled when he pictured the dainty white-gloved fist coming through the window. "You had the element of surprise on your side, but you didn't make a proper fist."

He took hold of her hand and showed her how. "Don't tuck your thumb underneath your fingers. You'll get it broken if you do. Put it here, on the outside, below your knuckles. Now squeeze tight," he ordered. "Let the force of the blow come from here," he added as he rubbed his finger back and forth across the tip of her knuckles. "Put your whole body into the action."

Sara nodded. "If you say so, Nathan."

"You need to know how to take care of yourself," he muttered. "Pay attention, Sara. I'm instructing you."

She hadn't realized she was feeling so insecure with

Nathan until that moment. "Don't you want to take care of me?" she asked.

His sigh parted her hair. "There will be times when I won't be with you," he reasoned. He was trying to be patient with her. "Now then," he added in a brisker tone of voice, "where you hit is just as important as how you hit."

"It is?"

She tried to turn around to look at him. Nathan pushed her head back on his shoulder. "Yes, it is," he said. "The most vulnerable area of a man's body is his groin."

"Nathan, you cannot believe I'd—"

He could hear the blush in her voice. He rolled his eyes heavenward in true exasperation. "It's ridiculous for you to be embarrassed. I'm your husband, and we should be able to discuss anything with each other."

"I don't think I could hit a man . . . there."

"The hell you couldn't," he countered. "Damn it, Sara, you will defend yourself because I command it. I don't want anything to happen to you."

If he hadn't sounded so irritated, she would have been pleased with his admission. Nathan hadn't sounded happy about the fact that he didn't want anything to happen to her, though. Lord, he was a complex man. He pushed and prodded her to do things she didn't know if she could do. "And if I can't hit a man there? Cowards don't defend themselves," she announced. "And I've already admitted that sin to you."

God, she sounded pitiful. Nathan tried not to laugh. "Explain to me why you consider yourself a coward," he ordered.

"I already did explain," she cried out. "My hands are still shaking, and every time I think about what could have happened I'm filled with terror. I can't even look at that gown without feeling sick to my stomach."

"What gown?" he asked.

She pointed to the blue dress on the floor. "That gown,"

she whispered. "One of those villains held it. I want you to throw it overboard," she added. "I'm never going to wear it again."

"All right, Sara," he soothed. "I'll get rid of it. Now close your eyes, and you won't have to look at it."

"You think I'm being foolish, don't you?"

He started to nuzzle the side of her neck. "I think you're experiencing aftermath," he whispered. "It's a natural reaction, that's all. It doesn't mean you're a coward."

She tried to concentrate on what he was saying to her, but he was making it very difficult. His tongue was teasing her ear, and his warm breath was making her warmer. The shivers were easing away, and she was beginning to feel drowsy.

"Do you ever have . . . aftermath?" she asked in a faint whisper.

His hand was caressing the underside of her breast. The rustling of silk against skin was arousing. "Yes," he told her.

"What do you do about it?"

"I find a way to vent my frustration," he answered. He pulled the ribbon free from the drawstring bow at the top of her chemise and then eased the straps down her shoulders.

Sara was feeling relaxed. Nathan's voice was soothing against her ear. She let out a little sigh of pleasure and closed her eyes again.

His hand rested on her thigh. When he began to caress the sensitive skin near the junction of her legs she moved against him restlessly.

His fingers slipped beneath the edge of her chemise, and he slowly began to stoke the fire in her. He knew just how much pressure to exert, just where to touch to drive her wild. She let out a ragged moan when his fingers thrust inside her.

"Easy, baby," he whispered when she tried to stop him. "Don't fight it, Sara. Let it happen."

He held her tight against him and continued his sweet

torture. His fingers were magical, demanding. Sara was soon mindless to everything but finding her release.

"I love the way you respond to me. You get so hot, so wet. It's all for me, isn't it, Sara?"

She couldn't answer him. He was becoming more forceful with his demands and she was coming unglued. She couldn't stop the climax. It happened before she realized it was going to happen. Her hands reached down to hold his hand between her thighs, and she tightened around him by drawing her knees up and squeezing him tight.

It was a shattering orgasm. Sara went limp from the wonder of it. She fell back against her husband's chest in blissful surrender.

As soon as her heartbeat slowed a little and she was able to catch a thought she became embarrassed. Her chemise was down around her waist, and Nathan was gently caressing her breasts.

"I didn't know that I could . . . that is, without you inside me, I didn't think it was possible. . . ." She couldn't go on.

"I was inside you," he whispered. "My fingers were, remember?"

He turned her around until she was on her knees facing him. God, he was sexy. Her breath caught in her throat, and she suddenly realized she wanted him again. Her gaze held his as she pushed the chemise down over her thighs.

She leaned forward until her breasts were pressed against his chest. He was already pulling his pants off. It was awkward, but in seconds they had both tossed their garments aside. Sara was once again kneeling between her husband's legs. She held his gaze as she reached down to touch him. His low groan told her he liked that boldness.

Then his hands were fisted in her hair, and he was pulling her toward him. "This, Sara, is how you get rid of the aftermath," he whispered. His mouth claimed hers, cutting off any reply she might have made. Sara didn't mind. He was, after all, instructing her, and she was his ever-attentive student.

They spent another hour together before Nathan went back to directing the repairs. Sara did a lot of sighing as she dressed. She collected her charcoals and her sketch pad and went up on deck to sit in the afternoon sun.

In little time the work had ceased, and she was surrounded by men who wanted her to draw their likenesses. Sara was happy to accommodate the men. They praised her work, and their disappointment seemed sincere when she'd used the last paper and had to quit.

Nathan was up on the spar deck, helping to strengthen one of the smaller sails that had been knocked loose when the cannon had hit. He finished that chore and then turned to go back to the wheel.

He paused when he spotted his wife. She was sitting on the wooden ledge below him. At least fifteen of his men were sitting on the deck by her feet. They seemed to be extremely interested in what she was saying to them.

Nathan moved closer. Chester's voice reached him. "Do you mean to say you were only four when you wed the captain?"

"She just explained it all to us, Chester," Kently muttered. "It were by the daft king's demand, weren't it, Lady Sara?"

"Do you wonder why the king wanted to end the feud?" Ivan asked.

"He wanted peace," Sara answered.

"What caused the rift in the first place?" another asked.

"No one can recall," Chester guessed.

"Oh, I know what caused the disagreement," Sara said. "It was the cross of gold that started the feud."

Nathan leaned against the post. He smiled even as he shook his head. So she believed that nonsense, did she? Of course she did, he thought to himself. It was a fanciful story, and Sara would certainly believe it.

"Tell us about this cross of gold," Chester asked.

"Well, it began when a Winchester baron and a St. James baron went on a crusade together. The two men were good friends. This was back in the early middle ages, of course, and everyone was out to save the world from infidels. The two barons' holdings were adjacent to each other, and the story has it that they grew up together in King John's court. I don't know if that was true or not, though. Anyway," she added with a shrug, "the two friends went to a foreign port. One of them saved the life of the ruler there, and in return he was given a gigantic cross made all of gold. Yes," she added when the men looked so impressed, "it was encrusted with large stones, too. Some were diamonds, others rubies, and it was said to be quite magnificent."

"How big was it said to be?" Matthew called out.

"As big as a full-grown man," Sara answered.

"But what happened then?" Chester asked. He was eager to hear the rest of the story and didn't like the interruptions.

"The two barons returned to England. Then the cross suddenly disappeared. The Winchester baron told everyone who would listen that he'd been given the cross and that the St. James baron had stolen it. The St. James baron gave the very same story."

"It weren't ever found, m'lady?" Kently asked.

Sara shook her head. "War broke out between the two powerful barons. Some say there never was a cross, and that it was used only as an excuse to gain the other's land. I believe the cross exists."

"Why?" Chester asked.

"Because when the St. James baron was dying he was said to have whispered, 'Look to the heavens for your treasure.'"

She nodded after making that statement. "A man doesn't lie when he's about to meet his Maker," she instructed. "Directly after saying those words he clutched his heart and dropped dead."

Her hand moved to her bosom, and she bowed her head. Some of the men started to applaud, then stopped themselves. "You aren't believing this story, are you, Lady Sara?"

"Oh, yes," she answered. "One day Nathan's going to find the cross for me."

Nathan thought his wife was a hopeless dreamer. He smiled, though, for he suddenly realized he liked that flaw in her.

"Sounds like the captain will have to go to heaven to find it," Chester said.

"Oh, no," Sara argued. "It was just a little clue the baron was giving when he said 'Look to the heavens.' He was being cunning."

The talk continued for a few more minutes. A storm was brewing, however, and the wind soon became too high to ignore. Sara went back to her cabin to put her charcoals away. She spent the remainder of the day with her Aunt Nora, but by nightfall Nora was yawning like an infant, and Sara took her leave so that her aunt could get her needed rest. The events of the long day had clearly worn her out.

In truth, Sara was just as exhausted. She started having the telltale back pains while she readied herself for bed. The pain was a sure indication that she was about to start her monthly.

An hour later the cramps came on with a vengeance. They were much worse than usual. She was in too much pain to worry that Nathan might find out about her condition. She was freezing, too. The pain did that to her, and it didn't matter at all that it was warm and humid inside the cabin. She was still chilled through to the bone.

She put on her heavy white cotton sleeping gown, then crawled into bed and covered herself with three quilts.

She couldn't get comfortable no matter what position she tried. Her lower back felt as though it had been broken in half, and the agony soon made her start whimpering.

Nathan didn't come down to the cabin until the night watch had changed. Sara usually left a candle burning for him, but the room was pitched into darkness.

He heard her groan. He quickly struck two candles and hurried over to the bed.

He still couldn't see her. She was cocooned beneath a mound of covers.

"Sara?"

His alarm was obvious in his tone of voice. When she didn't immediately answer him he jerked the covers away from her face.

Fear made him break out in a cold sweat. Her face was as white as the sheets. Sara pulled the covers back over her head.

"Sara, what in God's name is the matter?"

"Go away, Nathan," she whispered. Her voice was muffled by the quilts, but he understood her all the same. "I don't feel well."

She sounded near death. His worry intensified. "What's the matter with you?" he demanded in a rough whisper. "Does your face hurt now? Damn, I knew I should have killed that bastard."

"It isn't my face," she cried out.

"Is it fever, then?" He jerked the covers away again.

Oh, God, she couldn't explain her condition to him. It was too humiliating. She let out another low groan and rolled onto her side, away from him. Her knees were pulled up against her stomach, and she began to rock back and forth in an attempt to ease the pain in her back. "I don't want to talk about it," she said. "I just don't feel well. Please go away."

He wasn't about to do any such thing, of course. He put his hand on her forehead. It was cool, though damp, to his touch. "It isn't fever," he announced with an added grunt of relief. "God, Sara, I didn't hurt you this afternoon, did I? I know I was a little . . . rough, but—"

"You didn't hurt me," she blurted out.

He still wasn't convinced. "You're certain?"

She was warmed by his obvious worry. "I'm certain. You didn't cause this illness," she added. "I just need to be alone now."

A cramp claimed her full attention then. She let out a low moan, then added, "Let me die in peace."

"The hell I will," he muttered. Another black thought

gave him the chills. "You didn't make anything when you were in the galley, did you? You didn't eat something you prepared?"

"No. It isn't stomach upset."

"Then what the hell is it?"

"I'm not . . . clean."

He didn't know what in God's name that was supposed to mean. "You're sick because you aren't clean? Sara, that's got to be the most illogical illness I've ever heard of. Will you feel better if I order a bath made ready for you?"

She wanted to scream at him yet knew the effort would cost her more pain. "Nathan, it's a . . . woman's condition," she whispered.

"A what?"

Lord, he was going to make her spell it out for him. "I'm having my monthly," she shouted. "Oh, I hurt," she added in a whimper. "Some months are worse than others."

"You're having your monthly . . ."

"I'm not pregnant," she blurted out at the same moment. "Please go away now. If God is truly merciful, I'll die in just a few more minutes . . . if not from the pain, then from the shame of having to explain my condition to you."

He was so relieved she wasn't suffering from a life-threatening ailment, he let out a ragged sigh. Then he reached out to pat her shoulder. He pulled back before actually touching her, though. Damn, he felt awkward. Inadequate, too.

"Is there anything I can do to ease your pain?" he asked. "Do you want something?"

"I want my mother," she muttered. "But I can't have her, can I? Oh, just go away, Nathan. There isn't anything you can do."

She pulled the covers back over her face and let out another pitiful moan. Nathan must have decided to let her have her way, she decided when she heard the door shut. She burst into tears then. How dare he leave her when she was in such agony? She'd lied when she said she wanted her mother. She wanted Nathan to hold her, and the obstinate man should have been able to read her mind and know that was what she needed.

Nathan immediately went to Nora's cabin. He didn't bother to knock. As soon as he threw the door open a deep voice called out, "Who's there?"

Nathan almost smiled. He recognized Matthew's booming voice. The seaman was obviously sharing Nora's bed. "I have to talk to Nora," he announced.

Sara's aunt came awake with a start. She let out a gasp and pulled the covers up to her chin. Her blush was as high as the candle flame.

Nathan walked over to the side of the bed and stood there with his hands clasped behind his back, staring at the floor.

"Sara's ill," he announced before Nora could say a word.

Nora's embarrassment over being found in such a compromising position quickly faded in the light of that announcement.

"I must go to her," she whispered. She struggled to sit up. "Do you know what the ailment is?"

"Do you want me to have a look at her?" Matthew asked in a rush. He was already tossing the covers aside.

Nathan shook his head. He cleared his throat. "It's this . . . woman's thing."

"What woman's thing?" Matthew asked, genuinely perplexed.

Nora understood. She patted Matthew's hand but kept her gaze on Nathan's face. "Is she in much pain?"

Nathan nodded. "She's in terrible pain, madam. Now tell me what I can do to help her."

Nora thought he sounded very like a military commander, so brisk was his tone of voice. "A stiff drink of brandy sometimes helps," Nora suggested. "A gentle word wouldn't hurt either, Nathan. I remember becoming very emotional during that time of month."

"Isn't there anything else I can do for her?" Nathan muttered. "My God, Nora, she's in pain. I won't have it."

With extreme effort Nora was able to contain her smile. Nathan looked like he wanted to kill someone. "Have you asked her what might help?"

"She wanted her mother."

"How would that help?" Matthew asked.

Nora answered, "She needs her husband, dear. Nathan, she wants someone to comfort her. Try rubbing her back."

Nora had to raise her voice to give that last suggestion, for Nathan was already striding out the doorway.

As soon as the door closed behind him Nora turned to Matthew. "Do you think he'll tell Sara that you and I—"

"No, my love, he wouldn't say a word," Matthew interjected.

"I hate to deceive Sara, but she does tend to see everything in black or white. I don't think she'd understand."

"Hush now," Matthew soothed. He kissed Nora and pulled her into his arms. "Age will season her."

Nora agreed. She changed the topic then and whispered, "Nathan is beginning to care for Sara, isn't he? It won't be long before he realizes he loves her."

"He may love her, Nora, but he won't ever admit it. The boy learned a long time ago to protect himself against any true involvement."

Nora snorted over that remark. "Nonsense," she countered. "Given an ordinary woman, perhaps you would be right, Matthew, but surely you've noticed by now that my Sara isn't ordinary. She's just what Nathan needs. She thinks her husband loves her, and it won't take her long to convince him that he does. Just wait and see."

Sara didn't have any idea she was the topic of discussion. She was in the throes of self-pity.

She never heard Nathan come back into the cabin. He was suddenly touching her shoulder. "Sara, drink this. It will make you feel better."

She rolled over, saw the goblet in his hands, and immediately shook her head.

"It's brandy," he told her.

"I don't want it."

"Drink it."

"I'll throw up."

She couldn't be any blunter than that, he supposed. He hastily put the goblet on the desk and then got into bed beside her.

She tried to push him out. He ignored her struggle and her demands.

Sara rolled back onto her side again, facing the wall. She might as well pray for death, she supposed. It was an overly dramatic request she gave her Maker, and in the back of her mind she really hoped He wasn't listening, and that thought didn't make a lick of sense to her either.

She couldn't take the pain much longer. Then Nathan put his arm around her waist. He pulled her a little closer to him and began to rub her lower back. The gentle touch was heaven. The ache immediately began to lessen. Sara closed her eyes and scooted closer to her husband so that she could steal a little more of his warmth.

She barely noticed the rocking and pitching motion of the ship. Nathan noticed. His own stomach was in torment, and he wished to God he hadn't eaten anything. It was only a matter of time before he would turn completely green.

He kept rubbing her spine for fifteen minutes or so without speaking a word to her. He tried to concentrate on the woman cuddled up against him, but each time the ship rolled, so did his stomach.

"You can stop now," Sara whispered. "I'm feeling better, thank you."

Nathan did as she requested, then started to get out of bed. She waylaid that intent with her next request. "Will you hold me, Nathan? I'm so cold. It's chilly tonight, isn't it?"

It was as hot as blazes to him. His face was drenched in perspiration. He did as she asked, though. Her hands felt like ice, but in just a few minutes he'd hugged her warm again.

He thought she was finally asleep and was just easing himself out of her hold when she whispered, "Nathan? What if I'm barren?"

"Then you're barren."

"Is that all you can say? We can't have children if I'm barren."

He rolled his eyes heavenward. God, she sounded like she was going to cry again. "You can't possibly know if you're barren or not," he said. "It's too soon to jump to that conclusion."

"But if I am?" she prodded.

"Sara, what do you want me to say?" he asked. His frustration was almost visible. His stomach lurched again. Deep breaths weren't helping. He tossed the covers aside and tried to leave the bed again.

"Would you still want to be married to me?" she asked. "We won't get the land the king promised if I don't have a baby by the time—"

"I'm aware of the conditions of the contract," he snapped. "If we don't get the land, then we'll rebuild on the land my father left to me. Now quit your questions and go to sleep. I'll be back in a little while."

"You still haven't answered me," she said. "Would you still want to be married to a barren woman?"

"Oh, for God's sake—"

"You would, wouldn't you?"

He grunted. She took that sound to mean he would. She rolled over and kissed his back. He'd left the candles burning, and when she looked up at his face she saw how gray his complexion had turned.

She was quick to put two and two together. The ship was bouncing like an errant ball in the water. The goblet of brandy was pitched to the floor. Nathan closed his eyes and grimaced.

He was seasick. Sara was filled with sympathy for her poor husband, but that emotion was quickly squelched when he muttered, "I wouldn't be married to anyone if it wasn't for the damned contracts. Now go to sleep."

After grumbling out that remark he swung his legs over the side of the bed.

Sara was suddenly furious again. How dare he take that tone of voice with her? She was just as ill as he was, perhaps even more. She forgot all about the gentle way he'd treated her and decided to teach the man a lesson he wouldn't soon forget.

"I'm sorry I'm keeping you from whatever business you have to attend to," she began. "My back is feeling much better now, Nathan. Thank you. My stomach isn't upset either. I suppose I shouldn't have had that fish for supper. It tasted wonderful, though, especially when I put a little dab of chocolate on top. Have you ever tasted fish sweetened that way? No?" she asked when he didn't answer her.

He seemed to be in quite a hurry to get his pants back on. Sara held her smile. "I usually just put sugar on top, but I wanted to experiment tonight. By the way, the cook has promised to serve us oysters when we reach port. I love oysters, don't you? The way they sort of . . . slide down your throat . . . Nathan, aren't you going to kiss me good-bye?"

The door slammed shut before she'd finished her question. Sara smiled. She gained tremendous satisfaction from her sinful actions. It was high time her husband realized his good fortune in having her for his wife. High time indeed.

"Serves him right for being so obstinate," she muttered to herself. She pulled the covers up over her shoulders and closed her eyes. She was sound asleep in minutes.

Nathan spent most of the night hanging over the side of the ship. He'd gone to the usually deserted area, and no one paid him any attention.

The sun was easing up into the sky when he returned to the cabin. He felt as wrung out as a wet sail. He literally collapsed on the bed. Sara was bounced awake by that action. She rolled over and cuddled up against her husband's side.

He started snoring so she wouldn't start talking again. Sara leaned up and kissed the side of his cheek. In the soft candlelight she could see how pale he was. He was in dire need of a shave, too. He looked fierce with the dark shadow along his jawline. Sara reached up to touch the side of his cheek with her fingertips. "I love you," she whispered. "Even with all your flaws, Nathan, I still love you. I'm sorry I deliberately made you seasick. I'm sorry that you suffer from such an ailment."

Satisfied with her confession, especially because she knew he hadn't heard a word of what she'd just said, she rolled away from him. Her sigh was loud. "I do believe you should consider another line of work, husband. The sea doesn't seem to suit you."

He slowly opened his eyes, then turned to look at her. She appeared to be asleep again. She looked damned peaceful to him. Angelic.

He wanted to throttle her. His wife had somehow found out about his illness and had deliberately used that knowledge to get even with him. She must have taken exception to his remark about not being married at all if it weren't for the contracts.

His flash of anger dissipated in little time, and he found himself smiling. Little Sara wasn't such an innocent after all. She'd done exactly what he would have done if he'd had such a weapon at his disposal and wasn't strong enough to physically retaliate.

When he was angry he liked to use his fists. She used her head and it pleased him. Still, it was high time she understood just who was in charge of the marriage. High time indeed. She wasn't supposed to use cunning on him.

And Lord, she looked lovely. He suddenly wanted to make love to her. He couldn't, of course, because of her delicate condition, and he almost shook her awake to ask her how long this woman's thing lasted.

Exhaustion finally overcame him. Just as he was drifting off to sleep he felt Sara take hold of his hand. He didn't pull away. His last thought before falling asleep was a bit unsettling.

He needed her to hold him.

They were just two days away from Nora's home, and Nathan was once again beginning to think that the rest of the voyage might prove uneventful.

He should have known better.

It was late evening on the twenty-first of the month. There were more stars than sky above, and the breeze was every bit as pretty by a seaman's measure. The wind was gentle, yet coaxingly insistent. They were making good time—a clipping speed, in fact. The mighty ship set straight in the water and cut directly through the ocean without rocking or lurching to either side. A man could put a keg of grog on the rail without fear of losing it, so calm was the sea, and there was nary a worry to annoy a seaman's dreams.

Nathan stood next to Jimbo behind the wheel. The two men were in deep discussion over the plans to expand the Emerald Shipping Company. Jimbo was in favor of adding additional clippers to their fleet, while Nathan favored heavier, more durable ships.

Sara interrupted their conversation when she came rushing across the deck. She was dressed only in her nightgown and wrapper. Jimbo noticed that right away. Nathan's back was to his wife, however, and because she was barefoot he didn't hear her approach.

"Nathan, I must speak to you at once," she cried out. "We have a horrible problem, and you must take care of it right away."

Nathan had a resigned look on his face when he turned around, but that expression faltered as soon as he saw the pistol in his wife's hand. The weapon, he couldn't help but notice, was pointed at his groin.

Sara was in a high fit about something. She looked a sight. Her hair was in wild disarray around her shoulders, and her cheeks were bright.

Then he noticed her state of attire. "What are you doing strutting around the deck dressed in your nightclothes?" he demanded.

Her eyes widened over his rebuke. "I wasn't strutting," she began. She stopped herself with a shake of her head. "This isn't the time to lecture me about my attire. We have a serious problem, husband."

She turned her attention to Jimbo. The pistol made her curtsy awkward. "Please forgive my unladylike appearance, Jimbo, but I've had quite an upset, I can tell you, and I didn't take time to dress."

Jimbo nodded even as he dodged the pistol she was waving back and forth between Nathan and him. He didn't think she realized she was holding the weapon.

"You've had an upset?" Jimbo prodded.

"What in God's name are you doing with that pistol?" Nathan demanded at the same time.

"I might have need for it," Sara explained.

"Lady Sara," Jimbo interjected when Nathan looked as if he was at a loss for words, "calm yourself and tell us what has you so upset. Boy," he added in a growl, "get that damn pistol away from her before she shoots herself."

Nathan reached out to take the weapon from her hand. Sara backed up a space and put the pistol behind her back. "I went to see Nora," she blurted out. "I just wanted to say goodnight to her."

"And?" Nathan asked when she didn't continue.

She stared at Jimbo a long minute before deciding to include him in her explanation, then glanced over her shoulder to make certain no one else was within hearing distance. "She wasn't alone."

She'd whispered that statement and waited for her husband's reaction. He shrugged.

She wanted to shoot him. "Matthew was with her." She nodded vehemently after telling that news.

"And?" Nathan prodded.

"They were in bed together."

She waved the pistol again. "Nathan, you have to do something."

"What would you like me to do?"

He sounded very accommodating, but he was grinning. The man wasn't at all surprised by the news she'd just given him. She should have guessed he'd react that way. Nothing ever seemed to upset him . . . except her, of course. She always upset him, she admitted.

"She wants you to make Matthew leave," Jimbo interjected. "Isn't that right, Sara?"

She shook her head. "It's a little late to shut the barn door, Jimbo. The cow's already out."

"I'm not getting your meaning," Jimbo returned. "What do cows have to do with your aunt?"

"He dishonored her," she explained.

"Sara, if you don't want me to make Matthew leave Nora alone, just what do you think I should do?" Nathan asked.

"You have to make it right," Sara explained. "You're going to have to marry them. Come along with me, husband. We might as well get it done right away. Jimbo, you can serve as witness."

"You can't be serious."

"Quit your smile, husband. I'm very serious. You're captain of this vessel, so you can legally marry them."

"No."

"Lady Sara, you do come up with the most astonishing suggestions," Jimbo said.

It was obvious to her that neither man was taking her seriously. "I'm responsible for my aunt," Sara said. "Matthew has blemished her honor, and he must marry her. You know, Nathan, this will really solve another worry. My Uncle Henry won't come chasing after Nora for her inheritance once she's remarried. Yes, this could have a happy ending, to my way of thinking."

"No." Nathan's voice was emphatic.

"Sara, does Matthew want to marry Nora?"

She turned to frown at the seaman. "It doesn't matter if he wants to or not."

"Aye, it does," Jimbo argued.

She started waving the pistol around again. "Well, I can see I won't be getting any help from either of you."

Before the two men could agree with that statement Sara whirled around and started for the steps again. "I do like Matthew," she muttered. "It's a shame."

"What are you thinking to do, Lady Sara?" Jimbo called out.

She didn't turn around when she called out her answer. "He's going to marry Nora."

"And if he doesn't?" Jimbo asked, smiling over the matter-of-fact way she'd made that announcement.

"Then I'm going to shoot him. I won't like it, Jimbo, but I'll have to shoot him."

Nathan was right behind Sara. He put his arm around her waist, hauled her up against him, then reached over her shoulder and grabbed hold of the pistol. "You aren't going to shoot anyone," he told her in a low growl.

He handed the pistol to Jimbo, then dragged Sara down to their cabin. He shut the door behind him and continued on toward the bed.

"Unhand me, Nathanial."

"Don't ever call me Nathanial," he ordered.

She pushed away from him and turned to look at his face. "Why can't I call you by your given name?"

"I don't like it, that's why," he told her.

"That's a stupid reason," she argued. She put her hands on her hips and frowned at him. Her wrapper opened, and he was given a healthy view of her full breasts pressed against the thin nightgown.

"Sara, when is this condition of yours going to be over?" he asked.

She didn't answer that question but nagged him back to the topic of his name. "Why don't you like being called Nathanial?"

He took a threatening step forward. "I see red whenever I hear it, Sara. It puts me in a fighting mood."

That wasn't really a suitable explanation, but she wasn't about to point that out to him. "When aren't you in a fighting mood, husband?" she asked.

"Don't bait me."

"Don't yell at me."

He took a deep breath. It didn't calm him one bit.

She smiled. "All right," she whispered in a bid to placate him. "I won't ever call you Nathanial . . . unless I want you in a fighting mood. You'll know to be on your guard, husband. Agreed?"

He thought those comments were too ignorant to answer. He'd backed her over to the side of the bed. "Now it's your turn to answer me, Sara. When is this damned woman's thing finished?"

She slowly removed her robe. She took her sweet time folding the garment. "You aren't going to do anything about Nora and Matthew, are you?" she asked.

"No, I'm not," he answered. "And neither are you. Leave them alone. Do you understand me?"

She nodded. "I'm going to have to think about this long and hard, husband."

Before he could make a stinging remark about her ability to think much at all she pulled her nightgown up over her head and tossed it on the bed. "I have finished this damned woman's thing," she whispered shyly.

She was trying to be bold, but the blush ruined that effect. Nathan was making her feel awkward because of the way he was looking at her. His hot stare made her toes tingle. She let out a sigh and then moved forward into his arms.

He made her kiss him first. She was in an accommodating mood. She put her arms around his neck and tugged on his long hair to bring his mouth down to hers.

And Lord, did she kiss him. Her mouth was hot, her tongue wild, and it didn't take her any time at all to get the response she wanted.

Nathan took over then. He held her captive by making a fist in her hair, then slowly lowered his head again. His open mouth settled on hers, and his tongue thrust deep inside to mate with hers. Her breasts were pressed against his bare chest, and her arms were wrapped tightly around his waist.

He let out a low growl when she sucked on his tongue, so she did it again. The sound he made was as arousing to her as his kiss, and she couldn't seem to get close enough to him.

He pulled away to remove his clothes but stopped when she began to nibble on the side of his neck. He shuddered in reaction. His hands stroked her smooth shoulders. The feel of her silky skin against his rough, callused palms made him realize once again how very fragile she was. "You're so delicate," he whispered. "And I'm . . ."

He couldn't retain his thought, for she was making him forget everything but feeling. She kissed every inch of his chest. Her tongue tickled his sensitive nipples. When he gruffly ordered her to cease her torment she doubled her efforts to drive him beyond the brink of sanity.

She was forced to stop when he pulled on her hair and shoved the side of her face against his chest. He was taking deep, gulping breaths. Then her fingers circled his navel. He quit breathing. She smiled. "You make me feel so warm, so alive, so very strong. I want to show you how much I love you, Nathan. Will you let me?"

He understood her intent when she began to unbutton his pants. Her hands shook. Then she slowly disengaged herself from his embrace and knelt down. Nathan didn't remember much after that. His delicate little wife had turned into a blaze of sensuality. She was like the sun, scorching him with her soft mouth, her wet tongue, her incredibly arousing touch.

He couldn't take the sweet agony long. He wasn't very gentle when he pulled her up and lifted her high off the ground. He forced her legs around his waist as he captured her mouth for a long, intoxicating kiss.

"God, Sara, I hope you're ready for me," he whispered on a low groan. "I can't wait any longer. I have to be inside you. Now. Then I'll be able to slow down, I promise."

He tried to shift positions, but she pulled on his hair. "Nathan, tell me you love me," she demanded.

He answered her by kissing her again. Sara soon forgot all about wanting to hear his declaration of love. Her nails dug into his shoulder blades, and all she could think about was finding fulfillment.

His hands gripped the sides of her hips, and he began to ease slowly inside her.

Her head fell back. She let out a low whimper. "Please hurry, Nathan."

"I want to drive you crazy first," he ground out. "Like you drive me . . ."

She bit his neck. He thrust deep. He was shaking as much as she was. She squeezed him tight. He groaned with pleasure.

He braced their fall onto the bed with his knee, then covered her completely. His hands cupped the sides of her face, and he leaned up on his elbows and gently kissed her forehead, the bridge of her nose, her sweet lips.

"God, you always taste so good," he growled. He nibbled on the side of her neck, teased the lobe of her ear with his tongue, and the last thing he remembered saying to her was that he was going to set the pace this time.

But then she drew her knees up, taking even more of him inside her. She arched up against him. The provocation was too much for him to endure. He felt enveloped by her heat, her intoxicating scent . . . her love.

The bed squeaked with each deep thrust. He wanted their lovemaking to last forever. The fever of passion raged between them. Sara suddenly tightened even more around him. She cried out his name. Her surrender gave him his own. He poured his seed inside her with his last thrust. His deep, guttural growl drowned out their pounding heartbeats.

He collapsed on top of her, too weak to move, too content ever to want to move away from her. His head rested in the hollow of her neck. His breaths were still deep, shaky. So were hers. That fact made him smile inside.

As soon as she loosened her hold on him he rolled to his side. He took her with him for the simple reason that he couldn't seem to let go of her.

She couldn't quit crying.

It was a joyful interlude, but he knew it was just a matter of time before she started nagging him again to give her the words she longed to hear.

He didn't want to disappoint her, yet he wouldn't lie to her. And in the dark recesses of his mind fear took root. What if he wasn't capable of ever giving her what she wanted?

Nathan considered himself the master of the game when it came to hurting people. He'd had quite a lot of experience in that area. Yet when it came to loving someone he didn't have the faintest idea how. Just considering that problem scared the hell out of him. Damn if he'd allow himself to become so vulnerable, he thought. Damn if he would.

She felt him tense against her. She knew what would come next. He'd try to leave her. She wasn't going to let him this time, however, and she vowed that if she had to, she'd even follow him out the door.

How could her husband be so gentle, so giving, so wonderfully considerate when he made love to her and then turn into a statue of ice? What in God's name was going through his mind?

"Nathan?"

He didn't answer her. She expected that rudeness. "I love you," she whispered.

"I know you do," he muttered when she nudged him.

"And?" she persisted.

His sigh was long, drawn out. "Sara, you don't have to love me. It isn't a requirement in this marriage."

He thought he'd been very logical when he'd made that statement of fact. He'd skirted the true issue quite nicely, to his way of thinking.

Sara tried to shove him out of the bed. "You are the most impossible man I've ever known. Listen well, Nathan. I have something to say to you."

"How could I not listen, Sara?" he drawled. "You're screaming like a shrew again."

He did have a point there, she admitted to herself. She had been screaming. She rolled onto her back, pulled the light cover up over herself, and stared at the ceiling. "God's truth, you do frustrate me," she muttered.

He took exception to that remark. "The hell I do," he countered. He blew the candle flame out, then rolled onto his side and roughly pulled her into his arms. "I satisfy you every damned time I touch you."

That wasn't what she meant at all, but he sounded so arrogantly pleased with himself that she decided not to argue. "I still have something important to say to you, Nathan. Will you listen?"

"Will you promise to go to sleep directly after you've said this thing?"

"Yes."

He grunted. She guessed that sound meant he didn't really believe her. She was about to tell him what she thought about his rude behavior when he pulled her even closer to him and gently began to rub her back. His chin rested on the top of her head.

He was being extremely affectionate. Sara was astonished. She wondered if he even realized what he was doing.

She decided she didn't care if he realized or not. The

action was so telling, she couldn't contain the burst of joy that filled her heart.

Just to test him she tried to move away. He tightened his hold. "All right, Sara," he announced. "I'd like to get some sleep tonight. Tell me what's on your mind. Get it done so I can rest."

She couldn't quit smiling. That was quite all right, she told herself, because he couldn't see her expression. He'd pressed her face against the side of his neck. His fingers were gently stroking the hair away from her temple.

She had been quite determined to tell him that he loved her. She'd believed that once she'd told him, he'd realize she was right. Now she didn't want to say anything to ruin the moment. He wasn't ready to acknowledge the truth quite yet.

The revelation had finally settled in her mind. It stunned her a little. Nathan was afraid. She wasn't certain if he was afraid of loving anyone or just afraid of loving her . . . but he was afraid.

Lord, he'd go into a rage if she told him what she was thinking. Men didn't like to hear they were afraid of anything.

"Sara, damn it all, hurry up and get it said so I can go to sleep."

"Get what said?" she countered as her mind raced for a suitable topic to talk about.

"God, you make me daft. You said you had something important to tell me."

"I did," she agreed.

"Well?"

"Nathan, don't squeeze me so tight," she whispered. He immediately let up on his hold. "I seem to have forgotten whatever it was I wanted to tell you."

He kissed her forehead. "Then go to sleep," he instructed.

She snuggled up against him. "You're a fine man, Nathan." She whispered those words of praise and then let out a loud, thoroughly unladylike yawn. "You do please me most of the time."

His deep chuckle warmed her. It wasn't enough, though. "Now it's your turn," she instructed.

"My turn to do what?" he asked. He deliberately pretended not to understand just to prick her temper.

She was too tired to nag him any longer. She closed her eyes and yawned again. "Oh, never mind," she said. "You can have your turn tomorrow."

"You're a fine woman," he whispered. "You please me, too."

Her sigh of pleasure filled the room. "I know," she whispered back.

She fell asleep before he could give her a lecture on the merits of humility. Nathan closed his eyes. He needed rest, for God only knew what tomorrow would bring, with Lady Sara trying her damnedest to run things.

If Nathan had learned anything of value over the past weeks, it was never to expect the usual.

He had believed he would have to protect his wife from the world. Now he knew the truth. It had become his duty to protect the world from his wife.

It was an absurd revelation, of course, but the marquess still fell asleep with a grin on his face.

Chapter Eleven

❧

The day they dropped anchor in the deeper waters surrounding Nora's Caribbean home Sara found out her husband had more than two titles. He wasn't just the Marquess of St. James and the Earl of Wakersfield.

He was also Pagan.

She was so stunned by that bit of news, she literally collapsed on the bed. She hadn't deliberately set out to eavesdrop, but the trap in the ceiling of her room was open and the two seamen were talking rather loudly. It was only when their voices dropped to whisper level that Sara began to pay attention to what they were talking about.

She refused to believe what she heard until Matthew entered the conversation and spoke matter-of-factly about the booty they'd divided from their last raid.

She had to sit down then.

In truth, she was more terrified than horrified by the revelation. Her fear was solely for Nathan, though, and every time she thought about the chances he took when he set out to pirate another ship she got sick to her stomach.

One black thought led to another. She pictured him walking toward the gallows, but only once would she allow herself to imagine that terrible possibility. When the bile rose in her throat and she knew she was about to lose her breakfast she forced herself to stop her black thoughts.

Sara would have been in complete despair if not for the last comment she overheard Chester make. The seaman admitted he was damned happy his pirating days were behind him. Most of the men, he added, were ready to take on family life, and their illegal savings would give them all a nice start.

She was so relieved she started to cry. She wasn't going to have to save Nathan from himself after all. He had apparently already seen the error of his ways. Lord, she prayed he had. She couldn't bear the thought of losing him. She'd loved him for so long, and life without him grunting at her and shouting at her—and loving her—was too devastating to think about.

Sara spent most of the morning worrying about Nathan. She couldn't seem to rid herself of her fear. What if one of his men betrayed her husband? The bounty on Pagan's head was enormous at last posting. No, no, don't think about that, she told herself. The men were a fiercely loyal lot. Yes, she'd noticed that right away. Why borrow trouble? What would happen would happen, no matter how much fretting she did beforehand.

No matter what, she would stand beside her husband and defend him any way that she could.

Had Matthew confided his dark past to Nora? And if so, had he also told her that Nathan was Pagan? Sara decided she would never find out one way or the other. She wasn't about to tell anyone, not even her dear aunt, what she'd learned. That secret was going to go to the grave with her.

When Nathan came down to the cabin to collect his wife he found her sitting on the side of the bed, staring off into space. It was as hot as the inside of a furnace, but Sara was shivering. He thought she wasn't feeling well. Her face was pale, yet the more telling symptom was that she barely spoke a word to him.

His concern intensified when she sat quietly in the rowboat that took them to the pier. Her hands were folded in her lap, her gaze downcast, and she didn't seem to be at all interested in her surroundings.

Nora sat beside Sara and kept up a steady stream of conversation. The elderly woman mopped her brow with her handkerchief and used her fan to cool herself. "It will take a day or two to get used to the heat," she remarked. "By the way, Nathan," she added, "there's a lovely waterfall just a half mile or so from my house. The water comes from the mountain. It's as pure as a baby's smile. There's a gathering pool at the bottom, and you simply must make time to take Sara up there for a nice swim."

Nora turned to look at her niece. "Sara, perhaps now you can learn how to swim."

Sara didn't answer her. Nora nudged her to gain her attention.

"I'm sorry," Sara said. "What did you just say?"

"Sara, whatever are you daydreaming about?" Nora asked.

"I wasn't daydreaming." She stared at Nathan when she made that remark. She frowned, too.

Nathan didn't know what to make of that. "She doesn't feel well," he told Nora.

"I feel perfectly well," Sara countered.

Nora's concern was obvious in her expression. "You've been terribly preoccupied," she remarked. "Is the heat bothering you?"

"No," Sara answered. She let out a little sigh. "I was just thinking about . . . things."

"Any special thing in particular?" Nora prodded.

Sara continued to stare at Nathan. He raised an eyebrow when she didn't immediately answer her aunt.

Nora broke the staring contest when she asked her question once again. "I was suggesting that now would be an excellent time to learn how to swim."

"I'll teach you."

Nathan volunteered for that duty. Sara smiled at him. "Thank you for offering, but I don't believe I want to learn how. There isn't any need."

"Of course there is," he replied. "You'll learn before we leave for England."

"I don't wish to learn," she said again. "I don't need to know how."

"What do you mean, you don't need to know how?" Nathan asked. "You sure as hell do need to know how."

"Why?"

Because she looked so genuinely perplexed, he lost a little of his irritation. "Sara, you won't have to worry about drowning if you know how to swim."

"I don't worry about it now," she countered.

"Damn it all, you should."

She couldn't understand why he was getting so irritated. "Nathan, I won't drown."

That statement gave him pause. "Why not?"

"You wouldn't let me." She smiled.

Nathan braced his hands on his knees and leaned forward. "You're right," he began in a reasonable tone of voice. "I wouldn't let you drown."

Sara nodded. She turned to Nora. "There, do you see, Nora? There really isn't any need—"

Nathan interrupted her. "However," he announced in a louder voice, "what about those times when I'm not with you?"

She gave him an exasperated look. "Then I wouldn't go into the water."

He took a deep breath. "What if you fell into the water by accident?"

"Nathan, this is sounding very like the argument you gave me about defending myself," she said, her voice full of suspicion.

241

"It's exactly the same argument," he countered. "I don't want to have to worry about you. You're going to learn how to swim, and that's the end of this discussion."

"Nora, do you notice how he yells at me all the time?" Sara asked.

"Don't try to draw me into this discussion," her aunt said. "I won't take sides."

Husband and wife lapsed into silence. Not another word was exchanged until they reached the pier.

Sara finally took time to notice her surroundings. "Oh, Nora," she whispered. "Everything is even . . . greener and lusher than I remembered."

The tropical paradise was vibrant with every color in the rainbow. Sara stood on the pier and stared up at the rolling hills in the distance. The sun pierced the palm trees, shining bright upon the multitude of delicate red flowers sprinkling the way to the top of the mountain.

Clapboard houses painted in pastel shades of pink and green, with copper-colored tiled roofs, stood regal against the background of hills overlooking the harbor. Sara wished there was time to take her charcoals and paper in hand and try to capture the God-created canvas. She realized almost immediately that she couldn't possibly duplicate the masterpiece, and she let out a little sigh.

Nathan walked over to stand beside her. The innocent wonder on her face took his breath away.

"Sara?" he asked when he noticed the tears gathering in her eyes. "Is something the matter?"

She didn't take her gaze away from the hills when she answered him. "It's magnificent, isn't it, Nathan?"

"What's magnificent?"

"The painting God's given us," she whispered. "Look up at the hills. Do you see how the sun acts as the frame? Oh, Nathan, it truly is magnificent."

He never looked up. He stared down at his wife's face for what seemed an eternity. A slow heat seemed to permeate his heart, his soul. He couldn't stop himself from reaching out to touch her. The back of his finger slowly trailed a line down the side of her cheek.

"You are magnificent," he heard himself whisper. "You see only the beauty in life."

Sara was stunned by the emotional force in his voice. She turned to smile at him. "I do?" she whispered.

The unguarded moment was gone. Before she could so much as blink Nathan's manner changed. He became brisk when he ordered her to quit dallying.

She wondered if she was ever going to understand him. She walked by her aunt's side along the wooden planks that led to the street while she considered her husband's confusing personality.

"Sara dear, you're frowning. Is the heat beginning to bother you?"

"No," she answered. "I was just thinking what a confusing man my husband is," she explained. "Nora, he actually wants me to become thoroughly self-sufficient," she confessed. "Nathan has made me realize how dependent I try to make myself. I only thought I should," she added with a shrug. "I thought he was supposed to take care of me, but perhaps I was in error. I believe he would still cherish me even if I could defend myself."

"I believe he'd be very proud of your efforts," Nora answered. "Do you really want to be at a man's mercy? Consider your mother, Sara. She isn't married to a man as caring as Nathan."

Her aunt had given her something to think about. Sara hadn't considered the possibility that Nathan might have turned out to be a cruel man. But what if he had?

"I must think about what you've just said," she whispered.

Nora patted her hand. "You'll work it all out in your mind, my dear. Don't frown so. It will give you a headache. My, isn't it a lovely day?"

There were several men loitering along the pathway. They all stared at Sara when she strolled past. Nathan scowled at their blatantly lustful looks, and when one overly appreciative man let out a low whistle Nathan's temper ignited. When he walked past the man he casually slammed the back of his fist into the bastard's face.

The blow toppled the man into the water. Sara glanced back over her shoulder when she heard the splash. It was an absentminded action, for she was also trying to concentrate on what Nora was saying to her. She caught Nathan's eye. He smiled at her. She smiled back before turning around again.

All but one of the other men moved out of the way when Nathan walked past. The less cautious individual had a twiglike nose and a squint. "She's a fetching one, ain't she?" he remarked.

"She's mine," Nathan announced in a low growl. Instead of hitting the insolent man he simply shoved him off the pier.

"Boy, you're getting a mite protective, don't you think?" Jimbo drawled out. He grinned when he added, "She's just a wife."

"The woman doesn't realize her own appeal," Nathan muttered. "She sure as hell wouldn't walk like that if she noticed how the bastards were leering at her."

"Exactly how is she walking?" Jimbo asked.

"You know damn well what I'm talking about. The way her hips . . ." He didn't continue his explanation, but turned his attention to Jimbo's last remark. "And she isn't just a wife, Jimbo. She's my wife."

Jimbo decided he'd baited Nathan long enough. The boy was working himself into a fury. "I can already see from the looks of the place that we aren't going to be able to get the supplies we need to repair the mast."

That glum prophecy turned out to be true. After sending Sara with Nora and Matthew to get settled in Nora's house, Nathan went with Jimbo to explore the tiny village.

It didn't take Nathan long to agree that they'd have to sail to a larger port. According to the charts, the nearest supply port was a good two days away.

Nathan knew his wife wouldn't like hearing about his departure. On his way up the hill, he made the decision to tell her at once and get the inevitable scene over and done.

He was a bit surprised when he reached Nora's house. He'd expected to find a small cottage, but Nora's residence was three times that size. It was a large, two-story structure. The exterior was a pale pink. The verandah that circled the front and sides was painted white.

Sara was sitting in a rocking chair near the front door. Nathan climbed the steps and announced, "I'm leaving with half the crew tomorrow."

"I see."

She tried to control her expression. She was suddenly filled with panic. Dear God, was he going away on another raid? Nora had mentioned that her island home was close to the pirates' nest located just a little further down the coast. Was Nathan going to meet up with past associates and go on one last adventure?

She took a deep, settling breath. She knew she was jumping to conclusions, but she couldn't seem to stop herself.

"We have to sail to a larger port, Sara, in order to get the supplies we need to repair the *Seahawk*."

She didn't believe a word of that story. Nora lived in a fishing village, for God's sake, and the seamen would certainly have enough supplies on hand. She wasn't going to let Nathan know what she was guessing, though. When he was ready to tell her he was Pagan, he would. Until then she would pretend to believe him. "I see," she whispered again.

Nathan was surprised by her easy acceptance. He was used to arguing with her over every little matter. The change in her manner actually worried him. She had been acting peculiar all day long.

He leaned against the rail and waited for her to say

something more. Sara stood up and walked back into the house.

He caught up with her in the foyer. "I won't be gone long," he told her.

She kept right on going. She'd reached the second story when he grabbed hold of her shoulders. "Sara, what's gotten into you?"

"Nora has given us the second chamber on the left, Nathan. I only packed a few things, but perhaps you'd better have some of the men fetch my trunk."

"Sara, you aren't going to be staying here that long," Nathan countered.

"I see."

And if you're killed at sea, she wanted to scream at him. What then, Nathan? Would anyone even bother to come back here to tell me? Lord, it was too horrible to think about.

Sara shrugged off his hands and continued. Nathan once again followed her.

The bedchamber assigned to them faced the sea. Twin windows were open, and the lulling sound of the waves slapping against the rocks echoed throughout the spacious room. There was a large four-poster bed situated between the windows with a lovely multicolored quilt covering it. A large overstuffed green velvet chair sat at an angle near the wardrobe adjacent to the door. The color of the drapes matched the color of the chair exactly.

Sara hurried over to the wardrobe and began to hang her dresses inside.

Nathan leaned against the door and watched his wife for a minute. "All right, Sara. Something's the matter, and I want to know what it is."

"Nothing's the matter," she said, her voice shaking. She didn't turn around.

Damn, he thought, something was certainly wrong, and he wasn't going to leave the room until he found out what it was.

"Have a safe voyage, husband. Good-bye."

He felt like growling. "I'm not leaving until tomorrow."

"I see."

"Will you quit saying I see?" he bellowed. "Damn it, Sara, I want you to quit acting so damned cold with me. I don't like it."

She turned around so he could see her frown. "Nathan, I've asked you countless times to quit using blasphemies in my presence because I don't like it, but that doesn't stop you, does it?"

"That isn't the same," he muttered. He wasn't at all irritated with her near-shout. The fact that she was getting her temper back actually pleased him. She wasn't acting cold or uncaring.

Sara couldn't understand why he was smiling at her. He looked relieved. The man didn't make any sense to her at all. Nathan had obviously spent one too many days in the hot sun.

A plan formed in her mind. "Since you like using blasphemies so much, I shall have to assume that you gain immense satisfaction when you use such ignorant words." She paused to smile at him. "I've decided I'm going to use sinful words, too, just to test this theory. I'm also going to find out if you like hearing your spouse talk so commonly."

His laughter didn't bother her at all. "The only foul words you know are damn and hell, Sara, because those are the only blasphemies I've ever used in your presence. I was being considerate," he added with a nod.

She shook her head. "I've heard you use other words when you didn't know I was on deck. I've also heard the crew's colorful vocabulary."

He started laughing again. The thought of his delicate little wife using foul words was extremely amusing to him. She was such a feminine thing, such a soft, sweet lady, and he couldn't even begin to imagine her using a crude word. It just wasn't in her nature.

A shout from Matthew stopped their discussion. "Nora's

wanting both of you in the drawing room," he bellowed up the stairs.

"You go on down," Sara ordered. "I only have two more gowns to finish. Tell her I'll be right there."

Nathan hated the interruption. He had been thoroughly enjoying himself. He let out a sigh and started out the door.

Sara had the last word. Her voice was amazingly cheerful when she called out, "Nathan, it's a damned hot afternoon, isn't it?"

"Damned right it is," he called back over his shoulder.

He wasn't about to let her know he didn't like hearing her talk like a common wench. What Sara said to him in private was one thing, but he knew good and well she'd never use such blasphemies in public.

He was given a chance to put her to the test much sooner than he'd anticipated.

There was a visitor sitting beside Nora on the brocade settee in the drawing room. Matthew was standing in front of the windows. Nathan nodded to his friend, then strode over to Nora.

"Nathan, dear, I'd like to present the Reverend Oscar Pickering." She turned to her guest and added, "My nephew is the marquess of St. James."

It took all he had not to start laughing. The opportunity was simply too good to pass up. "You're a man of the cloth?" he asked with a wide smile.

Nora had never seen Nathan so accommodating. Why, he actually reached out and shook the vicar's hand. She'd thought he would be as ill at ease as Matthew. That poor dear looked as if he had a rash paining him.

Sara walked into the drawing room just as Nathan sprawled in one of the two chairs facing the settee. He stretched his long legs out in front of him and grinned like a simpleton.

"Oscar is the newly appointed regent for the village," Nora was telling Nathan.

"Have you known Oscar long?" Nathan asked before he spotted Sara standing in the doorway.

"No, we've only just met, but I did insist that your aunt call me by my given name."

Sara walked forward, then made a perfect curtsy in front of their guest. The new government official was a skinny man with rounded spectacles perched on the bridge of his nose. He wore a starched white cravat with his black jacket and breeches, and his manner was most austere. He seemed a little condescending to Sara, for his head was tilted back, and he was looking down through his spectacles at her.

He kept giving Nathan quick glances. There was a noticeable look of disdain on his face.

Sara didn't like the man one bit. "My dear," Nora began, "I would like to present—"

Nathan interrupted. "His name is Oscar, Sara, and he's the new regent for the village."

He'd deliberately left out mention that the man also happened to be the vicar.

"Oscar, this lovely young lady is my niece, and Nathan's wife, of course. Lady Sara."

Pickering nodded and motioned to the chair next to Nathan. "I'm pleased to meet you, Lady Sara."

Sara dutifully smiled. The man's spectacles must have been pinching his nose tight, she thought, as he had an unusually high, nasal voice.

"I should have sent a note requesting an audience," Pickering said, "but I happened to be out on my daily walk, and I couldn't restrain myself when I saw all the commotion going on up here. My curiosity, you see, got the better of me. There are several unsavory-looking men sitting on your verandah, Lady Nora, and I would advise you to have your servants chase them away. Mustn't mingle with the inferiors, you see. It isn't done."

Pickering frowned at Matthew when he made that last comment. Sara was quite astonished by the man's rudeness.

He wasn't as schooled as he'd have them believe, she knew, because he hadn't bothered to stand up when she'd walked into the room. The man was a fraud.

In her agitation she picked up a fan from the table, flipped it open with a flick of her wrist, and diligently began to wave it back and forth in front of her face.

"No one's chasing anyone away," Nathan announced.

"The men are part of the marquess's crew," Nora interjected.

Sara walked over to stand beside Matthew. It was a show of loyalty on her part, and Matthew's slow wink told her he knew what her game was. She smiled in reaction.

Then Nathan drew her attention. "My wife was just remarking on the heat," he drawled. His gaze was directed on Sara. His smile, she noticed, was devilish. "What was it you said, wife?" he innocently asked.

"I don't remember," she blurted out.

The look of satisfaction that came over her husband changed her mind. "Oh, yes, I do remember now. I said it was damned hot. Don't you agree, Mr. Pickering?"

The spectacles fell to the tip of the regent's nose. Matthew looked just as startled. Nathan, she noticed, had quit smiling.

Sara sweetened her smile. "The heat always gives me a hell of a headache," she announced.

She added up the reactions once again. Matthew was looking at her as though he'd only just noticed she had more than one nose on her face.

Her dear husband was glaring at her. That wasn't good enough. She was after total defeat, and with it the promise that he would never use foul words again.

She prayed Nora would be understanding when she explained her shameful conduct. Then she let out a loud sigh and leaned back against the window ledge. "Yes, it's a real pisser today."

Nathan bounded out of his chair. Like a man who'd just heard a foul suggestion and couldn't quite believe it, he demanded that she repeat herself. "What did you just say?" he roared.

She was happy to accommodate him. "I said it's a real pisser today."

"Enough!" Nathan shouted.

Matthew had to sit down. Nora started in coughing in a bid to cover her laughter. Mr. Pickering was out of his seat and hurrying across the room. He clutched a book in his hands.

"Must you leave so soon, Mr. Pickering?" Sara called out. Her face was hidden behind the fan so he wouldn't see her smile.

"I really must," their guest stammered.

"My, you're in a hurry," Sara said. She put the fan down and started for the foyer. "Why, you act as though someone just kicked you in the—"

She never got in the last word since Nathan's hand suddenly covered her mouth. She pushed his hand away. "I was only going to say backside."

"Oh, no you weren't," Nathan countered.

"Sara, whatever in heaven's name came over you?" Nora called out.

Sara hurried over to her aunt. "Do forgive me. I hope I didn't upset you overly much, Nora, but Nathan does like to use crude words, and I thought I'd give it a try. I didn't particularly care for this new government official anyway," she confessed. "But if you wish it, I will of course chase him down and apologize."

Nora shook her head. "I didn't like him either," she admitted.

Both ladies were pretending not to notice that Nathan was standing in front of them. Sara scooted a little closer to Nora. She felt as if she were going to be pounced on at any moment.

She didn't care for that feeling at all. She cleared her throat in a nervous action but valiantly held onto her smile when she said, "What was that book I noticed in Mr.

Pickering's hands? Did you lend him one of your novels, Aunt? I don't believe I'd trust him to return it to you. He doesn't seem the reliable sort at all."

"It wasn't a novel he was carrying," Nora said, her smile gentle. "It was his Bible. Oh, heavens, I really should have explained much sooner."

"Explained what?" Sara asked. "Do you mean to tell me that condescending man carries a Bible around with him? If that isn't hypocritical, I don't know what is."

"Sara, most of the clergy do carry Bibles."

She was slow to catch on. "Clergy? Nora, you told me he was the newly appointed regent."

"Yes, dear, he's a government official, but he also happens to be the pastor of the only church in the village. He stopped by to invite us to attend his Sunday services."

"Oh, my God." After wailing out those words Sara closed her eyes.

No one said a word for a minute. Nathan continued to glare at his wife. Sara continued to blush, and Nora continued to struggle not to laugh. Then Matthew's deep voice broke the silence. "Now that, Lady Sara, is a real pisser."

"Watch your mouth, Matthew," Nathan ordered. He grabbed hold of Sara's hand and pulled her from the settee.

"I can just imagine what the topic of his sermon is going to be come Sunday," Nora announced. She started laughing, and within a flash she needed to mop the tears from her cheeks. "Oh, Lord, I thought I'd die when you so casually remarked—"

"This isn't amusing," Nathan interjected.

"Did you know?" Sara demanded at the same time.

Nathan pretended ignorance. "Know what?"

"That Pickering was a man of the cloth?"

He slowly nodded.

"It's all your fault," Sara cried out. "I never would have disgraced myself if you hadn't prodded me. Now do you understand my point? Will you quit using blasphemies?"

Nathan threw his arm around his wife's shoulders and

hauled her up against his side. "Nora, I apologize for my wife's foul mouth. Now give me directions to this waterfall." He glanced down at Sara. "You're going to have your first swimming lesson, Sara, and if you use one more obscene word, I swear I'll let you drown."

Nora led them through the back of the house as she gave hes directions. When she suggested she have the cook prepare a nice picnic luncheon for them, Nathan declined. He grabbed two apples, handed one to Sara, and dragged her in his wake out the back door.

"It's too hot for a swim," Sara argued.

Nathan said nothing.

"I'm not suitably attired for the water," she continued.

"Too bad."

"I'll get my hair wet."

"That you will."

She gave up. His mind was set on this course of action, she supposed, and it was wasted effort to try to reason with him.

The broken path was narrow. She held onto the back of Nathan's shirt when the climb became steep. She was just beginning to get weary of their hike when the sound of the waterfall caught her attention.

Eager to see a bit of paradise, as Nora had called it, she passed her husband and took the lead.

The foliage was dense around them, and the sweet scent of wildflowers filled the air. Sara felt as though she was in the center of a kaleidoscope of colors. The green of the leaves was the most vivid color she'd ever seen, save for Nathan's beautiful eyes, she told herself, and the pink, orange, and bright red flowers sprinkled about by Mother Nature's whim seemed to blossom before her eyes.

It really was a paradise. That admission carried with it the worry of a serpent.

Nathan had just lifted a fat branch out of the path and motioned for Sara to go ahead.

"Should I worry about snakes?" she asked him in a whisper.

"No."

"Why not?" she asked, hoping he'd tell her there weren't any of the horrid reptiles on the island.

"I'll worry for you," he said instead.

Her fear increased. "What will you do if a snake bites you?" she asked as she passed him.

"Bite him back," Nathan drawled.

That ludicrous remark made her laugh. "You would, wouldn't you?"

She came to an abrupt stop and let out a gasp of pleasure. "Oh, Nathan, it's so lovely here."

He silently agreed with her. The waterfall poured down over the smooth rocks and fell into a froth in the pool at the bottom.

Nathan took hold of Sara's hand again and led her to the ledge behind the waterfall. The area was very like a hidden cave, and when they'd reached the center the water became a curtain shielding them from the world.

"Take your clothes off, Sara, while I see how deep it is here."

He didn't give her time to argue with that command but turned to lean against the rock to take off his boots.

Sara took his apple, added her own, and placed both on the rock behind her. She put her hand out to touch the water flowing down and was surprised that it wasn't overly cold to the touch.

"I'll just sit here and dangle my feet in the water," she announced.

"Take your clothes off, Sara."

She turned to argue with her husband and found he'd stripped out of all his garments. Before she could even blush he'd disappeared through the curtain of water into the pool below.

Sara folded her husband's clothes and put them way back against the wall. She then removed her dress, her shoes, her stockings, and her petticoats. She left her chemise on.

Then she sat down close to the edge and let the water pour over her feet. She was just about to relax when Nathan caught hold of her feet and pulled her into the water. It felt too wonderful to protest. The sun was bright, and the drops of water seemed to glisten on Nathan's bronzed shoulders.

The water came to the middle of his chest. It was so clear, she could see to the bottom. Nathan's muscular thighs drew her immediate notice. He was such a fit man, she thought to herself. He was terribly gentle with her when he pulled her into his arms.

She wrapped herself around him and rested the side of her face on his shoulder.

"You're very trusting," he whispered. "Stand up. Let's see if the water covers your head."

She did as he requested. The water reached her mouth, but when she tilted her head all the way back she could breathe without difficulty.

"This is nice, isn't it?" she asked.

Nathan was trying to concentrate on the swimming lesson he was about to give, but her soft body kept getting in his way. The thinner-than-air chemise she wore clung to her breasts, and all he really wanted to do was make sweet love to her.

Hell, he thought, he had the discipline of a gnat when she was near. "All right, then," he began in a brisk, no-nonsense voice. "The first thing you're going to learn is how to float."

Sara wondered why Nathan was frowning so, then decided he was being brisk so she wouldn't try to argue with him. "If you say so, Nathan."

"You're going to have to let go of me, Sara."

She immediately did as he ordered. She slipped under the water when she lost her anchor and her balance, and she came up sputtering. Nathan lifted her up by holding her around the waist, then ordered her to stretch out on her back.

Sara was floating without his assistance in little time. He

was more pleased over her accomplishment than she appeared to be. "That's enough instruction for one day," she announced. She grabbed hold of his arm to balance herself and then tried to nag him into taking her back to the ledge

Nathan pulled her into his arms. His touch was gentle as he brushed her hair out of her face. Her soft breasts rubbed against his chest. He took his time lowering the straps. Sara didn't realize her husband's intent until her chemise was down around her waist.

She opened her mouth to protest. He silenced her with a long wet kiss. The sound of the waterfall drowned out his low growl of desire. Her knees went weak when his tongue moved inside her mouth. He swept her resistance completely away. She threw her arms around his neck and held him tight.

Nathan worked the chemise down her legs, then lifted her higher until he was pressed tight against the junction of her thighs. She felt so incredibly good to him. Kissing her wasn't enough anymore. He pulled back and looked into her eyes.

"I want you."

"I always want you, Nathan," she whispered.

"Now, Sara," he said. "I want you now."

Her eyes widened. "Here?"

He nodded. "Here," he said in a low groan. "And now, Sara. I don't want to wait."

Even as he told her his intent he was pulling her legs up around his waist. He was kissing her wildly, demanding her response.

Oh, how easily he could make her want him, she thought. Sara was trembling with raw need when he asked her if she was ready for him. She couldn't even speak. Her nails scraped his shoulders in answer, and she let out a little sigh of pleasure when he began to ease inside her.

Nathan captured her mouth for a long kiss, and when her tongue touched his he thrust deep inside. She tightened around him.

They both almost drowned. Neither minded. And when

they found their fulfillment they were both left spent from the bliss they'd just shared.

Sara didn't have the strength to walk to the ledge. Nathan carried her there and placed her on the rock next to the waterfall. The sun beat down on her, but Sara didn't mind the heat. She was still feeling happy and lethargic from their lovemaking.

Nathan lifted himself up on the ledge and sat beside Sara. He couldn't stop himself from touching her. He kissed the top of her head, then the ticklish spot behind her ear. She fell back against the rock and closed her eyes. "It's quite remarkable what happens when we make love, isn't it, Nathan?" she whispered.

He rolled to his side, propped himself on one elbow, and stared down at her. His fingers slowly circled her breasts, smiling when he saw the goosebumps his touch caused.

Sara had never felt so wonderful. The heat from the rock against her back warmed her, and her husband's touch made her shiver at the same time. She didn't think it was possible for her to want him again so soon, but when he began to nuzzle the valley between her breasts desire flared again.

She couldn't stop herself from arching up against him. He was driving her mad with his light, teasing caresses. He bathed each breast with his mouth, his tongue, and when he next looked into her eyes he saw the passion there, the need. His fingers tickled a path down her stomach. He teased her navel. She drew her stomach in. His hand moved down lower, and when his fingers slipped inside her she let out a low groan.

"You're wet for me, aren't you, Sara?"

She was too embarrassed to answer him. She tried to move his hand away. He wouldn't let her. And then he leaned down and began to make love to her with his mouth. His tongue made her lose her control. She writhed beneath him. She never wanted the sweet torture to end.

Her movements made him hard again. Just when he felt her tighten around him he moved between her legs and thrust deep inside her. Sara found her release then. The climax was so shattering, so consuming, she thought she'd died and gone to heaven.

Nathan was there with her. He let out a low groan and poured his seed into her.

Sara was too weak to move. Nathan thought his weight must be crushing her. With extreme effort he braced himself up with his elbows.

When he saw her bemused expression he smiled. "If we fall into the water now, we're going to drown."

She smiled up at him through her tears. She reached up and touched his mouth. "You wouldn't ever let anything happen to me. Do you have to go away tomorrow?"

He had started to turn away from her but her question stopped him. "Yes," he answered.

"I see."

God, she sounded forlorn. "What exactly do you see?" he asked. He nudged her chin up when she tried to turn her face away. "Sara?"

Because she couldn't come right out and ask him if he was going pirating, she decided not to say anything at all.

"Are you going to miss me, wife?" he asked.

She was nearly undone by the tenderness in his gaze. "Yes, Nathan," she whispered. "I will miss you."

"Then come with me."

Her eyes widened in astonishment. "You would let me come with you?" she stammered out. "But that means you aren't going . . . I did jump to conclusions. You have put it all behind you."

"Sara, what are you rambling about?"

She pulled his head down for a kiss. "I'm happy you would let me come with you, that's all," she explained. She sat up and leaned against his side. "I don't need to go with you now. It's quite enough to know you'd let me."

"Quit talking in circles," Nathan ordered. "And while I'm thinking about it, I want you to explain what was going on in your head earlier today. You were upset about something. Tell me what it was."

"I was afraid you wouldn't come back for me," Sara blurted out. It was a lie, of course, but her arrogant husband couldn't possibly know that. In fact, he looked quite pleased by her statement.

"I would never forget to come back for you," he countered. "But I'm talking about before, Sara."

"Before what?"

"Before you even knew I was leaving to get supplies. You were acting oddly then."

"I was feeling sorry for myself because my time with Nora was soon going to end. I shall miss her, Nathan."

He gave her a fierce look while he tried to make up his mind if she was telling the truth or not. Then she smiled at him and told him she was once again ready to go back into the water. "I haven't quite mastered this floating business yet," she said.

Husband and wife stayed in the pool most of the afternoon. They ate their apples as they made their way back down the mountain. Sara's delicate skin was already beginning to burn. Her face was as red as the sunset.

When Nathan put his arm around her shoulder she let out a squeal. He was immediately contrite.

Nora met them at the kitchen door. "Matthew and Jimbo and I held dinner so that . . . goodness, Sara, you're as red as a beet. Oh, child, you're going to suffer tonight. Whatever were you thinking of?"

"I didn't think about the sun," Sara replied. "I was having such a good time."

"What were you doing? Were you swimming all the while?" Nora asked.

"No," Nathan answered when his wife glanced up at him. He smiled at her and then turned back to Nora. "As a matter of fact, we were—"

"Floating," Sara blurted out. "I'll just be a minute, Aunt,

while I change my clothes and brush my hair. You really shouldn't have waited for us," she added over her shoulder as she rushed toward the stairs.

Nathan caught her at the bottom step. He slowly turned her around, then tilted her chin up and kissed her. It was a long, lingering kiss that made her feel she was going to swoon. It wasn't like him to show such affection in front of others, she realized, and he never kissed her unless he wanted to make love to her . . . or shut her up, she knew. Since he looked too exhausted to make love again, and since she hadn't been arguing with him, she could come to only one conclusion. Nathan was being affectionate just because he wanted to.

She was further confused when he leaned down and whispered into her ear, "I thought what we did all afternoon was called making love, wife, but if you prefer to call it floating, that's fine with me."

Her face was too sunburned for anyone to know if she was blushing or not. She smiled up at him even as she shook her head at him. He was teasing her. Good God, Nathan had a sense of humor, too. It was too much to take in all at once.

Then he gifted her with a slow wink. She knew she'd died and gone to heaven then. The sunburn didn't matter any longer, nor did her audience of Jimbo, Matthew, and Nora. Sara threw herself into Nathan's arms and kissed him soundly. "Oh, I do love you so," she cried out.

She wasn't even disappointed when he grunted in reply and didn't shout his love for her then and there. It was too soon for him to tell her what was in his heart, she decided. The feelings were too fresh, too new, and Nathan was quite stubborn. It might take him another six months before he could finally say the words she wanted to hear. She could wait, she told herself. She was, after all, patient and understanding. Besides, in her heart she already knew he loved her, and the fact that he wasn't ready to know it didn't bother her at all.

She didn't make it downstairs for dinner. Once Nathan

had helped her remove her gown she seemed to swell up, and the thought of putting any clothing against her burning skin made her want to scream.

Nora provided a bottle of green paste. Sara carried on something fierce while Nathan gently applied the sticky lotion to her back and shoulders. Fortunately the front of her hadn't been burned. She slept on her stomach, and when she couldn't stand the shivers she slept on Nathan.

The next day Nathan didn't make a single rude remark when he kissed Sara good-bye. He pretended he didn't mind looking at the mask of green paste covering her face.

Sara spent the next two days with her aunt. The Reverend Mr. Pickering came back for a second visit. He was much more civil. Sara explained the reason she'd used such foul words in his presence. Pickering broke into a smile. He looked relieved by her confession, and his manner toward Aunt Nora warmed considerably.

During the course of their visitation the reverend mentioned that there was a ship leaving for England the following morning. Sara immediately went to her aunt's desk and penned a letter to her mother. She told all about her adventure, how happy she was, and boasted that Nathan had turned out to be a kind, considerate, loving husband. Reverend Mr. Pickering took the missive with him to give to the captain of the vessel.

When Nathan came back the following morning Sara was so happy to see him that she burst into tears. They spent a peaceful day together and fell asleep wrapped in each other's arms.

Sara couldn't believe it was possible to be so happy. Being married to Nathan was like living in paradise. Nothing could ever destroy their love. Nothing.

She wished everyone could be as happy and made that remark to Nora and Matthew late one evening. The three of them sat in wicker chairs on the verandah while they waited for Nathan to return from an errand.

"I believe Matthew and I know exactly what you're

talking about," Nora announced. "One doesn't have to be young to experience love, my dear. Matthew, are you ready for a brandy?"

"I'll fetch it," Sara volunteered.

"You'll stay put," Nora countered. She stood up and started for the door. "Your burn's still tender. Keep Matthew company. I'll be right back."

As soon as the door closed behind Nora Matthew whispered, "She's too good for me, Sara, but I'm not going to let that stand in my way. As soon as I put my affairs in order I'm coming back to live out my days with your aunt. How are you feeling about that?"

Sara clasped her hands together. "Oh, Matthew, I think that's wonderful news. We must have the wedding ceremony before we leave for England. I don't want to miss the celebration."

Matthew looked uncomfortable. "Well, now, Sara, I didn't exactly mention marriage, did I?"

She bounded out of her chair. "You'd best mention it now, Matthew, or you aren't ever coming back here. A single night of passion is one thing, sir, but a plan to live out the rest of your days in sin is quite another. Think of Nora's reputation!"

"I am thinking about Nora's reputation," Matthew defended. "She couldn't marry me. It wouldn't be right. I'm not worthy enough."

The seaman stood up and stared out toward the sea. Sara walked over and jabbed him in his stomach with her finger. "You bloody well are worthy enough. Don't you dare insult yourself to me, sir."

"Sara, I've led a . . . speckled life," Matthew stammered.

"And?" she asked.

"And I'm only a seaman," he said.

Sara shrugged. "Nora's first husband was a groom. He was probably just as speckled as you think you are," she added. "Nora was blissfully happy with her Johnny. She must like speckled men. Nora confessed to me that you are a dear, tenderhearted man, Matthew. I know you love her. She must love you, too, if she let you into her bed. As I said to Nathan not long ago, this would solve many problems. Uncle Henry wouldn't send anyone after Nora if he knew she had someone strong to protect her. You'll look after her interests. And I would be so very proud to call you Uncle."

Matthew was humbled by her faith in him. He let out a happy sigh. "All right," he said. "I'll ask Nora. But you have to promise me you'll accept it if Nora says no. All right?"

Sara threw her arms around Matthew's neck and hugged him tight. "She won't say no," she whispered.

"Wife, what the hell are you doing? Matthew, unhand her."

Both Sara and Matthew ignored Nathan's brisk order. Only after she'd placed a chaste kiss on Matthew's cheek did she move away from him. She walked over to the top step where Nathan stood and gave him a sassy grin. "We have to go upstairs now, husband. Matthew wants to be alone with Nora."

She had to pull him into the house and up the stairs. He wanted her to explain why he'd found her draped all over his seaman. "I'll explain everything when we're in our bedroom."

They passed Nora on their way across the foyer. Sara bid her aunt goodnight, then went upstairs. She paced while she waited to find out if Matthew had asked his question and if Nora had given him her answer. When Nathan grew weary of watching her wear out the carpet he captured her in mid-pace, tossed her on their bed, and made wild, passionate love to her. They fell asleep wrapped in each other's arms.

The announcement was made the following morning. Nora had agreed to become Matthew's wife. Sara guessed that much as soon as she saw her aunt's radiant smile.

Matthew explained that he would have to return to England for a short while, in order to straighten out his affairs and sell his cottage. He wouldn't take Nora with him, of course, for her life would be in jeopardy if the Winchesters sniffed out her presence in England. The older seaman wanted to get married before he left, and since Nathan was determined to set sail within a week, the wedding was scheduled for the following Saturday. It was a simple ceremony. Sara wept her way through the event and Nathan spent most of his time mopping at her tears.

He thought she was the most exasperating woman.

Nathan stood there watching his gentle little wife as she whispered and laughed with her aunt, and he realized then the joy she brought to others.

He heard her tell Matthew that her most fervent wish was that their marriage would be as perfect as hers was. He laughed then. Sara really was a hopeless romantic.

She was ridiculously tenderhearted.

She was outrageously innocent.

She was . . . perfect.

Chapter Twelve

There was more than one serpent slithering around in Sara's paradise, just waiting for her return to England.

The voyage back to London was uneventful, however. Ivan took Sara under his wing and tried to teach her how to make a proper soup. The woman couldn't seem to grasp the knack of using just a pinch of seasoning, but Ivan couldn't bring himself to tell her the truth. The rest of the men wouldn't tell her either. They praised her considerably, yet the minute she turned her back on them they tossed the soup overboard. Their empty stomachs weren't nearly as important to them as Sara's feelings.

Sara then wanted to try her hand at making biscuits. The ones stored in the wooden tins were filled with vile little creatures called weevils. The crew didn't mind the insects. They merely pounded the biscuits on the floor a couple of times to shake the weevils loose, then ate the biscuits whole.

Since Ivan had all the ingredients needed, he decided to let Sara make a batch. She worked all morning on the biscuits. The men pretended to be appreciative, but the things were as hard as stones, and they were afraid they'd break their teeth if they tried to take a bite out of one.

Chester had become Sara's greatest champion. He scoffed at the other men, then soaked his biscuit overnight in a full cup of grog. Come morning, even he had to whisper defeat. The biscuit was still too hard to chew.

Matthew suggested they use the leftovers for cannonballs. Nathan laughed at that remark. Sara happened to overhear the banter and took immediate exception. She retaliated that evening by eating the most disgusting meal ever put together by man. She made certain Nathan was watching her, too. The sour cucumbers soaked in strawberry jam did the trick. Nathan barely made it to the railing before he lost his supper.

Sara did seem to have an iron stomach and less than ordinary discrimination regarding food. Nathan watched her every move, and it wasn't long before he realized how enjoyable it was to have her around. He liked the sound of her laughter.

And then they reached London.

Nathan immediately took Sara to the Emerald Shipping office. He was eager for her to meet Colin.

It was midmorning when they walked down the crowded wharf. The sun was shining bright enough to make a person squint. It was warm, too. The door to the office was propped open to let the sweet breeze inside.

When they were just a half a block away from the entrance Nathan pulled Sara aside, leaned down, and whispered, "When you meet Colin, don't mention his limp. He's a little sensitive about his leg."

"He has a limp? What happened to the poor man?"

"A shark took a bite out of him," Nathan answered.

"Good Lord," she whispered in a rush. "He's fortunate to be alive."

"Yes, he is," he agreed. "Now promise me you won't say anything."

"Why would you think I'd mention his limp to him? What kind of woman do you think I am? Nathan, I do know what's proper and what isn't. Shame on you for thinking I'd say a word."

"You screamed when you saw my back," he reminded her.

He would have to bring that up. "For heaven's sake, that was different."

"How?" he asked, wondering what outrageous explanation she would give him.

She shrugged. "It was different because I love you," she said, blushing.

God, she was exasperating, he thought. Pleasing, too. He was becoming accustomed to hearing her tell him how much she loved him. Shaking that thought away, he continued. "And now that you know about Colin's leg you won't be surprised, and you therefore won't say anything to embarrass him. Isn't that right?"

Even as she nodded agreement she tried to get in the last word. "Lord, you're insulting."

He kissed her just to gain a moment's peace, but before he could stop himself he'd properly hauled her into his arms and let the kiss get completely out of hand. She opened her mouth before he would have forced her. His tongue swept inside to rub against hers. He didn't mind at all that they were standing in the center of the busy crosswalk, didn't care either that several passersby stopped to watch them.

Jimbo and Matthew came rushing down the walk but stopped when they saw the couple. Jimbo let out a snort of disgust. "For God's sake, boy, now isn't the time to be pawing your woman. We've got business to see to before the day's completely gone."

Nathan reluctantly pulled away from his wife. She sagged against him. He had to smile over that telling reaction. Then she noticed the group of strangers watching her. The mist of passion quickly evaporated.

"You forget yourself," she whispered to Nathan.

"I'm not the only one who forgot myself," he answered.

She ignored that truth. "I'm about to meet your business associate, and I would appreciate it if you wouldn't distract me so."

She turned her back on him before he could think of a suitable retort. While she smoothed her hair over her shoulders she smiled at Jimbo and Matthew. "Are you coming along with us?"

The two men nodded in unison. Sara took Jimbo's arm. "You may escort me, sir, and you as well, Matthew," she added when he offered his arm to her. "I'm most anxious to meet Nathan's friend. He must be quite a man to put up with my husband. Shall we go?"

Nathan had only enough time to get out of the trio's way as they continued down the walk. He trailed behind, frowning over the high-handed way his wife had taken charge.

"And by the way," he heard Sara say, "whatever you do, please don't mention Colin's limp to him. He's very sensitive about that topic, I can assure you."

"I thought you hadn't met him yet," Jimbo said.

"I haven't," Sara replied. "But Nathan has advised me. My husband is proving to be very tenderhearted when it comes to his friend's feelings. Now if I could only get him to show me like consideration, well, I assure you, I would be most grateful."

"Quit trying to provoke me," Nathan said from behind. He shoved Jimbo out of his way, grabbed hold of his wife's hand, and dragged her forward.

She was highly insulted by that command. She wasn't the ill-natured partner in the marriage. Since she was so sweet-natured, she decided not to take issue with Nathan. She'd wait until later to set him straight.

Besides, she was eager to meet his friend.

Colin was sitting behind his desk, sorting through a mound of papers. As soon as Sara and Nathan walked inside he stood up.

THE GIFT

Nathan's friend was an extremely good-looking man, and it didn't take Sara long to realize his character was just as charming. He had a nice, genuine smile. There was a devilish sparkle in his hazel-colored eyes. He was handsome, though certainly not as handsome as Nathan. Colin didn't have the height, either, or the muscle. Sara did have to look up at him, of course, but she didn't get a crick in her neck as she always did when Nathan was standing close to her and nagging her to look him in the eye.

She guessed it was rude of her to stare at the man and immediately made a formal curtsy.

"At last I'm allowed to meet the bride," Colin said. "You're even more beautiful close up, Lady Sara, than from the distance at which I last saw you."

After giving her that compliment Colin walked over to stand directly in front of her. In a gallant action he formally bowed to her, then lifted her hand and kissed it.

She was quite impressed with his manners.

Nathan wasn't. "For God's sake, Colin, you don't have to put on a show. You won't impress her."

"Yes, he will," Sara announced.

"He's impressing me, too," Jimbo announced with a deep chuckle. "I've never seen the Dolphin act so fancy." He nudged Matthew in the ribs. "Have you?"

"Can't say that I have," Matthew replied.

Colin didn't let go of Sara's hand. She didn't mind. Nathan obviously did. "Unhand her, Colin," he muttered.

"Not until you've made a proper introduction," Colin announced. He winked at Sara and almost laughed when she blushed in reaction.

Not only was Nathan's wife exquisitely beautiful, she was also charming, Colin thought to himself. Had Nathan realized his good fortune yet?

Colin turned to his friend to ask just that question, then decided to find out for himself. "Well?" he said.

Nathan let out a long sigh. He leaned against the window

ledge, folded his arms in front of him, and then said, "Wife, meet Colin. Colin, meet my wife. Now let go of her, Colin, before I smash your face in."

Sara was appalled by the threat. Colin laughed. "I wonder why you don't like me holding your wife," he drawled.

He hadn't let go of Sara's hand but kept his gaze fully directed on his friend. Nathan, he decided, looked extremely uncomfortable.

Sara's comment turned his attention back to her. "Nathan doesn't like anything, sir," she announced with a smile.

"Does he like you?"

She nodded before Nathan could order Colin to quit his teasing. "Oh, yes, he likes me very much," she said matter-of-factly. She tried to extricate her hand from his grasp, but Colin held tight. "Sir, are you deliberately trying to provoke Nathan's temper?"

He slowly nodded. "Then I believe we have something in common," Sara said. "I always provoke his temper."

Colin threw back his head and laughed. Sara hadn't thought her remark was that amusing, and she wondered if he wasn't laughing about something else altogether.

He finally let go of her hand. She immediately clasped her hands behind her back to keep them safe from his grasp. Nathan noticed that action and found his first smile. Then Colin soured it. "You didn't need a reprieve after all," he told Nathan. "Sooner would have been better than later."

"Leave it alone," Nathan ordered. He knew Colin was referring to his past remark that he wanted to leave the chore of collecting his bride until the last possible minute.

"Sir, have we met before?" Sara asked. "You did mention that from a distance . . ."

When he shook his head at her she stopped her question. "I happened to see you one afternoon, but alas, I wasn't given the opportunity to make my presence known to you. I was on a mission, you see, to determine if a certain possession would fit through a window."

"I'm not amused, Colin," Nathan muttered.

Colin's grin indicated he was vastly amused. He decided that he'd prodded his friend enough for the moment. "Let me move those papers from the chair, Lady Sara, and you can sit down and tell me all about your voyage."

"It isn't a happy story, Dolphin," Jimbo interjected. Since there weren't any other chairs available, he leaned against the wall. His gaze was directed on Sara. "We met with one sorry disaster after another, didn't we?"

Sara gave him a dainty shrug. "I thought it was a lovely voyage," she announced. "Very uneventful, as a matter of fact. Jimbo," she added, "it's impolite to snort when you don't agree with someone."

"Uneventful, Sara?" Matthew asked. He grinned at Colin. "The enemy stalked us at every turn."

"What enemy stalked us?" Sara asked. "Oh, you must mean those horrid pirates."

"They were only a small part of the mischief," Matthew remarked.

Sara turned back to Colin. "Pirates attacked the ship, but we chased them away quick enough. As for the rest of the voyage, I declare it was quite peaceful. Don't you agree, Nathan?"

"No."

She frowned at him to let him know his rude denial wasn't appreciated.

"You're forgetting the parasols," he reminded her.

Colin thought he'd lost track of the conversation. "What are you talking about?"

"Sara's parasols turned out to be our greatest enemies," Matthew explained. "There were three of them . . . or was it four? I can't remember. I tend to block unpleasant memories. I get the shivers."

"Will someone explain?" Colin demanded.

"It isn't significant," Sara blurted out. She wasn't about to let her men drag out her venial sins like soiled linen to be scrubbed clean in front of company. "Matthew's just jesting with you. Isn't he, Nathan?"

The worry in her gaze wasn't lost on her husband. "Yes," he agreed with a sigh. "He was just jesting."

Colin let the topic drop when he noticed how relieved Sara looked. He decided to wait until he and Nathan were alone to find out the story behind the parasols.

He lifted the stack of papers from the chair and hurried over to the far side of the office. After placing the stack on top of the cabinet he went back to his chair, sat down, and propped his feet up on the edge of the desk.

Sara watched him closely and couldn't help but notice that he hadn't limped at all. "Nathan, Colin doesn't have a—"

"Sara!"

"Please don't raise your voice to me in front of your associate," she ordered.

"What don't I have?" Colin asked.

Sara sat down, adjusted the folds in her gown, and then smiled at Colin. She could feel Nathan's frown. "A surly nature," she announced. "I can't imagine why you and Nathan are such good friends. You seem very different to my way of thinking, sir. Yes, you do."

Colin grinned. "I'm the civil one in the partnership," he told her. "Is that what you're thinking?"

"I dare not agree, of course, for it would make me disloyal to my husband," she replied. She paused to smile at Nathan, then added, "But you notice that I'm not disagreeing either."

Colin was noticing a whole lot more than that. Nathan couldn't seem to take his gaze off his wife. There was a warm glint in his eyes Colin had never seen before.

"You don't have to call me sir," Colin said to Sara. "Please call me Colin, or even Dolphin like the men do, if that will suit you." A mischievous look came into his eyes, and he glanced over at Nathan before asking, "And what might I call you, Lady Sara, that isn't quite so formal? After all, you are part of this enterprise now. Does Nathan have a special nickname for you that I might also use?"

Nathan thought the question was ridiculous. He didn't particularly like the way Colin was fawning over his wife. He trusted his friend completely, of course, and aside from that fact, Nathan would never allow himself to care too much about his wife, at least not to the point where he was actually jealous. Odd, though, he was still getting damned irritated. "Colin, I call her wife," he announced. "You can't."

Colin leaned further back in his chair. "No, I don't suppose I can," he drawled. "Pity you haven't given her any other nicknames."

"Like what?" Sara asked.

"Like sweetheart, or love, or even—"

"Hell, Colin," Nathan interrupted, "will you quit this game?"

Sara straightened her shoulders. She was frowning at her husband. Nathan thought it was because he'd accidentally slipped in a blasphemy. He almost apologized, then caught himself in time.

"No, Colin, he has never called me by any endearments," Sara announced. She sounded properly appalled. Nathan rolled his eyes heavenward.

"Even if I did," Nathan said, "you damned well couldn't. Partners or not, Colin, you aren't calling my wife sweetheart."

"Why would it bother you?" Colin innocently prodded.

So that was his game, Nathan thought. He's trying to find out just how much I care about Sara. He shook his head at his friend, then added a glare so that Colin would be sure to get his message to let the topic drop.

"Nathan does have a special nickname he uses when he addresses me," Sara announced then, drawing her husband's attention. "You have my permission to use it, too."

"Oh?" Colin asked. He caught the surprised look on Nathan's face and became all the more curious. "And what might that be?"

"Damn it, Sara."

Colin couldn't believe he'd heard correctly. "Did you say—"

"Nathan usually addresses me as Damn It Sara. Don't you, dear?" she asked her husband. "Colin, you may also—"

As if on cue, Nathan muttered, "Damn it, Sara, don't push me. I . . ."

Even he saw the humor then and joined in the laughter. Then Matthew once again reminded them that there was business to attend to and that they'd best get on with it.

The teasing banter ended. Sara sat quietly while she listened to Colin give Nathan a catch-up on the firm's activities. She smiled when Colin announced that they had five more contracts to ship supplies to the Indies.

"Nathan, does that mean we're . . ."

"No, we aren't rich yet."

She looked crestfallen.

"We'll all be rich when you—"

"I know what my duty is," she blurted out. "You don't have to explain it in front of my staff."

Nathan smiled. Colin shook his head. "I haven't followed any of that," he admitted. "What is the duty you have to perform that will make us rich?"

From the way Lady Sara blushed, Colin concluded the matter was of a personal nature. He remembered that Nathan had told him the king's treasure wouldn't be handed over until Sara gave her husband an heir. Because of Sara's obvious discomfort, however, Colin decided to let the topic drop.

"For the love of God," Matthew muttered, "quit this chitchat. I'm itching to get going, Colin. I've got some personal dealings to settle before the week's out."

"Are you going somewhere?" Colin asked.

"Oh, heavens, Matthew, you haven't told Colin about Nora," Sara interjected

"Who is Nora?"

Sara was happy to explain. She hadn't realized the details she'd given until she was finishing up her explanation. "I cannot say more, Colin, about the quickness of the wedding, for to do so would damage my aunt's reputation."

"Sara, you already told him everything," Nathan interjected dryly.

From his position behind the desk Colin had a clear view of the street beyond the open doorway. Sara had just begun to explain why she hadn't truly revealed her aunt's unusual circumstances when a black carriage swayed to a stop across the street. There were five men on horseback escorting the vehicle.

Colin recognized the seal on the side door. It was the Earl of Winchester's family crest. He gave Nathan a barely perceptible nod, then returned his attention to Sara.

Nathan immediately moved away from the ledge, motioned to Jimbo and Matthew, and then casually walked outside.

Sara didn't pay any attention to the men. She was determined to convince Colin that her aunt was a decent woman and that she would never have become so passionately involved with Matthew if she hadn't loved him with all her heart. She also wanted his promise not to repeat a word of what she'd inadvertently blurted out about her aunt.

Just as soon as he gave her the promise she wanted she started to turn around to see what her husband was doing. Colin stopped her by asking another question.

"Sara, what do you think of our office?"

"I don't wish to injure your feelings, Colin, but I do believe it's rather drab. It could be very attractive, though. We need only paint the walls and add drapes. I'd be happy to supervise this task. Pink would be a lovely color, don't you think?"

"No," he said, in such a cheerful tone of voice that she wasn't at all offended. She became a little uneasy, however, when he opened the center drawer of the desk and took out a pistol. "Pink's a woman's color," Colin said then. "We're men. We like dark, ugly colors."

His grin indicated he was jesting with her. Besides, she reasoned, although she didn't know him at all well, she was certain he wouldn't shoot her just because he didn't care for the color she'd suggested. Nathan wouldn't let him.

As to that, where was her husband? Sara stood up and started for the doorway. She spotted Nathan standing between Jimbo and Matthew across the street. The trio was blocking the door of a black carriage. Sara couldn't see the seal. Jimbo's large bulk blocked it. "Who are they talking to, I wonder. Do you know, Colin?"

"Come and sit down, Sara. Wait for Nathan to come back inside."

She was about to do just that when Jimbo shifted positions and she saw the crest. "That's my father's carriage," she cried out in surprise. "How in heaven's name did he know so soon that we were back in London?"

Colin didn't answer her, for Sara had already rushed out the doorway. He shoved the pistol into his pocket and hurried after her.

She hesitated at the curb. Her stomach suddenly tightened up. Oh, God, she hoped her father and Nathan were getting along. And who were those other men?

"Don't borrow trouble," she whispered to herself. She took a deep breath, picked up her skirts, and rushed across the street just as her father climbed out of the carriage.

The earl of Winchester was considered by many to be a distinguished-looking gentleman. He still had a full head of hair, though most of it was silver-colored, and his belly was more firm than round. He stood two inches below six feet in height. He had the same shade of brown eyes Sara did, but that was the only resemblance they shared. Her father's nose was eagle-sized. When he frowned, or squinted against the sun, as he was doing at that moment, his eyes disappeared behind narrow slits. His lips, when pressed together, were as thin as a finely drawn line.

Sara wasn't afraid of her father, but he did worry her, for the simple reason that he wasn't at all predictable. She never knew what he was going to do. Sara hid her concern and rushed forward dutifully to embrace her father. Nathan noticed how the earl stiffened in response to Sara's touch.

"I'm so surprised to see you, Father," Sara began. She stepped back and took hold of Nathan's arm. "How did you know we were back in London so soon after our arrival? Why, our trunks haven't even left the ship yet."

Her father quit frowning at Nathan long enough to give her an answer. "I've had my men watching the water since the day you left, Sara. Now come along with me. I'm taking you home where you belong."

The anger in her father's voice alarmed her. She instinctively moved closer to her husband. "Home? But Father, I'm married to Nathan. I must go home with him. Surely you realize . . ."

She stopped trying to explain when the carriage door opened and her older sister Belinda climbed out.

God's truth, Sara was sorry to see her. Belinda was smiling. That wasn't a good sign. The only time Belinda ever appeared to be happy was when there was trouble brewing. She smiled a lot then.

Belinda had gained a considerable amount of weight since Sara had last seen her. The gold-colored walking dress she wore was straining at the seams. Her sister was heavy-boned and given to fat anyway, and the extra pounds she'd put on had settled around her midriff. She looked more pregnant than not. As a child Belinda had been the pretty sister. The men in the family doted on her. She had curly sun-yellowed hair, a dimple in each cheek, and adorable blue eyes. As she'd grown into womanhood, however, the dimples had been swallowed up in her overly rounded cheeks. Her glorious hair had turned into a mousy brown. The darling of the Winchester family wasn't the center of attention any longer. Belinda's answer to that change in status was to console herself with food.

Sara, on the other hand, had been a rather plain, lanky-legged child. She was terribly awkward, and her permanent teeth had seemed to take forever to come in straight. For almost a year she spit whenever she spoke. No one except her nanny and her mother ever doted on her.

It was a sin not to love her sister, and for that reason alone Sara loved Belinda. She thought she understood her sister's cruel streak. It had been born out of all the disappointments she'd suffered, and Sara always tried to be patient and understanding with her. When Belinda wasn't in a snit about something she could actually be quite pleasant.

Sara tried to concentrate on her sister's good qualities when she called out her greeting. Her grip on Nathan's arm was at great odds with her cheerful tone of voice. "Belinda, how nice it is to see you again."

Her sister rudely stared at Nathan while she returned her sister's greeting. "I'm happy you're finally home, Sara."

"Is Mother with you?" Sara asked.

The earl of Winchester answered her question. "Your mother's at home, where she belongs. Get into the carriage, daughter: I don't want trouble, but I'm prepared for it," he added. "You're coming with us. No one knows you've been with the marquess, and if we—"

"Oh, Papa," Belinda interrupted, "you know that isn't true. Everyone knows. Why, consider all the notes of sympathy we've received since Sara left."

"Silence!" the earl roared. "Dare you contradict me?"

Sara moved so quickly Nathan didn't have time to stop her. She pulled Belinda away from her father's side and positioned herself between them. "Belinda didn't mean to contradict you," Sara said.

Her father looked somewhat mollified. "I won't tolerate insolence," he muttered. "As to the few who do know about your disgraceful conduct, daughter," he continued, addressing his frown and his full attention to Sara, "they'll keep their mouths shut. If a scandal breaks before I've settled this matter, I'll face it."

Sara was more concerned than ever. When her father acted so sure of himself there was always mischief afoot. "What scandal, Father?" she asked. "Nathan and I haven't done anything to cause gossip. We're obeying all the conditions set down in the contract."

"Don't mention the contract to me, daughter. Now get into the carriage before I order my men to draw their weapons."

The ache in Sara's stomach intensified. She was going to have to defy her father. It was a first for her. Oh, she'd often stood up to him, but it was always in defense of her mother or her sister, never herself.

She slowly backed away until she was once again standing next to Nathan. "I'm sorry to disappoint you, Father, but I cannot go with you. My place is with my husband."

The earl was infuriated. To have his daughter openly defy him in front of witnesses was humiliating. He reached out to slap her. Nathan was quicker. He grabbed hold of the earl's wrist and started to squeeze. Hard. He wanted to break the bone in half.

Sara stopped him by merely touching him. When she sagged against his side he immediately let go of her father and put his arm around her shoulder. He could feel her trembling and became all the more furious.

"She isn't going anywhere, old man," Nathan announced in a low, controlled voice.

The denial was obviously the signal the earl's men needed. The pistols were drawn and pointed at Nathan.

Sara let out a gasp. She couldn't believe what was happening. She tried to put herself in front of Nathan to protect him. He wouldn't let her move. He tightened his hold and continued to stare at her father. He smiled. Sara didn't know what to make of that reaction.

Surely he understood the severity of the situation. "Nathanial?" she whispered. She used that name as a method to put him on his guard. She leaned up and then whispered, "You don't have a pistol. They do. Please take notice of the odds, husband."

Nathan quit his smile and looked down at her. He knew what she did not—that the odds were indeed on his side. At least eight of his loyal crew had come running at the sight of the carriage. They were lined up behind Sara, ready and armed for a fight.

There was also the fact that her father was bluffing. The look in his eyes indicated to Nathan that he didn't have the mind or the courage for a direct confrontation.

"This has gotten completely out of hand," Sara told her father. She was so upset, her voice shook. "Order your men to put their weapons away, Father. Nothing will be solved by hurting Nathan or me."

The earl of Winchester didn't give the order quickly enough. "I won't let you hurt my husband," Sara cried out. "I love him."

"He won't hurt him," Colin called out. "I'll put a hole through his forehead if he tries."

Sara turned to look at Nathan's friend. The transformation in Colin was so stunning to her, she caught her breath. Colin's stance looked relaxed, and there was a smile on his face, but the coldness in his eyes clearly indicated he'd carry out his threat without suffering a moment's qualm.

The earl immediately motioned for his men to quit their positions. When their weapons were back inside their waistbands he tried a different approach to gain victory. "Belinda, tell your sister about your mother. Since Sara refuses to come home, she might as well hear the truth now."

Belinda had moved back to her father's side. He gave her arm a little prod to get her started. "Sara, you really must come home with us," Belinda blurted. She glanced over at her father, received his nod, and then continued. "Mother's taken gravely ill. That's the reason she didn't come with us."

"She's longing to see you again," her father interjected. "Though after the way you've worried her, I can't understand why."

Sara shook her head. "Mother isn't ill," she said. "This is just trickery to get me to leave Nathan, isn't it?"

"I would never use your mother in such a manner," her father muttered with indignation.

He nudged Belinda again. Nathan noticed the action and knew the scene he was witnessing had been rehearsed. He hoped his wife was astute enough to notice, too.

Belinda took a step forward. "Mama took ill right after you left, Sara. Why, for all she knew, you could have been drowned at sea, or killed by . . . pirates."

"But Belinda, Mother . . ." Sara stopped. She wasn't certain her father knew she'd left a note explaining to her mother that she was going to help Nora get back home. Her mother might have hidden the letter from her father. "I mean to say, I sent a long letter to Mama when Nathan and I reached our destination. Mama should have received the missive by now."

Nathan was surprised by that news. "When did you write?"

"When you left to get supplies," Sara explained.

"Yes, we received both of your letters," the earl interjected.

Sara was about to argue that she'd only sent one letter, but she wasn't given a chance before her father continued. "And of course, I was pleased with the information you gave me. Still, daughter, the matter is not quite resolved, and for that reason we must continue to use discretion."

She didn't know what he was talking about. "What information?" she asked.

Her father shook his head at her. "Don't play the fool with me, Sara." He straightened his shoulders, then turned to pull the carriage door wide. "Your mother is waiting."

Sara looked up at Nathan. "Will you take me to see Mother? I'll worry until I've spoken to her."

"Later," Nathan replied.

Sara turned back to her father. "Please tell Mother we'll come to visit her as soon as Nathan finishes his business here."

The earl of Winchester had planned to wait until he'd gotten Sara away from the marquess before putting his plan into action. He didn't like direct conflicts. It was much more satisfying to have surprise on his side, and less dangerous as well. Yet when the marquess told him to take his leave, his rage exploded. "The prince regent has all the information before him now," he shouted. "It's only a matter of time till he decides you've violated the contract. Just you wait and see."

"What the hell are you rambling about?" Nathan demanded. "You're demented if you think I've violated any conditions. This marriage will not be invalidated. I've slept with my wife. It's too late."

The earl's face turned a blotchy red. Sara had never seen him in such a fury.

"Father, please calm yourself. You're going to make yourself ill."

"Sara, do you know what your father's talking about?" Nathan asked.

She shook her head. She and her husband both turned back to the earl again.

"This is a private conversation," Sara's father announced. He nodded to his men. "Wait at the corner."

He turned to Nathan again. "Dismiss your men," he ordered, "unless you wish for them to overhear what I'm about to say."

Nathan shrugged. "They stay."

"Father, I'll be happy to explain," Belinda volunteered. She smiled while she waited for their escort to leave. When the men were out of earshot she turned to Nathan. "Sara wrote to us. We never would have known if she hadn't told, you see."

"What wouldn't you have known?" Sara asked.

Belinda let out a mock sigh. "Oh, Sara, don't act so innocent. It isn't necessary now." She looked up at Nathan again and smiled. "She told us about your father. We know all about the earl of Wakersfield now. Yes, we do."

"No," Sara cried out. "Belinda, why—"

Her sister couldn't let her continue. "Of course, Sara only gave us the bare bones, but once we had that information— well, Papa had his important friend do a little investigating, and the rest was ferreted out. When Papa's finished, everyone in London will know that your husband's father was a traitor."

The earl let out a snort of disgust. "Did you think you could keep that filth swept under the carpet?" he asked Nathan. "My God, your father nearly toppled our government. Machiavelli was a saint in comparison to your father. Those sins are now on your shoulders," he added with a brisk nod. "When I'm finished you'll be destroyed."

"Father, quit these threats," Sara cried out. "You can't mean them."

Her father ignored her plea. His gaze was directed on Nathan. "Do you honestly believe the prince regent will force my daughter to spend her life tied to an infidel like you?"

Nathan was so astonished by the earl's comments that a fury he'd never felt before began to burn inside him. How had the bastard found out about his father? And God, when it was made public, how would his sister Jade react?

It was as if the earl had read Nathan's mind. "Think about your sister," he announced. "Lady Jade's married to the earl of Cainewood, isn't she? She and her husband have become the darlings of the set. That will soon change," he added with another snort. "The shame is going to make your sister a leper in society, I promise you."

Sara was terrified on Nathan's behalf. How had her father found out about the earl of Wakersfield? When Nora had confided that secret to her she'd told her no one would ever find out. The father's file was locked away inside the War Department's vault. No one could breach that sanctuary.

And then the full truth of what her father and her sister were trying to do settled in her mind. They wanted Nathan to believe she'd betrayed him.

She immediately shook her head. No, that didn't make sense, she told herself. How could they guess that she'd found out? "I don't understand how you learned about Nathan's father," she whispered. "But I—"

Belinda interrupted her. "You told us. You don't have to lie any longer. As soon as Papa read the shocking news he did as you instructed, Sara. For heaven's sake, you should be happy now. You're going to be free very soon. Then you can marry a gentleman worthy of you. Isn't that what you said, Papa?"

The earl of Winchester quickly nodded. "If the contract is set aside, the duke of Loughtonshire would still be willing to take you for his wife."

"But Belinda's pledged to him," Sara whispered.

"He prefers you," her father muttered.

The pain in Sara's stomach was so acute it almost doubled her over. "Is that why you're lying, Belinda? You don't want to marry the duke, and you've made a pact with Father, haven't you?"

"I'm not lying," Belinda countered. "You gave us the information we needed. Papa says he's going to demand that all the land the marquess inherited from his father be confiscated. When Papa's finished," she added with a sarcastic slur in her voice, "the marquess will be a pauper."

Sara shook her head. Tears streamed down her cheeks. She was so humiliated that her family would act in such a cruel, sadistic manner. "Oh, Belinda, please don't do this."

Nathan hadn't said a word. When his arm dropped away from Sara's shoulders the earl guessed that his gamble had paid off. He felt like gloating with victory. He'd heard what a cynical, hardheaded man the marquess of St. James was, and now he knew the rumors were true.

Sara needed to hear her husband tell her he believed her. She couldn't tell anything from his expression. "Nathan? Do you believe I wrote to my mother and told her about your father's sins?"

He answered her with a question of his own. "Did you know about my father?"

God save her, she almost lied to him. He looked so bored, so unconcerned. Yet his voice shook with anger.

He condemned her.

"Yes, I did know about your father," she admitted. "Nora told me."

He took a step away from her. She felt as though he'd just struck her. "Nathan? You cannot believe I would betray you. You cannot!"

Colin spoke up. "Why shouldn't he? It's damn telling evidence against you. That secret's been safe a long time. Then you find out, and—"

"So you find me guilty, Colin?" she interrupted.

He shrugged. "I don't know you well enough to judge if I can trust you or not," he said. He was being brutally honest with her. "But you are a Winchester," he added with a meaningful glance in her father's direction.

Colin looked at Nathan. He knew the anguish his friend must be going through yet doubted that anyone else was aware of that pain. Nathan had that uncaring look on his face. His friend had become a master at concealing his reactions. Ironically, it had been a woman who had first taught him how to protect his heart. Now another woman seemed to be proving Nathan's cynicism was more than justified.

Sara's anguish was apparent, however. She looked devastated, defeated. Colin began to have doubts about his quick judgment. Was Sara capable of such fakery? "Why don't you ask Nathan again?" he suggested in a softer tone of voice.

She shook her head. "He should have enough faith in me to know I'd never betray him."

"Get in the carriage," her father ordered again.

She whirled back to confront her father. "I've been such a fool about so many things, Father," she announced. "I actually made excuses for your sinful conduct, but Nora was right after all. You aren't any better than your brothers. You disgust me. You let your brother Henry dole out the punishment whenever you're displeased. Your hands stay clean that way, don't they? Oh, God, I never want to see you again." She took a deep breath, then added in a harsh whisper, "I'm no longer your daughter."

She turned her attention to Belinda next. "As for you, I hope you get down on your knees and pray God's forgiveness for all the lies you've told today. You may tell Mother I'm sorry she isn't feeling well. I'll come to see her when I'm certain neither one of you is home."

After making that speech Sara turned her back on her family and walked across the street. Colin tried to take hold of her arm. She pulled away.

Everyone watched her until she'd walked inside the office and shut the door behind her.

The earl of Winchester still wasn't ready to give up. The argument became fierce again and lasted several minutes before Nathan finally took a step forward.

Sara's father tried to go toward the office then. He shouted his daughter's name in such a booming voice that the veins in the side of his neck stood out. Nathan blocked his path. That action proved threatening enough.

No one said a word until the Winchester carriage rounded the corner. The men on horseback trailed after the vehicle. Then everyone started talking at once.

Jimbo and Matthew both argued in Sara's defense. "She might have told," Matthew said, "but only the way she told about Nora and me. Inadvertent like."

"I'm saying she didn't tell at all," Jimbo muttered. He folded his arms across his chest and glared at Colin when he made that emphatic statement. "You didn't help, Dolphin," he added. "You could have swayed the boy's mind if you'd argued in our Sara's defense."

"The last time I argued in a woman's defense Nathan damn near got killed," Colin replied.

"He was young and stupid back then," Matthew said.

"He still is," Jimbo stated. "You aren't at all surprised, are you?" he said then. "With your cynical heart, I imagine you expected our Sara to fail you. Isn't that right?"

Nathan wasn't listening to his friends. His gaze was centered on the corner where the carriage had last been seen. With a shake of his head he pulled himself out of his musings and turned to walk away.

"Where are you going?" Matthew called out.

"Maybe he came to his senses," Jimbo said when Nathan started across the street. "He might be going to apologize to Sara. Did you see the look on her face, Matthew? It tore me up to see such torment."

"Nathan wouldn't apologize," Colin said. "He doesn't know how. But he might be calm enough to listen to her now."

Sara had no idea Jimbo and Matthew had come to her defense. She believed everyone had damned her. She was so upset she couldn't stop pacing. She kept picturing the expression on Nathan's face when she'd admitted that she'd known the truth about his father.

He believed she had betrayed him.

Sara had never felt so alone. She didn't know where to go, whom to turn to, what to do. She couldn't think. Her fantasy of living in paradise with the man she'd always believed loved her was gone.

Nathan had never loved her. It was just as her relatives had told her. He was only after the king's gift. She'd thought those often-repeated reminders were lies meant to turn her heart against him. She knew better now.

God, what a fool she'd been.

The pain was simply too much, too overwhelming to

think about. Sara remembered the vile threat her father had made against Nathan's sister Jade. Her heart went out to the sister, and even though she'd never met the woman she knew it was her duty to try to warn her so she could prepare herself.

The plan gave her a mission, a reason to move. No one noticed when she walked outside. They were occupied shouting at each other. She walked to the corner, but as soon as she was out of sight she started running. She lost her way almost immediately, yet she kept on running until she was out of breath.

God took mercy on her, for when she couldn't go another step she spotted a hack in the middle of the street only half a block away. A passenger was getting out of the vehicle. While he sorted through his pockets for his coins Sara hurried forward.

She didn't have any shillings with her. She didn't know the address of her destination either. She couldn't worry about the lack of funds, though. She decided the coachman would have to be responsible for finding the address on his own.

"The earl of Cainewood's townhouse, if you please," she called out. She got inside the vehicle and pressed herself into the corner. Her fear was that Nathan might have sent one of his men to chase after her.

The coachman directed the hack to what he referred to as the fancy-pants section of town, yet he still had to ask directions from a passerby before he found the address his fare had requested.

Sara used the time to calm her queasy stomach. She took deep, gulping breaths and prayed she wouldn't be sick.

Nathan had no idea Sara wasn't waiting for him inside the office. He tried to rid himself of some of his anger before he spoke to her again. He didn't want to add to her upset. God help him, he couldn't imagine what her life must have been like living with such vile relatives.

Jimbo began to nag him in earnest. "I don't condemn her

for telling," Nathan said. "I understand her flaws. I wasn't surprised. Now, if you'll quit your hounding, I'll go and tell her I've forgiven her. Will that satisfy you?"

Jimbo nodded. Nathan strode across the street and went inside the office. It didn't take him any time at all to realize his wife wasn't there. He looked inside the back storage area just to make certain.

Panic filled him. He knew she hadn't left with her father, and that meant that she had literally walked away.

The picture of just what could happen to an unattended woman in that section of the city terrified Nathan. His roar echoed through the streets. He had to find her.

She needed him.

Chapter Thirteen

S ara cried her way to her destination. When the hack came to a stop in front of a brick-front townhouse she forced herself to gain a little control. Her voice barely cracked when she ordered the coachman to wait for her. "I won't be but a minute," she promised. "I have another destination after I've finished here, and I'll double your fare if you'll kindly be patient."

"I'll wait as long as it takes," the driver promised with a tip of his hat.

Sara rushed up the steps and knocked on the door. She wanted to get inside the townhouse before she was spotted by her relatives. She was also afraid her courage would desert her before she'd completed her mission.

The door was opened by a tall, arrogant-looking man with deep wrinkles at the corners of his eyes. He was quite homely in appearance, but the sparkle in his dark eyes indicated he had a kind nature.

"May I be of assistance, madam?" the butler inquired in a haughty tone of voice.

"I must see Lady Jade at once, sir," Sara answered. She

gave a quick look over her shoulder to make certain she wasn't being watched, then said, "Do let me in."

The butler only had enough time to get out of her way. Sara rushed past him, then demanded in a whisper that he shut the door and bolt it against intruders.

"I pray your mistress is here," she said. "I don't know what I will do if she isn't home."

That possibility was so distressing, her eyes filled with tears. "Lady Jade is home today," the butler told her.

"Thank God for that."

A smile softened the elderly man's expression. "Yes, madam, I often thank God for sending her to me. Now," he continued in a brisker tone of voice, "may I tell my mistress who has come calling?"

"Lady Sara," she blurted out. She suddenly grabbed hold of his hand. "And please hurry, sir. I'm growing more cowardly by the second."

The butler's curiosity was caught. The poor distressed woman was trying to squeeze the bones right out of his hand. "I shall be pleased to hurry, Lady Sara," he announced. "Just as soon as you let go of me."

She hadn't realized she was holding on to him until that moment, and she immediately pulled away. "I'm very upset, sir. Please forgive my boldness."

"Of course, m'lady," the butler returned. "Is there perchance a last name to go with the first?" he asked.

The question proved to be too much for her. Much to the servant's consternation, she burst into tears. "I used to be Lady Sara Winchester, but that changed, and I became Lady Sara St. James. Now that's going to change, too," she cried. "Come morning, I don't know what my name will be. Harlot, I would imagine. Everyone will believe I lived in sin, but I didn't, sir. I didn't," she whispered. "It wasn't sinful."

She paused in her explanation to mop the tears away from her eyes with the handkerchief the butler handed her. "Oh, you might as well call me harlot now and get it over with. I'll have to get used to it."

Sara realized she was making a complete fool of herself. The butler was slowly backing away from her. He probably thought he'd let a deranged woman into his employer's sanctuary.

The earl of Cainewood had just strolled into the foyer from the back of the house where his library was situated when he heard his man Sterns ask their guest what her full name was. Her bizarre answer had made him stop in his tracks.

Sara tried to skirt her way around the butler. She handed him the soggy handkerchief and said, "I shouldn't have come here. I realize that now. I'll send a note to your mistress. Lady Jade is certainly too busy to see me."

"Catch her, Sterns," the earl called out.

"As you wish," the butler replied. His hands settled on Sara's shoulders. "Now what, m'lord?" he inquired.

"Turn her around."

Sterns didn't have to force Sara. She moved without any prodding. "Are you Lady Jade's husband?" she asked when she saw the tall, handsome man leaning against the banister.

"May I present my employer, the earl of Cainewood?" the butler announced in a formal voice.

Her curtsy was instinctive, born from years of training. The butler made her stumble, though, when he added, "M'lord, may I present Lady Sara Harlot?"

She almost fell to her knees. Sterns reached out to steady her. "It was just a jest, m'lady. I couldn't restrain myself."

Jade's husband came forward. He was smiling at her. That helped. "You may call me Caine," he told her.

"I'm Nathan's wife," she blurted out.

His smile was so tender, so kind. "I guessed as much," he said, "as soon as I saw how upset you were. I also caught the part of your explanation about becoming a St. James," he added when she looked so bewildered. "Welcome to our family, Sara."

He took hold of her hand and gave it an affectionate squeeze. "My wife is most eager to meet you. Sterns, go and fetch Jade, will you? Sara, come along with me into the drawing room. We can get to know each other while we wait for my wife."

"But sir, this isn't a social call," Sara said. "When you learn the reason for my visit you'll both want to throw me out."

"Shame on you for thinking we'd be so inhospitable," he countered. He winked at her, then pulled her along by his side. "We're family now, Sara. Call me Caine, not sir."

"I won't be part of the family long," she whispered.

"Now, now, don't start crying again. It can't be as bad as all that. Have you come to tell on Nathan, then? What's he done, I wonder."

His smile indicated he was teasing her. The mere mention of her husband started the tears again. "He hasn't done anything," she said between sobs. "Besides, I would never tell on my husband if he displeased me. It wouldn't be loyal."

"So loyalty is important to you?" he asked.

She nodded. Then she frowned. "So is having faith in your spouse," she muttered. "Some do, others don't."

He wasn't certain he knew what she was talking about. "Do you?" he asked.

"Not anymore I don't," she announced. "I've learned my lesson."

Caine still didn't know what the conversation was about. "I haven't come here to talk about Nathan," she declared. "Our marriage will soon be over. You might as well understand that right away."

It took considerable effort for Caine to keep his smile contained. So it was a marital disagreement after all. "Nathan can be a bit difficult," he said.

"That he can, husband."

Both Caine and Sara turned toward the doorway just as Lady Jade came strolling into the room.

Sara thought Nathan's sister was the most beautiful

woman she'd ever seen. She had such glorious auburn hair. Her eyes were as green as Nathan's, and her complexion was porcelain-perfect. Sara felt completely inadequate by comparison.

She forced herself to put the matter of appearances aside and began to pray in earnest that Jade didn't share her brother's cranky disposition. "I've come with distressing news," she blurted out.

"We already know you're married to Nathan," Caine drawled. "There can't be anything more distressing to you than that, Sara. You have our sympathy."

"How very disloyal of you," Jade replied. Her smile indicated she wasn't at all irritated by her husband's remark, however. "Caine loves my brother," she told Sara. "He just hates to admit it."

She walked over and kissed Sara's cheek. "You aren't at all what I expected," she said. "That pleases me. Where are my manners? I'm so pleased to finally meet you, Sara. Where is Nathan? Will he be joining you soon?"

Sara shook her head. She suddenly had to sit down. She collapsed into the nearest chair. "I never want to see him again," she whispered. "Except to tell him that I never want to see him again, of course. Oh, I don't know where to begin."

Jade and Caine exchanged a look, then Caine mouthed the words "marriage problems" as his guess as to what the problem could be. Jade nodded before she sat down on the brocade settee and patted the cushion next to her. Caine immediately joined her.

"No matter what he's done, Sara, I'm certain the two of you will be able to work this out to your mutual satisfaction," Caine said.

"My husband and I fought all the time when we were first married," Jade added.

"No, love, we fought before we were married, not after," Caine said.

Jade was about to argue over that ridiculous remark when

Sara blurted out, "I haven't come to discuss my marriage. No, I've . . . why aren't I what you expected?"

Jade smiled. "I worried that you would be . . . restrained. Many of the ladies in our society tend to be superficial. They go to great lengths to pretend boredom. You, on the other hand, appear to be refreshingly honest in your reactions."

"You must be giving Nathan fits," Caine said before he could think better of it.

"I refuse to talk about Nathan," Sara said. "I've come here to warn you. You must prepare yourselves for the scandal."

Caine leaned forward. "What scandal?"

"I should start at the beginning so that you'll understand," Sara whispered. She folded her hands in her lap. "Do you happen to know about the conditions set down in the contract between Nathan and me?"

They both shook their heads. Sara let out a sigh. "King George, bless his broken mind, was determined to end the feud between the St. James family and the Winchesters. He forced a marriage between Nathan and me and then sweetened the vinegar in that action by setting aside a large fortune in gold and a tract of land that is situated between the two families' country estates. The feud dates back to the early middle ages," she added. "But that isn't important now. The land is actually more coveted than the gold, for it's fertile, and the mountain water that flows directly down the middle of the tract feeds the fields of both estates. Whoever owns the land could effectively ruin the other by withholding the water supply. According to the contract, the treasury goes to Nathan as soon as he collects me for his wife. After I give him an heir, the land will also come to us."

Caine looked incredulous. "How old were you when this contract was signed?"

"I was four years old. My father signed in my stead, of course. Nathan was fourteen years old."

"But that's . . . preposterous," Caine said. "It can't be at all legal."

"The king decreed it legal and binding. The bishop was with him, and he blessed the marriage."

Sara couldn't look at Caine or Jade. The easy part of her explanation was over, and it was time to get to the heart of the matter. She turned her gaze to her lap. "If I walk away from the contract, Nathan gets everything. And if he were to walk away, then I—or rather, my family—would receive everything. It was a very cunning game the king played with us."

"You and Nathan were his pawns, weren't you?" Caine said.

"Yes, I suppose we were," Sara agreed. "I think the king's motives were pure, though. He seemed obsessed with making everyone get along. I try to remember that he had our best interests at heart."

Caine didn't agree with that evaluation, but he kept his opinion to himself. "I've made you digress," he said. "Please continue with your explanation, Sara. I can see how upsetting this is for you."

She nodded. "Nathan came to get me over three months ago. We sailed away on his ship and only just returned to London. My father was waiting for us."

"What happened then?" Caine asked when she didn't continue.

"My father wanted me to come home with him."

"And?" he prodded again.

"Caine," Jade interjected, "it's obvious she didn't go home with her father. She's here with us, for heaven's sake. Sara, I'm having trouble understanding why your father would want you to return to his home. You'd be breaking the contract, wouldn't you? Why, Nathan would win it all, and I can't imagine the Winchesters allowing that to happen. Besides, I assume that you and Nathan have been living together as husband and wife. It's too late, isn't it—"

"Sweetheart, let Sara explain," Caine suggested. "Then we'll ask our questions."

"My father has found a way to break the contract and win the gift," Sara said.

"How?" Jade asked.

"He found out something terrible about your father," Sara whispered. She dared a quick look up and saw the alarm that came into Jade's eyes. "Did you know about your father's activities?"

Jade didn't answer her. "This is very difficult," Sara whispered.

Caine wasn't smiling. "Exactly what did your father find out?"

"That the earl of Wakersfield betrayed his country."

Neither husband nor wife said anything for a minute. Caine put his arm around his wife's shoulders in an attempt to comfort her.

"I'm so sorry to have to tell you about your father," Sara whispered. Her anguish was apparent. "But you must try not to condemn him. You can't possibly know the circumstances that led him toward the path he took."

Sara didn't know what else to say. The color had left Jade's face, and she looked as if she was going to be ill. Sara felt the same way.

"It was bound to come out sooner or later," Caine said.

"Then you knew?" Sara asked.

Jade nodded. "Nathan and I have known about our father for a long time." She turned to her husband. "You're wrong, Caine. That secret should never have had to come out." She turned back to Sara. "How did your father find out?"

"Yes, how did he find out?" Caine asked. "That file was locked away in the vault. I was assured that no one would ever find out."

"Nathan believes I found out and wrote the news to my family," Sara said.

"Did you know?" Jade asked.

"That was the very question your brother asked me," Sara said. The sadness in her voice indicated her pain. "I almost lied to Nathan because he was looking at me in such a frightening way."

"Did you know?" Jade asked again. "And if so, Sara, how did you find out?"

She straightened her shoulders. "Yes, I did know about your father, Jade. I can't tell you how I found out, though. It would be disloyal."

"Disloyal?" Jade would have bounded out of her seat if her husband hadn't restrained her. Her face was flushed pink. "Telling your family is what I call disloyal," she cried out. "How could you do such a thing, Sara? How could you?"

Sara didn't even try to defend herself. If her own husband didn't believe her, why should his sister?

She stood up and forced herself to look at Jade. "I felt it was my duty to come here to warn you," she said. Her voice was flat. "I would apologize for my family, but I've decided to disown them, and it wouldn't ease your torment anyway. Thank you for listening to me."

She walked to the foyer. "Where are you going now?" Caine called out. He tried to stand up, but his wife was pulling on his attention by tugging on his hand.

"I must make certain my mother is all right," Sara explained. "And then I'm going home." With that, Sara opened the door and left.

"So much for disowning her family," Jade muttered. "Caine, let her leave. I never want to see her again. Oh, God, we have to find Nathan. He must be terribly upset over this treachery."

Caine gave his wife a good scowl. "I can't believe what I'm hearing," he said. "If you're referring to the scandal about to break, Nathan won't be upset. Jade, the St. James men thrive on disgrace, remember? For God's sake, reason this through. You never used to give a damn what others thought. Why the sudden change?"

"I still don't care what anyone thinks, except you, husband. I was talking about Sara's treachery. She betrayed my brother, and that's why I believe Nathan must be very upset."

"So you've found her guilty, have you?"

That question gave her pause. She started to nod, then shook her head. "Nathan judged her," she said. "Sara told us he believed she betrayed him."

"No," Caine said. "She said he asked her if she knew about his father. Jade, you can't possibly know what he's thinking until you ask him. Your brother's one of the most cynical men I've ever known, but damn it, wife, I expect better from you."

Jade's eyes widened. "Oh, Caine, I did find her guilty, didn't I? I just assumed . . . and she didn't defend herself."

"Why should she?"

"She did tell us she was going home. For a woman who claims she just disowned her family . . . you think she's innocent, don't you?"

"I have only formed one conclusion thus far. Sara loves Nathan. All you have to do is look at the woman to know that. Would she have bothered to come to warn us if she didn't care about your brother, my sweet? Now unhand me, please. I'm going after her."

"You're too late, m'lord," Sterns called out from the foyer. "The hack has already left."

"Why didn't you stop her?" Caine asked as he rushed toward the door.

"I was occupied eavesdropping," the butler admitted. "I also didn't know you wanted me to stop her." He turned his gaze to his mistress. "I hope you don't mind that I gave your sister-in-law a few shillings. Lady Sara was without funds and needed to pay the fare to her next destination."

The pounding on the front door stopped the conversation. Before Sterns or Caine could open it the door was flung wide, and Nathan came striding into the foyer. There were few men who could intimidate Sterns, but the marquess of

St. James was one of them. The butler immediately got out of the big man's path.

Nathan acknowledged both men with a brisk nod. "Where's my sister?"

"It's good to see you again, too, Nathan," Caine drawled. "What brings you here today? Have you come to see your godchild? Olivia's sleeping, but I'm certain your bellowing will wake her in no time at all."

"I don't have time to be sociable," Nathan replied. "Olivia's all right, isn't she?"

As if in answer to that inquiry the sound of the infant's wailing came floating down the stairwell. Sterns frowned at the marquess before starting up the steps. "I'll see to the babe," he announced. "She'll be wanting me to rock her back to sleep."

Caine nodded agreement. The butler was far more family than servant and had taken over the care of little Olivia. The two got along extremely well, and Caine wasn't certain who was more firmly wrapped around the other's fingers.

Caine turned to give Nathan a proper set-down for disturbing his daughter's sleep, but when he saw the expression on his brother-in-law's face he changed his mind. It was a look Caine had never seen before on Jade's brother's face. Nathan looked afraid.

"Jade's in the drawing room," he told Nathan.

His sister stood up as soon as her brother came into the drawing room. "Oh, Nathan, thank heavens you're here."

Nathan walked over to stand directly in front of his sister. "Sit down," he ordered.

She immediately complied. Nathan clasped his hands behind his back, then said, "Brace yourself. The Winchesters found out all about our father, and it's only a matter of time before you're properly humiliated. Got that?"

As soon as she nodded he turned and tried to leave.

"Wait," Jade called out. "Nathan, I must talk to you."

"I don't have time," her brother called back.

"You always were a man of few words," Caine said. "Why the hurry?"

"I've got to find my wife," Nathan told him in a near bellow. "She's missing."

He was already out the front door before Caine's announcement caught him. "Your lovely wife was just here."

"Sara was here?"

"For God's sake, Nathan, must you roar every time you open your mouth? Come back inside."

The sound of little Olivia wailing again was followed by the loud slam of a door above the stairs. Sterns was obviously sending them a message to keep their voices down.

Nathan walked back into the foyer. "What was my wife doing here?"

"She wanted to talk to us."

"Why did you let her leave, man? Damn it, where did she go?"

Caine motioned his brother-in-law into the drawing room and pulled the doors closed before giving his answer. "Sara came to warn us. She wasn't quite as blunt as you were," he added dryly.

"Did she tell you where she was going?"

Jade hurried over and grabbed hold of Nathan's hand so he couldn't disappear on her. She started to answer his question, then caught herself when Caine shook his head at her.

"We'll tell you where Sara went after you sit down and talk to us," Caine announced. "For once, Nathan, you're going to be civil. Got that?"

"I don't have time for this. I've got to find Sara. Do I have to break your arm to get the information I need?"

"Sara's safe enough," Caine said. Unless wolves really do eat their young, he qualified to himself. He put his arm around Jade's shoulders and led her back to the settee.

He noticed Nathan wasn't following them. "Sit down," he ordered in a much firmer voice. "I've got a couple of questions to ask you, Nathan, and I'm not telling you where Sara went until I get some answers."

Nathan knew it was pointless to argue. Beating his brother-in-law into a bloody pulp wouldn't do him any good either. Caine would just bloody him up, too. Precious time would be wasted, and when the fight was over Caine would still remain stubborn.

It was just one of several reasons Nathan admired his sister's husband.

"Why the hell can't you be more like Colin?" he asked. He sat down and glared at Caine. "Jade, you married the wrong brother. Colin's a damn sight more agreeable."

His sister smiled. "I didn't fall in love with Colin, Nathan."

She looked up at her husband then. "I don't believe I've ever seen Nathan this upset. Have you?"

"All right," Nathan muttered. "Ask me your questions."

"Tell me how the Winchesters found out about your father."

Nathan shrugged. "It isn't important how the truth was found out."

"The hell it isn't," Caine interjected.

"Do you believe Sara told her family?"

"She probably did," Nathan said.

"Why?" Jade asked.

"Why did she tell or why do I believe she told?" Nathan asked.

"Why do you believe she told?" Jade qualified. "And quit fencing with me, Nathan. I can see you're uncomfortable with this topic. I'm not going to let it go, so you might as well answer directly."

"Sara's a woman," Nathan said.

He realized the foolishness in that statement almost as soon as his sister did.

"I'm a woman," Jade said. "What does that have to do with the issue under discussion?"

"Yes, of course you're a woman," Nathan answered. "But you're different, Jade. You don't behave like one."

She didn't know if she'd just been insulted or complimented. She looked at her husband to judge his reaction.

Caine's expression showed his exasperation. "Nathan, haven't you learned anything about women in all the time you spent with Sara?"

"Caine, I don't condemn her," Nathan argued. "I'm still a little angry with her, but only because she wouldn't admit to me that she had told them. She shouldn't have lied to me. Still," he added, "she probably—"

"Let me guess," Caine interrupted. "She probably couldn't help herself."

"Your views about women are appalling," Jade said. "I had no idea you'd become so misdirected." She realized she'd raised her voice and forced herself to calm down when she asked, "Is it because she's a Winchester that you have so little faith in her?"

Caine let out a snort. "Isn't that a little like the pot calling the kettle black? If Nathan doesn't have any faith in his wife because of her background, she sure as hell shouldn't have any faith in him."

Nathan was becoming more uncomfortable with each question. His family was forcing him to reevaluate beliefs he'd held for years.

"Of course Sara has faith in me," he muttered. "As I said before, I don't condemn her."

"If you say again that she probably couldn't help herself, I do believe I will try to strangle you, Nathan," Jade announced.

Nathan shook his head. "These questions are pointless."

Nathan started to stand up, but Caine's next question stopped him. "What if she's innocent? Nathan, don't you realize what that means?"

It was more the tone of voice than the question itself that caught Nathan's attention. "What are you suggesting?" he asked.

"I'm suggesting that if you happen to be wrong about Sara, then someone else got hold of your father's file. And that means that someone got into the War Department, breached the inner sanctuary, and got into the vault. We could damn well be dealing with another traitor. England's most carefully guarded secrets are kept inside that safe. Nathan, your file's there, and so are Colin's and mine. We're all at risk."

"You're jumping to conclusions," Nathan announced.

"No, brother, you've jumped to conclusions," Jade whispered. "Caine, you must find out the truth as soon as possible."

"Damned right I will," Caine announced. He looked at Nathan again. "Sara told us she was going home. It was a contradiction, though. She said she wanted to see her mother, and then she was going home."

"She also told us that she'd disowned her family. I got the feeling that you were included in that remark, Nathan," Jade said.

Her brother was already striding toward the foyer. "If I have to tear apart the Winchester's townhouse from rafter to cellar, by God I will," he bellowed.

"I'm coming with you," Caine announced. "There might be more than one Winchester waiting to greet you."

"I don't need your help," Nathan replied.

"I don't care if you need it or not," Caine argued. "You're getting it."

"Damn it, I don't need anyone to fight my battles."

Caine wasn't deterred. "I'll let you fight the bigger battle all on your own, brother, but I'm going with you to the Winchesters'."

Sterns had just started down the stairs when Nathan bellowed, "What the hell are you talking about, Caine?"

The infant's wail of distress echoed throughout the foyer. Without breaking his stride Sterns turned around again and started back up the stairs.

"What's the bigger battle?" Nathan demanded to know as he opened the front door and started out.

Caine was right on his heels. "The battle to win Sara back," he answered.

A tremor of worry nagged Nathan. He pushed the feeling aside immediately. "Damn it, Caine, lower your voice. You're upsetting my godchild."

Caine suddenly wanted to throttle his brother-in-law. "Nathan, I hope Sara makes you suffer. If there's any justice in this world, she'll bring you to your knees before she ever forgives you."

Nathan didn't tear down the rafters of the Winchester residence, but he did break through a couple of locked doors. While Caine kept watch from the foyer Nathan quite methodically searched every room from top to bottom. Luck was on his side. Both the earl and his daughter Belinda were away from the townhouse, no doubt searching for Sara, Nathan surmised, and at least he didn't have to put up with their interference. It wouldn't have stopped him, of course, but it might have slowed him down a little.

Sara's mother stayed out of his path, too. The fragile-looking gray-haired woman hovered next to the fireplace inside the drawing room and simply waited until the marquess had finished his task.

Lady Victoria Winchester could have saved Nathan considerable time by simply telling him that Sara had paid a brief visit and had already left, but the marquess of St. James overwhelmed the timid woman, and she couldn't seem to find her courage or her voice.

Caine and Nathan were leaving when Sara's mother called out to them. "Sara was here, but she left a good twenty minutes ago."

Nathan had forgotten the woman was in the drawing room. He walked toward her but stopped in the center of the room when she cringed away from him. "Did she tell you where she was going?" he asked softly. He took another step forward, then stopped again. "Madam, I'm not going to harm you. I'm worried about Sara, and I would like to find her as soon as possible."

His gentle voice helped her regain her composure. "Why do you want to find her? She told me you don't care for her, sir."

"She's been telling me these past weeks that I do," he countered.

Sara's mother slowly shook her head. The sadness in her eyes was apparent. Superficially, she looked like her sister Nora, but Nora had a zest for life, while Sara's mother looked like a frightened, defeated woman.

"Why do you want to find Sara?"

"Why? Because she's my wife," Nathan replied.

"Is it true you only want Sara back so that you can have the king's gift? My Sara's determined to find a way for you to have both the land and the treasure, sir. But she doesn't want anything from you."

Tears filled the elderly woman's eyes. "You've destroyed her innocence, m'lord. She had such faith in you all these years. We have both wronged my Sara."

"Sara has always had kind words for you, madam," Nathan said. "She doesn't believe you've ever wronged her."

"I used to call her my little peacemaker," she said. "When she was older she often took up my battles for me. It was so much easier, you see."

"I don't understand," Nathan said. "What battles?"

"Just family squabbles," she answered. "My husband Winston often dragged his brother Henry into our personal disagreements. Sara put herself in front of me to weight the odds more equally."

Nathan shook his head. He decided that Sara's mother had a little spirit left inside her when she suddenly straightened her shoulders and frowned at him. "Sara deserves to find peace and joy for herself. She won't settle the way I did. She won't be coming back here, either. She's very disappointed in all of us."

"Madam, I have to find her."

His anguish got through to her. "You are worried about her, then? You do care, if only just a little?"

Nathan nodded. "Of course I'm worried. Sara needs me."

Lady Victoria actually smiled. "Perhaps you also need her," she remarked. "She told me she was going home," she added. "I assumed she meant she was returning to you. She said there were several details she needed to see to before she left London again."

"She isn't leaving London." Nathan made that statement in a hard voice.

Caine walked forward. "Could Sara have gone to your townhouse?" he asked his brother-in-law.

Nathan frowned at him. "I don't have a townhouse, remember? It was burned to the ground by a few of my father's associates."

Caine nodded. "Hell, Nathan, where else could she have gone? Where is your home?"

Nathan turned back to Sara's mother. "Thank you for giving me your help. I'll send word to you as soon as I've found Sara."

The woman got teary-eyed again. She reminded Nathan of Sara, and he smiled at her. He knew where his wife had inherited her trait for weeping at the slightest provocation.

She put her hand on Nathan's arm and walked by his side to the front door. "Since my Sara was a little girl she's loved you. Oh, she would only admit it to me, of course. The rest of the family would have ridiculed her. She was always given to fantasy. You were her knight in shining armor."

"He's getting more tarnished by the minute," Caine said.

Nathan ignored that insult. "Thank you again, Lady Winchester."

Caine was astonished by the tenderness in Nathan's voice. When he bowed formally to the elderly woman Caine did the same.

They were both out the door and halfway down the steps when Sara's mother whispered from behind, "His name is Grant. Luther Grant."

Both Caine and Nathan turned around. "What did you say?" Nathan asked.

"The man who found out about your father," Sara's mother explained. "His name is Luther Grant. He works as a guard, and my husband paid him handsomely to look into the files. That's all I chanced to overhear," she added. "Will it help you?"

Nathan was speechless. Caine nodded. "Thank you. It saves considerable time, I assure you."

"Why did you tell us?" Nathan asked.

"Because it was wrong. Winston went too far this time. My husband gets caught up in his greed, and he doesn't consider what his plans will do to others. I cannot let Sara be his scapegoat again. Please don't let anyone know I told you. It would be difficult for me."

Sara's mother closed the door before either man could give her his promise.

"She's terrified of her husband," Caine whispered. "It sickens me to see such sadness in her eyes. No woman should have to live her life in fear."

Nathan nodded. His mind wasn't on Sara's mother, though, and when he turned to Caine he couldn't hide his fear. "Where do I look for her now, Caine? Where could she have gone? My God, if anything happens to her, I don't know what I'll do. I've grown accustomed to having her around."

It was as close as Nathan was going to come to admitting the truth, Caine realized. He wondered then if his stubborn-headed brother-in-law knew he loved Sara.

"We'll find her, Nathan," he promised. "I think we should go back to the wharf first. Colin might have some news for us. One of the men might have spotted her."

Nathan grabbed at that thread of hope. He didn't say another word until he and Caine had reached their destination. His fear was tearing at his nerves. He couldn't seem to think straight.

It was sunset when they reached the waterfront. The streets were cast in orange shadows. Candles burned bright inside the Emerald Shipping office. As soon as Nathan and Caine walked inside Colin bounded to his feet so quickly that shooting pains radiated up his injured leg.

"Did anyone find Sara yet?" Caine asked his brother.

Colin nodded. "She found us," he said. His forehead was beaded with perspiration, and he was taking deep breaths in an attempt to ease the pain. Neither Caine nor Nathan remarked upon his obvious distress, for they both knew their sympathy would only irritate the proud man.

Nathan waited until Colin lost some of his grimace, then asked, "What do you mean, she found us?"

"Sara came back here."

"Then where the hell is she now?" Caine asked.

"She demanded to be taken home. Jimbo and Matthew escorted her. Sara's back on board the *Seahawk*."

Caine's sigh of relief filled the room. "So she considers the *Seahawk* her home, does she?"

The tightness inside Nathan's chest began to loosen up. He was so relieved to know that Sara was safe, he literally broke out in a cold sweat. He snatched the linen handkerchief Colin had pulled from his vest pocket and wiped his brow. "It's the only home we've shared," Nathan muttered in a low, gruff voice.

"I guess that means Sara isn't holding a grudge," Caine

said. He leaned against the edge of the desk and grinned at his brother. "Pity, that. I was really looking forward to watching Nathan practice."

"Practice what?" Colin asked.

"Getting down on his knees."

Chapter Fourteen

N athan couldn't stand the idle chitchat long. He had to get to Sara. He needed to see for himself that she was all right. It was the only way he would be able to calm his racing heartbeat. He had to know she was safe.

Without a word of farewell he left Colin and Caine and rowed out to the *Seahawk*. He was surprised to find that most of the crew had already boarded. The men traditionally spent the first night back in port getting drunk enough to fight anything that moved.

A portion of the crew stood guard on the three decks while the others took up their positions in the wardroom area. Some of the men had strung their hammocks up between the hooks in the ceiling and slept with their knives on their chests for the sake of readiness.

The hammocks were used only in foul weather or when it was too cold to sleep on deck. It was warm that day— exceedingly so, as a matter of fact—and Nathan knew the men were there solely for protective purposes. They were watching over their mistress.

As soon as they spotted him they rolled from their swinging cots and filed up the steps.

The door to the cabin was unlatched. When Nathan went inside he spotted Sara at once. She was sound asleep in the center of his bed. She was holding his pillow against her chest. She'd left two candles burning in their glass globes on the desk, and the soft glow from the light played against the angles of her face like dancing shadows.

He'd have to have another talk with her about the worries of fire, he thought to himself. The woman was forever forgetting to douse the candle flame.

Nathan quietly shut the door, then leaned against it. He was so hungry for the sight of her, he stood there for a long while just watching her sleep until his panic finally dissipated and it didn't hurt so much to breathe.

Every now and again she let out a little hiccup, and Nathan realized she must have cried herself to sleep.

The sound made him feel as guilty as hell.

He couldn't imagine living his life without her by his side. God help him, he cared for her.

That acknowledgment wasn't nearly as painful as he'd imagined it would be. He didn't feel as though his soul had just been snatched away from him. Just as amazing as the admission itself, he hadn't been struck by lightning.

Caine had been right after all. He had been a fool. How could he have been so blind, so indifferent? Sara would never try to manipulate him. Sara was his partner, not his enemy. The thought of spending the rest of his life without getting to shout at her again was simply too monstrous to think about.

Her love gave him renewed strength. Together they could face any challenge, he knew, be it from the St. James camp or the Winchester den. As long as he had Sara by his side Nathan didn't think he could ever be defeated.

His thoughts moved on to ways he could please his wife. He was never going to raise his voice to her again. He'd start calling her by those ridiculous endearments he'd heard other men call their wives. Sara would probably like that.

He finally took his gaze away from her and looked around the room. There was clutter everywhere. Sara's dresses were hanging between his shirts on the hooks.

She'd made the cabin her home. Her possessions were everywhere. Her ivory brush and comb, along with a multitude of colored hairpins, littered his desktop. She'd washed out some of her feminine undergarments and had hung them up to dry on a rope she'd hooked from wall to wall across the room.

He had to dodge the damp clothing when he took his shirt off. He could think of nothing but finding the right words to use when he told her he was sorry. God, it was going to be difficult. He'd never apologized to anyone before, but he was determined not to muck it up.

He bent over to take off his boots and knocked the makeshift clothesline. One of Sara's silk chemises was jarred free. Nathan reached out to catch the garment before it fell to the floor and only then realized just what his wife had used for her rope.

"You used my whip for your clothesline?"

He really hadn't meant to shout. It had just caught him off guard. His bellow of outrage didn't wake her up, though. Sara muttered in her sleep, then flipped over on her stomach.

It only took him a minute to calm down. Then he was actually able to see the humor in the situation. He couldn't quite smile, but he wasn't grimacing any longer. Tomorrow, he decided, right after he talked to her about fire hazards, he'd mention his special attachment to his whip and ask her not to use it for such demeaning chores.

He stripped out of the rest of his clothes and stretched out next to Sara. She was exhausted from the heartache both he and her Winchester relatives had put her through. She needed her rest. She didn't even stir when he put his arm around her.

313

He didn't dare pull her close to him, knowing full well that as soon as she cuddled up against him he wouldn't be able to stop himself from making love to her.

His intentions were honorable. His frustration, however, soon became damned painful. Nathan considered it due penance for the agony he'd caused her. The only thought that got him through the long dark night was the promise he made to himself that as soon as morning arrived and Sara was awake he'd show her how much he cared for her.

Nathan didn't fall asleep until the sun was starting to rise. He awoke with a start several hours later, then rolled over to take his wife into his arms.

She wasn't there. Her clothes were gone, too. Nathan pulled on his pants and went up on deck to look for her.

He found Matthew first. "Where's Sara?" he demanded. "God, she isn't in the galley, is she?"

The seaman motioned toward the wharf. "Colin rowed out earlier with some papers for you to sign. Sara and Jimbo went back with him to the office."

"Why the hell didn't you wake me?"

"Sara wouldn't let us disturb you," Matthew explained. "She said you were sleeping like the dead."

"She was being . . . considerate," Nathan muttered. "I appreciate that."

Matthew shook his head. "She was bent on avoiding you, if you want my opinion," he said. "And after the way we each took a turn lighting into her yesterday when she came back to the wharf, well, we were all feeling a little guilty, and so we let her have her way today."

"What are you talking about?"

"As soon as Jimbo saw Sara climbing out of that hack he started in lecturing her about the dangers of the city for an innocent woman traveling alone."

"So?"

"Then Colin had to have a turn," Matthew continued. "Next Chester gave her what for . . . or was it Ivan? I don't recall now. God's truth, Nathan, the men were all lined up waiting their turn to lecture her. It was a sight I thought I'd never see."

Nathan pictured the scene and couldn't help but smile. "The men are loyal to her," he announced. He started to turn back to the steps. He fully intended to go after his wife and bring her back. He paused suddenly and turned around. "Matthew? How was Sara feeling this morning?"

The seaman glared at Nathan. "She wasn't crying, if that's what you're wondering. Now, if you ask me how she was acting, I'd have to say she acted damned pitiful."

Nathan walked back over to his friend and stood by his side. "What the hell does that mean?"

"Defeated," Matthew muttered. "You've broken her heart, boy."

Nathan suddenly pictured Sara's mother in his mind. She was certainly a defeated woman, and Nathan knew that her husband, Winston, had been responsible for breaking her spirit. God help him, was he just as bad?

That thought terrified him. Matthew was watching Nathan's expression and was astonished to see the vulnerability there. "What the hell am I going to do?" Nathan muttered.

"You broke it," Matthew countered. "You fix it."

Nathan shook his head. "I doubt she'll believe anything I say. God, I can't blame her."

Matthew shook his head. "Do you still have so little faith in our Sara?"

That question gained a glare. "What are you saying?" Nathan asked.

"She's loved you for a heap of years, Nathan. I don't believe she can stop so suddenly, no matter what dastardly thing you've done to her. You've only got to let her know you have faith in her. If you stomp on a flower, you kill it. Our Sara's heart is like that flower, boy. You've hurt her, and that's a fact. Best find a way to show her you're caring. If you don't, you'll lose her for good. She asked me if she could accompany me back to Nora's island."

"She isn't leaving me."

"You don't need to shout, boy. I hear you fine." Matthew had to struggle to hide his smile. "She mentioned that you'd mind if she left."

"Then she realizes that I have begun to"—Nathan suddenly felt like an awkward schoolboy—"care."

Matthew snorted. "No, she hasn't recognized that," he said. "She's thinking you want the land and the treasure. She called herself the extra baggage that went along with the king's gift."

In the beginning that was all he'd been interested in, but it hadn't taken him long to realize that Sara was far more important to him.

And he was losing her. He had broken her heart, but God help him, he didn't know how to fix it.

He needed advice from an expert.

After ordering Matthew to take charge of the *Seahawk* for the day he finished dressing and went into London proper. He knew Sara would be safe with Jimbo and Colin looking after her, and so he went directly to his sister's house. He didn't want to see Sara until he knew exactly what he would say to her.

Jade answered the front door. "How did you find out so soon?" she asked her brother when he rushed past her.

"I've got to talk to Caine," Nathan announced. He looked inside the drawing room, saw that it was empty, and then turned back to his sister. "Where is he? Damn, he didn't go out, did he?"

"No, he's in the study," Jade answered. "Nathan, I've never seen you in such a state," she added. "Are you worried about Sara? She's all right. I just settled her in the guest chamber."

Nathan was halfway down the hallway before Jade had finished her explanation. He turned around then. "She's here? How did—"

"Colin dragged her back to us," Jade explained. "Nathan, please lower your voice. Olivia has just gone down for her afternoon rest, and I believe that if you wake her this time, Sterns will come after you with a hatchet."

That statement got a quick grin from Nathan. "Sorry," he whispered.

He started back toward Caine's study. Jade called out, "I've apologized to Sara because I shamelessly jumped to the wrong conclusion. Have you, Nathan?"

"Jumped to the wrong conclusion?" he asked.

She ran after him. "No," she snapped. "I want to know if you've apologized for finding her guilty of betrayal, brother. I know she couldn't have done it. She loves you, Nathan. She's set on leaving you, too."

"I'm not letting her go anywhere," Nathan bellowed.

Caine heard his brother-in-law's booming voice. He sat down behind his desk and pretended to be absorbed in reading the dailies.

Nathan didn't knock. He barged inside, then shut the door with a slam from the back of his boot. A baby's shrill cry followed that noise.

"I've got to talk to you."

Caine took his time folding his paper. He was trying to give Nathan a few moments to calm down. He motioned for him to sit. "Would you like some brandy?" he asked. "You look like you could use some."

Nathan declined the offer. He didn't sit down either. Caine leaned back in his chair and watched his brother-in-law pace until his patience ran out. "You said you wanted to talk to me?" he prodded.

"Yes."

Another good five minutes went by before Caine tried again. "Spit it out, Nathan."

"It's . . . difficult."

"I've already gathered that much," Caine returned.

Nathan nodded, then resumed his pacing.

"Damn it, will you sit down? I'm getting dizzy watching you."

Nathan suddenly stopped. He stood in front of Caine's

desk. His stance was rigid. Caine thought he looked ready to do battle.

"I need your help."

Caine wouldn't have been surprised if Nathan had lost his supper then and there. His brother-in-law's face had turned gray, and he looked like he was in acute pain.

"All right, Nathan," Caine said. "I'll help you any way I can. Tell me what you want."

Nathan looked incredulous. "You don't even know what I need, yet you immediately promise to help me. Why?"

Caine let out a long sigh. "You've never had to ask anyone for anything, have you, Nathan?"

"No."

"It's damned difficult for you, isn't it?"

Nathan shrugged. "I've learned not to depend on others, but I can't seem to think straight now."

"You've also learned never to trust anyone either, haven't you?"

"Meaning?"

"Sara says you expected her to betray you. Is she right?"

Nathan shrugged again.

"Look," Caine said. "When I married your sister, you became my brother. Of course I'll help you. It's what family's all about."

Nathan walked over to the window and stared outside. His hands were clasped behind his back. "I believe Sara might have lost some of her faith in me."

Caine thought that had to be the understatement of the year. "Then help her find it again," he suggested.

"How?"

"Do you love her, Nathan?"

"I care for her," he answered. "I've come to realize that she isn't my enemy. She's my partner," he added in a brisk tone of voice. "She has my best interests at heart, just as I have her best interests at heart."

Caine rolled his eyes heavenward. 'Colin's your partner Nathan. Sara's your wife."

When Nathan didn't comment, Caine continued prodding him. "Do you want to spend the rest of your life with Sara? Or is she just a nuisance you have to put up with in order to receive the king's gift?"

"I cannot imagine living without her," Nathan said in a low, fervent voice.

"Sara's a little more than just a partner, then, isn't she?"

"Of course she is," Nathan muttered. "She's my wife, for God's sake. Colin's my partner."

The two men were silent for a moment.

"I had no idea this . . . caring thing could be so irritating. I've ruined everything, Caine. I've destroyed Sara's faith in me."

"Does she love you?"

"Of course she loves me," Nathan immediately answered. "Or at least she used to love me. She would tell me almost every day." He let out a sigh, then said, "Matthew was right. All this time Sara's given me her love without reservation. It's like a flower, and I've stomped on it."

Caine tried not to smile. "Like a flower, Nathan? God, you have taken a fall. You've become . . . eloquent."

Nathan wasn't paying him any attention. "She thinks of herself as extra baggage I have to put up with in order to get the land and the coins. That was true at first, but everything's changed now."

"Nathan, simply tell her how you feel."

"Sara's so delicate," Nathan announced. "She deserves better than me, but I'll be damned if I'll let anyone else touch her. I've got to fix this. I've stomped on her . . ."

Caine cut him off. "I know. I know. You've stomped on her flower."

"Her heart, damn it," Nathan muttered. "Get it right, for God's sake."

Since Nathan wasn't looking at him, Caine felt it was safe to smile. "So what are you going to do?" he asked.

Another five minutes passed in silence. Then Nathan

straightened his shoulders. He turned around to look at Caine. "I'm going to restore her faith in me."

Caine didn't think it would do him any good to remind Nathan that he'd suggested that very action not ten minutes earlier.

"That's a sound idea," he said instead. "Now tell me how you plan to achieve this—"

"I'm going to show her," Nathan interrupted. "Hell, why didn't I think of this before?"

"Since I don't know what you're thinking, I can't answer you."

"It's so simple, an imbecile could figure it out. I'll need your help to pull it off."

"I already said I'd help you."

"Now I need some advice, Caine. You are the expert on women," he added in a matter-of-fact tone of voice.

That announcement was news to Caine, and he was about to ask Nathan how he had come to that conclusion, but his brother-in-law answered him before the question was asked. "Jade never would have settled. If anything, my sister is discriminating."

Caine started to grin, then frowned instead when Nathan casually added, "I still can't figure it. You must have something only she can . . . appreciate."

Caine wasn't given a chance to respond to that barb. "I need your help with Luther Grant," Nathan announced.

"For God's sake, Nathan, will you quit jumping back and forth between issues? You just asked for advice concerning women, and now you're—"

"Grant's got to talk to us," Nathan insisted.

Caine leaned back in his chair. "I was going after the bastard anyway, Nathan. He'll get what's coming to him."

"He might be on the run," Nathan said.

"Don't borrow trouble," Caine said. "We'll find out soon enough."

"He has to admit his part in this scheme before

Farnmount's ball. If Grant has taken off, that only gives us two days to find him."

"We'll have his signed confession before then," Caine promised. "But why is Farnmount's ball your deadline, Nathan?"

"Everyone comes back to London to attend, that's why."

"You never attend."

"I will this year."

Caine nodded. "You know, Nathan, I always enjoy the affair. It's the only ball your friendly St. James relatives attend."

"It's the only ball they're ever invited to attend," Nathan drawled. He leaned against the window ledge and smiled at his brother-in-law.

Caine still didn't understand what Nathan was planning. He knew prodding wouldn't do him any good. Nathan would tell him when he was ready. "Everyone's afraid to go to the ball for worry that he will be your Uncle Dunnford's next victim," Caine remarked. He smiled when he added, "But they're also afraid to miss the fiasco. Dunnford does provide some refreshing entertainment. He reminds me of Attila the Hun dressed in formal attire. Now that I think about it, so do you, Nathan."

His brother-in-law barely heard what Caine was rambling on about. His mind was centered on his plans. Another minute or two passed before he said, "The prince regent always attends the party, too."

A sudden gleam came into Caine's eyes. He leaned forward in his chair. "Yes," he agreed. "And so do all the Winchesters, now that I think about it."

"I'm only interested in one Winchester," Nathan said. "Winston."

"Do you think that's when he plans to spring his scandal about your father? Hell, yes, it is," Caine continued. "What better opportunity?"

"Can you set up a meeting with Sir Richards? I want to fill him in on the facts as soon as possible."

"The director of our War Section already knows about Grant. I spoke with him just this morning. He should be visiting with the bastard right about now."

"Unless he's gone into hiding," Nathan muttered.

"He doesn't have any reason to think we know about him. Quit worrying about Grant and tell me what you plan to do."

Nathan nodded. He then proceeded to explain what he wanted to do. When he finished Caine was smiling. "If luck is on our side, we should be able to set the meeting as early as tomorrow afternoon, Nathan."

"Yes," his brother-in-law answered. He straightened away from the window. "Now, about Sara. Someone has to keep a close watch on her until this has been resolved. I don't want the Winchesters to get hold of her while I'm seeing to the details. If anything happened to her, Caine, I don't know what . . ." He didn't go on.

"Jimbo's in the kitchen, eating the shelves dry. He already made it clear he's protecting Sara. He won't let her leave here. Jade and I will also keep a close watch. You don't think you'll make it back here before tonight?"

"I'll try," Nathan said. "Right now I've got to talk to Colin. It's only fair that my partner agree to my plan before I proceed."

"At the risk of sounding completely ignorant, why does Colin need to give his agreement about Grant?"

"I'm not talking about Grant now," Nathan explained. "I'm talking about Sara. God, Caine, pay attention."

Caine let out a long sigh. "I'm trying."

"I have one more favor to ask you."

"Yes?"

"You're always calling Jade by those ridiculous endearments."

"Jade likes hearing those ridiculous endearments," he muttered.

"Exactly my point," Nathan said with a quick nod. "Sara will like them, too."

Caine looked incredulous. "You want me to call Sara by the same endearments I call my wife?"

"Of course not," Nathan snapped. "I want you to write them down on a piece of paper for me."

"Why?"

"So I'll know what the hell they are," Nathan bellowed. "Damn, you're making this difficult. Just write them down, all right? Leave the paper on the desk for me."

Caine didn't dare laugh. He did smile, though. The picture of Nathan referring to notes while he tried to woo Sara was quite amusing. "Yes, I'll leave it on the desk for you," he said when Nathan glared at him.

Nathan started to leave. "Are you even going to look in on Sara before you go?" Caine asked.

Nathan shook his head. "I have to get everything ready first."

The worry in his voice wasn't lost on Caine. "The love words aren't necessary, Nathan, if you just tell her what's in your heart."

His brother-in-law didn't respond to that suggestion. Caine finally understood. "You're afraid to confront her, aren't you?"

"The hell I am," Nathan roared. "I just want it to be right."

Jade was just passing by the library door when she heard her husband's laughter. She paused to listen, but the only snatch of conversation she caught didn't make any sense to her.

Nathan had just announced that come hell or high water, he was going to fix his flower. He just needed time to find out how.

Now what in heaven's name did that mean, Jade wondered.

Chapter Fifteen

Sara spent the afternoon in the guest bedroom. She sat in a chair near the window and tried to read one of the leather-bound books Jade had brought up for her. She couldn't concentrate on the story, though, and ended up staring down at the small flower garden behind the townhouse. All Sara could think about was Nathan and what an ignorant country mouse she'd been to love him.

Why couldn't he love her?

She asked herself that painful question every ten minutes or so but never did come up with a proper answer. The future terrified her. She'd already made up her mind to break the contract so that her family couldn't have the king's gift; but once the scandal was made known about Nathan's father, wouldn't the prince regent be placed in the position of having to withhold the royal gift from Nathan as well?

Sara couldn't allow that. Her father had used trickery and deceit to gain the advantage over Nathan. Sara was determined to find a way to even the odds. She didn't want to live with a man who didn't love her, so she decided to strike a bargain with Nathan. In return for her signature giving up all rights to the gift Nathan would let Matthew take her with him when he returned to Nora's island.

Lord, there was so much to consider. The unfairness of what her father had done shamed her. She decided then that her only hope was to gain the prince regent's support. The thought of having to plead her case to him sent a shiver down her spine.

George, the future king of England once his father died or was, as the rumors were whispering, officially declared insane, was a handsome, well-educated man. Those were, unfortunately, his only good points. Sara disliked him immensely. He was a spoiled, pleasure-seeking fop who rarely placed his country's concerns above his own. His worst flaw, to Sara's way of thinking, was his trait of changing his mind on any matter. Sara knew she wasn't the only one who disliked the prince. He was extremely unpopular with the masses, and just a few months past she'd heard that the windows of his carriage had been broken by angry subjects. George was in the conveyance at the time, said to be on his way to Parliament.

Still, she didn't have anyone else to turn to, and so she penned a note to the prince requesting an audience the following afternoon. She sealed the envelope and was just about to go into the corridor to ask Sterns to send a messenger over to Carlton House when Caine intercepted her.

He'd come to fetch her for dinner. Sara was most polite when she refused his invitation, insisting that she really wasn't hungry. Caine was just as polite when he insisted that she eat something. The man wouldn't take no for an answer. He told her so as he coaxed her along the hallway.

Jimbo was waiting in the foyer. Sara handed him the envelope and asked him to deliver the letter for her. Caine reached over Sara's head and plucked the letter out of the seaman's hands before he could agree to undertake the errand.

"I'll have one of the servants take it over," Caine explained. "Jimbo, escort Lady Sara into the dining room. I won't be a minute."

As soon as Jimbo and Sara turned the corner Caine opened the envelope, read the letter, and put it in his pocket. He waited another minute or two and then strolled into the dining room.

Jimbo sat next to Sara at the long table. Jade was seated directly across from her. Caine took his place at the head of the table and then rang for the servants to begin.

"Though it was probably very rude of me to notice, I did see that the letter was addressed to our prince regent," Caine began.

"I don't know of anyone else living in Carlton House," Jimbo interjected.

Caine frowned at the seaman. "Yes, but I didn't realize Sara was on personal terms with the prince."

"Oh, I'm not on personal terms with the prince," she rushed out. "I don't even like . . ." She stopped in mid-explanation, then blushed. She lowered her gaze to the table. "I apologize. I do tend to blurt out whatever's on my mind," she confessed. "As far as the note is concerned, I requested an audience. I hope that the prince will see me tomorrow afternoon."

"Why?" Jade asked. "Sara, the prince is certainly in your father's camp."

"I do hope you're wrong, Jade."

"I'm afraid my wife's correct in that evaluation, Sara," Caine said. "When the prince made it known he wanted to divorce his wife, Caroline, your father was one of a handful who supported him."

"But won't the prince put personal considerations aside and come to a loyal subject's aid?"

Her innocence was both refreshing and alarming. Caine didn't want her to be disappointed. "No," Caine said. "His own considerations always come first. The man changes his views as often as he changes his ministers, Sara. Anything he would promise you shouldn't be counted on. I'm sorry to sound disloyal, but I'm being completely honest with you. I don't want you to get your hopes up only to have them dashed. Let Nathan fight this battle, Sara. Stand by his side and let him handle your father."

She shook her head. "Do you know I refused to learn how to swim?" she blurted out. "I thought I shouldn't have to know how, you see, because it was Nathan's duty to make certain I didn't drown. I've been perfectly willing to take care of everyone but myself. Now you suggest I let Nathan fight my battles. It's wrong, Caine. I've been wrong. I don't want ever to cling to anyone. I should have enough strength to stand on my own. I want to be strong, damn it."

She turned bright pink after she'd finished her impassioned speech. "Please excuse my gutter language," she whispered.

An awkward silence followed that remark. Jimbo filled the space with a couple of spicy stories about his sea adventures.

The dessert tray was just being removed from the table when Jade asked, "Have you seen our beautiful daughter yet?" She'd blurted out that question in an attempt to keep Sara at the table awhile longer. She wanted to bring the conversation around to Nathan, of course. Jade was determined to interfere. It was such a heartache to see Sara looking so desolate and alone.

Sara actually smiled at the mention of the infant. "I've heard your daughter," she confessed. "But I've yet to see her. Sterns has promised me that this evening he'll let me hold Olivia."

"She's such a delightful baby," Jade announced. "She's smiling all the time now. She's very intelligent, too. Caine and I noticed that right away."

Jade continued to expound on her three-month-old's considerable accomplishments. Sara noticed that after each of Jade's boasts, Caine immediately nodded his agreement.

"Olivia's blessed to have such loving parents."

"Nathan will make a wonderful father," Jade interjected. Sara didn't comment.

"Don't you agree, husband?" Jade asked Caine.

"If he ever learns to lower his voice, he will."

Jade kicked her husband while she continued to smile at Sara. "Nathan has so many wonderful qualities," she announced.

Sara didn't want to talk about Nathan, but she felt it would be rude not to show some interest. "Oh? And what might those qualities be?" she asked.

Jade opened her mouth to answer, then stopped. She looked as if she'd forgotten the topic. She turned to Caine for assistance. "Explain Nathan's wonderful qualities to Sara."

"You explain them," Caine replied as he reached for another sweet biscuit.

That statement earned him another kick under the table. He glared at his wife, then said, "Nathan's trustworthy."

"He might be trustworthy, but he certainly doesn't trust anyone else," Sara said. She started to fold her napkin.

"The boy's got courage," Jimbo blurted out. He grinned, too, for he was inordinately pleased to have come up with something.

"He's remarkably . . . tidy," Jade said. Even as she gave that bit of praise she wondered if she was right.

Sara neither agreed nor disagreed. Caine decided they were taking the wrong approach. His hand covered Jade's, and when she looked over at him he gave her a conspiratorial wink. "Nathan's probably the most stubborn man I've ever known."

"He might be a little stubborn," Sara immediately countered, "but that certainly isn't a sin." She turned her gaze to Jade. "Your brother reminds me of a beautifully sculptured statue. On the outside he's so handsome, so perfect, but inside his heart is as cold as marble."

Jade smiled. "I never considered Nathan beautiful," she said.

"Sara can't possibly consider him beautiful." Caine squeezed his wife's hand before adding, "Nathan's an ugly bastard, and everyone knows it. His back is covered with scars, for God's sake."

Sara let out a loud gasp, but Caine held his grin. At last they were getting her to show a little emotion.

"It was a woman who scarred Nathan's back," Sara cried out. "And it was this same woman who scarred his heart."

She tossed her napkin on the table and stood up. "Nathan isn't ugly, sir. He's incredibly handsome. I think it's dreadful that his own brother-in-law would say such insulting things about him. Now, if you'll excuse me, I'd like to go upstairs."

Jimbo frowned at Caine for upsetting Sara, then chased after her to make certain she did in fact go back above the stairs.

"Caine, you've upset her to the point where you're going to have to apologize," Jade told her husband.

Just then, Jimbo came rushing back into the dining room. "Sara's looking in on the little mite now," he said. "Tell me why you snatched her letter out of my hands. You weren't thinking I'd actually deliver the thing, were you?"

"The letter's in my pocket," Caine said. "I took it from you because I wanted to read it."

"Caine, that's an invasion . . . what did it say?" Jade asked.

"Just what Sara told us she'd written," Caine answered. "She requests an audience to discuss the contract."

"I'm assuming the boy's put together some sort of plan," Jimbo interjected.

"Yes," Caine answered.

"What did Sara mean when she said it was a woman who scarred Nathan's back? Who planted that misinformation in her mind? It was the fire that trapped him inside the prison."

"But wasn't Ariah responsible for having him locked up?"

"She was," Jimbo admitted. "It happened so many years ago, I doubt Nathan even holds a grudge. He came through it seasoned, to my way of thinking, and we didn't leave the island without a full booty to share amongst ourselves."

Caine stood up. "I've got a couple of details of my own to see about. I won't be home until late, Jade. Sir Richards and I have a little business to discuss."

"Why do you need to talk to the director of the War Department?" she asked. She couldn't hide her fear. "Caine, you haven't started back doing secret work for our government without discussing the matter with me first, have you? You promised—"

"Hush, love," Caine soothed. "I'm helping Nathan sort out a little matter, that's all. I'm fully retired and have no desire to return to the cloak-and-dagger days."

Jade looked relieved. Caine leaned down and kissed her. "I love you," he whispered before he started for the doorway.

"Just one minute," Jade called out. "You still haven't explained to me why you deliberately riled Sara up. Caine, we already know she loves him. All you have to do is look at her face to know that."

"Yes, we know she loves him," Caine said. "I just wanted to remind her," he continued. His grin turned devilish. "Now, if you'll excuse me, I've just thought of a few more endearments, and I want to write them down before I leave."

He left Jimbo and Jade staring after him.

For the first time that day Sara was able to stop thinking about Nathan. Little Olivia took her full attention. She was a beautiful infant. One minute she was smiling and drooling, and the next she was bellowing like an opera singer.

Olivia had her mother's green eyes. The sprinkle of dark hair on her crown looked like it might curl just like her father's. Sterns hovered by Sara's side the entire time she held the baby.

"I fear my little love has inherited her Uncle Nathan's inclination to bellow. She can be as loud as he is," Sterns confessed with a smile. "Olivia's wanting immediate gratification," he explained when the babe began to fret in earnest.

He took Olivia back into his arms and held her close. "Shall we go and find your mama, my little angel?" he crooned to the infant.

Sara was reluctant to go back to her room. It was lonely there, and she knew her problems would once again overpower her.

She went to bed early that night, and because she was so emotionally distraught she slept the full night through. She vaguely remembered cuddling up against her husband, knew he had slept next to her, for his side of the bed was still warm, and she came to the sorry conclusion that Nathan was still too angry with her to bother waking her up. He must still believe she'd betrayed him, she thought to herself.

Needless to say, that possibility infuriated her all over again. She worked herself into a rage by the time she'd finished her bath. Even though she'd rested long, uninterrupted hours she felt as refreshed as an old, wrung-out hag. She thought she looked like one, too.

There were dark half circles under her eyes, and her hair was as limp as her spirits. Sara wanted to look her best when she went to plead with the prince regent. She fretted over which gown to wear, just to take her mind off the real issue at hand, and finally settled on a conservative, high-necked pink walking dress.

Like a wallflower at a formal ball Sara sat in the corner of the bedroom all morning long, waiting for the invitation that never arrived.

She refused luncheon and spent a good portion of the afternoon pacing her room while she tried to figure out what her next step would be. It was terribly upsetting to her that the prince regent had ignored her urgent request. Caine had been right, she decided, when he'd said that the prince wasn't interested in the problems of his subjects.

Caine knocked on her door then, interrupting her thoughts. "Sara, we have a little errand to do," he said.

"Where are we going?" she asked. She started to put on her white gloves, then stopped. "I shouldn't go out," she explained. "The prince regent might still send word to me."

"You have to come with me," Caine ordered. "I don't have time to explain, Sara. Nathan wants you to meet him at the War Department offices in a half hour's time."

"Why?"

"I'll let your husband explain."

"Who else is going to be there? Why do we have to meet at the War Department?"

Caine was terribly smooth when it came to evading her questions. Jade was waiting in the foyer. Olivia was draped over her shoulder. "It's all going to turn out just fine," she told Sara. She was diligently patting her daughter's back.

The baby let out a loud belch. The sound made everyone smile. Caine kissed his wife and daughter good-bye, then gently nudged Sara out the front door.

"I'll have your gowns pressed and put in the wardrobe while you're doing this errand," Jade said.

"No," Sara blurted out. "I'll only be staying one more night."

"But where will you and Nathan be going?" Jade asked.

Sara didn't answer her. She turned around and walked down the three steps. Caine held the door to the carriage open. Sara sat across from her brother-in-law. He tried to engage her in casual conversation but quickly gave up when she gave him only whispered yes or no answers.

The War Department was situated in a tall, ugly, gray stone building. A musty smell permeated the stairwells. Caine took Sara up to the second floor. "The meeting's going to take place in Sir Richards's office. You'll like him, Sara. He's a good man."

"I'm certain I will," she said, just to be polite. "But who is he, Caine, and why does he want this meeting?"

"Richards is the director of the department." He opened the door to a large office area and motioned for Sara to go inside.

A short, heavy-bellied man was standing behind a desk. He had thin gray hair, a beak nose, and a ruddiness to his complexion. As soon as he looked up from the paper he was holding in his hand and spotted Sara and Caine he started forward.

"There you are now," he announced with a smile. "We're about ready. Lady Sara, what a pleasure it is to meet you."

He was such a nice gentleman, she thought. He formally bowed to Sara and then took her hand in his own. "You must be quite a lady to have captured our Nathan."

"She didn't capture him, Sir Richards," Caine interjected with a smile of his own. "He captured her."

"I fear you're both incorrect," Sara whispered. "King George captured the two of us. Nathan was never given a choice in the matter, but I would like to find a way to—"

Caine wouldn't let her go on. "Yes, yes," he interrupted. "You'd like to find Nathan, wouldn't you? Where is he?" he asked the director.

"Waiting for the papers," Sir Richards explained. "He'll be back in just a minute. My assistant is quite speedy. Don't worry, my dear, it will all be legal."

She didn't know what the director was talking about but didn't want to appear completely ignorant. "I'm not at all certain why I'm here," she admitted. "I—"

She quit speaking when the side door to the office opened and Nathan walked in. She couldn't remember what she was saying then, and when the pain in her chest started throbbing she realized she was holding her breath.

He didn't even acknowledge her but strode over to the desk and dropped two papers on top of a stack. Then he walked over to an elongated window seat and stood there staring at her.

She couldn't take her gaze off him. He was a rude,

impossible-to-understand, stubborn-headed man whose manners were no better than a hedgehog's, she thought.

A knock sounded at the door, and a young man dressed in a guard's black uniform looked inside. "Sir Richards, the prince regent's carriage is down front," he said.

Sara heard the announcement, but she still couldn't take her gaze away from Nathan. He didn't seem to be at all surprised that the prince was on his way up the steps. He didn't appear overly nervous either, for he leaned against the wall and continued to look at her.

If he wasn't going to speak to her, then by God, she wasn't . . .

He crooked his finger at her. She couldn't believe his arrogance. Both Sir Richards and Caine were in deep discussion over some topic or other. Their low voices were still quite close to her, and she wondered if she'd been included in the conversation. Then Nathan crooked his finger at her again. It would be a burning day in heaven before she obeyed that rude command, she told herself, even as she started walking toward him.

He wasn't smiling at her. He wasn't scowling either. Nathan looked so serious, so . . . intense. She stopped when she was facing her husband, just a foot or so away.

God help her, she thought, she couldn't start weeping. He wasn't making her torment any easier to bear. He looked so damned satisfied. And why shouldn't he? she asked herself. All the man had to do was crook his finger at her, and she came running.

She turned and tried to walk away from him. He reached out and pulled her back. He put his arm around her shoulder and leaned down to whisper in her ear. "You will have faith in me, wife. Do you understand me?"

She was so astonished by his command, she let out a little gasp. She looked up at him to make certain he wasn't jesting with her. Then she remembered that Nathan rarely jested about anything. Sara was immediately consumed with anger. How dare he demand anything from her? At least she had enough faith in him to lose some, she thought to herself. Her eyes filled with tears almost immediately, and all she could think about was getting out of the room before she completely disgraced herself.

Nathan suddenly grabbed hold of her chin and forced her to look up at him again. "You love me, damn it."

She couldn't deny it, and so she said nothing at all.

He stared at her for a minute. "And do you know why you love me?"

"No," she answered in a voice to match his. "Honest to God, Nathan, I haven't the faintest idea why I love you."

He wasn't at all irritated by the anger in her voice. "You love me, Sara, because I'm everything you could ever want in a husband."

A tear slipped out from the corner of her eye. He caught it with his thumb.

"Dare you mock me by turning my own words against me? I haven't forgotten that I said the very same words to you when we set sail for Nora's island. Love can be destroyed. It's fragile, and . . ."

She stopped trying to explain when he shook his head at her. "You aren't fragile," he told her. "And your love can't be destroyed." His fingers gently caressed her cheek. "It's what I've come to value most, Sara. I wasn't mocking you."

"It doesn't matter," she whispered. "I know you don't love me. I've accepted it, Nathan. Please don't look so concerned. I don't fault you. You were never given a choice."

He couldn't stand to see her anguish. God, how he wished they were alone so he could take her into his arms and show her how much he loved her. He was going to have to prove himself to her first. "We'll discuss this later," he announced. "For now I have but one order, Sara. Don't you dare give up on me."

She didn't understand what he was asking her.

Nathan turned his attention to the door when the prince

regent walked inside the office. Sara immediately moved away from her husband, bowed her head as any loyal subject should, and patiently waited for her leader to address her.

The prince was of medium height and had dark, handsome looks. He wore his arrogance like a cloak around his shoulders.

Each man bowed to the prince when he was greeted, and then it was Sara's turn. She made a low curtsy. "It's always a pleasure to see you, Lady Sara."

"Thank you, my lord," she replied. "And thank you, too, for granting me this audience."

The prince looked bewildered by that comment. He nodded, however, and took his place behind Sir Richards's desk. The two men accompanying him took up their positions as sentinels behind their leader.

Caine was concerned that Sara might make another comment about the letter she'd written to the prince. He strolled over to stand next to her. "Sara, I never sent your note to the prince. It's still in my pocket."

Sir Richards was discussing the meeting with the prince, and since neither man was paying them any attention Sara felt it wasn't overly rude to whisper back. "Why didn't you send the letter? Did you forget?"

"No, I didn't forget," Caine said. "The letter would have interfered with Nathan's plans."

"Then it was Nathan who requested this meeting?"

Caine nodded. "Sir Richards also put in his request," he said. "You'd better sit down, Sara. It's going to get a little rocky. Keep your fingers crossed."

Nathan was leaning against the wall, watching her. He heard Caine's suggestion that she sit down and waited to see what Sara would do. There was a wingback chair across the room and an empty window seat next to him.

Sara glanced over to the wingback chair, then turned and walked over to Nathan. He was arrogantly satisfied with her instinctive show of loyalty.

And then he realized he'd come to depend upon that quality.

Nathan sat and pulled her down beside him in the space of a second. He almost leaned down then and there to tell her how much he loved her. He stopped himself just in time. It had to be right, he told himself. In just a few more minutes he would show her how much he loved her.

Sara edged away from her husband so that she wouldn't be touching him. She didn't think it would be appropriate to sit so close in the presence of the prince.

Nathan thought otherwise. He wasn't at all gentle when he hauled her back up against his side.

"I'm ready to begin," the prince announced.

Sir Richards motioned to the guard standing by the front entrance. The man opened the door, and Sara's father came rushing into the office.

As soon as she saw her father she instinctively moved closer to her husband. Nathan put his arm around her waist and held her close.

The earl of Winchester bowed to the prince, then frowned when he spotted the others.

He was about to request that the office be cleared, for the matter to be discussed was a confidential one, but the prince spoke first. "Do sit down, Winston. I'm eager to get this matter settled."

The earl immediately took one of the chairs facing the prince. He sat down and leaned forward at the same time. "Have you looked over the evidence I sent to you?"

"I have," the prince answered. "Winston, have you met our esteemed director of War Operations?"

Winston turned to Sir Richards and gave a quick nod. "We met a time or two," he said. "May I ask why he's here? I don't see that the matter has any bearing on his department. It's a question of breaking a contract, nothing more."

"On the contrary," Sir Richards interjected. His voice was as pleasant, as smooth as sugared ice. "Both the prince and I are very interested in just how you came by this information about the earl of Wakersfield. Would you care to enlighten us?"

"I must protect the person who told me," Winston announced. He'd turned to look at Sara when he'd made that statement. His gaze deliberately lingered there a minute. Then he turned back to the prince. "How isn't important, my lord. Surely, after reading the facts, you've come to realize that my daughter can't live her life with the son of a traitor. She'd be shunned by society. The marquess's father didn't act in good faith toward the king or the Winchesters when he signed the contract binding his son to my daughter. I therefore demand that Sara be freed from this ludicrous commitment and that the gift be given over to her as payment for the embarrassment and humiliation she's had to suffer."

"I'm afraid I'm really going to have to insist that you tell us who gave you the information about Nathan's father," Sir Richards said again.

Winston turned to the prince for support. "I would rather not answer that demand."

"I believe you must answer," the prince said.

Winston's shoulders sagged. "My daughter," he blurted out. "Sara wrote to us. She gave us the information."

Sara didn't say a word. Nathan gave her a gentle squeeze. It was an awkward attempt to give her comfort. She didn't protest at all.

Don't give up on him, she thought. Those were his very words. Sara tried to concentrate on the important discussion underway, but Nathan's whispered command kept getting in the way.

Her father was giving one excuse after another as to why his daughter would share that damning information about Nathan's father. Sara didn't want to listen to those lies.

The prince caught her attention when he motioned to one of the men standing behind him. The guard immediately went over to the side entrance and pulled the door open. A short, thin man holding a dark cap in his hands came into the office.

Sara didn't recognize the man. It was obvious, though, that her father did. He couldn't quite hide his surprise. "Who is this man intruding upon our discussion?" he asked.

His paltry attempt to bluster his way through the ordeal didn't work. "He's Luther Grant," Sir Richards drawled. "Perhaps you've met him, Winchester. Luther used to work as a senior attendant in our department. He was so trustworthy, he was given charge of the vault. It was his sole duty to keep England's secrets safe."

The director's tone of voice had turned biting. "Luther's going to be protecting the walls of Newgate Prison from now on. He'll have his very own cell to watch over."

"The game's over," Caine interjected. "Grant told us you paid him to look at Nathan's file. When he couldn't find anything damning there, he looked at Nathan's father's file."

Winston's expression showed only disdain. "Who cares how the information was found out?" he muttered. "The only thing that matters is that—"

"Oh, but we do care," Sir Richards interrupted. "You've committed an act of treason."

"Isn't that a hanging crime?" the prince asked.

From his expression Sara couldn't tell if he was goading her father or if he really didn't know.

"Yes, it is a hanging crime," Sir Richards said.

Winston shook with fury. "I have never been disloyal to the crown," he announced. He stared at the prince regent. "When every other politician in this city has ridiculed you, I've stood firmly by your side. My God, I even argued in your defense when you wanted to rid yourself of your wife. Is this how I'm repaid for my loyalty?"

The prince's face turned red. It was obvious that he didn't like being reminded of his unpopularity or of his attempt to rid himself of his wife. He glared at Winston even as he shook his head. "How dare you speak to your prince regent with such insolence?"

Winston realized he'd gone too far. "I apologize, my lord," he blurted out, "but I am desperately trying to protect my daughter. The marquess of St. James isn't good enough for her."

The prince took a deep breath. His color remained high, but his voice was much calmer when he said, "I disagree with you. I've never taken an active interest in the War Department, for it bores me immensely, but once I read the facts about Nathan's father I asked Sir Richards to give me the son's file as well. Nathan isn't responsible for his father's sins. No man should have to be." His voice rose an octave when he added, "My subjects could blame me for my own father's weak condition if that was the case, isn't that so?"

"They don't hold you responsible for your father's illness," Winston assured him.

The prince nodded. "Exactly so," he muttered. "And I don't hold Nathan responsible for his father's errors. No, the marquess isn't responsible," he repeated in a weary voice. "But even if he were, he more than proved his loyalty by all the courageous deeds he accomplished on England's behalf. If the secrets could all be revealed, Nathan would be knighted for his heroic acts. As to that, I'm told that the earl of Cainewood would deserve like treatment. Reading the files took up most of my evening, Winston, and I now say that having all the facts before me, I feel honored to be in the same room with these loyal, distinguished men."

No one said a word for a minute. Nathan could feel Sara trembling. He noticed that she was watching her father, and he wanted to whisper to her that it was all going to be all right, that he'd never be able to frighten her again.

The prince spoke once more. "Sir Richards refuses to allow the information to be made public, however, and I have decided to bow to his superior wisdom in this matter. Suffice it to say that these men have my gratitude. I now have a bargain to put to you," he said. His gaze had turned to rest on the director. "If Winston assures us that he won't speak a word about Nathan's father, I suggest we don't lock him up."

Sir Richards pretended to mull over that suggestion. "I would rather see him hanged. However, the decision is up to you. I am but your humble servant."

The prince nodded. He looked at Winston again. "I know that certain members of your household are aware of the information about Nathan's father. It will be your duty to keep them silent. You'll be responsible for defending Nathan against any such scandal, for if a hint of a rumor reaches me, you'll be charged with treason. Do I make myself clear?"

Winston nodded. He was so furious he could barely speak. The prince's revulsion was apparent. The earl of Winchester knew he wouldn't be included in any of the more important functions in future. As soon as the prince gave him the cut direct everyone else would follow suit.

Sara could feel her father's rage. Her throat closed up, and she thought she was going to be sick. "May I have a glass of water, please?" she whispered to Nathan.

He immediately got up and left the room to fetch a drink for her. Caine also moved from his chair and took Luther Grant out the side door.

Winston turned to Sir Richards. "I could challenge this. It's still Grant's word against mine."

The director shook his head. "We have other evidence," he lied.

The earl of Winchester stood up. He obviously believed the director's bluff. "I see," he muttered. "How did you find out about Luther?" he asked the prince.

"Your wife told us," the prince answered. "She came to her daughter's aid, Winston, while you tried to destroy her. Leave, Winston. It pains me to look at you."

The earl of Winchester bowed to the prince, turned to stare at his daughter for the briefest of seconds, and then left the office.

Sara had never seen such black fury on her father's face. She was filled with terror. She knew her mother would soon bear the brunt of his anger.

Dear God, she thought, she had to get to her first.

"Will you please excuse me?" she cried out as she rushed toward the door.

Sara had barely received the prince's nod before she'd closed the front door behind her.

"Do you think she's ill?" Sir Richards asked.

"I can't imagine why she wouldn't be," the prince answered. "Richards," he added in a softer tone of voice, "I know how the various department heads whisper their contempt for me. Oh, I have my spies to keep me informed. I also know you've never said a word against me. Although I've incorrectly been judged as a ruler who changes his mind whenever the whim comes over me, I tell you now that it isn't so. I won't change my mind about this issue with Winston, I assure you."

Sir Richards walked to the door with the prince. "You do realize, my lord, that I lied when I told Winston we had other evidence against him. It really is Grant's word against his, and if he were to push this issue . . ."

The prince smiled. "He won't push anything," he assured the director.

Nathan walked in by way of the side entrance with a glass of water in his hand and Caine by his side. The prince had just taken his leave. "Where's Sara?" Nathan asked.

"She went to the washroom," Sir Richards explained. He went back to his desk and collapsed in the chair. "By God, that went smoothly. I couldn't be certain how the prince regent would behave. He was on the mark this time, wasn't he?"

"Will he stay on the mark?" Caine asked. "Or will Winston be back in his camp come tomorrow?"

The director shrugged. "I pray that he won't change his mind, and my feeling is that he'll keep his promise."

Caine leaned on the edge of the desk. "I cannot believe you let him read the files, Richards."

"Then don't believe it," his director answered, grinning. "I gave him only a brief summary of some of the lesser deeds accomplished. Quit your frown, Caine. Nathan, for God's sake, quit pacing with that glass in your hand. Most of the water's on the carpet now."

"What's taking Sara so long?"

"I believe she wasn't feeling well. Let her have a few more minutes of privacy."

Nathan let out a sigh. He went to refill the glass while Sir Richards caught Caine up on activities within the department.

Nathan tried to be patient, but when another ten minutes went by and Sara still hadn't returned to the office he decided to go after her. "Where the hell is the washroom? Sara might need me."

Sir Richards gave him directions to the floor above. "Are the papers ready for signatures?" Caine asked when Nathan turned to leave.

"They're on the desk," Nathan called over his shoulder. "As soon as I get my hands on Sara we can get this over and done with."

"He's quite a romantic," Caine drawled out.

"Actually, what he's about to do for his wife indicates to me that he really is a romantic at heart. Who would have thought Nathan would fall in love?"

Caine grinned. "Who would have thought anyone would have him? Sara's as much in love with him as he is with her. Nathan's determined to start over," he added with a nod toward the papers.

"Ah, love in bloom," Sir Richards said. "Sara will certainly be pleased with his thoughtfulness. God knows she's deserving of some happiness. It was hard on her today. Why, the look on her face when the prince made mention of her mother nearly broke my heart, Caine, and I'm certainly not given to emotion as you well know. Lady Sara looked so frightened. I wanted to reach out to her, to pat her and tell her it would all wash out. I'm not usually so demonstrative, but I tell you I had to restrain myself from going over to her."

Caine looked bewildered. "I don't recall the prince mentioning Sara's mother."

"I believe both you and Nathan were out of the room at the time," Richards said. "Yes, that's right," he added with a nod. "Sara sat all alone. Nathan had gone to fetch some water for her."

"Sara isn't in the washroom," Nathan bellowed from the doorway. "Damn it, Richards, where'd you send her? Down the street, for God's sake?"

Caine stood up. "Nathan, we might have a problem." His voice was harsh from worry. "Sir Richards, tell us exactly what the prince said about Sara's mother."

The director was already pushing his chair back so that he could stand up. He wasn't certain what the danger was, but the scent was there, permeating the air.

"Winston demanded to know who told us about Grant. The prince told him it was his wife who gave us the name."

Both Nathan and Caine were already running out the door. "Surely Winston wouldn't dare touch his wife or his daughter," Sir Richards muttered as he chased after the two men. "You're thinking that's where Sara went, aren't you? Charles," he shouted over his shoulder, "bring the carriage around."

Nathan reached the ground level with Caine right on his heels when Sir Richards turned the corner of the landing above. "Nathan, you don't believe Winston is capable of hurting either his wife or his daughter."

Nathan threw the door open and ran out onto the sidewalk. "No," he shouted over his shoulder. "Winston won't touch them. He'll leave it to his brother to mete out the punishment. That's how the bastard operates. Damn it,

344

Sara took your carriage, Caine. God, we've got to get to her before Henry does."

A hack was racing down the street. Nathan seized his opportunity. He wasn't about to wait for the director's carriage. He ran into the street, braced himself for the struggle, and grabbed the reins of the two horses.

He threw his shoulder into the side of the horse closer to him. Caine added his strength, and the vehicle came to a screeching stop.

The driver was thrown on top of the vehicle. He started shouting. The fare, a blond-headed young man with spectacles and a squint, stuck his head out the window to see what all the commotion was about just as Nathan pulled the door open. Before the man knew what had happened Nathan had tossed him to the pavement.

Caine shouted directions to the driver while Sir Richards helped the stranger to his feet. The director was being very solicitous until he realized he was about to be left behind. He rudely shoved the man back to the ground and jumped inside the hack before Caine could pull the door closed.

No one said a word on the ride over to the Winchesters' townhouse. Nathan was shaking with terror. For the first time in his life he rebelled against the isolation he'd always enforced upon himself. He needed her, and dear God, if something happened to her before he could prove to her that he could be worthy, could love her as much as she deserved to be loved, he didn't think he could go on.

In the space of those long, unbearable minutes Nathan learned how to pray. He felt as unskilled as an atheist, couldn't remember a single prayer from childhood days, and so ended up simply begging God's mercy.

How he needed her.

The ride over to her mother's residence wasn't quite as traumatic for Sara. She wasn't in a panic because she knew she had enough time to get to her mother first. Her father would have to go to his brother's townhouse. That ride would take him at least twenty minutes. Then he'd have to spend at least fifteen more minutes working his brother into a rage for the injustices dealt to him. Assuming that Henry would certainly be in the throes of his daily hangover, it would take him time to clear his head and get dressed.

There was also the oddly comforting fact that surely in that amount of time Nathan would put the pieces together and figure out she wasn't in the washroom. She knew he'd come after her.

Don't give up on me. His whispered command once again intruded upon her thoughts. She immediately tried to get angry over the insulting demand. How dare he think she'd given up on him. How dare he . . .

She couldn't work herself up into a proper fury, for in her heart she wasn't at all certain she had the right to be outraged. Had she given up on him? No, of course not, she told herself. The simple fact was that Nathan didn't love her.

He had shown her consideration, though. She'd give him that much. She remembered how he'd rubbed her back when she'd been in such embarrassing agony with her monthly cramps. His touch had been so gentle, so soothing.

He was a gentle lover, too. Not that he'd ever given her loving words when he was caressing her. But he'd shown her kindness, patience, and never once had she truly been afraid of him. Never once.

But he didn't love her.

He'd spent long hours teaching her so many little things he thought she needed to know to become self-sufficient. She thought it was because he didn't want to watch out for her. And while she did consider it her duty to protect those she loved, like her mother, she left the task of her own protection to her husband.

Like her mother . . .

Dear God, Nora had been right. Without realizing it Sara had been following in her mother's path. She had been determined to become dependent on her husband. If Nathan had turned out to be a cruel, selfish man like her father, would Sara have learned how to cringe whenever he raised his voice to her?

She shook her head. No, she would never allow any man to terrorize her. Nathan had made her realize her own strength. She could survive alone, and she certainly could stand up for herself.

He hadn't taught her how to defend herself because he didn't want to be bothered with the chore of watching out for her. He just didn't want anything to happen to her.

He was a kind man.

Sara burst into tears. Why couldn't he love her?

Don't give up on me. If he didn't love her, why did he care if she gave up on him or not?

Sara was so consumed with her thoughts, she didn't realize the carriage had stopped until Caine's driver shouted down to her.

She asked the driver to wait, then hurried up the steps.

The butler, a new man hired by her father, told her that both her mother and her sister had gone out for the afternoon.

Sara didn't believe him. She pushed her way past the servant and hurried up the stairs to the bedroom level to see for herself.

The butler sniffed at her lack of manners and retired to the back of the house.

The bedrooms were empty. Sara was at first relieved, then she realized she would have to find her mother before either of the Winchester men did. She went through the stack of invitations on top of her mother's writing table, but none gave her a clue as to the afternoon activities.

She decided to go back downstairs and force the information out of the servants. Surely one of them knew where her mother had gone.

Sara had just reached the landing when the front door opened. She thought it was her mother returning home and started down the steps. She stopped midway when Uncle Henry strutted into the foyer.

He saw her at once. The sneer on his face made her stomach lurch.

"Father went directly to you with his anger, didn't he?" she called out, contempt evident in her voice. "I knew he would," she added. "It's the only thing he's predictable about. He thinks he's so cunning to let his drunken brother dole out the punishment whenever he's upset. Father's waiting at White's, isn't he?"

Her uncle's eyes narrowed into slits. "Your mother should have her tongue cut out for turning against her husband. This isn't your business, Sara. Get out of my way. I'm going to have a word with your mother."

Sara shook her head. "I won't let you speak to her," she shouted. "Not now, not tomorrow, not ever. If I have to force Mother, I will, but she's going to leave London. A nice visit with her sister will be just the thing. She might even realize she doesn't want to come back here again. God, I hope so. Mother deserves a little joy in her life. I'm going to see that she gets it."

Henry kicked the door shut behind him. He knew better than to strike Sara, for he remembered the threat her husband had made when he'd walked into the tavern to get his bride.

"Go back to the cur you're married to," he shouted. "Victoria," he added in a screech. "Get down here. I'm wanting a word with you."

"Mother isn't here. Now *you* get out. The sight of you makes me ill."

Henry started toward the steps. He stopped when he

spotted the brass umbrella stand in the corner. He was too furious to consider the consequences. The chit needed to learn a lesson, he thought to himself. Just one good hit to rid her of her insolence.

He reached for the ivory-tipped walking stick. Just one good hit . .

Chapter Sixteen

She damn near killed him.

Tortured screams echoed into the street. The carriage hadn't come to a complete stop before Nathan jumped to the pavement and started up the steps. The god-awful screaming made him crazed with fear for his Sara—so crazed, in fact, that he didn't stop to notice it was a man's voice making all the noise. He didn't stop to open the door, either. He went through it. The frame bounded off his shoulder and landed with a thud on Henry Winchester's head. The heavy piece of wood muffled some of the louder cries.

Nathan wasn't at all prepared for the sight he came upon. He was so stunned, he stopped dead in his tracks. Caine and Sir Richards crashed into his back. Caine let out a low grunt. He felt as though he'd just run into a block of steel. Both he and Sir Richards recovered their balance and moved to the side to see what held Nathan transfixed.

It was difficult for the men to take in. Henry Winchester was shriveled up in a fetal position on the floor in the center of the large foyer. His hands were clutching his groin. The man was literally writhing about in agony, and when he rolled over their way Sir Richards and Caine immediately noticed his bloody nose.

Nathan was staring at Sara. She was standing at the bottom of the steps. She looked thoroughly composed, absolutely beautiful, and completely unharmed.

She was all right. The bastard hadn't gotten to her. Yes, she was all right. Nathan kept repeating that fact inside his mind in an attempt to calm down.

It didn't work. His hands were shaking. He decided he needed to hear her tell him she was all right before he could start breathing normally again.

"Sara?" Nathan whispered her name in such a hoarse whisper, he doubted she could hear him above the racket her Uncle Henry was making. He tried again. "Sara? Are you all right? He didn't hurt you, did he?"

The anguish in her husband's voice was almost her undoing. Tears filled her eyes, and she realized that Nathan was just as misty. The look on his face made her heart ache. He looked so . . . scared, so vulnerable . . . so loving.

Dear God, he did love her. It was so apparent to her.

You love me, she wanted to shout. She didn't, of course, because there were other people present. But he loved her. She couldn't speak, couldn't quit smiling.

She started toward her husband, then remembered her audience. She turned to Caine and Sir Richards and made a perfect curtsy.

Caine grinned. Sir Richards was in the middle of an acknowledging bow when he caught himself. "What happened here?" he demanded in a fluster of authority.

"Damn it, Sara, answer me," Nathan strangled out at the same time. "Are you all right?"

She turned her gaze to her husband. "Yes, Nathan. I'm quite all right. Thank you for inquiring."

She looked down at her uncle. "Uncle Henry had a little mishap," she announced.

The director bent on one knee and lifted a remnant of the

door away from Henry's chest. "I surmised as much, my dear," he said to Sara. He tossed the piece of wood aside, then frowned at Henry. "For the love of God, man, quit that weeping. It isn't dignified. Did the door fell you when Nathan came charging through? Speak up, Winchester. I can't catch a word of your blubbering."

Caine had already put the pieces together. Sara was rubbing the back of her right hand in what appeared to be an attempt to work out the sting. Henry was clutching his groin.

"Uncle Henry had his mishap before the door fell on him," Sara explained. She sounded incredibly cheerful, and she was smiling at Nathan when she made that statement. Nathan still wasn't calm enough to reason it through. He couldn't understand why his wife looked so damned pleased with herself. Hadn't she realized the danger she'd been in? Hell, his nerves still felt as raw as a fresh wound.

Then she was slowly walking toward him, and all he could think about was taking her into his arms. He was never going to let go of her, not even when he lectured her on her sinful habit of taking off on her own.

Caine's smile proved catching. The director found himself smiling, too, though he still didn't know what was so amusing. He stood up and turned to Sara. "Please satisfy my curiosity and tell me what happened."

She wasn't about to explain. If she told him exactly what she'd done, the director would certainly be appalled by her unladylike behavior.

Nathan wouldn't be appalled. He'd be proud of her. Sara couldn't wait until they were alone and she could give him all the details, blow by satisfying blow.

"Uncle Henry tripped over a walking stick," she said, unable to stop smiling.

Nathan finally came out of his stupor and took a good look around him. Sara had just reached his side when he grabbed hold of her and stared intently at the red splotches on the back of her right hand.

That low growl she found adorable was working its way up Nathan's throat. She could also see the rage coming over him. She wasn't at all frightened, however, for she knew he would never turn his anger against her.

She didn't want him to get all worked up on her behalf. Sara wrapped her arms around her husband's waist and hugged him tight. "I'm really all right, Nathan," she whispered. "You mustn't worry so."

She rested the side of her face against his chest. The hammering of his heart indicated that her soothing words hadn't calmed him at all. Yet his voice was deceptively calm when he asked, "Did you have the walking stick, or did he?"

"He had the stick when he started up the steps to get me," she explained. "He grabbed it from the umbrella stand."

Nathan pictured it in his mind. He tried to peel her hands away. "Nathan? It's over now. He didn't strike me."

"Did he try?"

She felt as if she were clinging to a statue, so rigid had his stance become. She let out a little sigh, increased her hold on him, and then answered, "Yes, but I wouldn't let him hit me. I remembered your instructions, and I evened the odds, just as you promised I would in such a situation. As to that," she added, "I also had the element of surprise on my side. Uncle Henry isn't at all used to having women defend themselves. He looked . . . astonished when he fell backwards."

"Caine? Take Sara outside and wait for me. Richards, go with them."

All three of them told Nathan no at the same time. They all had different reasons. Caine didn't want the mess of getting rid of the body. Sara didn't want Nathan to go to the gallows. Sir Richards didn't want the paperwork.

Nathan was still rigid with fury when they'd finished giving him their arguments. He couldn't get Sara out of his arms long enough to rip the Winchester bastard apart. He found the situation extremely frustrating. "Damn it, Sara, if you'll just let me—"

"No, Nathan."

His sigh was long. She knew she'd won. She was suddenly in a hurry to get him alone so that she could win another victory. Come hell or his hide, she would get him to tell her he loved her.

"Nathan, we can't leave until I know Mama's going to be safe," she whispered. "But I want to go home with you now. What are you going to do about this problem?" She didn't give him time to answer. "I meant to say, Nathan, what are we going to do about this problem?"

Her husband wasn't one to give up easily. He still wanted to kill her uncle. He considered his plan a perfectly logical one. It would not only eliminate Sara's worry about her mother's safety, but it would also give him the tremendous satisfaction of putting his fist through the man's face. He kept staring at the walking stick and thinking of the damage a man could inflict with such a weapon. Henry could have killed her.

Caine came up with a nice solution. "You know, Nathan, Henry looks in need of a long rest. Perhaps a sea voyage to the colonies would be just the ticket to improve his health."

Nathan's mood immediately brightened. "See to it, Caine."

"I'll give him to Colin and let him arrange the details," Caine said. He lifted Henry up by the nape of his neck. "A few ropes and a gag are all the baggage he'll be needing."

Sir Richards nodded agreement. "I'll wait here until your mother returns, Sara. I'll explain that your uncle had a sudden desire to take a long trip. I'm also going to wait for your father. I want to have a few words with him, too. Why don't you and Nathan run along now? Take my carriage and have my driver return for me later."

Henry Winchester had regained enough of his sensibilities to make a doubled-over dash for the doorway. Caine deliberately shoved him toward his brother-in-law.

Nathan seized his opportunity. He slammed the back of his fist into Henry's stomach. The blow sent Sara's uncle back to the floor for another bout of writhing.

"Feel better, Nathan?" Caine asked.

"Immensely," Nathan answered.

"What about the papers you had drawn up?" Sir Richards asked Nathan.

"Bring them to Farnmount's ball tonight. We'll borrow Lester's library for a few minutes. Sara and I should get there around nine."

"I'll have to go back to the office to fetch them," the director said. "Set the meeting for ten, Nathan, just to be on the safe side."

"May I ask what it is you're discussing?" Sara interjected.

"No."

Her husband's abrupt answer irritated her. "I don't want to go out tonight," she announced. "I have something most important to discuss with you."

He shook his head. "You will have faith in me, woman," he muttered as he dragged her out the doorway.

She let out a gasp. "Of all the galling things to say to me . . ."

She stopped when he turned and lifted her into the carriage. His expression looked bleak. She noticed his hands were shaking, too.

He wouldn't let her sit next to him but took his place across from her. When he stretched out his long legs she was trapped between them.

As soon as the carriage started forward he turned and stared out the window.

"Nathan?"

"Yes?"

"Are you having . . . aftermath now?"

"No."

She was disappointed, for she hoped he'd need to vent his frustration the way she had when she'd experienced aftermath. The memory of just how her husband had helped her get over her tension made her face turn pink.

"Don't men have aftermath after they fight?"

355

"Some do. I shouldn't have hit Henry in front of you," he said. He still wouldn't look at her.

"Do you mean that if I hadn't been there, you wouldn't have hit him, or that you regret—"

"Hell, yes, I would have hit him," Nathan muttered. "I just shouldn't have struck the bastard in front of you."

"Why?"

"You're my wife," he explained. "You shouldn't be a witness to . . . violence. In future I will refrain from—"

"Nathan," she interrupted, "I didn't mind. Truly. There are times when it will happen again. I am opposed to violence," she added in a rush, "but I will admit that there are times when a sound punch is just the thing. It can be quite invigorating."

He shook his head. "You wouldn't let me kill the pirates, remember?"

"I let you hit them."

He shrugged. Then he let out a loud sigh. "You are a lady. You're delicate and feminine, and I will behave like a gentleman when I'm with you. That's the way it's going to be, Sara. Don't argue with me."

"You've always been a gentleman with me," she whispered.

"The hell I have," he countered. "I'll change, Sara. Now cease this talk. I'm trying to think."

"Nathan? Were you worried about me?"

"Hell, yes, I was worried."

He'd bellowed his answer. She held her smile. "I really would like you to kiss me."

He didn't even look at her when he responded, "No."

"Why not?"

"It has to be right, Sara."

What in heaven's name did that mean? "It's always right when you kiss me."

"I'll ruin everything if I kiss you."

"You aren't making any sense."

"Tell me what happened with Henry," he ordered.

She let out a little sigh. "I hit him . . . there."

A soft smile changed his frown. "Did you remember how to make a proper fist?"

She decided she wouldn't answer him until he looked at her. A long moment passed before he finally gave in.

He was fighting one hell of a battle to keep his hands off her. He thought he was winning the fight, too, until she smiled at him and whispered, "I knew you would be proud of me. Most gentlemen would have been appalled, though."

He roughly pulled her into his lap. His fingers were already twisting into her hair. "I'm not most," he said an instant before his mouth came down on hers. His tongue swept inside her mouth to taste, to caress, to tease. He couldn't get enough of her, couldn't get close enough, soon enough.

He kissed the side of her neck while he worked on the buttons at the back of her dress. "I knew if I touched you, I wouldn't be able to stop."

He'd lost all control. The carriage stopped, but only Sara realized that fact. She made him button her up again. It took him much longer, for his hands were shaking.

Nathan dragged her by her hand inside the townhouse. Jade smiled at the couple when they went flying up the stairs.

Nathan regained a little of his control by the time they reached their bedroom. He opened the door for her. Sara was already reaching behind her back to get the buttons undone again on her way over to the bed. She stopped when she heard the door slam.

She turned around to find that she was all alone. Nathan had left her. She was too astonished to react for several minutes. Then she let out an outraged scream. She pulled the door open and went running down the hallway.

Jade caught her at the landing. "Nathan just left. He said to tell you to be ready to leave by eight. He also suggested I lend you a gown, since your trunk is still on board the *Seahawk*."

"How could he have told you all that and ~~have~~ left already?"

Jade smiled. "My brother acted as though he had the devil on his tail," she said. "He finished his instructions from the walkway out front. He's going to meet us later, Sara. He must have some business to attend to—at least I think that's what he added when he jumped into Caine's carriage and took off."

Sara shook her head. "Your brother is rude, inconsiderate, arrogant, stubborn . . ."

"And you love him."

Her shoulders sagged. "Yes, I love him. I believe he might love me, too," she added in a mutter. "He might not truly realize it yet, or he might just be a little afraid. Oh, I don't know anymore. Yes, of course he loves me. How can you believe he doesn't?"

"I'm not arguing with you, Sara. I believe Nathan loves you, too," she added with a nod. "It's quite obvious to me, as a matter of fact. He's so . . . rattled. He's always been a man of few words, but now he doesn't even make sense when he mutters."

Sara's eyes filled with tears. "I want him to tell me he loves me," she whispered.

Jade was full of sympathy. She patted Sara's hand and led her to her bedroom.

"Do you know that I'm everything Nathan could ever want in a wife? No one could love him as much as I do. Please don't consider me inferior. I'm really not. I'm just very different from you, Jade."

Nathan's sister turned from the wardrobe to stare incredulously at Sara. "Why would you think I would ever consider you inferior?"

Sara stammered out her explanation of how the men on board the *Seahawk* had constantly compared her to Jade, and how she'd always lost the contest. "And then the pirates attacked, and I was able to redeem myself in their eyes."

"I would imagine so," Jade agreed.

"I also have courage," Sara said. "I'm not boasting, Jade. Nathan did convince me that I'm very courageous."

"We're both loyal to our husbands, too," Jade said. She turned back to her wardrobe and continued to sort through, looking for an appropriate gown.

"Nathan only likes me to wear high-necked gowns," Sara said.

"That's telling, isn't it?"

"I usually try to be accommodating."

Jade didn't dare let Sara see her expression. The anger in her sister-in-law's voice made her want to laugh. The poor love was getting all worked up again.

"Perhaps, Jade, that is the problem," Sara announced. "I've been too accommodating. I'm always telling Nathan how much I love him. And do you know what his answer always is?" She didn't give Jade time to guess. "He grunts. Honest to God, that's what he does. Well, no more, thank you."

"No more grunting?" Jade asked.

"No more accommodating. Find me the lowest-cut gown in your closet."

Jade did laugh then. "That should push Nathan right over the edge."

"I do hope so," Sara answered.

Five minutes later Sara held an ivory-colored gown in her arms.

"I only wore the dress once, and not out of the house, so no one's seen it. Caine wouldn't let me keep it on."

Sara loved the gown. She thanked Jade several times, then started out of the room. She suddenly stopped and turned around. "May I ask you something?"

"We're sisters now, Sara. You may ask me anything."

"Do you ever cry?"

Jade hadn't expected that question. "Yes," she answered. "All the time, as a matter of fact."

"Has Nathan ever seen you cry?"

"I don't know if he has or not."

From Sara's crestfallen expression Jade realized that wasn't the answer she was hoping for. "Now that I think about it, yes, he has seen me cry. Not as often as Caine, of course."

"Oh, thank you for sharing that confidence with me. You have no idea how happy you've just made me."

Sara's smile was radiant. Jade was pleased, though she admitted to herself she still didn't know exactly what Sara was so thrilled about.

Two hours later Jade and Caine patiently waited in the foyer for Sara to make her appearance. Jimbo paced back and forth by the front door.

Jade was dressed in a dark green silk gown with embroidered cap sleeves. The neckline showed only the barest hint of bosom. Caine still frowned over it before he muttered that she looked beautiful. He wore his formal attire, and she told him he was the most handsome devil in the world. Then Jimbo started nagging them about making certain someone stayed by Sara's side all evening.

"Don't let her out of your sight until Nathan shows up to take over," Jimbo ordered for the fifth time.

Sara drew everyone's attention when she started down the steps. Jimbo let out a low whistle. "Nathan's going to see red when he gets a look at our Sara."

Both Jade and Caine agreed. Sara looked magnificent. Her hair was unbound, and the soft curls swayed about her shoulders with each step she took.

The virginal-colored dress was extremely low-cut and ended in a deep V between her breasts. It was the most provocative gown Caine had ever seen. He remembered it, too. "I thought I tore that thing when I helped you get undressed," he whispered.

His wife blushed. "You were in a hurry, but you didn't tear it."

"Nathan's going to," Caine whispered back.

"Then you think my brother will like it?"

"Hell, no, he won't like it," Caine predicted.

"Good."

"Jade, sweet, I'm not so certain this is such a good idea. Every man at the ball is going to be lusting after Sara. Nathan's going to have a fit."

"Yes."

Sara reached the foyer and made a curtsy to her audience.

"You needn't be so formal with us," Caine said.

Sara smiled. "I wasn't," she said. "I was just making certain I wouldn't fall out of this dress when I do have to curtsy."

"What about when your husband has his hands around your neck and he's strangling you?" Jimbo asked. "Will the gown prove sturdy enough, do you suppose?"

"I'm going to find her a cloak," Caine said.

"Nonsense," Jade argued. "It's too warm for a cloak."

The argument continued even after they were on their way.

The duke and duchess of Farnmount lived a scant mile outside of London proper. Their home was gigantic in diameter, with impressive manicured lawns circling the terraces. Hired servants held torches along the side of the road, lighting the way.

"Rumor has it that the prince has tried to buy Farnmount's residence," Caine said. "He won't give it up, of course."

"Yes," Jade agreed, though she was barely paying attention to her husband's remarks. She was watching Sara. "You look flushed to me," she said. "Are you feeling well?"

"She's fine," Caine said.

Sara wasn't fine, though. Her mind raced with her worries. "The Winchesters will be there tonight," she suddenly blurted out. "None of the men would dare offend the duke and duchess. I don't understand, though, why this is the only affair the St. James family attends."

Caine grinned. "It's the only affair they're invited to attend," he explained.

"I worry about Nathan," Sara suddenly blurted out.

"Jimbo, I wish you could come inside, too. Caine may need your assistance watching out for my husband."

"The boy will be all right," Jimbo answered. He patted Sara's hand. "Quit your fretting."

No one said another word until the carriage drew to a stop in front of the mansion. Jimbo jumped down, then turned to assist Sara. "I'll be standing right beside this carriage. When you've had enough, just step outside the front door, and I'll spot you."

"She'll stay with us until Nathan arrives," Caine said.

Sara nodded. She took a deep breath, lifted the hem of her skirt, and went up the steps.

The ballroom was located on the top level of the four-story structure. The stairway leading up was a blaze of candles and fresh flowers.

A butler stood next to the entrance to the ballroom. There were three steps leading down to the dance area. Caine handed his invitation to the servant, then waited until the bell was dutifully rung. It was a signal to the other guests crowding the floor. Few paid attention, other than to give a quick look up toward the entrance, for a waltz was in progress, and they were busy concentrating on their foot-work.

"The earl of Cainewood and his wife, Lady Jade," the butler announced in a loud, booming voice.

It was Sara's turn next. She handed the man the invitation Caine had given her, then stood by his side until the introduction was made.

"Lady Sara St. James."

He might as well have shouted fire. The announcement had just the same force. A low murmur began in the middle of the crowd, and by the time everyone had added their whisper the sound had increased to earthquake proportions.

One couple actually bumped into another as the man and woman strained to get a better look at Sara.

She held her head high and stared down at the crowd. She prayed she looked composed. Then Caine took hold of her hand. Jade moved to Sara's other side and took hold of her other hand.

"Sara, dear, have you noticed that the Winchesters are all squeezed up together on the right side of the ballroom, and the St. James are all on the left? One might be led to conclude that the two families don't get along."

Jade had made those remarks. Sara broke into a smile. Her sister-in-law had sounded so perplexed. "Rumor has it they don't particularly like each other," Sara teased back.

"I think we'll take up the middle so as not to show partiality," Caine announced as he led the ladies down the steps.

"Nathan isn't here yet, is he?" Jade asked. "Sara, do keep smiling. Everyone's gawking at you. It's the dress, I imagine. You look positively stunning tonight."

The next hour was a trial. Sara's father was in attendance. He made quite a show of giving his daughter the cut direct. When she looked over to the Winchester side of the ballroom the guests turned their backs on her.

Everyone noticed the slight, of course. Caine was furious on Sara's behalf until he looked at her face and saw that she was smiling. He relaxed then.

Dunnford St. James hadn't missed the cut, either. The leader of the St. James clan let out a loud snort, then strolled over to speak to his nephew's wife.

Dunnford was a large, square-framed man with far more muscle than fat. His hair was gray, thinning, and cut as short as a squire's in olden days. He had a full beard, broad shoulders, and looked ill at ease in his formal black attire and crooked starched cravat.

Caine thought he was prettier than his wife.

"What do we have here?" he bellowed when he stopped directly in front of Sara. "This be Nathan's woman?"

"You know perfectly well who she is," Caine answered. "Lady Sara, have you met Dunnford St. James?"

Sara made a formal curtsy. "It is a pleasure to meet you," she said.

Dunnford looked bewildered. "Are you jesting with me?"

Now she looked confused. "I beg your pardon?"

"She has manners, Dunnford. Surprising in a St. James, isn't it?"

A sparkle entered the older man's eyes. "She just became a St. James. She'll have to prove herself before I'll welcome her."

Sara took a step toward Dunnford. That surprised him more than the curtsy had. He was used to having women back away from him. They never smiled, either. This one, he concluded bleakly, was different.

"How shall I prove myself to you?" Sara asked. "Should I shoot one of your brothers to gain your approval, do you suppose?"

She was jesting. He took her suggestion to heart. "Well, now, I suppose it would depend upon which brother you shot. Tom's always a good choice."

"For God's sake, Dunnford, Sara was teasing you."

Dunnford grunted. "Then why'd she offer?"

Caine shook his head. "It was a jest in reference to the time you shot your brother," he explained.

Dunnford rubbed his beard. His grin was devilish. "So you heard about that little misunderstanding, did you? Tom doesn't hold a grudge," he added. "Pity, that. A good feud livens up a family."

Before anyone could remark upon that outrageous remark Dunnford let out a low growl. "Where's your husband? I'm wanting a word with him."

"He should be here any minute," Caine said.

"Where is your wife?" Sara asked. "I would like to meet her."

"Whatever for?" Dunnford countered. "She's probably in the dining room seeing about my meal."

"Aren't you going to say hello to me?" Jade asked her uncle. "You're pretending I'm not even here. Are you still upset because I gave Caine a daughter and not a son?"

"You carrying again yet?" Dunnford asked.

Jade shook her head.

"Then I ain't speaking to you until I get a nephew." He turned to Caine. "You bedding her proper?" he demanded.

Caine grinned. "Every chance I get," he drawled out.

Sara turned red with embarrassment. She noticed that Jade was trying not to smile. Dunnford was giving Nathan's sister a hard glare. Then he turned to Sara again, and suddenly the older man reached out and clasped the sides of her hips with his big hands.

"What are you doing?" Caine demanded in a whisper. He tried to push Dunnford's hands away.

Sara was too astonished by the bold action to move. She simply stared down at his hands.

"I'm taking her measure," Dunnford announced. "She don't look wide enough to bring a babe into the world. The skirt could be deceiving," he added with a nod. "Aye, you might be wide enough."

He was now staring at her chest. Sara's hands immediately covered her bosom. She wasn't about to let him measure anything else.

"I can see you got yourself enough to feed the babe. Are you carrying yet?"

Her face couldn't possibly turn any hotter. She took a step forward. "You will behave yourself," she whispered. "If you touch me again, sir, I will strike you. Are you completely without manners?"

Dunnford guessed he was. When he said so, Sara took yet another step toward him. Caine was amazed by her boldness. Just as astonishing was the fact that Dunnford actually backed up. "I would like a cup of punch, Uncle Dunnford," Sara said then. "It would be proper for you to fetch it for me."

Dunnford shrugged. Sara let out a sigh. "I do suppose I could ask one of the Winchesters to fetch it for me," she said then.

"They'd spit on you first," Dunnford announced. "You're swaying toward our side of the family, aren't you?"

She nodded. He grinned. "I'll be happy to fetch a drink for you."

Sara watched her uncle force his way through the crowd. There was a line waiting for the servant to ladle out a portion of the pink punch. Dunnford pushed the line of guests aside with a hard shove.

"I wouldn't drink any of the punch if I were you," Caine drawled out after Dunnford picked up the giant punch bowl and took several long gulps. He put the bowl back on the table, then dunked a cup into the liquid and turned to walk back across the room.

He wiped his beard with the back of his hand when he presented the cup to Sara.

Caine noticed there was no longer a line in front of the punch bowl. He reached out and grabbed the punch so that Dunnford couldn't accidentally spill the pink liquid on Sara.

"Tell Nathan I'm wanting a word with him," Dunnford announced once again. He added a frown to his reminder, then turned his back and walked over to the far side of the room where his relatives were standing.

Sara noticed the other guests made a wide path for the man. She decided then that he was very like Nathan.

"The marquess of St. James."

The shouted announcement drew everyone's attention. Sara turned to look up at the entrance. Her heart started beating frantically at the sight of her husband. She'd never seen him dressed in formal attire before. It was a bit overwhelming. His hair was bound behind his neck, and he wore the black jacket and pants like a mighty king. The arrogance in both his stance and his expression made her knees weak.

She instinctively started to walk toward him.

It was easy for Nathan to find his wife in the crowd. As

soon as his name had been announced the guests had all moved toward the corners. Sara stood all alone in the center of the dance floor.

She looked magnificent to him. She was so delicate, so exquisite, so . . . damned naked.

Nathan bounded down the stairs toward his wife. He was already taking his jacket off.

As soon as Nathan came down the steps the Winchesters started forward. The St. James men immediately imitated that action.

Caine nudged Jade. "Go sit down," he whispered. "There could be trouble, and I don't want to have to worry about you."

Jade nodded. She wanted Caine's mind solely on protecting her brother. Then she spotted Colin coming down the steps. From the bulge under his jacket she surmised he was armed for any eventuality.

Nathan had his jacket off, but when he reached Sara he couldn't remember what he was supposed to do with it.

"Sara?"

"Yes, Nathan?"

She waited for him to say something more.

He seemed content to stand there and stare at her. Her love was so apparent in her gaze. Her smile was tender. Dear God, he thought, he was unworthy of her, and yet she loved him.

He broke out in a cold sweat. He started to reach for the handkerchief Colin had stuffed in his pocket, then realized he was holding the coat in his hands. He couldn't imagine why. He put it back on. He couldn't take his gaze off his beautiful wife, and his arm got all caught up in the sleeve, but he finally righted the thing.

Sara stepped forward and adjusted his cravat just so, then moved back again.

And still he couldn't speak to her. God, it had to be right, he told himself. She deserved that much. No, no, it had to be perfect for her, not just right, he decided once again. He'd take her down to the library, get the papers signed, and then he'd . . .

"I love you, Sara." His voice sounded as if he'd just had a taste of her soup.

She made him tell her again. Her eyes were filled with tears, and he knew she'd heard him the first time. "I wasn't supposed to say that—not yet, anyway," he muttered. "I love you."

Her expression didn't change. His did. He looked as though he was going to be sick.

She took pity on him. "I know you love me, Nathan. It took me a long while to realize it—almost as long as it took for you to come and fetch me—but I know now. You've loved me for a long time, haven't you?"

His relief was obvious. "Why didn't you tell me you knew?" he demanded in a whisper. "Damn it, Sara, I went through hell."

Her eyes widened, and her face turned pink. "You went through hell? You're the one who refused to have any faith in me. You're the one who would never tell me what was in your heart. I told you all the time, Nathan."

He shook his head. His grin was sheepish. "No, Sara, not all the time. You told me once a day. Some days you waited until after dinner. I'd find myself getting nervous."

She took a step toward him. "You waited each day for me to tell you I loved you?"

He could tell from her expression that she was pleased with his confession. "Will you marry me?" he asked her in a fervent whisper. He'd leaned down until he was almost touching her forehead. "I'll get down on one knee if you want me to, Sara. I won't like it," he added in a rush of honesty. "But I'll do it. Please marry me."

She had never seen her husband so rattled. Telling her what was in his heart was obvious torture for him. It made her love him all the more, of course. "Nathan, we're already married, remember?"

Their audience was enthralled. The couple staring so lovingly into each other's eyes was such a romantic spectacle. Women dabbed at their eyes with their husbands' handkerchiefs.

Nathan had forgotten all about the other guests. He was desperately trying to get his plan completed so he could take Sara home.

"We have to go down to the library," he announced. "I want you to sign a paper breaking the contract."

"All right, Nathan," she answered.

Her ready agreement didn't surprise him. She'd always had such trust in him. He was still humbled by her faith. "My God, Sara, I love you so much, it . . . hurts."

She solemnly nodded. "I can see that it does," she whispered. "Are you getting seasick?"

He shook his head. "After you sign your paper, I'll sign mine," he stated.

"Why are you signing papers?" she asked.

"I'm also going to break the contract. I don't want the inheritance. I already have the greatest gift of all," he whispered. "I have you." His smile was filled with tenderness when he added, "You're everything I could ever want."

She started crying. He couldn't stop himself from pulling her into his arms. He leaned down and kissed his wife. She kissed him back.

A collective sigh came from the women in the crowd.

Yet Nathan's hope that the evening would turn out to be perfect for his wife was not completely fulfilled. By the St. James family's standards it was a huge success. By everyone else's standards it was a nightmare.

No one, however, would ever forget the brawl.

It began innocently enough when Nathan turned to take Sara to the library. She tugged on his hand to make him stop.

"I believe you love me, Nathan," she said when she had his full attention again. "You don't have to give up the king's gift just to prove it."

"Yes, I do," he returned. "I want to show you how much I love you. It's the only way you're going to believe me. You've given me your love for so long, and I've given you nothing but aggravation. It's penance, Sara. I have to do this."

She shook her head. "No, you don't have to do this. Nathan, you will show me you have faith in me and my love by not giving up the gift. You waited long years for that inheritance, and you're going to keep it."

"My mind's made up, wife."

"Unmake it," she countered.

"No."

"Yes."

She could tell from the set look on his face that he was determined to make a noble sacrifice for her. She was just as determined not to let him.

"And if I don't sign my paper?" she asked.

She folded her arms in front of her and frowned up at him while she waited for his answer.

Dear heaven, how she loved him, she thought. And how he loved her, too. He looked like he wanted to throttle her. She felt like laughing.

"If you don't sign the paper, Sara, then your family can have the king's gift. I don't want it."

"I won't have it."

"Now, Sara . . ."

He didn't realize they were shouting. She did. She turned to look over the St. James section of the crowd until she found the man she wanted. "Uncle Dunnford?" she called out. "Nathan wants to give up the king's gift."

"Oh, hell, Sara, why'd you do that?"

She turned around and smiled at her husband. Nathan was already taking his jacket off. Then Sara noticed Caine and Colin were doing the same thing.

She started to laugh. God help her, she'd already turned into a St. James.

Nathan didn't look sick anymore. A sparkle had come

into his eyes. He was such a fit man. And she was just the woman to manage him. He was glaring at her chest. Then his jacket was around her shoulders, and he was demanding that she put her arms through the sleeves. "If you ever wear that gown again, I'll tear it off you," he whispered. "Hell, here they come."

The St. James men were moving forward like a troop of soldiers set on war. "I love you, Nathan. Do remember not to tuck your thumb under your fingers. You wouldn't want to break it."

Nathan raised an eyebrow over that suggestion. She retaliated by giving him a slow, sexy wink. He grabbed her by the lapels of his jacket, kissed her hard, and then pushed her behind his back.

It was, without a doubt, a night to remember. The duke and duchess of Farnmount, both surely in their late sixties, couldn't have been more pleased with the entertainment. Their little gathering would provide enough talk to keep everyone well fed in the gossip department for a good long while.

Sara remembered seeing the stately couple perched on the top step. They each held a goblet of wine, and after the first punch was landed the duke of Farnmount directed the orchestra to begin playing a waltz.

In truth, however, Sara liked the aftermath much better than the brawl. As soon as the fight was over Nathan dragged her out into the night. He didn't want to waste time taking her back to the ship, and so he took her back to Caine's and Jade's townhouse.

He was frantic to touch her. She was just as frantic to let him. Their lovemaking was passionate, wild, and filled with love.

Sara was sprawled on top of her husband in the center of the bed. Her chin was propped on top of her folded hands, and she was staring down into his beautiful eyes.

He looked thoroughly content. He was gently rubbing her backside in a haphazard way. Now that they were all alone

Nathan was able to tell her how much he loved her without turning gray at all. He was a bit of a romantic. He opened the drawer of the table next to the bed, pulled out a piece of paper, and handed it to her.

"Pick out the ones you like," he ordered.

She chose "sweetheart," "my love," and "my sweet" from the list of endearments on the sheet. Nathan promised to memorize them.

"I used to be a little envious of Jade," she told him. "I didn't think I could ever be like her, and my staff kept making comparisons."

"I don't want you to be like anyone else," he whispered. "Your love has given me such strength, Sara."

He leaned up to kiss her. "I have come to rely on your love. It became my anchor. It was the one certainty I had, and it took me a long while to realize it."

"How long will it take for you to have complete faith in me?" she asked.

"I already have complete faith in you," he argued.

"Will you tell me all about your past?"

He looked a little wary now. "In time," he finally agreed.

"Tell me now."

He shook his head. "It would only upset you, sweetheart. I've led a rather black life. I've done a few things you might consider . . . worrisome. I think it would be better if I just tell you one story at a time."

"Then it is only out of consideration for my tender feelings that you hesitate to tell me about your past?"

He nodded.

"Were some of these things . . . illegal?"

Her husband looked highly uncomfortable. "Some would say they were," he admitted.

It took all she had not to laugh. "I'm happy you're so concerned about my feelings, husband, and now I know you only hesitate to tell me about your past because I might worry, and *not* because you think I might accidentally blurt out anything of significance."

The sparkle that came into her eyes puzzled him. She was up to something, but he couldn't imagine what it could be. He wrapped his arms around her waist and let out a loud, satisfied yawn. He closed his eyes. "I know you love me," he whispered. "And in time—say five or ten years, my love— I'll tell you everything. By then you should have become accustomed to me."

She did laugh then. He was still a little scared. Oh, she knew he trusted her, knew he loved her, but it was all so new for Nathan, and it was going to take him time to rid himself of all his shields.

She didn't have any such problems, of course. She'd loved him for the longest time.

Nathan blew out the candle and nuzzled his wife's ear. "I love you, Sara."

"I love you too, Pagan."

Add these

JULIE GARWOOD

---

books to your collection:

Mercy

✳

Heartbreaker

✳

Guardian Angel

✳

Come the Spring

✳

Ransom

✳

Pocket
Books

2418-02

Visit

JULIE GARWOOD

online!

For a preview excerpt of Julie Garwood's upcoming hardcover, *Heartbreaker*, go to:

www.SimonSays.com/juliegarwood

Read excerpts from her other books, find a listing of future titles, and learn more about the author!